AN ASHLEY PARKER NOVEL

PLAGUE TOWN

BOOKS BY
DANA FREDSTI

THE ASHLEY PARKER NOVELS
Plague Town
Plague Nation
Plague World

Murder For Hire: The Peruvian Pigeon

The Spawn of Lilith (coming June 2017)

AN ASHLEY PARKER NOVEL

PLAGUE TOWN

DANA FREDSTI

TITAN BOOKS

PLAGUE TOWN
Print edition ISBN: 9780857686350
E-book edition ISBN: 9780857686381

Published by Titan Books
A division of Titan Publishing Group Ltd
144 Southwark St, London SE1 0UP

First edition: April 2012
9 8 7 6 5 4 3

Visit our website: www.titanbooks.com

Did you enjoy this book? We love to hear from our readers.
Please email us at readerfeedback@titanemail.com or write to us at Reader
Feedback at the above address.

To receive advance information, news, competitions, and exclusive offers online,
please sign up for the Titan newsletter on our website: www.titanbooks.com

A CIP catalogue record for this title is available from the British Library.

Printed and bound in the United States.

To Jack Young and
Norman David Morris

Jack, you taught me to lock and load...
and always reach for the sky.

David, you were a wonderful friend and
the best "big brother" a girl could want.

I wish you were both here to read this.

PROLOGUE

"That's how it always begins. Very small."

Egg Shen, *Big Trouble in Little China*

"Just the flu," Maggie murmured, stirring a large pot of homemade chicken soup. "That's all it is."

Nothing to worry about, *Dr. Albert had explained.* Unless you're very young or very old.

He called it Walker's flu, said that like any virus, it exploited weaknesses in the immune system. But Josh and their son Jason were perfectly healthy—they could fight off anything Mother Nature threw their way. Just in case, though, the doctor had given them both the usual anti-virals. He'd also insisted that she have a shot, although considering how much vomit and Kleenex she'd waded through in the last few days, it was pretty much a case of shutting the barn door after the horse was long gone.

Everything will be fine, *she told herself silently.*

Not that you could tell from the way Josh was acting. This was the first serious illness her husband had experienced since he'd contracted the mumps as a child. It was all she could do not to laugh when her usually stoic spouse reverted to a childish whiner in his sick bed. Though Jason was only seven, he was soldiering though it better than his father.

Still, her hands were full nursing them and she was exhausted.

Their fevers had to break soon. They'd both had brief periods of relief where their temperatures had dropped and their appetites had returned, but the respite had been short-lived—an hour or so at most.

Maggie didn't like the way the whites of their eyes had gone yellow, either—a sickly color shot through with red lines. She worried that it was a sign of jaundice. Didn't that mean the liver was infected?

No, if they weren't on the mend by the morning, she'd have to load them into the car and make the long, winding drive down the mountain into Redwood Grove for another visit with the doctor. In the meantime, she'd continue to bring them chicken soup, saltines, and ginger ale, even if the food just sat on the nightstand, untouched.

If only they would eat.

"Mom?" Jason's voice, a thin echo of its usual healthy tone, came through the baby monitor she'd placed next to his bed. "Mom, my throat hurts. I'm so thirsty."

Maggie hit the speaker button.

"Be right there, baby," she said. "I'll bring you some water."

Jason coughed in reply, issuing a wet, phlegmy sound that would have alarmed her if she hadn't heard it so many times the last few days. Still, it seemed as if he was coughing up a lung.

Stirring the soup a few more times, Maggie turned down the burner under the pot, tightened her robe, grabbed a glass, and filled it with tap water. Then she headed up the stairs in what must have been her fiftieth trip of the day.

She sighed.

Who needs the gym?

Walking down the hallway to Jason's room, she sniffed and wrinkled her nose. The smell of stale, sweat-soaked linens hung in the air, tinged with urine. Hopefully she'd be able to wash the sheets in the next day or two.

Pushing Jason's door open with her free hand, Maggie stepped into her seven-year-old son's room… and stopped dead in her tracks.

"Dear Jesus…"

Jason lay in his bed in his Spider-Man pajamas, eyes wide open, unnaturally dark blood trickling out from his tear ducts, nostrils, ears, and mouth. His skin was cyanotic blue and the corneas of his eyes were fish-belly white.

The glass slipped from Maggie's hand, shattering on the hardwood floor, sending water and shards flying everywhere. She didn't notice, her attention entirely on her son.

"J...Jason?" She took another step into the room, glass crunching beneath her shoes. "Baby?"

No response. Her little boy lay there unmoving, the blood seeping out onto the pillow, creating a dark halo around his corn-silk blond hair.

A deep primal wail stuck in Maggie's throat, a hair's breadth from emerging and shattering the silence with its pain. Part of her refused to accept the evidence of her eyes, and she shoved the cry back, somehow knowing that voicing her loss would make it real.

Josh, she thought instinctively. I have to get Josh. He'll know what to do.

She backed out of Jason's room and spun, sprinting to the master bedroom where Josh had spent the last four days lying in misery. The door was ajar, and she stumbled past it.

"Josh," she choked. "It's Jason, I think he's... he's not breathing, and—" The words caught in her throat.

Josh lay on his back, his head turned toward the sound of Maggie's voice, but there was nothing but pain in his gaze. He coughed, and blood sprayed out of his mouth. More dribbled from his nostrils, ears, and eyes. It was as if his insides were dissolving.

Before Maggie could do more than gasp in horror, her husband's jaw fell open and a rattling noise emerged—a wheezing, liquid vibration coming from deep in his throat.

He's choking, she realized. Suffocating on his own blood. She flew across the room, grabbing him by the shoulders and lifting him in an attempt to raise his head and clear out his esophagus. She could feel the fever radiating from his body like heat rising from asphalt on a summer day.

"C'mon honey, breathe!" she said, shifting into emergency mode. "Breathe, god dammit!" But Josh's head just lolled to one side, his eyes quickly glazing over with the same milky film as Jason's.

"Ohjesusohjesusohjesus..."

Maggie's head shook back and forth in denial even as she lowered Josh back onto the bed and reached for the phone on the bedside table. This isn't happening, she told herself as her fingers stabbed out 9-1-1. Dr. Albert said it was just the flu. Where's all the blood coming from? There had to be an answer, a cure, something that would bring back her husband and son.

She listened to the ringing on the other end of the line, waiting for a calm, soothing voice to pick up and tell her what to do.

"Hurryhurryhurry," she chanted, averting her eyes from Josh's body. Five, six, seven times, and no one answered. She raised her arm, ready to hurl the phone across the room, when a thumping noise in the doorway stopped her short.

Her little boy, her Jason, lurched into the room, one hand slamming unheedingly against the doorframe.

Maggie gave a choked sob of joy. She dropped the phone and reached for his small form as he staggered toward her. His arms stretched out pleadingly, his mouth agape.

Maggie's eyes widened as she saw her son with sudden clarity. The still-bluish tint of his skin... his milky eyes, like those of a blind man. Her skin crawled, and instinctively she started to draw back.

No! He needs me.

She reached for him again with the age-old reflexes of a mother.

By the time her heart caught up with her brain and Jason had sunk his teeth into her arm, it was too late.

Because Josh was awake now, too. And so was his appetite.

CHAPTER ONE

I slapped the head of my giant panda alarm clock, sending a metal spike into its adorable panda skull. Normally I'd feel guilty about assaulting an endangered species, but *anything* to stop the hideous ringing.

I hate getting up.

I mean, *really* hate it. I'd sleep until noon if I had my way, but *some*one thought it was a good idea to start the day in the morning.

I'm too old for this, I thought through the cobwebs. Try as I might to schedule my first class at a reasonable hour, there was an asshole out there who'd decided that "Pandemics in History" were best studied at 8 a.m.

Sadist. Like I really needed to read about the Black Death, or debate love during the time of cholera, with just a single cappuccino under my belt.

One... two... three!

I threw off the down comforter and rolled out of bed, taking my time standing up. I'm never particularly perky before 10 a.m. In fact, I'm the anti-perk. But I was especially slow to start these days.

Bad enough that I was at least ten years older than anyone else in the class. Who would have thought a decade could make such a difference? On top of that, I'd already missed the first week of my sophomore year thanks to a case of genuine, bona fide Walker's flu; named, by the way, after the first guy to catch the disease. I could think of better ways to be immortalized.

Damn, it had kicked my butt. It left me weak and cranky. *Really* cranky.

I hardly ever get sick, but it'd slipped in right after a nasty case of food poisoning. Dr. Albert—our family GP since I was in diapers—said I probably caught it because of my weakened immune system.

That didn't make me feel any better about it. Weirdly enough, the doc had seemed almost *cheerful* at the thought, until I'd refused a shot of flu vaccine.

Dr. Albert was a big believer in flu shots. Kind of like an evangelistic drug pusher… except legit. I'd missed the free flu vaccine clinic while I'd been puking up my guts due to some bad sushi—I should have known eating at a fast food place called Sushirama was a bad idea.

So he'd tried to shoot me up when I crawled into his office, but I'd said *no way*. I mean, I was already sick, so putting more nasties into my system seemed like a bad idea.

Now, as I stood up on unsteady legs, I wondered if maybe I should have listened to him.

My roommate Zara was already gone for the day, leaving the bathroom free and clear, thank goodness. I mean, I liked her, but honestly, the girl took an hour to put on make-up, and that was after all the scrubbing, exfoliating, creaming, and toning. And the vegetable and fruit drawers in our little fridge were stuffed full of leaking jars of face goo. Our apples and carrots may have smelled funny, but they had the best skin in town.

I stared at my face in the bathroom mirror.

Euwww.

At least I wouldn't get carded if I wanted to buy booze. I looked old enough to be my mother. My skin had this kind of pale olivey cast, the same color as those scary babies in Italian Renaissance paintings. And my eyes looked dull—more gray than green, like brackish swamp water.

Okay, maybe not that bad, but points for using "brackish" in a sentence before my first cup of coffee.

Glancing guiltily at Zara's magic potions, I pried one open and used it to try and hide the dark circles under my eyes. Applied something called "Sun-Kissed Beige Glow" to try to change the sickly tone of my skin to an artificially natural tint. The result surprised me.

Definitely better.

A little mascara and some lip-gloss brightened my face enough to pass inspection. That left the thick, tawny mess I call hair. I pulled it back and used an industrial strength metal clip made in the shape of a butterfly. The violet and red crystals set in the wings caught the sunlight shining through the bathroom window. At least part of me sparkled. Although not in a *Twilight* way.

Personally I thought Edward was kinda… well… gay. Not that there's anything wrong with that, but I prefered my vamps like Christopher Lee or the cute Billy Idol clone in *Buffy*. Not bothering with all the torturey-angst, just happy to sip blood from some sexy women.

Uh-oh. Couldn't let Matt know about that. Just a hint of encouragement, and he'd be trying for a threesome.

Which made me smile, in spite of myself. After all, my boy toy was wicked cute in a button-down collar kind of way. He was on the swim team, which made him all toned and tan in the right places. If only he was just a little bit older…

Then again, that was part of the appeal, wasn't it? Proving I could attract someone as hunky as Matt at twenty-nine, after my ex had dumped me for an eighteen-year-old.

Here's to you, Mrs. Robinson.

I finally pulled on some jeans, a long pink tank top, baby-doll T-shirt in a darker pink, and a violet hoodie. Like most Nor-Cal coastal communities, Redwood Grove was cool and foggy the majority of the time, but you never knew when the sun was going to burn through the fog. Layering was usually the safest bet.

I didn't have too far to walk to my first class—the apartment was just a couple blocks away from the campus proper—but today it felt like miles. I'd lost some weight during my double-whammy, and while, sure, it was great to have my clothes comfortably loose, I felt as if a strong gust of wind would blow me away. Every once in a while I'd still get hit with a hot flash that made me want to turn around and crawl back in bed.

I hate being sick.

Fog shrouded the campus this morning, condensation dripping from roof eaves and plants. The tops of the redwoods vanished into the mist. I inhaled deeply, loving the smell of leaves, mulch, and a hint of salt air. Then a coughing fit hit me, reminding me that I'd have to enjoy nature a little less enthusiastically for a while.

I walked past the two-story Victorian house I'd shared with my ex-husband, a former professor at Big Red, and flipped it off.

I smiled. While I was sick, I'd had to forego my daily ritual. I'd missed it.

Next I stopped at one of Big Red's many coffee kiosks for an extra-hot, wet double cappuccino and a blueberry muffin. It cost me an extra five minutes, but if I didn't eat something I'd spend the next hour clutching my stomach every time it growled, pretending it wasn't me. And if I didn't have my caffeine, I might as well have stayed in bed.

By the time I reached D. B. Patterson Hall, the corridors were pretty much cleared out, which meant I was definitely in the late zone. At room 217 I opened the door as quietly as possible, hoping to sneak into the auditorium and find a seat in the back row.

Unfortunately, the door was badly in need of WD-40, and room 217 was one of the smaller auditoriums. It announced my arrival. Loudly.

From where I stood, conspicuous in layers of pink and violet, I could see that almost every seat was filled—including the back row.

"Excuse me… miss?"

A deep male voice hailed me from the front of the room. A tall, drop-dead gorgeous blond guy in his late twenties stood near the lectern. Nice to see someone my own age in class, even if he *was* a teacher. Learning about buboes and black vomit might be fun after all.

When I say "blond," I'm talking the kind of hair people describe as freshly minted gold. I couldn't tell the color of his eyes, but I was betting on sky-blue. His features were regular, other than a bump in his otherwise perfect nose. He looked like an archangel who'd gone a round or two with Rocky Balboa. A little young to be a professor, but I wasn't about to complain.

Damn, he was pretty.

He'd been fussing with papers and a laptop, but now he was just staring. I gave him my most charming smile and did a little toast with my cappuccino cup.

He looked totally uncharmed.

"Any reason you can't take a seat and join us?" he asked loudly.

Okay, now, no need for sarcasm. But I kept the smile.

"Um, not seeing any empty seats?" I replied.

He pointed to one in the front row.

"Please, be my guest."

Great. I did my best to ignore the giggles and whispers that followed me down the aisle. I noticed a couple of girls looking very pleased at my embarrassment. Dimes-to-donuts they were hot for teacher.

And the cute asshat wasn't done yet. As I sat down, he leaned forward from the lectern.

"Any particular reason you're late, Miss…"

"Ashley," I said, deciding that was all he deserved to know.

"Miss Ashley?"

"Close enough," I answered, shooting for calm and collected. And speaking of close enough, I could see his eyes now. They were, indeed, a very pleasing shade of denim blue. Much more pleasing than his personality—if that was what you could call it.

He pulled a piece of paper out of a notebook and ran a finger down it.

"Ashley Parker?"

Crap.

I nodded and bit into my blueberry muffin. Now that he had my name, maybe he'd drop it.

"So-o-o..." He drew the word out, and I knew that couldn't be good. "What made you decide to join us today, given that the first week of class wasn't to your liking?"

"Not my fault," I protested. "I've been sick," I added, hoping that would shut him up.

No such luck.

"And now you're late."

"Like I said, I've been sick." He raised an eyebrow. "Walker's," I added, hoping that might be my "Get Out of Jail Free" card.

The look on his face told me he couldn't care less.

"Ah, yes, Walker's," he said. "The new substitute for, 'the dog ate my homework.'" That sent a titter through the class.

Did you wake up on the wrong side of bed, or are you always in permanent fucktard mode? I took a deep breath before replying. No way I'd give him the satisfaction of hearing my voice break.

"I sent in a doctor's note."

Still no mercy.

"That doesn't explain today," he replied, pinning me with those beautiful baby blues.

I'd give my hair a soccer mom cut before I'd cry in front of this jerk.

"It's still hard to get moving in the morning," I said between gritted teeth.

"If you didn't stuff yourself with processed sugar and caffeine, you'd have a healthier immune system." He stared at my double, extra-hot, wet cappuccino. "I'd think that at your age, you'd know better." More titters.

I'm going to have to kill him, I thought. *What a waste of perfectly good man flesh.*

"In fact," he said, turning to the rest of the class, "Miss Parker here is a perfect example of what *not* to do if you want to keep up a healthy immune system. She would be one of the first to die in a pandemic."

I gaped at him. What a tool!

"Excuse me," I said, "but didn't a lot of the victims of the Spanish flu die be*cause* they had healthy systems? Didn't their immune response go way over the top, and cause inflammation of the lungs?" Lying in bed for a week, you have a lot of time to read for your classes. My addiction to the History Channel didn't hurt either.

Jerkwad, however, didn't bat an eye before shooting back.

"True, but they didn't have the medical resources we do today," he countered. "And I *guarantee* that an uncompromised immune system, coupled with modern medicine, will serve you better than a double latte when fighting the pandemics of the future."

I swear the girl next to me scooted over. I resisted the urge to sneeze on her Coach handbag.

As I did so there was another loud creak, and a short and skinny little Goth girl slipped in through one of the side doors. She was all decked out in black and purple, with pale pink hair floating around her face like a pastel dandelion. Her black, buckled platform boots said "tough girl," but her bright smile seemed free of 'tude. She scurried straight over to my new arch-nemesis.

"Hey, Gabriel," she said. "Sorry I'm late. My car broke down and I had to take the bus the rest of the way from Maberry."

Gabriel, huh? Like the nasty angel in *Prophecy*, always

blowing his own horn and causing trouble. It fit. And now he had a new victim. I took a sip of my coffee and waited for him to rip her a new one. *Then don't drive cars. I don't.*

But "Gabriel" just gave her a half-smile.

"At least you made it," he said.

I almost choked on my cappuccino. How come Miss Hot Topic got a free pass?

Then he turned and addressed the class.

"Everyone, this is Jamie Ackerman, Professor Fraser's new intern."

Ah, so dickwad isn't the professor? The plot thickened.

"She'll be helping out in class for the rest of the semester," he added. The girl next to me, a total *Mean Girls* type, raised her hand and spoke in a high voice.

"Does this mean *you* won't be helping any more?" Great, I was sitting next to Betty Boop, and she was hot for teacher, too. Now I *really* wanted to sneeze on her bag. Yet she gave me hope…

"No, I'll still be assisting Professor Fraser, as well," he announced.

Damn.

A nearly audible sigh of relief rippled through the auditorium as students whispered amongst themselves.

The side door opened again and the conversations immediately died down. Gabriel practically stood at attention while Jamie turned toward the newcomer like a flower seeking the sun. This *had* to be Professor Fraser.

A tall, elegant woman with patrician features, clear grass-green eyes, and blond hair drawn up in a French twist, she commanded attention immediately. Her outfit was a tailored, hunter-green trumpet skirt and jacket with a nipped-in waist. Very retro. She could have been anywhere between forty and fifty-five. Cate Blanchett would play her in the movie.

She strode to the lectern and surveyed all of us with a cool green stare. Her gaze fell on me and she raised an eyebrow. Her Vulcan forefathers would have been proud.

"You're new."

"Ashley Parker," I said.

"Ah, yes, I received the note from Dr. Albert." She stared at me sharply, and I wondered why. "Walker's, yes?"

"Er… uh-huh." I braced myself for another lecture on nutrition and the evils of caffeine.

"You still look a bit pale," she said. "Make sure to get plenty of sleep." With that she clapped her hands together and smiled. "So, who's ready to learn about buboes and the difference between bubonic, pneumonic, and septicemic plagues?

"Everyone? Excellent!"

Maggie was hungry.

The chunks of flesh missing from her arms didn't bother her. She didn't notice that both breasts were gone or that her intestines poked through the gaping hole in her abdomen. And even though her left leg was shredded and barely bore the weight of what remained of her torso, she didn't care. The hollow, gnawing sensation inside was the only thing Maggie registered.

Staggering down the stairs, she made her way to the front door and began her slow, lurching march toward food.

CHAPTER TWO

"…That jerk had the nerve to humiliate me in front of the entire class and he wasn't even the *professor*!"

"Sounds like a total bag o' douche." Matt dropped a comforting kiss on the top of my head. Seeing as he was six foot and then some, it was easy for him to do. I'm just five-seven in my stocking feet.

"I should've kicked him in the *cajones*," I grumbled.

"Should've," Matt said agreeably. "If he had any."

I smiled up at him, taking a moment just to admire how damn cute he was. Our five-year age difference didn't quite make him my boy toy, but it was enough to make me feel slightly naughty. Matt reminded me of a cross between Owen and Luke Wilson, hair between blond and brown, hazel eyes, and that body… He did more for Gap jeans and white cotton shirt than most men did for a tux.

We moved up another foot in the line.

As usual, Che Cafe was crowded. It had the advantage of being in the student union, the central hub of Big Red, and the food was pretty damned tasty. You could get a veggie burger or a big honkin' buffalo burger. Pizza, decent Thai and Middle Eastern food, sandwiches, a burrito/taco bar, tofu, steamed veggies, and salads. Something for everyone.

I'd been living on miso soup, chicken broth, saltines,

and watered-down Gatorade for what seemed like forever. I caught the smell of red meat and practically started drooling. My appetite was back with a vengeance.

Finally we reached the front.

"What do you want, babe?" Matt grinned down at me, an endearingly cocky grin known to melt the panties off entire sororities. "My treat, to make up for your sucky TA."

"Ooh, buffalo burger with double cheese. And onion rings." I snuggled against him. He may not have been the smartest guy on campus, but Matt never failed to make me feel special.

"No wonder you got sick, eating like that."

Oh, you have got *to be kidding me...*

I looked around and there was the douchebag himself. And in spite of myself, I confirmed that he did as much as Matt for jeans and a plain white cotton shirt. Maybe even a little bit more. He was about as tall, too.

There is no justice.

Had he been standing there the entire time? I mean, could I be that clueless? Judging from his expression, the answer to both those questions was a big old *yes*.

Ugh.

Okay, the only defense at this point was a good offense. Disengaging myself from Matt, I crossed my arms.

"What the hell do you care about what I eat?"

Gabriel smirked down at me from his superior height.

"Not a hell of a lot," he replied, "except for the fact you're wasting Professor Fraser's time, and a seat in class that could belong to someone who deserves it."

Matt bristled behind me.

"Ash, is this the douchebag?" he growled. I waved him back.

"I'll handle this, sweetie." This was my war.

I took a step toward Gabriel.

"Are you for real?" I demanded. "I mean, do you just wake up every morning and say 'Today I will be an asshole to the first innocent bystander who crosses my path? Or did I kill your puppy or something? 'Cause I'd really like to know."

"I just don't like the idea that the university is wasting time trying to improve people who can't be improved," he countered. "Anyone who's too stupid to live properly shouldn't be cluttering up the system."

"Hey, asshole…" Matt said, and I heard him step forward.

"It's cool, babe," I told him over my shoulder. Then I turned back to my new archenemy. "Two things," I said. "One, class hadn't even started yet, and you know it." My teeth were clenched so tight I bet I could have made a diamond from a lump of coal. "The professor—the *real* one—wasn't even there."

"That's not the point, now, is it?" he replied. "Class is supposed to start at eight. Professor Fraser is there to teach the students. You're not there to teach her. So the least you can do is show her the respect of showing up on time."

"Maybe you're right," I said. "I missed seeing how you stack your notes. Damn. There goes the midterm now."

Gabriel narrowed those gorgeous blue eyes.

Stop it! I told myself.

"Two," I continued, determined to have my say. "Did anyone tell Westborough Baptist one of their judgmental pricks is missing?"

His nostrils flared. Score.

"Why are you even taking Professor Fraser's class?" he demanded.

"Because it sounded interesting," I shot back. "Did I need a better reason?"

"You're a Liberal Arts major, aren't you?"

"And that's supposed to mean *what*?"

"That you don't know what you want to be when you grow up, so you're wasting our time while you figure it out." He gave me a dismissive once-over. "Your slot could be occupied by someone who's worth the time and effort." He followed this up with a look so condescending, it was all I could do not to punch him in the face.

The fact that he might be right didn't help.

Matt, on the other hand, felt no such restraint. Testosterone crackled and before I knew what was happening he'd stepped in front of me and straight-armed Gabriel with a hand to the chest.

"Back off, asswipe!" Matt growled.

I'm not exactly sure what happened next, but next thing I knew there was yelling, Matt was on the ground with one arm twisted up behind him, and Gabriel's foot was braced against his back.

"You *jerk*!" I yelled. Never mind that Matt had thrown the first... er... shove.

I smacked Gabriel on the side of his head as hard as I could. He whipped around and his expression very nearly got an "I'm sorry" out of me. His pupils were dilated so they were more black than blue, and he honestly looked as though he'd kill me without a second thought. Talk about Jekyll and Hyde.

I was just stubborn enough—and hungry enough—to stand my ground. Low blood sugar is a great equalizer.

"Let go of him *now*!" I demanded. Then I prepared for the worst.

To my surprise and relief Gabriel slowly backed off, lifting his foot and releasing Matt's arm at the same time. He moved out of the way as Matt rolled onto his back and then jumped to his feet, fists clenched. I quickly stepped in-between them just in case Matt decided to take another swing.

I needn't have worried.

Evidently Matt's surge of protective testosterone had faded as quickly as it'd come. What he said next floored me.

"Damn, that was *fast*!" He peered at Gabriel, and his fists uncurled. "Judo?"

Gabriel shook his head.

"Aikido." His expression was almost sheepish. "Are you okay?"

Matt nodded.

"Just a little embarrassed," he said. "It's not cool being taken down in front of my girlfriend."

"Don't be," Gabriel said. "It wasn't a fair match. I've been training for fifteen years."

I couldn't resist.

"Training at what? Being a black-belt pain in the ass?"

Gabriel's lip twitched in what might have been a smile if it'd had a chance to grow a little.

"Perhaps I owe you an apology."

I waited.

"I'm... sorry." The words didn't quite stick in his throat, but they tried. "I'm working on five hours sleep over the last three days, and it's made me short-tempered." He faced Matt when he spoke, so I didn't think I was meant to be the recipient of his *mea culpa*.

"Oh, dude, that sucks," Matt said. "I did a couple of all nighters for mid-terms last year. Totally screwed with my head. I'm sorry I swung at you."

I rolled my eyes. Enough with the male bonding already.

"Um, *Matt*?" I said, maybe a little too sharply. "Can we get some food please?"

Matt stared at me blankly for a second.

"Huh? Oh, sure." He moved back toward the counter, paused, and then looked at me again.

"What did you want?"

The testosterone-drenched fun fest didn't end there. Gabriel ended up sitting with us during lunch. Normally I'd be totally jazzed to be sitting with two guys that hunky—especially considering the envious stares of co-eds much younger than me—but I'd had enough crap for one day. And there was something *really* irritating about how fast Matt went from protective boyfriend to total man-crush.

I stared at Gabriel and openly savored a juicy bite of my buffalo burger, but he seemed to be out of self-righteous snark for the time being.

"So you don't eat any meat?" Matt took a big bite of his burger, oblivious to the irony of his question.

"No meat, no poultry, no dairy."

"No fun," I muttered, dipping an onion ring in ketchup.

"Not true," Gabriel replied. "You'd be amazed."

"I bet I would," I said. "What about onion rings? There are no animal products in onion rings, are there?" I waved one at him.

"Vegan diets are free of cholesterol, and are generally low in saturated fat." He sounded as if he were reciting from the Vegan Bible or something. "So no, no onion rings."

I shook my head. "Like I said," I replied, "no fun."

———

Maggie made slow but steady headway toward Redwood Grove. Some instinct kept her moving in the right direction even when she left the winding road, taking a more direct path through the woods.

She fell often, the lack of connective tissue around her left knee making balance a problem. Her feet were bare and the flesh was torn, but she felt no pain, not even when she landed face first in a bush and a broken branch punctured an eyeball. It snapped off with the force of her fall, leaving Maggie with a stick jutting out of her ruined eye socket, vitreous egg-white oozing from the puncture and sliding down her cheek like thickened tears.

Inexorably pulling herself to her feet, she began moving

again. Not far away there was the sound of an automobile pulling to a stop, the engine shutting off. Maggie shifted direction abruptly, following the echoing slam of a car door. The trees thinned out, revealing a small building, carved redwood bears and other items lined up on its raised porch. Several cars were parked in front.

There were splotches of blood leading up the stairs and into the souvenir store. A stuffed bear lay in a pool of congealing gore.

Her attention focused on the oblivious young man who was fiddling with one of the gas pumps. He wore shorts, despite the chill weather, and his legs were strong and tanned.

An ululating moan emerged from Maggie's mouth, a call of dreadful desire having nothing to do with sex. She stumbled down a small slope leading to the parking lot, sprawling full length on the gravel in her awkward rush.

"Ma'am, are you okay?"

The sound of his voice made her moan again, the sound muffled against pine needles and gravel.

"Ma'am?" Closer now. "Ma'am, are you hurt?"

She heard the crunch of his shoes on gravel.

"Jesus..." His footsteps quickened. "Don't move, let me help you!" An arm curled around her shoulders as he tried to help Maggie to her feet.

She clutched at him with eager hands, mewling noises mixing with the moans as he lifted her.

"Jesus, we need to get you to the hospital and—" He stared into her face, punctured eyeball and all. Before he could react, she sunk her teeth into his cheek, ripping a strip of flesh from his cheekbone to his jaw line.

"Jesus fuck!" Screaming, the man shoved her away and back-pedaled, hand clasped to his face as blood poured between his fingers and ran down into the collar of his gray Big Red sweatshirt. Maggie staggered after him, arms lifted as if imploring him to hold her again.

"Oh fuck, oh fuck!" Still clutching his face, the man backed away toward his car, not taking his eyes off of her as she followed *him. He slammed into the rear passenger door and ran around the back of the car, only to catch his foot on the gas hose.*

He went down hard, his skull smacking against the edge of a pump island, then lay there dazed for a minute, shaking his head. By the time he could move, Maggie had staggered around the car. She fell on him.

Before his screams had fallen silent, Maggie was joined by two other figures that shared her feast. Josh and Jason had been busy eating inside the gift shop. They were still hungry, however, and joined Maggie for a family meal.

CHAPTER THREE

"Ash, have you seen my exfoliating scrub?" Zara asked weakly, followed by a rattling coughing fit. My poor roomie had been bitten hard by Walker's, but even bedridden she insisted on following her skin care regimen, come hell or high water.

I hustled into the kitchen where she was huddled in front of the open fridge, feebly digging through apples and Diet Cokes. She looked terrible, the circles under her eyes so dark her face seemed bruised, and the rest of her skin sickly pale. Her dark-brown hair hung in sweat-soaked hanks down her back, stray strands plastered to her face.

All the exfoliant in the world wasn't going to help.

"Zara, get back into bed!" I said. Putting an arm around her shoulders, I led her back to the twin bed across from mine. "You can exfoliate later, okay?"

Zara lay down, coughed again, then smiled weakly up at me.

"You'll find it for me, though, right?"

I held up my right hand and crossed my heart.

"By the time you're ready for a facial, I will have unearthed your Sassy scrub from wherever it's hiding."

Zara heaved a sigh, as though a heavy burden had been lifted from her soul, and fell sound asleep. I felt her forehead; it was hot and clammy. She'd been really sick for three days now, despite having gotten the flu vaccine. If she wasn't any better tomorrow, I'd get Matt to help me drive her to see Dr. Albert.

With all the fuss about the latest flu, I'd heard that maybe, what, around six hundred people had actually died from it so far. Yeah, six hundred isn't exactly a small number, but thousands of people die every year from the regular bug. Given the population of California—let alone the rest of the country—Walker's didn't seem too alarming.

Even Gabriel had been out sick, despite his vegan miracle diet. Since I'd been fit as a fiddle for two weeks now, it was something I planned to exploit mercilessly as soon as he returned. But while I was a little concerned about Zara, I pretty much assumed she'd get over it, like I had.

Still, I'd keep an eye on her.

Speaking of sickness and death, I mused, *I'm going to be late for Pandemics if I don't leave right away.* So I grabbed my bag and dashed out the door.

There was only one other person in line at the coffee kiosk; an androgynous-looking hipster with a pixie cut, American Outfitters hoodie, and distressed jeans tucked into L.L. Bean boots. The smell of cloves tipped me off to his cigarette even before he raised it to his mouth for a long inhale.

He started hacking right after the puff, a deep, rattling cough that made me step back a foot. I didn't think I could catch Walker's again, but still…

While I waited for the girl in the kiosk to make the hipster's foamy double extra-hot vanilla latte, I looked around. There were surprisingly few people, given that the outbreak had been going on for more than a month.

But we had to be in the home stretch. Hopefully by the next week most of them would be back, and the campus would return to its usual beehive of activity. I hoped so, 'cause for the moment it resembled a ghost town.

I ordered my usual double cappuccino and blueberry muffin.

"Is it just me, or is it even deader than usual today?" I commented.

The girl tamped down two shots of espresso with an expert hand.

"It's *crazy* dead today. You're, like, my fifth customer this morning. Normally we have a total mad rush by eight." Frothing the non-fat milk, she made my cappuccino as automatically as a robot would. Android *barista*.

"Weird," I said. "I mean, I know a lot of people have been sick the last couple weeks, but you'd think they'd be back in class by now."

She handed me my cap.

"I heard the ER's still hopping."

"Seriously?"

She nodded, using tongs to pull a fat streusel-encrusted blueberry muffin out of the case. I tried not to drool.

"Yup," she added. "And from what I've heard, some people have been getting kind of crazy."

"Crazy like how?"

She shrugged, putting the bag on the counter.

"Fights and stuff. Really sick people attacking folks in the hospital and on the street."

"Wow."

"Yeah."

"I haven't heard any of this stuff."

She glanced around, then leaned closer.

"My brother works for the Redwood Grove PD. He says it's no big deal, but the cops are trying to keep it quiet so people don't freak out."

My turn to nod.

"Yeah, I can see why they wouldn't want to have that getting around." Forking over four fifty, I stuffed a buck in the tip jar and headed to D.B. Patterson Hall, dodging a gaggle of grim-faced ROTC types in full-on military gear jogging across the grass in front of the student union.

Be all that you can be, and all that.

I hoped Gabriel was back today. I couldn't wait to ask him how his diet of fruit, nuts, soy and whole grain had worked out for him.

Granted, our student-TA relationship had improved since that contentious first day, but we still sniped at each other. His sanctimonious attitude definitely brought out the worst in me. And if I behaved badly… well, he started it.

I made it to room 217 at five minutes before eight, plenty of time to have my pick of seats. From the look of things, I probably could have arrived at eight-thirty and still picked a seat pretty much wherever I wanted. The classroom was only half full.

Jamie—whom I still thought of as Miss Hot Topic— stood in Gabriel's usual spot at the lectern, getting the projector set and doing whatever else Gabriel did to make himself feel important before class

Meow.

She looked up at the sound of the door creaking, but when she saw it was me, she went back to her work without acknowledging my presence.

Jamie did not like me. I'd figured this out after three consecutive classes where my efforts to talk to her had been studiously ignored. Maybe she had a crush on Gabriel or something.

Whatever.

I took out my copy of Professor Fraser's *The Black Death to Ebola: Plagues Through History,* and pulled out my trusty NEO AlphaSmart. A lot of students used laptops, but if there was one thing I *didn't* need during class was an excuse to distract myself with stuff like Facebook, Twitter, and random web surfing.

The AlphaSmart gave me word processing, but no Internet. If I had access, I'd do it. My mind was willing, but my attention span weak.

By the time Professor Fraser arrived, looking like a forties movie star in wide-legged black trousers and a white silk blouse, we were still missing at least a third of the class, and of the two thirds there, half were coughing miserably.

The professor stood at the lectern and surveyed the class, with Jamie a couple steps behind her like a worshipful shadow.

"So, how many here feel perfectly healthy today?"

About ten of us raised our hands.

"And how many would rather be home in bed?"

Everyone raised his or her hands. We all laughed, followed by more of those nasty coughing fits.

Professor Fraser smiled and shook her head.

"Let me rephrase that. How many of you feel like death warmed over?"

This time the number of hands counted for at least half of the students in the room.

"Excellent!" she said. "I'd like all of those who just raised their hands to go home immediately."

A few students laughed, but from the expression on Professor Fraser's face, it became obvious that she wasn't joking.

"*Now*, please," she said. "You are ill, and should not be here. The irony—of germ-infested students attending a lecture on pandemics—is not lost on me. But the germs you carry *should* be—so please take them away." People still hesitated. "If you're worried about your grades, I guarantee that anyone who misses any portion of this class due to illness will be given every opportunity to make up the work they've missed.

"After all, intimate contact with a potentially lethal virus should count as part of your grade." She clapped her hands together briskly. "Now go!" As much as she was trying to be upbeat, I had the feeling she wasn't just being a good Samaritan.

I didn't blame her.

At least half the class slowly rose and trailed out through the doors. The rest of us stayed where we were.

"Jamie?" Professor Fraser gave a nod to her intern, who promptly grabbed a box and started handing out small packets to all of the remaining students. She dropped mine on the little foldout desk that was attached to my chair.

According to the label on the packet, it was a Clean-'n'Wipe sanitizing towelette. When everyone had one, the professor spoke again.

"I suggest you all use these to wipe down your hands, desks, and the desks of those who sat next to you."

Nobody argued with her.

"Miss Parker, you're looking much healthier this week." The professor smiled at me approvingly.

"I think I pretty much kicked Walker's' butt," I said.

"Good." Professor Fraser nodded. "You're very lucky."

I caught Jamie glaring at me, and suddenly her animosity made sense. Total *girl* crush going on here. I'd been on her shit list since day one, ever since Professor Fraser had told me to take care of myself.

Did I mention *whatever*?

When I stopped back at the dorm to check on Zara, she was still asleep. Her breathing seemed kind of thick and uneven, but her fever had gone down and her color was less "moldy cheese" and "more living co-ed."

I heated up some chicken broth on our hot plate, and when I brought it to her, she stirred. I propped some pillows under her so she could eat.

"You sure you're okay if I'm out tonight?" I asked, hoping desperately that she would say "yes."

Zara nodded, taking a few tentative sips of the broth.

"Yeah. I'm okay." She ate some more soup and had a swallow of ginger ale. "Thanks for making this."

"No prob. Just stay in bed, okay?"

"I promise."

I handed her a tube of apricot and olive oil exfoliant. "It was behind the tomatoes. Just don't try and use it tonight."

Zara yawned.

"You're the best, Ash."

My cell phone beeped. Matt, texting he was waiting for me downstairs.

"Gotta go. Call me on my cell if you need anything!"

But Zara had already curled back up and dropped off, clutching the tube of face scrub like it was a teddy bear.

I smiled as I headed out the door. She was definitely on the mend.

Josh and Jason had suffered less mutilation than Maggie. They traveled with her, some atavistic bond keeping them near even though their corpses were capable of moving much more quickly.

They were all hungry. Their last meal had been a week ago when they'd stumbled across one of the houses scattered through the mountains above Redwood Grove. There had only been one skinny teenager at home when they'd arrived, and by the time the three had eaten their fill, all the girl's reanimated remains would be able to do was flop and wriggle about on the floor.

Still their hunger persisted.

The sound of motors turned the trio toward a break in the trees. Vehicles painted in forest camouflage rumbled by on the road below.

Food.

Two weeks stumbling through dense forests had taken its toll on Maggie, and she quickly fell behind as Josh and Jason moved with a swift, single-minded purpose down a steeply graded hill that ended in a sheer drop-off. Neither had the coordination needed to stop from tumbling over the edge.

Landing on the rock-strewn canyon below, Josh shattered all of his limbs, while Jason got lucky and fell on what used to be his father, rolling off without damage. Driven by mindless appetite, he slowly got to his feet and lurched off into the forest, leaving Josh to writhe hungrily on the ground.

Meanwhile, Maggie veered off in a different direction as the sound of trucks moved off into the distance.

Lights shone down below the tree line.

Lights meant food.

CHAPTER FOUR

"Mmmm, baby, you smell so good."

I giggled as Matt nuzzled against me, sniffing up and down my neck and shoulders. It tickled, and he sounded like a Saint Bernard with asthma. Disgusting and cute at the same time.

I thought I heard a rustling sound, and jumped. Pushing Matt away, I ignored his pout, pulled my sweater back down and jeans back up, scanning for any passers-by wandering the woods behind campus after dark. Not too likely, really, especially when the weather was chilly and overcast. Plus the grove of redwoods where we'd spread our blanket was pretty much private.

So I turned and shot him my sweetest smile, hoping to salve his bruised male ego.

"Pass the champagne, 'kay?"

Matt still pouted a little, but filled a little glass flute with some Italian bubbly.

"It's Prosecco, not champagne, Ash," he said with a light air of condescension. "It's not champagne—"

"—Unless it *comes from Champagne*," I finished for him. "I know, I know." I didn't have the heart to tell him that my ex had exposed me to top quality wine back in the day. I didn't complain about Matt's enthusiasm, though. I got to taste some prime stuff without suffering through the cheap white zins of the world.

Yeah, all in all, I'd rather be seduced with sparkling wine than Pabst Blue Ribbon.

Right on cue, Matt decided he'd sulked long enough and shot me his winning grin.

"Enjoying the picnic, Ash?"

I nodded. How could I not? I mean, how many college guys took the time to pack full-on picnics? We're not talking a bucket of KFC and a six-pack. Nope, roast chicken, bread, brie, and bubbly. Bread knife, cutting board, *and* cloth napkins. He'd even brought a small camp lantern, but had turned it down in order to be less conspicuous. My ex had never gone to this much trouble.

I wonder what Gabriel serves his dates, I mused somewhat guiltily. *Soy wine?* I took another sip and used my free hand to hide a delicate little belch that bubbled out of nowhere.

Bubbly burp, I thought, and I started giggling.

Whoa, tipsy much? I probably should have had more of the food before diving straight into the alcohol.

Matt didn't mind.

"What's so funny?" he asked, not really expecting an answer. Good thing, 'cause I couldn't stop giggling now that I'd started.

He started nuzzling my neck again, making low growling noises that vibrated pleasantly against the sensitive skin, both tickling me and turning me on. One thing led to another and we were soon happily back where we'd left off.

Then he added something new to the repertoire. It was a weird, low, moaning sound—but not the usual "Oh, baby" and "You're turning me on." No, this noise was strange enough to break through my lust-and-alcohol haze.

I stopped in mid-kiss.

"What was that?"

"What was what?" The sound had stopped, and it was pretty obvious Matt that hadn't heard a thing.

He continued stroking my hips, insinuating his hand between my thighs, stroking me through the denim. I squirmed with pleasure even as my ears strained to pick up anything out of the ordinary.

Nothing except the cracking of ancient redwood branches. The forest gave off an almost-sour loamy smell tonight, causing me to wrinkle my nose a bit.

Giving a mental shrug, I turned my attention back to my boy toy, specifically the bulge beneath his jeans. I teased him, rubbing one hand along the outline of his erection while nibbling gently on his neck in a way I knew he liked. His free hand caressed my breasts, first one, and then the other, thumb softly flicking against the nipples, a move guaranteed to drive me wild.

We were both moaning with desire at this point, all panting with eagerness to take things to the next level... when suddenly his hand squeezed my left breast way too hard.

"*Ow!* That hurt!" I smacked him on the shoulder, hard.

"Huh?" Matt lifted his mouth from my earlobe. "What the hell did you do *that* for?"

But he squeezed again, nails digging in this time. A rattling moan sounded close to my ear. The ear *not* next to Matt's mouth.

Suddenly the forest smelled *rank*.

"What the fuck?" I said. "Get off me!" I shoved Matt and rolled away from the moaning. The hand on my breast stayed there, accompanied by a nasty tearing noise, like the sound of a drumstick being ripped off a whole chicken.

Matt grabbed the lantern and turned it up. I looked down and gasped in grossed-out disbelief. The glow revealed a rotted hand clutching my 34-C, ragged nails digging into the flesh. Even worse, said hand was attached to an equally gross arm...

And nothing else.

"Omigod, *that's disgusting*!" I suppressed the urge to hurl the contents of my stomach.

"Jeez, babe, what *is* your damage?" Matt sat up, sounding mortally offended.

I didn't have time to deal with his petulance. I was too busy dislodging what looked like a cheap Halloween prop from my boob. It didn't take much effort; the thing seemed to have lost all of its *oomph*.

As Matt lifted the lantern, I found out why.

The top half of what was once a young woman squirmed on the mossy ground next to our blanket. Her torso trailed off into strings of intestines and other bits of unidentifiable organs. Chunks of flesh were missing from her face and neck.

Two spooky, milky-white eyes stared at me from above a bloody hole, chewed gristle sticking out where her nose used to be. Her mouth opened and closed hungrily as she used her remaining arm to pull herself onto the blanket.

I choked back a definitely hysterical laugh as I wondered if this counted as a lesbian encounter. Then my stomach twisted in serious knots, and I threw up.

"Holy shit!" Matt got a good look at our visitor as she pulled herself slowly, relentlessly towards us. "Holy shit! What the fuck *is* that?"

I shook my head, holding back my own "holy shits" through the sheer force of willpower.

"I don't know," I said, trying to stay calm. "But it's ugly and it felt me up and I think it's trying to eat us." I fumbled in the picnic basket and grabbed the bread knife.

"What are you doing, Ash?" Matt's voice rose an octave as I turned back to what had to be the grossest picnic crasher ever.

I didn't say anything, though. I just brought the knife down as hard as I could into one of Miss Thang's ears, shoving with all of my strength to push the serrated blade deep into whatever was left of her brain... and hoped that the movies didn't lie.

Kill the brain, kill the zombie.

And it worked. She... it... stopped wriggling and chomping, like a really gross mechanical doll with the batteries removed.

Matt stared at me as though he didn't know who I was.

"What did you just do?"

I shrugged, my body still thrumming with adrenaline. I felt oddly detached from reality, possibly because reality had just received a new and totally fucked-up definition.

"I think I just killed a zombie." Yeah, that definitely didn't sound like something I would say.

"There's no such thing as zombies!" Matt's voice was unnaturally high, as if he'd regressed.

"Well, what the hell would you call *this?*" I added emphasis with another shove of the bread knife. Matt winced. He opened his mouth to answer, but suddenly the night was filled with a moaning chorus.

This could *not* be good.

CHAPTER FIVE

Matt jumped up, nostrils flaring like those of a panicked horse.

Bracing one hand against the... *thing's* head, I tried to extract the knife, but I'd jammed it in there well and good, and it wasn't budging.

Eerie moans floated through and above the trees, drifting with tendrils of fog coming in from the ocean.

I needed more leverage.

Scrambling to my feet, I grabbed the knife with both hands, and pulled. The blade came up slowly, reluctantly. A horrible squelching sound and the knife gave way, nearly sending me back on my ass with the suddenness of its release.

"We have to get out of here," Matt said unnecessarily. He started gathering up the picnic gear. I just stared at him.

"Are you *crazy*? Leave this shit behind!"

"This *shit* cost me over a hundred bucks." Matt tossed the champagne flutes into the basket. I heard one of them break as it hit a china plate.

"We'll come back for it later!" I grabbed the lantern and shoved it into his hand. "*Now*, Matt." Latching onto his arm, I pulled him out of the grove. We used the lantern's light to navigate uphill through the trees as milky fog poured in like a bad special effect. The only thing missing was the blue backlighting.

The moaning grew louder as we neared the top of the hill. At the summit the old redwood growth gave way to an overgrown field with a trail leading back to campus through blackberry bushes and bracken. All we had to do was follow the trail and call the cops when we reached Big Red.

We reached the top and paused to catch our breath. Mine stuck in my throat as the smell hit again, but stronger. A thick, coppery mix of blood, rot, and shit. In my mind's eye I pictured decayed flesh oozing out with stuff meant to stay inside… like intestines.

The moon hit a break in the clouds and I scanned the field. Tendrils of fog drifted across the landscape, but not enough to obscure the sight of at least two dozen—maybe more—ambulatory figures staggering through the bushes and on the path. One of them spotted us and staggered in our direction, its moans growing louder.

This set off a chain reaction and pretty soon the entire crowd moaned in discordant harmony, some internal zombie GPS system set on me and Matt. A couple of them were close enough that we could see strips of flesh and white bone glistening in the moonlight.

"How are they moving?" Matt's breath rasped, in and out, in and out. "They should be dead!"

"I think they are." I fought the impulse to puke up what was left of my Prosecco.

"Then they shouldn't be walking!" Matt's well-ordered world view had been smashed to hell and back, and he was having serious trouble dealing. I couldn't blame him. I mean, if the dead could walk, then what other nasties from our nightmares were waiting to appear?

But there was no time for this.

"Well, they *are* walking, Matt," I said harshly, "and we need to get out of here. We don't have time for you to freak out!"

"We should go back through the woods!"

I shook my head.

"We don't know how many of those things are in there. At least here we can see them… and it's a straight shot to campus."

Matt nodded, visibly struggling to keep a grip. I suppose everyone has areas outside of their comfort zone. I wasn't sure why zombies weren't outside of mine.

The same thing must have occurred to him. He looked at me as if I were a stranger.

"Why aren't *you* freaking out?"

I didn't have a real answer.

"I guess I'll freak out later," I offered, "when we're safe."

His expression made me wonder if our relationship would survive the night, even if *we* did, but I didn't have time to dwell on it. The zombies lurched closer with every second. Classic George Romero ghouls, thank god, not the ones that could sprint. Still…

There was a loud *crack* as a branch broke like a gunshot. At least I hoped it was a branch. Time to run. I seized Matt's hand.

"GO!" I shouted, and hauled ass down the trail for all I was worth, Matt right beside me.

There were more of them than I had realized. Rotting, diseased hands clutched at us from either side, like the gauntlet scene in *The Last of the Mohicans* except with zombies instead of Hurons.

We shook off the first of them, barreling through the ones that stepped in front of us with the velocity of a well-thrown bowling ball smashing into ninepins. The blackberry bushes helped us—they grew all around the path and even at their sparsest, the brambles clutched at the encroaching undead.

But they kept coming. For each one we knocked down, two more would stagger out of the brush, leaving bits of themselves behind as they pushed through the thorns, oblivious to pain.

I'm not much of a runner—jogging is last on my list

of exercise options—so I got winded pretty quickly. Matt, on the other hand, quickly outdistanced me, sprinting down the path with one arm outstretched like a fullback smashing through the opposition. He sent a few zombies flailing back into the blackberries, but several landed their decomposing asses on the path… right in front of me.

I leapt over the first one, what was once a skinny woman with chunks of her arms and legs missing. A broken branch stuck out of one milky eyeball, indefinable goo all jellied and gross below it. She wore a robe, thankfully zipped up the front. I so did not want to see zombie boobies.

Barely eluding her grasping fingers as they skimmed my ankle, I stumbled, recovered, and then tripped right over a fat businessman type, suit still surprisingly intact. I know this because I fell right on top of him.

Ugh. Squishy.

He clutched me with implacable strength before I could move. I looked right into his dead eyes, and smelled decomposition wafting out of the gaping maw of his mouth.

I shrieked as the zombie brought his gore-drenched teeth toward my neck, and shoved my left arm in-between us without thinking. He growled and sunk his teeth into my sweater-clad forearm. I screamed bloody murder and managed to jerk away from him.

A chunk of my arm and sweater stayed behind.

Fatty reached for me again, but this time I threw myself back to the ground before he could take another bite out of me. I crab-scuttled away from him as quickly as I could, the bite in my arm burning as if it was on fire. I scuttled right into the woman I'd vaulted over—she was just getting to her feet. Clawed fingers seized my hair. I flailed wildly, sacrificing a handful of hair to get away, but she got a bite of my shoulder anyway.

God, that hurts.

I wailed in pain and terror, my screams mixing with

the moans of more zombies closing in for their share of the feast.

"Ashley!"

I heard Matt shout my name from what seemed miles away, along with what sounded like footsteps pounding my way. Then his voice.

"Get off me, you motherfucker!"

A loud thud as several bodies hit the ground. And then the screams began.

Matt kept screaming for what seemed forever, shrieks of unimaginable pain accompanied by the sound of teeth rending flesh.

I didn't know guys could scream so high, I thought vaguely as I struggled to my feet, the world fading out around the edges. I knew I was dead, but part of me refused to give up, even as what seemed like hundreds of undead hands reached for me again.

I backed away into the blackberry bushes, hemmed in by zombies on both sides of the path. No retreat, no way forward. Thorns dug into my back, poking through the fabric of my sweater and jeans, and grabbed at my arms. My hair snarled in some branches, trapping me as effectively as a fly in a spider web, no matter how hard I tried to pull free.

Death closed in from all sides, reaching for me with implacable hands and ravenous mouths.

I gave one last scream of despair mixed with fury. This was *so* not how I wanted to die. I mean, zombie chow?

Fuck my life.

A red light suddenly danced in the center of the closest zombie's forehead. Just as suddenly, there was a loud burping sound. A neat little hole replaced the light and the zombie fell to the ground, the back of its head a gaping wound.

The rest of the ghouls were dispatched with similar

efficiency as I cowered against the blackberry bushes, nearly fainting with fear and pain. The closer ones fell one by one, while those that were further away fell before a fusillade of bullets.

Suddenly I was harboring the smallest hope I might make it out of this alive.

A tall figure appeared in front of me, dressed entirely in black. I shrieked again and struck out with my fists. Strong, gloved hands caught me by the wrists and a deep male voice yelled.

"This one's alive!"

Maybe not for long, though, I thought as the blackness around the edges pushed inward. I gave up, and let it take over completely.

CHAPTER SIX

I struggled to find my way back to consciousness, swimming through a sea of fever, pain, and nausea, all wrapped in a battening of cotton around my brain. I knew I felt like shit, but either shock or some sort of medication prevented me from feeling the full effects of what had happened to me.

What *had* happened to me?

I opened my eyes and stared blearily at my surroundings. I was lying on a bed of sorts, covered by a lightweight blanket. The room looked like some sort of temporary hospital ward, something out of a war movie or *M*A*S*H* reruns. I think they called it a triage unit.

A dozen or so flimsy-looking cots occupied with moaning, weeping patients; intravenous fluid set-ups; lots of people in olive drab hazmat suits—the kind meant to protect you against chemical or biological nasties. I couldn't see anyone's face through the protective goggles and faceplates. Some carried medical gear.

Others held firearms.

WTF?

I tried to move, but it hurt so much that I stopped trying, shut my eyes, and lay back, becoming more aware of every ache and pain in my body with each passing second.

White-hot poison bubbled inside my right shoulder and arm. Itching, burning sensations coursed through the skin, muscles, and blood vessels. I wanted to rip out the pain and the itching, but I couldn't move my arms, so I just suffered in a fog of confusion.

Someone groaned nearby, and the sound became more frantic. I slowly turned my head until I could see the cot next to me. The man occupying it thrashed in apparent agony, head whipping back and forth so fast that his features blurred.

"She's awake."

I jumped, and pain flashed through my shoulder, causing me to groan. Someone was standing at the head of my bed. I couldn't tell if it was a man or a woman—everything was filtered through the bass drum that was pounding in my head.

"Ashley?" the muffled voice said right next to my ear. "Are you hungry?" I forced my eyes open and saw one of the faceless hazmat wearers standing next to my cot. He/she/it held a styrofoam container holding a chunk of raw, bloody meat, waving it in front of my nose as if it were a gourmet dish.

I gagged at the sight, trying desperately not to puke.

"Get that away from me!" I tried to move my left arm so I could get the nauseating thing out of my face, but something held me down. I tugged violently against whatever restrained me, and the movement was enough to send shards of glass burrowing into my head. My vision blurred and my eyelids slammed shut as someone yelled.

"We've got another wild card!"

Another wild what? I thought before passing out again.

When I woke up again, I still hurt… but the pain was less intense, as if someone had kindly poured Novocain inside all of my wounds. I knew it was there, but it was muted. Almost bearable.

"Ashley." It was a familiar voice that I couldn't quite place. "Ashley, can you hear me?"

I opened my eyes, and blinked once or twice in the glare of a stark fluorescent ceiling light. My eyelids hurt and my vision was blurry, but at least no one was shoving raw meat in my face.

"Ashley?"

I focused on the figure in front of me, trying to place the voice. Blurred lines and features slowly coalesced into the familiar smile of Professor Fraser, still dressed like Katharine Hepburn, sitting in a chair next to me.

Her presence made no sense. Yet I found it oddly comforting.

"H... Hi," I stammered. *Ohhh*. It hurt to talk. My throat felt as if I'd swigged a glass of Drano. Probably from all the screaming I'd done.

Professor Fraser looked down at me.

"How do you feel?"

Like shit, I thought. I struggled to sit up, but quickly realized it was a bad idea when a wave of nausea and weakness swept over me.

"Crappy," I said.

"Not surprising." The professor laid a cool hand on my forehead; it felt good. "You've been through an experience most people don't survive." She picked something up off of a tray. "Here." She held a straw to my mouth. I sipped and was rewarded with a mouthful of cold ginger ale.

I don't think anything in the world ever tasted as good.

A few more sips settled my stomach, and I risked moving my head to look around me. The surreal movie-set med ward had been replaced by an equally surreal small room, windowless except for a little view panel in the door. Sterile white walls, no closet, no bathroom, no other furniture except the chair occupied by Professor Fraser, my bed, and a little stand next to it.

"Where am I?" I asked, and I totally expected some bullshit answer. *This is a secret facility, and I can't tell you...*

"You're in a lower level of the med lab behind Patterson Hall."

Okay, not so secret. I decided to press my luck.

"What's going on?"

"What do *you* think is going on?"

Ah, and there's the bullshit.

Professor Fraser stared at me, waiting for an answer. If only I'd had one.

"What is this?" I countered. "Psych 101?"

"No. I'd just like to hear your take on what happened to you."

"My take?" I *so* was not in the mood for head games. "My boyfriend and I were having a picnic and…" I stopped short, flashing back to the sound of screams. *Ohmigod, Matt. What happened to Matt?* I started again, trying to keep my voice from trembling.

"Matt and I were having a picnic, and we were attacked by… zombies." The word just hung there.

"Zombies?" She continued to study me, and for the life of me I couldn't tell if she was taking me seriously, or ready to have me committed. Hell, even *I* couldn't decide whether or not to have me committed.

Too bone-weary and sick to be defensive, I shrugged, then immediately wished I hadn't. I had another swallow of ginger ale before I tried to talk again.

"Yeah. Zombies. Unless you have a better word for people who look dead, smell dead, and act dead, except for the whole walking-around-and-trying-to-eat-flesh part." I blanched at the all too recent memory of teeth sinking into my shoulder and arm. My chest tightened as delayed panic started to set in.

I forced myself to breathe.

"No, that works," Professor Fraser said, "though traditionally zombies were thought to be created through a combination of voodoo and a special powder containing textrodotoxin, the same poison found in pufferfish. This combination was said to create a state of living death in its victims. The etymology of the word 'zombie' is in and of itself absolutely fascinating, and—"

I stared at her and she stopped.

"Erm, yes. Zombie is an adequate term to describe the creatures that attacked you. Although," she couldn't resist adding, "ghoul is another popular word in the nomenclature assigned to the reanimated dead."

Uh-huh. Mercifully, curiosity was replacing the memories. Professor Fraser's calm, academic observations were as soothing as Valium.

"So you're telling me these things are real. You're not gonna tell me I'm crazy or on crack or whatever?"

Professor Fraser shook her head.

"No. You experienced something outside of the norm… but unfortunately, not outside of reality."

"And those were really dead people walking around? Hungry dead people."

A hesitation.

"Yes. I'm afraid so."

I lay back, taking a deep breath. Looked at my bandaged arm, felt the throb in my neck and shoulder. I had enough pop culture savvy to know what that meant.

"Am I… that's going to happen to me, isn't it?" She didn't answer right away. I reached out and grabbed her hand. "You're going to have to shoot me in the head, aren't you?"

"No," Professor Fraser said, "but that's a very good response on your part."

"What the hell are you talking about, Professor?" It was official—I'd entered the "anger" stage. "I've been bitten, so whatever infected those people, whether it's voodoo or puffer fish toxins or whatever—it's gonna happen to me, too, isn't it?"

"Simone."

"Huh?"

"My name is Simone." That took me by surprise. Professor Fraser gently extracted her hand from mine, but then took my hand in hers and peered at me steadily. "We'll be working together now, and probably for the foreseeable future. There's no need for things to stay so formal."

"Working together?" I had no idea what she was talking about. My head suddenly pounded to the rhythm of my heartbeat, my arm and shoulder throbbed, and I wanted more painkillers. "I'm not dying?"

Professor Fraser shook her head, and I didn't think she was bullshitting me any longer.

"No," she answered. "You need to rest and let your wounds heal. That's all."

"But how do you know?" My face flushed with fever heat as my anxiety ramped up another notch. "How can you be sure I'm not gonna die, and try to eat you?" I struggled to sit up again, but she placed a firm hand on my uninjured shoulder.

"Trust me, Ashley, I've seen this before—"

Of course you have, I thought furiously. *Nothing to see here, folks, 'cause this happens every day!*

Then I stopped myself.

What if it *did*, but most people were lucky enough to never know about it?

"And you exhibit none of the clinical indications we've come to associate with reanimation," she continued.

Clinical indications?

I searched Professor Fraser's face for some sign that she was lying, and saw nothing but certainty there. She was so calm, it was both disconcerting and yet oddly comforting.

I lay back down.

"What… what about Matt?" I asked, not sure I wanted to know the answer. "Is he here, too?"

Was it my imagination or did she hesitate before replying?

"Yes," she said. "He's in another part of the lab."

Oh, thank god… I'd thought for sure he'd been ripped to pieces.

"Is he okay?" There was a definite hesitation this time. My skin began to crawl. *So much for comforting.*

"He's still alive," she said.

"Can I see him?"

Professor Fraser... Simone... shook her head.

"Not right now," she said, and I thought I saw cracks appearing in that composure. "You need to rest."

"I don't want to rest," I protested. "I've *been* resting. I want to know what's—"

"I know you do," she said, and she pressed a small button next to the bed. "We'll explain everything to you when you're more up to it."

We?

The pulsing in my head increased. I was about to force the issue when the door opened to admit a skinny, ginger-bearded, and vaguely rodent-featured man in his early fifties.

"Doctor Albert?"

He jumped a little, as if startled.

"Oh, hello, Ashley."

"What are you doing here?"

Dr. Albert smiled soothingly.

"I'm the head of University Medical Services," he said, as if that explained everything. Before I could respond, he took something out of his pocket. A syringe. "Now Ashley, this will help you with the pain, and let you sleep a bit more."

This is a load of crap, I thought. I wanted to know what happened to me. I wanted to know what happened to Matt! But I was too weak to resist as he administered the shot and my protests died before they'd begun.

The effects hit almost immediately, and a wave of numbing drowsiness washed over me. Without a word, I drifted back off to sleep.

Josh lay on the ground, mouth opening and closing in mindless hunger. Footsteps crunched on pine needles and dirt a short distance away.

"Any sign?"

"Piece of terrycloth. Dried blood on it."

Cartridges were slapped into place and rounds chambered as the footsteps sped up to a slow jog, heading in Josh's direction. He moaned again, the sound rising up and echoing through fog-shrouded trees.

"Think I've got a zed over here, sir!"

Footsteps crunched on pine needles.

"Oh, man, that is seriously fucked up..." Someone coughed, almost dry heaving. Josh moaned, clawing hungrily at the dusty black boots a foot or so away from his head.

"Zed identified, sir!"

"Fire!"

"On the way!"

There was a clap of thunder and Josh's second life disintegrated, along with his head.

CHAPTER SEVEN

I don't know what the doctor shot me up with, but whatever it was, I slept like the un-reanimated dead—a long and dreamless sleep.

Waking up was better this time; I could open my eyes without sending ground-glass pain shooting into the lids and sockets. In the nasty glare of the fluorescent lights, everything looked much as it had before, except the chair where Simone had been sitting was unoccupied.

The door to my little room was closed, but I could hear an occasional voice and the sound of footsteps. My anxiety, although muted by the lingering effects of the sedative I'd been given, rose a notch. A borderline claustrophobic, I didn't much like the closed space.

Was I a patient here, or a prisoner?

I pushed myself up to a seated position with much more success than my last attempt. My shoulder and arm still throbbed under their bandages, but other than that, I felt pretty damn good… which in itself was pretty damn weird.

I was wicked thirsty—probably dehydrated from the drugs, not to mention the hundred-yard zombie dash I'd done—but I actually felt rested. It was like the first good sleep-in of summer vacation. Except I usually didn't start my summer vacation with chunks of flesh missing from my body.

That's gonna suck come tank-top weather.

A glass sat on the bedside table, condensation frosting its sides. I reached for it with my left hand, wincing when the move put pressure on wound.

The pain was totally worth it, though, once I took a swallow of cold ginger ale. The taste reminded me of childhood and being home sick, with my mom bringing saltines and glass after glass of soda to settle my stomach.

My mom...

Was this zombie thing happening all over the place, or just around Redwood Grove? My parents were up in Lake County. Would they be safe on their ranch?

I needed to call them, but my iPhone was gone, probably lying somewhere in the woods or the field, covered with blood and intestines. I fought the urge to leap out of bed, mainly because I'd likely collapse if I tried to do anything that quickly. So I pushed the blankets off me and very slowly and carefully swung my legs over the side of the bed, pausing to see what the rest of me thought of this movement.

My head felt a little woozy, and I doubted my bite wounds would like *anything* at this point, but... not too bad.

Better living through drugs.

Encouraged, I set my feet on the ground and stood up.

Whoah. Suddenly I knew how Dorothy felt. I held onto the rickety metal bed frame and waited for things to stop spinning, or at least slow down a bit. Closing my eyes helped.

"What the *hell* are you doing out of bed?"

The voice came out of nowhere: male, angry and horrifyingly familiar. My eyelids flew open and I let out a startled yelp, letting go of the bed frame.

Bad move.

Things started to go gray and my knees went wobbly. My face and the floor were on a collision course, but strong arms stopped the fall just before impact, scooping me up like I weighed five pounds instead of, well, whatever. My visitor carefully set me on the bed while cursing under his breath.

I lay there for a minute until I was sure I wasn't going to pass out, and then took another look. I prayed this was just another nightmare, or the after-effects of the drugs.

Gabriel glared at me, arms folded. He wore green fatigues and a black T-shirt, and looked about ten pounds lighter than the last time I'd seen him. The weight loss didn't harm his good looks; his cheekbones were more defined than ever.

"What are *you* doing here?" I said, shooting for authoritative. But my voice sounded feeble and kind of petulant, even to my own ears.

"Stopping you from falling flat on your face, it would seem," he replied with that familiar holier-than-thou attitude. I would have rolled my eyes if I didn't think it would hurt. Instead I settled for a glare of my own.

"I only fell because you startled me."

"You shouldn't be out of bed," Gabriel said as he plunked himself down in the room's only chair. "Professor Fraser sent me to check on you."

"But why are you dressed like Rambo?" The dizziness passed, and I started to sit up, only to have him put a restraining hand on my shoulder. He ignored my admittedly snarky question.

"You need to rest," he said.

"I've been resting for…" Then I stopped, realizing I had no idea how long I'd been asleep. "Gabriel, I need to call my parents. I need to find out what happened to Matt. I need to find out what happened to *me*."

An unreadable expression flashed across his face, but was quickly replaced by a stoic mask.

"No phones," he said flatly.

"What do you mean, no phones?" I knocked his hand off my shoulder and struggled up to a sitting position. "There are *always* phones!"

"Not here, not now there aren't."

"That's a shitty answer!"

"It's all you're going to get." He crossed his arms again and stared straight ahead.

Bedside manner? Epic fail.

Maybe he's pissy because Professor Fraser doesn't let him call her Simone. Whatever the reason, I matched him, glare for *son-of-a-bitch* glare until he stood up.

"I'm going to get the professor," he said. "Now that you're awake, she'll want to talk to you."

Way to pass the buck.

"Wait!" I said.

Gabriel paused, hand on the doorknob.

I opened my mouth to ask about Matt, but that wasn't what came out.

"I need to use the bathroom." Was it just the light or did Gabriel's face just turn red?

Yup, definitely some embarrassment going on there.

"Professor Fraser said you needed to stay in bed."

It was like talking to a call center in Bangalore. He couldn't deviate from the script.

Resistance is useless...

"Look, that's all well and good, but I need to pee, okay? Unless you have a bedpan handy, I really need to get to a bathroom—like *now.*"

Gabriel opened his mouth to argue, came to his senses and snapped it shut again without further discussion. When I started to stand up, he helped me to my feet. And for just a moment, the strength of his arm around my shoulders was a momentarily safe haven against the uncertainty rocking my world.

He opened the door and led me out into a hallway which was lit by the same unforgiving fluorescent bulbs. Down at one end a pair of double doors swung open and I could see the makeshift medical ward. People in hazmat suits and others dressed like Gabriel were bustling around, and a low hum of continual conversation was clearly audible. I also heard moans, and some screams. Disturbing splashes of red were clearly visible on the floor and bedclothes.

"Come on."

Gabriel steered me in the other direction. The hallway was lined with doors sporting little view-panels like the one in the door to my room. We reached the restrooms, clearly marked with the ubiquitous man-in-pants and woman-in-dress outlines. Gabriel stopped outside of the women's room.

"Will you be okay on your own?" He sounded suspiciously sincere.

I nodded and stepped away from the security of his arm. I wobbled slightly, but used the door handle to steady myself before he could grab me again. I didn't care if I passed out; no way was Gabriel coming in with me. There are some things a girl has to do on her own.

I did my business as quickly as possible and washed my hands thoroughly, as if to scrub away what had happened. Splashing water on my face, I made the mistake of looking at myself in the mirror. A ghastly pale face with hollowed eye sockets stared back at me, total "heroin chic."

The bandages on my shoulder were flecked with red at the point of the wound. Not too badly, though. Just a few dots of blood soaking through the gauze to remind me of what lay beneath.

I poked experimentally at the still pristine dressing covering my forearm. *Ouch!* Yes, it still hurt, but no blood came through. I flashed back to the moment when the fat zombie had sunk his teeth into my flesh. At the time it'd felt like he'd torn away half my arm, but maybe it wasn't so bad.

I shivered, and noticed that my backside and legs were colder than the rest of me. That brought the realization I was wearing one of those flimsy hospital gowns that tied at the back, leaving the butt hanging out when the two sides inevitably flapped open. And at some point or another someone had removed all of my clothes, leaving only my pink lace thong.

Great.

A fist pounded on the door, sending a surge of adrenaline through me.

"You okay in there?" Gabriel's voice, sounding more impatient than ever.

Jeez frickin' Louise, can't a girl pee in private?

"Yeah, I'm fine," I said. "Give me a sec."

I had a perverse desire to take my sweet time. But I really needed to lie back down, so I stifled my petty impulse and rejoined Gabriel in the hall.

He put an arm around my shoulders again, but any hint of warmth was gone. If I hadn't needed his arm for support, I would've shoved it off.

Before we reached my room, the double doors at the end of the hall crashed open and a gun-toting, hazmat-suit-clad soldier burst into the hallway. He called out to Gabriel.

"Captain! We have a situation!"

Captain? Since when did a teacher's aide earn a rank? I filed this away for later.

Gabriel's arm immediately dropped from my shoulders.

"I'll be right there." He turned to me. "Ashley, go back to your room." Not bothering to wait for an answer, he took off after the soldier, leaving me swaying unsteadily in the hallway.

I wanted to lie down, and really should have gone back to my room. But I've never been much for following orders, especially with so many questions left unanswered. So I waited a moment, and then followed him into the makeshift medical ward.

CHAPTER EIGHT

The screams I'd heard from the hallway hit me like a wave of sound the instant I slipped into the ward. Eerie moans echoed above the screaming, a real life chorus of the damned. The smell in the room was thick, coppery, and rancid. I did *not* want to know what the source was. There were a dozen or so cots, all occupied by thrashing people. None of them looked good. Sallow, greenish-yellow skin tone, like jaundice with a bad case of mold. Blood and other fluids leaking from their mouths, noses, and ears. Some had raw wounds on their arms or legs while others had bandages seeping through with blood—or in some cases, nasty, foul-smelling blackish ooze. Most of them had restraints strapped across their arms, waists, and legs, along with metal collars around their necks. The straps were totally disturbing, and the collars were strangely decorated with a bunch of rings. It was just plain creepy.

There was a commotion at the far end of the room, lots of shouting and guys brandishing guns. Most of the hazmat brigade were down there, along with Gabriel. Like me, he wasn't wearing protective gear.

I briefly wondered why, but then the woman in the cot nearest me started convulsing. Dark blood poured from her mouth and nose in scary quantities. Her eyes snapped open and for an instant we locked gazes. The whites of her eyes looked like bloody egg yolks; sickly yellow streaked with red veins. Thick red tears oozed out from under her lashes and trickled down her face. She opened her mouth and croaked out something.

I think it was "Help me."

Then a fresh flow of blood caused the words to rattle and distort in her throat.

"I... I'm sorry..."

I backed away from her, wanting only to escape from the horror of the moment. My legs hit cold metal and I nearly toppled back onto another cot, this one holding a skinny African-American kid covered in red-soaked sheets. His eyes and mouth gaped open, blood oozing thickly from the corners. I would have thought he was dead, except for the occasional tremor wracking his body.

Pressing a hand to my mouth to force back the bile rising in my throat, I stumbled to the middle of the room, trying not to look any more as my ears filled with the grotesque sounds of throats closing up, then vomiting out foul-smelling liquids.

Why isn't anyone doing something for these people?

Someone at the far end of the room growled, and it was a guttural, feral sound. My attention snapped back there in time to see one of the hazmat guys raise his gun, tugging back on a lever that made a nasty *ch-chak*, like the noise a shotgun makes in the movies when they rack a shell into it.

"Hold your fire." Gabriel barked the order in a tone that cut through the chaos. "Don't shoot it. We need to contain as many of these specimens as possible."

Specimens?

"Use the poles. Just keep away from its teeth."

I slowly approached the cluster of soldiers and medics, and saw that one of the creatures was loose. He... it was wearing one of the collars. The soldiers had poles, about six feet in length with spring-loaded clasps on the ends. No one noticed me as two or three of them tried to hook their clasps into one of the metal rings on the collar. The thing's head was snapping from side to side, but I could see that he had once been a good-looking guy in his twenties. He wore the torn, bloody remnants of jeans and a white cotton, button-down shirt.

Wounds were visible through the shredded fabric, deep gouges in gangrenous sallow-green flesh.

"Matt…?"

My voice came out as barely a croak.

Matt's head stopped moving as if my voice triggered an off switch. Everyone froze around him, seeming afraid that they would set him off again. Then he slowly turned to the side to stare at me with milky white pupils, the whites themselves yellowed and bloodshot.

One hand stretched out toward me and for a heartbeat I thought he recognized me. Then a feral snarl distorted his features and he… *it* lunged for me, mindless hunger the only thing evident in those dead eyes as it plowed unheedingly through the soldiers who stood between us.

A bolt of paralyzing grief hit me, so strong and painful that it felt as if someone plunged a knife into my chest. I just stood there as my now undead boyfriend knocked soldiers aside in a driving hunger for my flesh that had nothing to do with sex.

Zombie Matt's fingers actually grazed my shoulders when one of the pole clasps suddenly snagged the collar around its neck, stopping it in its tracks. I looked up to see Gabriel holding the other end of the pole, muscles tensing as he fought to pull Matt away from me. Everyone else scattered as it bucked and lunged, hands grasping and slipping off hazmat suits, guttural moans and growls spilling out of its mouth along with that rank black fluid.

"Some help here!" Sweat poured off Gabriel's brow.

Without thinking, I grabbed up one of the poles dropped by the soldiers and shoved the business end up against the ring on the other side of Matt's collar. The clasp opened and shut with a snap. The resulting jerk on my arms and shoulders nearly made me pass out. All that kept me upright was the knowledge that if I fainted, I would probably die.

Gabriel shot me an unreadable look.

"Someone grab that pole—*now!*" he barked.

Thankfully, someone grabbed the pole from my hands. Someone else caught me as I started a slow collapse to the floor.

This is getting monotonous, I thought as everything faded to black.

The last thing Annie wanted to do was open the store. Her throat felt like raw meat, what with all the coughing, and she could buy stock in Kleenex. But with Lily currently unreachable and her mom out of town, someone had to keep things running.

At least she had a job, Annie told herself as she went through the morning routine. And when she didn't feel like hammered shit, it was a job she loved, with a great boss and a sweetheart of a co-worker.

Maybe Lily had lost her cell phone, Annie mused as she counted out the bank for the register. It wasn't like her to ignore calls, especially when the store was involved. She sneezed for the umpteenth time in two days, getting her sleeve up just in time to prevent her from spraying the contents of the register. She was blowing her nose when the first screams ripped through the air outside.

Annie froze in front of the register. Then the unmistakable shriek of a child came from the courtyard out front, unlocking her paralysis. Grabbing the shop key, she dashed to the front door, jammed the key in the lock, and turned the tumblers.

Out in the courtyard a little boy in dinosaur-print pajamas cowered on the lawn as two men and a woman converged on him, all three looking—and smelling—like they'd spent the night in a dumpster.

Annie didn't stop to think. She threw herself through the door, yelling in outrage as she ran toward the little boy.

"What are you people doing? Get away from him!"

The woman ignored her, reaching for the child, who cringed away in terror.

"Mommy, no, please!"

The two men turned toward Annie, who stopped short in disbelief and dawning horror as she saw their faces for the first time. Black fluid dripped from their ears, noses, and mouths, their eyes were a combination of sickly yellow whites and milky corneas. One had a chunk of flesh missing from his cheek; the other looked like he'd gone a round with a grizzly, and lost.

Both moaned and lurched in her direction. She stumbled back a step, looking over at the child, who was now screaming steadily as the woman grabbed hold of him despite his efforts to scramble away.

"Mommy, nooo! Mommeeee!" His shrieks rose in pitch and intensity as the woman bit into his arm.

Annie took a step toward him, the desire to save him warring with the gut-wrenching fear that was flooding through her. When one of the things drew close enough to brush her with its bloodied fingertips, she ran back to the door of the shop, the boy's screams stabbing into her heart.

Clutching the handle, she turned it. It stopped halfway, locked from the inside. And the key was hanging from the lock on the other side of the door.

She spun around as hands reached for her, holding her, tearing at her. Teeth sunk into her neck as she was borne to the ground under the weight of reeking bodies. Something tore into her stomach, but soon the unbearable pain faded into blackness.

I woke up—again—in my little sterile room. To my surprise, Gabriel sat in the chair next to the bed. His eyes were shut and I thought he was asleep. He looked haggard, as exhausted as I felt.

Although…

Honestly, I didn't feel nearly as shitty as I should have. I ached a little, sure, but the fever? Gone. The bite wounds itched, and that was irritating, but shouldn't they have hurt a lot more?

I poked at the fresh bandage covering the bite on my forearm, resulting in about as much pain as if I'd bruised it sometime in the last couple of days.

This isn't right.

I began to think about what had happened before my blackout.

Matt.

I didn't want to go there. So to distract myself, I unhooked the little butterfly clasp holding the bandage in place and slowly unwound what seemed like a large intestine's length of gauze. I winced and closed my eyes as I revealed the arm itself, prepared for a gaping, ragged hole where the zombie's teeth had ripped away the flesh.

Giving in to the inevitable, I opened my eyes, and to my surprise the wound wasn't that bad. I could see tooth marks, sure, but I'd expected a major loss of flesh, and it just wasn't there.

"You feeling okay?"

I jerked, and Gabriel sat up, eyes open, bloodshot yet still startlingly blue.

"Yeah…" I sat up without any residual light-headedness. "I feel pretty good, actually. I don't get it."

Looking uncomfortable, Gabriel got to his feet.

"Professor Fraser will be here in a minute," he muttered. He opened the door and started to leave.

"Wait." I regretted it as soon as I said it.

He stopped in the doorway.

"What?"

"What—" I choked, afraid of the question I was about to ask. "What happened to Matt?"

He hesitated. His uncertainty was freaking me out, to the point that I actually missed the egotistical posturing.

"Professor Fraser will explain," he said. He turned to leave again, then paused and looked back at me.

"I'm really sorry about your boyfriend, Ashley."

The door shut behind him.

I drank some more ginger ale from the tray on my bedside stand, then lay back. About five minutes later the door opened and Simone entered, bearing a tray which she put on the bed stand. She sat down next to me and gave me an encouraging smile.

"Are you hungry, Ashley?"

I shook my head.

"Not really." I smelled chicken broth and my stomach growled. Okay, I lied. But I didn't *want* to be hungry. Matt was dead. Or should be dead. And somehow the fact that my body still wanted food seemed like a betrayal.

Simone reached out and brushed a lock of hair back from my forehead. The simple kindness of the gesture brought tears to my eyes.

"I know you're hurting... both physically and emotionally." She leaned back. "No one should have to go through what you've experienced in the last twenty-four hours. But you should try and eat something. You need to get your strength back. And you *did* lose some blood, you know."

"I want to call my parents," I said, trying hard not to cry. Suddenly I wanted to hear my mom's voice so badly it hurt. Some things didn't change with age.

"I'm sorry, Ashley, but that's just not possible." Simone looked sympathetic, but didn't give any ground. "Outside communications have been heavily restricted. We have a center handling all calls in and out of the quarantine zone."

"Quarantine zone?" My voice took on a new urgency. "Let me talk to my parents! I need to know if they're okay!"

"Where do they live?" she asked.

"Lake County."

A reassuring look settled on her face.

"So far the infection has been contained in Redwood County," she said. "They should be safe."

"But what if they contact this call center?" I pressed. "How will they know *I'm* okay?"

"They'll be told that you're recovering from a relapse of the flu, but need to remain in quarantine for a while longer. And that you're getting the best possible care." Simone patted my shoulder. "They'll still worry, of course, but not too badly."

I shut my eyes and heaved a reluctant sigh of relief.

Maybe I'll eat a little something after all.

Opening my eyes again, I looked at her.

"How did this happen?" I asked. "For that matter, what the hell happened?"

She shook her head.

"I don't know. *We* don't know."

"Who's 'we'?"

"Ah." Simone picked up the tray and set it carefully across my stomach. "Eat something, and I'll tell you what I can."

Chicken noodle soup, saltines, and more ginger ale. A very familiar menu, and definitely comfort food. Right now I needed all the comfort I could get. So I crumbled crackers into the soup, picked up the spoon, and ate while Simone talked.

"This isn't the first time an outbreak of this sort has occurred." She settled into professorial mode, lacking only her lectern and laser pointer. "Throughout history," she continued, "there have been outbreaks of the reanimated dead, also referred to as zombies, the walking dead, the living dead, and by numerous other colloquial and hyperbolic descriptions. It really all depends on the time period, locale, and average I.Q. of the local populace. 'Walking death' has been a popular term for the condition, though."

A part of me couldn't believe what I was hearing. I

wanted to scream, *What kind of idiot do you take me for?* Then again, I'd had chunks of flesh ripped out of my arm and had come face to face with my undeniably zombified boyfriend.

So I just let her continue.

"It's been difficult to isolate the root cause," she admitted. "It acts like a virus, spread via contact with the bodily fluids of an infected person. But as to how it originated? No idea. The religious implications alone are staggering." Simone paused, but then shook her head.

"Some of the outbreaks have been minor, quite easily contained. In those cases, patient zero was easily located and—"

"Patient zero?"

"The index case. The first patient whose discovery indicates the existence of an outbreak."

"Outbreak." I nodded. "Like in the movie, the guy who let the monkey go, he'd be patient zero, right?"

"Erm…" She struggled with that for a moment. Then, "Ah, yes. At least for the mutated Ebola virus they—" Simone stopped and looked at me askance. "That was a terrible movie, you know."

"It had Dustin Hoffman," I said in defense. I liked *Outbreak*.

Simone just looked at me.

"Don't judge me," I muttered, and drank some more ginger ale.

Redwood Bear Market and Gas was typical of the rest stops found off the little highway that cut through the forest a few miles west of Redwood Grove. Folksy billboard with a friendly anthropomorphized bear, carvings and furniture made of redwood burls lining the porch around the store, signs advertising espresso.

"It looks deserted."

Sergeant Willard Gentry glanced over at the speaker, PFC Knowles, the newest—and Gentry's least favorite—addition to their squadron. Knowles was far too cocky for such a skinny little shithead with breath like the back end of a buzzard, even if he did have what it took to make it through the demanding Zed Tactical Force selection process.

Their commander, Lt. Kaplan held up a hand.

"Get the wax out of your ears, private. All of you, listen."

All eight men in the squad obeyed their leader's command, freezing in place, ears cocked toward the building.

Gentry's scrotum tightened as if squeezed by an icy fist as the first moans reached his ears, the sound muffled by wood and glass, but still ball-shriveling no matter how many times he'd heard it before. It was even worse for the three men new to the ZTF.

Knowles looked like he was going to puke.

"This building has been compromised," Kaplan snapped. "Gentry, Jenkins, Knowles, stack on Private Atherton. The remaining—" He stopped as a wet cough rattled in his throat. He'd been fighting a bug for a few days, and it sounded like the flu was winning. This Walker's shit was nasty.

As if on cue Pvt. Atherton doubled over with a racking cough of his own.

Looks like the flu shots they gave us weren't worth shit.

Lt. Kaplan coughed one more time, spat a wad of phlegm onto the ground and finished.

"The remaining Alpha team secure the grounds and keep an eye out for hostiles exiting the building or approaching from the woods." As the four soldiers lined up against the wall by the door, Kaplan added, "Remember, use speed, surprise and violence of action."

Atherton kicked the door in. Gentry heard something fall as he dashed inside and peeled to the left while Jenkins went right. Knowles jinked off to the left a step or two away from the doorway and Atherton followed, still coughing.

Gentry trained his M-4 on a male zombie that had been knocked down during their entrance, and yelled.

"Zed identified!"

"Fire!"

"On the way!" Gentry put several shots into the zom's head, then scanned for the next target. Half a dozen zombies lurched through the aisles of tourist souvenirs.

"Jesus…" Knowles swallowed several times, probably trying not to lose his lunch. Gentry knew how he felt; he'd been there himself on his first mission.

Shots rang out as the four men took out the enemy. The percussion of gunfire mixed with Atherton's coughing.

Gentry tapped him on the shoulder

"You okay, man?"

"Fine. Just need me some cough syrup or something."

Gentry caught a glimpse of very dark blood as Atherton wiped his mouth with the back of one hand. That did not look good. But before he could pursue the matter, fire lit up the back of his calf as something tore through his pants and into the flesh beneath.

"Motherfucker!"

Gentry looked down to see what was once a little boy in diapers and a Sponge Bob T-shirt chewing on his right leg. The sergeant immediately raised the stock of his M-4 and smashed it into the zombie toddler's skull. Once, twice, three times, until it fell to the ground, a mouthful of flesh and camo fabric clenched between its teeth.

"Motherfucker." Gentry whispered it this time. He knew what a bite meant.

No time to feel sorry for himself, though. More zeds were pouring out from the back of the shop, at least ten of them. He heard Knowles scream as he was borne to the ground, caught by surprise. Atherton moved in to help, but was incapacitated by another coughing fit. Three zombies swarmed him before he could recover.

Gentry would take out as many zeds as he could before the virus took him. He hoped at least one of his teammates survived to do right by him.

CHAPTER NINE

"As I was saying," Simone continued, moving past my taste in movies, "many of the outbreaks were easily brought under quarantine. Since this virus wasn't airborne, pandemics were rare. In the past, limited travel options made it more difficult to spread any virus, especially in isolated pockets of civilization.

"And then—" Simone paused. "Three outbreaks occurred with the potential to become apocalyptic. Drastic quarantine measures were taken in each case. For instance, Pompeii and its sister town of Herculaneum were so heavily infected that we believe Vesuvius was deliberately caused to erupt."

I stared at her.

"You have *got* to be kidding. I mean, what? A bulimic volcano? Did someone stick a finger down its throat?"

Simone laughed abruptly, as if the sound was startled out of her.

"You have a unique way of viewing things, Ashley."

"But what *really* happened?"

"Well, we know it was the plan, but as to whether or not they succeeded, or the eruption was just a lucky coincidence, that information was lost. Regardless, the plague was wiped out."

"Seriously?"

Simone nodded.

"You see, there have been small groups over the centuries that have been aware of the existence of the zombie virus. Over the centuries these various splinter groups have joined together, and they've taken whatever steps were necessary to insure that the disease didn't run out of control. You've heard of Atlantis, yes?"

I assumed it was a rhetorical question, but nodded anyway.

"There's a reason it's under twenty leagues of saltwater."

"No way."

"Oh, yes." Simone didn't look or sound as if she was joking. "Those who fought to keep the zombie plague contained took measures to... er... pull the plug when the infection's spread couldn't be stopped. They did so at the cost of their own lives."

Okay, this was just too much.

"No way," I repeated.

"They opened a series of flood ports in ever increasing circles until the water flowed in, which further unbalanced several unstable fault lines."

"What I don't get," I said, still struggling to wrap my brain around everything she'd told me so far, "is how historical events that big have been covered up. I mean, it's not like they had the CIA back in those days."

Simone looked at me with an expression that seemed like pity.

"There have been cover-ups as long as there have been governments, organizations, and politicians, Ashley, ever since the first Cro-Magnon figured out that he could smooth-talk his neighbor out of a hunk of mammoth meat instead of beating it out of him.

"Although, there will always be those who prefer the beating to the talking."

"But *why* cover it up?" I asked. "Why not just tell people what's going on, so they could deal with it if it happened again?"

"I suppose it's because some things are too horrific for the average person to cope with without losing his or her sanity. The concept of the living dead would crack the walls of reality for many people."

"Or maybe it's because there's always some arrogant asshat who wants to decide what people do and don't need to know," I snapped.

"You're absolutely right," Simone said. "But some things will never change. Like the infantilizing of the masses by those in power."

"Whatever you call it, it sucks," I muttered.

"It does indeed," Simone agreed. "But on the other hand, imagine the uncontrollable panic that would erupt if it became known that the dead walked. Especially amongst extremely superstitious societies. A great many people would die needlessly.

"No," she said, shaking her head, "better to get the situation under control as quickly and quietly as possible, spin a plausible story for the survivors, and avoid the chaos of mass hysteria."

"So what's the cover story for this outbreak?"

"Er... the virulent outbreak of a new Ebola strain." She actually looked embarrassed as she continued. "Caused by an infected laboratory monkey on campus." I stared at her, and she added, "It wasn't my idea."

I finished my soup, thinking about what she'd said. She stayed silent, and I spoke up again.

"But what if there's an outbreak that gets out of hand?" I asked. "What if there are no volcanoes or whatever they did to sink Atlantis?"

Simone's gaze darted to the side for just an instant before she replied.

"So far, humans are the only viable host, which is a blessing. If it could be spread by another vector—the way fleas spread what started as the bubonic plague— well, 75 million people were claimed by the Black Death between 1347 and 1351. "

"No offense, but that doesn't really answer my question."

"No... no, I suppose it doesn't." Simone leaned back in her chair, pushing her hair off her forehead as she massaged her temples.

I glared at her.

"So stop 'infantilizing' me."

"I'm sorry, Ashley." She looked sincere. "Habits of a lifetime are hard to break. I'll try to answer your questions as best I can."

I nodded, somewhat mollified. I began to speak, but something she'd said sidetracked me.

"What do you mean, 'started as' the bubonic plague?"

"I mentioned three outbreaks. The plague reached Sicily in October 1347, along with an outbreak of the walking death. Both diseases spread throughout Europe, nearly wiping out civilization. That catastrophe was, point of fact, what brought the splinter groups together."

"So what if there's an outbreak that can't be contained?" I repeated. "Nuke time?"

"I hope not." Simone stared at me grimly. "In this instance, special units trained to deal with this were mobilized immediately after the first sighting. But—" She paused, a frown furrowing her brow. "Something's different this time. We haven't located the source of this particular outbreak. It's showing up spontaneously in pockets of populations, which would suggest that it's mutated to an airborne pathogen. But so far tests have negated the possibility."

"So you don't know why it's spreading?"

"No," she admitted. "And to make things worse, the symptoms start out very much like a bad case of the flu. Specifically, Walker's."

That sent a shiver down my spine, and I stared at her, horrified. Zara's eyes had shown the same jaundiced, bloodshot whites. I wondered if my roommate was still alive, or if she'd died in blood-soaked agony, only to reanimate as a hungry, walking corpse.

The door opened and Gabriel dashed in. He addressed Simone as if I wasn't even there.

"Professor Fraser, Alpha Team found another pocket in a tourist stop ten miles up the road." He paused and added, "It's definitely spreading."

"Any more symptoms amongst the teams?"

Gabriel nodded.

"Three more Alphas are showing initial symptoms and another was bitten. I've quarantined them."

Simone took a deep breath and then let it out slowly.

"Damn. This isn't good. We're running out of manpower far too quickly."

"I know. But I think we may also have another wild card—the soldier who was bitten." He paused, then added, "It's Gentry."

Simone blanched.

"Oh, I hope you're right. He's a good man. I'd hate to lose him."

"He has a nasty wound on one leg, but seems to be shaking off the infection. Just like Ashley." Gabriel nodded at me, his gaze skittering away when I made eye contact. "The outcome looks good."

Simone immediately brightened.

"That *is* good news. I'll be along to see him after I've finished briefing Ashley."

Gabriel nodded and left the room.

"Briefing?" I tried to laugh, but it came out more like a feeble cough. "That sounds awfully military."

Simone sighed.

"It is, Ashley. Which leads me to the real reason you're here."

I didn't like the sound of that, but I waited for her to elaborate. She didn't disappoint me.

"You are part of less than point-zero-zero-one percent of the population who can survive being bitten by a zombie." She stared intently at me. "You are what we refer to as a wild card."

I tried not to laugh.

Do we all get membership cards and decoder rings with our Dr. Tachyon fan club?

"Not only does some genetic predisposition enable you to survive a bite without becoming one of the walking dead," she continued, "but the virus also enhances your natural strength, speed, and reflexes."

Now I had to laugh.

"So, what?" I asked. "I'm, like, a mutant or something?"

Simone shook her head.

"I'm quite serious, Ashley," she persisted. "Wild cards are hard to kill and heal fast. Surely you've noticed that your wounds aren't nearly as bad as they should be so soon after the initial trauma.

"And with a fever and infection as extreme as the ones you had twelve hours ago, you shouldn't be able to sit up on your own, let alone help subdue a zombie."

I glanced at her, surprised.

"Oh, yes, Gabriel told me about your quick thinking with... well, with your boyfriend." She looked at me, probably to see how I reacted to that, but at this point my emotions were pretty much on hold. "You're quite a remarkable young woman, Ashley. And not just because of your immunity to the zombie virus. You're exactly the type of person we need."

I was starting to get pissed off with all of the dancing.

"Who the hell is 'we?'" I demanded. "Some kind of secret government zombie squad?"

Simone gave an indelicate snort.

"Zombie squad indeed," she said, then tilted her head to the side. "It sounds rather like a Disney movie.

"But we call ourselves the *Dolofónoi tou Zontanoús Nekroús.*" Seeing my blank look she added, "Loosely translated, killers of the living dead." She shook her head and continued. "The government *is* involved, in that the *Dolofónoi* has members placed in all key nations at the very highest level. 'Black ops' doesn't begin to cover the amount of secrecy involved."

"Let me guess," I said. "Since you told me, now you have to kill me?"

She smiled, shook her head.

"On the contrary, Ashley, you are now one of our most valuable assets. You see, because of the random spread of infection, the increasing frequency with which our teams are developing symptoms, and our current inability to pinpoint the cause, we are dangerously short-handed.

"We could easily lose control of the situation," she added, and the look on her face told me she wasn't exaggerating.

"What about bringing in more military from the outside?" I asked.

"Until we figure out why our people are developing these seemingly spontaneous symptoms, we can't risk bringing in more people, just to increase the number of walking dead. You wild cards are our last, best hope of containing this infection." She hesitated, then continued. "More than that, your blood—and that of other wild cards—coupled with modern technology, may hold the cure to a scourge that's threatened mankind for centuries."

I didn't like the sound of that.

"So I'm some sort of guinea pig now?"

"Of course not, but—"

"But you *are* an American."

What the hell?

CHAPTER TEN

A loud, brusque voice cut Simone off.

She and I both looked toward the door, now opened to reveal a lantern-jawed man in a military uniform, stripes, stars, and assorted medals dripping off the shoulders and above the left breast pocket.

Striding into the room, he came straight out of one of Syfy Channel's 'original' movies. The ones where a cast of assorted sexy twenty-somethings get stuck on an island, forced to battle a giant snake, tarantula, or alligator created by science gone terribly wrong. Racing against the clock because some military dude wants to blow up the evidence.

Well, this was the military dude with the itchy trigger finger.

He stopped at the foot of my bed, legs planted firmly apart in what I'm sure he thought was a heroic stance. He had this total middle-aged Charlton Heston thing going on, all craggy features and stern expression.

I didn't trust him.

Judging from her expression, he wasn't on Simone's list of favorite people, either.

"General Heald." Her voice was flat.

"Professor Fraser." He nodded briefly, as if conveying a favor.

Wow. Condescending much? For a fleeting moment I wondered if he was related to Gabriel.

General Brasshole turned back to me, steel gray eyes glinting with patriotic fervor beneath thick, unruly eyebrows.

"So, Miss Parker," he asked, "*are* you an American?"

No, I'm a Commie Pinko Bastard, I thought, remembering one of my dad's favorite expressions from the seventies. But I didn't say it out loud. Instead, I gave his question the answer it deserved.

I said nothing.

"Miss Parker, as Professor Fraser has explained, you are a very special young lady," he said. "Your enhanced physical abilities and immunity to the plague make you the ideal soldier to help us control this outbreak." He gave me a paternal smile. "Your country needs you, Miss Parker. Ideally I'd like to see you trained and put in the field as soon as possible."

I stared at him.

What the fuck?

"What the fuck?" Somehow, it seemed worth saying out loud. "Do I look like Lady Rambo here?"

Leaning forward, the General tapped me on one blanket-covered knee.

"Young lady, when we're done training you, you'll make Rambo look like a pussy." He gave me a conspiratorial smile.

I wasn't buying it.

"What if I don't *want* to make Rambo look like a pussy?

"I mean, No one's asking me if I want this training," I continued. "You're just telling me what I'm going to do. But it's my choice, right?"

General Heald's bushy eyebrows shot up. "Surely, Miss Parker, you'd want to do what's best for your fellow Americans, and perform your patriotic duty."

Simone shut her eyes.

"Oh, that's helpful," she muttered under her breath, not quite loud enough for the General to hear clearly.

I folded my arms across my chest and looked at him.

"I bet you can see Russia from your house."

He glared at me.

"Just what are you trying to say here, Miss Parker?"

"That you're a jingoistic idiot." Yeah, I said the quiet part loud. I blame the pain meds. But there's no way I was letting this medal-heavy moron lecture me about my duty to my country, without giving me the chance to make up my own mind.

"America, land of the free, remember?" I continued. "That means I get to choose." I looked at Simone. "Last time I checked, we didn't have a draft going on for this zombie squad droolphoney thingy, am I right?"

"We're not yet taking those measures, no," she answered, and something in her voice sounded as if she enjoyed it.

General Heald took a deep breath and maintained his composure.

"Yes, young *lady*—" The sarcasm dripped as thick as crystallized honey. "—you do indeed have a choice. But before you make that choice, please allow me to show you what you stand to gain if you decide to do the right thing."

He glared at Simone.

"Bring her to the lab so she can see the holding pens."

Simone started to protest.

"Ashley needs to rest up before—"

"Just do it, Professor Fraser." With that he turned on his heels and stalked back to the door, stopping to shoot me a withering glance. "We don't have time for this bullshit."

"That's *commie pinko bitch* bullshit to you," I muttered as he slammed the door behind him. Then I turned to Simone. "Is he for real?"

She nodded.

"And unfortunately, not without influence."

"Why does he want me to see the lab?" I asked. "What does he mean, 'holding pens'? And how the hell are they going to show me what I 'stand to gain' by joining this zombie-hunting team of yours?"

Simone looked me straight in the eyes.

"Ashley, there's one area in which I agree with General Heald," she said. "I think you're a very strong person. And you're going to need all of that strength in the time to come. So—"

The door opened and Gabriel walked in.

Ah, great. More attitude.

"Sorry to interrupt, Professor, but General Heald said he wants the two of you in the lab. He said Ashley might need some assistance."

Wow. I was *so* not touched by General Brasshole's concern. Judging from the look on Simone's face, she was equally unimpressed. But she nodded politely.

"Thank you, Gabriel," she said. "It probably wouldn't hurt to have some extra support for this."

Support for what? I was getting pretty sick of riddle-speak.

Gabriel didn't look at me. Something seemed different about him. He wasn't the same as he had been before all this shit hit the fan. Before he'd gotten sick, in fact.

Grimmer, maybe.

"Are you ready, Ashley?" he asked.

For what? I thought. But I just nodded, because ready or not, I had to go the lab. But first…

"Is there some kind of robe I can put on so I'm not flashing my butt?"

I felt rather than saw Gabriel's discomfort.

Heh.

Simone ducked out, and in record time procured a set of drab green scrubs for me. Not as cozy as a warm terrycloth robe, but better than the breeze-up-my-ass hospital gown. Gabriel turned his back while I slid on the pants and top, baggy enough to fit me half over. Little sock slippers went with them. It felt comforting to have something between my feet and the floor, even if it was just a layer of polycotton.

I stood, shaking off a Groundhog Day sense of déjà

vu as I wondered for an instant if I was going to pass out again.

"You okay?" Gabriel asked gruffly.

"I think so," I said, and I meant it. "But I swear, if I friggin' faint again, I'm gonna change my name to Satine."

"Huh?"

"Moulin Rouge," Simone said.

Give the lady a pop culture reference point.

Gabriel gave a small sound that might have become a laugh had it lived a few more seconds. I wonder how many of those things he'd suffocated the moment they were born.

CHAPTER ELEVEN

We had to go through the med ward to get to the lab. Gabriel marched grimly in front while Simone stayed by my side as I tried my best to keep my gaze straight ahead toward the door at the other end of the room. But the smells and sounds were unavoidable.

I just wanted out.

Out of the corner of my eye I caught sight of a couple of empty cots, blood- and black-bile-soaked sheets the only sign of their former occupants. I stumbled over twisted linen trailing off the end of a cot, and Simone steadied me with a hand under my elbow.

Gabriel immediately dropped back to my other side, ready to catch me should I faint again.

"Are you all right?"

I nodded.

"Just tripped," I answered. "Let's just get out of this room, okay?" A line from *Ed Wood* ran through my head: *"You've got to get through that door."*

Steeling myself, I took the lead until we were out of the room. Then Gabriel moved to the front again, heading down a hallway, through a door on the left, and down a stairwell. Our footsteps clanged on the metal stairs until we reached the next floor. This door was locked, with a little access pad on the wall next to it. Gabriel pulled a lanyard from around his neck, revealing a plastic card key that had been tucked into his shirt.

One swipe of the card and we were through, entering what looked like a very sterile antechamber. A double door in front of us had a number pad set in the center.

"Pretty tight security for a college campus," I observed.

Simone nodded.

"You'd be surprised at what you'd find behind the scenes in a lot of places... and not just colleges."

"I don't think much of anything would surprise me right about now." I felt pretty cynical as Gabriel finished punching in a lengthy sequence. The doors opened.

The smell was the first thing to hit me—a nasty-ass stew of diseased blood and rotting flesh, similar to the stink in the med ward. The odor here, however, was wrapped up in a falsely reassuring layer of bleach and antiseptic.

It was a large room, the size of a lecture hall but without theater-style seating. Metal tables all held groaning, moaning, teeth gnashing zombies strapped down at the wrists, ankles, and neck. Tubes and needles were stuck into their bodies at various points. Fluids pumping in and out of rotting flesh.

Hazmat-suit-clad techs, all wearing sidearms, were cutting away thin slices of flesh like Dad carving the turkey at Thanksgiving. Those strips were put under microscopes or into carefully marked containers.

I recognized both the African-American kid and the woman who'd asked me to help her in the med ward. All remnants of humanity were gone from their faces as they writhed against the straps, unmindful as the tough canvas rubbed away skin and flesh.

At the far end of the room were cages, with thick iron bars spaced close together. In those cages were more of the living dead, all jammed up against the bars, trying to shove their hands and arms through the narrow gaps to reach the hazmat-wrapped meals walking around the room.

Those had to be the holding pens.

"What the hell is this?" I whispered to no one in

particular. The scope of it all was beginning to sink in, and I didn't like the feeling.

"Research." Simone kept her volume low as she answered my question. "Regrettable, but necessary if we're ever to isolate the root cause or—more importantly—find a cure."

"So all the people you rescued… they're just research animals?"

"The ones who don't make it, yes." There was pain in her expression, but I couldn't find it in myself to feel sympathy.

"So if I wasn't one of your friggin' wild cards, I'd be strapped to one of these tables getting pieces carved out of me, right?" For some reason, this horrified me—and made me angry—more than anything else I'd seen.

"That's right, Miss Parker."

Great. Even through the weird, tinny filter of a hazmat helmet, I recognized General Brasshole's pompous tone as he strode into the room and stared at me through his plexiglas visor with what I can only describe as a leer of triumph.

"And this is what will happen to your former boyfriend," he added, "if you don't cooperate." That caught me by surprise.

"Exactly what the fuck are you saying?"

"Simply that if you join our group, your boyfriend will be given a swift and painless death." He smiled, and it was *so* not a nice smile. "Or to be more accurate, a swift and *final* death. As far as we can tell, zombies don't feel pain."

"And if I don't join your little militarized knitting circle," I said with something approaching a snarl, "you'll use him as a zombified lab rat."

He smirked and turned to Simone.

"You're right. She's not stupid."

Simone kept her cool.

"No," she said. "She's not."

Gabriel stayed silent throughout all of this, just as you'd expect from a good little soldier. A slight tic in his right cheek was the only sign of emotion.

A sudden, tinny yelp caused us all to jump. A tech was trying to wrestle a glove away from one of the zombies. He had been reaching across its face to adjust something on the other side. It snapped at him and its teeth caught in the glove before he could yank the hand away.

The creature worried the glove like an attack dog. The tech smacked the zombie on the head with his other hand and tugged the glove free, desperately inspecting it for rips in the fabric.

General Heald harrumphed his disapproval.

"That kind of carelessness will get you killed, soldier!"

"With all respect," the man replied, "I'm not a soldier, sir."

"No excuse! It's civilians like you who cost me good men."

As the General shook his gloved finger in the tech's face, I turned, catching Simone with a look of eye-rolling exasperation. Gabriel was expressionless.

"Question," I said quietly. "If this disease isn't airborne, then why are the suits necessary at all?"

Gabriel broke his silence to answer me.

"You've seen the amount of blood and vomit an infected person generates." I nodded, and he continued. "If it spattered on your skin or clothes, you'd be fine. But get any of it into an open sore, your eyes, or mouth, or accidentally swallow it… well, you might as well have been bitten."

Simone chimed in.

"During previous episodes the zombie virus was spread solely through bodily fluids that got into mucus membranes or open wounds, mainly via bites and scratches." A frown crossed her face. "Yet this time, without any such contact, several members of our team have come down with symptoms. Not enough to convince me that it's gone airborne, but still, it's worrisome."

Worrisome. That's one way to put it.

"So why are we the only ones *not* wearing protective gear?" I asked.

"Ah," Simone said. "As wild cards, you and I don't have to worry about contamination."

My eyes widened in surprise. So Simone knew what it was like to be bitten by one of those things and survive. My already considerable respect for her shot up another notch.

"What about Gabriel?"

Simone hesitated.

"Gabriel is different."

No shit.

"That's one word for it," I said. Gabriel shot me a look. "I mean, different *how*?" Before she could answer, General Heald stepped between us.

"Well, *Miss* Parker?" He moved into my personal space, trying to intimidate me by towering all of two inches above me.

I shot him a deadly look.

"Don't rush me."

"We don't have time to spare. Every moment we lose increases the odds that this epidemic will go global." He slapped a hand against a nearby table, rattling the metal. "Is it really such a tough decision, Miss Parker? You do the right thing, and your ex will be given a hero's funeral.

"After all, he died trying to save—" He poked me in the sternum with a forefinger. "—you.

"You owe it to him."

Oh, you total bastard, I thought. But he was right. Matt died when he came back for me. If he hadn't, he'd still be alive, instead of rotting in his Levis.

Still, if the General poked me again, I'd break his finger.

I looked at the cages, wondering if one of them held

what was left of Matt. A greenish-gray hand thrust its way between two bars. Was that Matt's class ring on one rotting finger?

"Is…" The words caught in my throat. "Is he in here?"

"Oh, yes," Heald said grimly. "Would you like to see him?" The bastard was enjoying this, and totally expecting me to say "no."

Simone had had enough.

"General, I don't see how this is necessary—"

"Yes," I said.

They both looked at me in surprise.

"Ashley, are you sure?" Simone put a hand on my arm.

I nodded.

"I want to see Matt," I said. "I need to. Then I'll make my decision." Part of me wanted to do it out of machismo, just to show Heald that I could take it. Another part of me needed to say good bye. And I needed to know what I was up against. To know what it was like to see someone I cared about come back as one of those things, and really *feel* it. It would help me decide what to do, although I already had a pretty good idea what my answer would be.

"Fine then," the General said brusquely. "Right this way, Miss Parker." He waved his hand toward the cages. I slowly moved past him, once again looking neither left or right so I wouldn't see the Mengele-esque experiments on the tables.

Heald trailed after me, no doubt wanting to see my face when I saw Matt again. I held up a hand.

"No way," I said. "You stay back here."

"Miss Parker," he replied with deadly calm, "you do not give the orders around here!"

"If you ever want me to obey *any* orders, especially yours, you'll back off and give me my space."

Heald drew in a breath, but Gabriel stepped in front of him.

"I'll show her, sir," he said. "It's safer for me." His tone was respectful, but I got the feeling he wouldn't back down if challenged.

"I suppose you're right." Heald sounded pissed, though, as if agreeing gave him indigestion. "Just make it quick."

Choke on it, pal.

CHAPTER TWELVE

Gabriel took me by the arm, his hand right above my elbow, and led me to the back of the room.

We stopped in front of the cage farthest from the lab entrance and stood a good three feet away from the bars. As we did so, agitated moans filled the air. A capture pole rested on the wall next to the cage, the hook end spattered with blood.

"Is he in there?" Stupid question. I just wanted to put off the moment of truth a few seconds longer.

Gabriel shook his head.

"No," he said. "*It* is in there. It's not Matt any more. Try and remember that. It'll make things easier if you can avoid humanizing them."

I bit my lip and turned to the cage. The size of a large closet, it contained four zombies, all male. The way they all focused on me, hands clutching between the bars, pupils what I'd come to recognize as Corpse Dead White.

The latest Crayola crayon color.

His point seemed like a good one, especially as Matt stared at me with those dead eyes, no recognition there whatsoever. Every bit of personality had left the building. And yet… even though his only expression was mindless hunger, he still looked enough like himself that it hurt my heart to see him.

It.

Shit, I couldn't do this. No way I could let what remained of Matt end up on one of those cold metal tables. There might not be anyone home, but what *had* been there had died trying to save me.

As though he read my mind, Gabriel suddenly leaned in close and spoke quietly in my ear.

"It's not true, Ashley."

I looked up at him, startled.

"Huh? What's not true?"

"The General was lying to you. Matt wasn't coming back to save you." He kept his voice pitched low so no one else would hear him.

"What do you mean?" My volume rose slightly and Gabriel's hand tightened on my arm, eyes flicking back toward the General. I dropped my voice and continued. "I heard him call my name when he was running back toward me."

"Ashley, the only reason he was heading back in your direction was that a half dozen zombies were blocking his escape route."

"You're lying." Even as I said this, I knew Gabriel had no reason to lie, at least not about this. But I still didn't want to believe him.

"Stay back from the bars," he said loudly. "They can reach through if they try hard enough." He dropped his voice back down. "I'm not lying. And you shouldn't think badly of him either for running away. Not everyone can handle it. Matt panicked. Wasn't thinking clearly. Otherwise he wouldn't have left you to begin with."

"Why are you telling me this?" I asked. "I mean, what's the point?"

He peered closely at me.

"You deserve to make your decision based on the truth. And the thing in this cage… it's not Matt any more. There's nothing left of him but a rotting shell. It won't know you, or thank you for saving it from the vivisectionist's knife."

I searched those denim blue eyes for any sign of a hidden agenda. Either he was the world's best liar, or Gabriel was being straight with me.

"Is it vivisection if they're already dead?" The words came out without thought. Weird, the things that pop into your head in times of stress.

Gabriel took it in stride.

"Now you're getting into philosophy."

I looked at Matt again, wondering if I'd have gone back for him, if the situation had been reversed. I think I would have. Did that make me braver than him, or just stupid?

Either way, I still knew what I had to do.

And apparently the General had reached the limits of his patience, which was approximately that of a two year old with attention deficit disorder.

"Well, Miss Parker?" he said, stepping up from behind. "Do you like what you see?"

I will remember all of this, I thought. *And I will pay back this shitty excuse for a man. Pay back for all of it.*

I looked up at him.

"Now that you're here, no," I replied.

I turned my back on him and stared at Matt, remembering our times together. It's not like I'd thought we'd end up married or anything. If asked whether or not I loved him, I'd probably have said no. But he'd been a decent boyfriend, and had done a lot to help me heal my trashed self-esteem.

He didn't deserve this.

"I'm sorry, Matt," I said softly.

The zombie cocked its head as if it understood me, and that freaked me out. It shoved one hand through the bars, ignoring or unaware of the skin sloughing off as it reached for me. I knew better than to react.

General Brasshole, however, did not. He reached past me and smacked the hand with his gloved fist.

"Looks like your boyfriend wants to hold hands, Miss Parker."

I'd had enough. I rounded on him, grabbing him by the front of his hazmat suit.

"What *exactly* are you trying to accomplish by being a total prick?" I demanded. "Piss me off?" He tried to push me away, but I was too strong. "Well, good job!" I continued, my voice rising. "But with an asshole like you in charge, *why the hell would I want to join your team?*"

Gabriel grabbed my arms while the General helplessly— and furiously—thrashed in my grasp. He did his best to pull me off Heald without hurting me. Several techs tried to pry my hands away.

"Ashley, let go!"

I registered Simone's voice even through the curtain of red that had descended on me. Don't ask me why, but for some reason I listened to her and dropped Heald as swiftly as I'd grabbed him. The techs caught the jerk before he fell against the cage.

Gabriel pulled me backward, holding me in case I decided to go for it again. He needn't have bothered; all of my rage-fueled energy evaporated and I sagged against him, sick at heart and exhausted in mind, body, and spirit.

His grip changed from restraining to supporting almost immediately.

"Are you all right?" Simone put a hand on my forehead. "You're running a fever again. You need to be in bed."

"Bed?" Even through the distortion of the helmet I could hear the icy rage in Heald's voice. "The little bitch needs to be put in one of these cages!" He shook off the techs and straightened up, either ignoring or unaware of several pairs of zombie hands pawing at him through the bars. Fingers grazed his hazmat suit without finding purchase.

"While I don't condone it, her attack on you was provoked," Simone said with forced calm. "This girl has been through hell, and cannot be expected to adjust to the situation instantly. She needs time."

"Time is a luxury we don't have, Professor Fraser." Heald glared at me. "Get it through your little Barbie head, Miss Parker. These things are a threat to the human race." He seized the capture pole from its resting place against the wall, thrusting the business end into the cage and into the nearest zombie.

The wood and metal clasp penetrated Matt's chest by about an inch before Heald pulled it back out. There was a squelching sound that I could've gone the rest of my life without hearing.

"Do you see that?" He shook the pole at me. "It didn't feel a thing. It is not human any more, it is the *enemy*." He gave a flourish with the pole, like a poor man's Darth Maul, flipping it so the butt end now faced the cage. "And the sooner you get this through your empty head, the more chance you'll have of surviving!" He punctuated his last sentence with another vicious thrust of the pole into the cage.

I don't know if what happened next was an accident or some dim recollection of motor skills past. As the pole stabbed towards its chest, what was left of Matt seized it clumsily with both hands and shoved back. The business end hit Heald's faceplate, shattering it as the bloodied hook and clasp went through to slice the General's forehead.

The General yelped in surprise and pain, staggering back at the sudden impact. Bits of plexiglas fell to the floor along with the pole as he reached through the broken faceplate and clasped one hand to the wound.

"Damn it!" He turned to one of the techs hovering nearby. "Get me some antiseptic for this, soldier!" He shot me a venomous look as if his stupidity had been my fault.

"Sir…" The tech just stared at the gash on Heald's forehead, then at the gore-spattered clasp on the end of the pole.

"Well?" Heald snapped. "Get the lead out!"

The techs exchanged terrified glances through their respective faceplates. The first one spoke up again.

"Sir," he said slowly, "you're infected."

"What?" Heald shook his head. "Nonsense! It's a scratch from this—" He indicated the shattered plexiglas. But as he did, his face went pale.

The first tech shook his head slowly, almost reluctantly.

"Sir, I saw the pole make contact with your face," he said. "It has hot blood on it."

"Bullshit!" Denial rang loud and clear in Heald's voice. "None of the blood touched me. This—" He gestured furiously at the cut on his forehead. "—is from the *faceplate*. Now get me that antiseptic!"

Another tech surreptitiously drew his firearm while the first guy continued to speak.

"Sir, we need to take you into quarantine."

"That's ridiculous," Heald blustered, but he seemed to be losing steam.

"No," Simone said quietly, "it's protocol." She turned to the techs. "Get Dr. Albert down here immediately."

The General whipped his head toward her, nostrils flaring like a panicked horse. This gave the techs the distraction they needed to move in, flanking him on either side as they grabbed his arms before he could reach for his own gun.

"I'm sorry, sir," said tech number one, "but you need to come with us."

The expression on Heald's face, as reality overwhelmed denial, would have been comical if the situation hadn't been so serious. I almost found it in myself to pity him.

Almost.

As they manhandled him towards the door at the back of the room, he locked eyes with me, upper lip curling back from his teeth like a mad dog.

"This is your fault, you bitch." If he could have killed me at that moment, I'm certain he would have. "I'll be back, and I'll take care of you once and for all."

All sympathy I might have had for him vanished.

"Yeah, you'll be back, all right," I said coldly as a third tech punched in a code to open the back door. "On one of these tables." Even as I said—and meant it—I couldn't quite believe that the words were coming out of my mouth. But damm me if the son-of-a-bitch hadn't asked for everything he'd gotten.

Heald lunged for me, breaking the grip of tech number two. Gabriel immediately swung me around to place himself between us. I'm not sure how he managed it so quickly, but one arm wrapped around my waist while his free hand suddenly held a gun.

"That's far enough, sir."

The techs regained their grip and General Heald was dragged from the room, thrashing and fighting his escorts every step of the way, screaming curses at me even after the door shut behind them.

After a long silence, I finally spoke.

"I want a nap," I said to no one in particular.

Simone gave a little shake of her head, as if clearing her mind.

"I need to check on the General," she said, and I couldn't tell what she was feeling. "Will you be all right, Ashley?"

I nodded. "I just want to sleep for awhile."

"Gabriel, would you take her back to her room? And get Doctor Albert to examine her again. I want to make sure the fever doesn't spike any further."

I felt rather than saw Gabriel nod. More than ever, his arm around me was reassuring. I glanced toward Matt in the cage, and tried not to feel guilty.

Simone turned to leave, stopped, and then turned back to me.

"Ashley, you don't need to make any decisions right now, no matter what the General—"

"I don't need any more time," I said, cutting her off.

"You should sleep on it."

I shook my head.

"I'm in," I said. "It's what I want."

Simone put a hand on my shoulder.

"You're sure?"

I nodded and took a deep shuddering breath.

"Yeah. I'm sure." Then I shrugged. "I mean, what else am I gonna do with a Liberal Arts degree?"

It took a few minutes for Gabriel's coughing fit to subside before he could escort me back to my room.

Jason made his slow relentless way through the trees, up another slope, his Spider-Man pajamas shredded and falling off his emaciated body. Low hanging branches and prickly bushes snagged his flesh, leaving gouges in arms, legs, and torso, but he didn't notice or care. He was hungry and following the sounds and scent of warm, living flesh from somewhere above.

He was finally rewarded by the sight of a tall, sturdily built man using a pair of long-handled bolt cutters on a chain-link fence at the top of the slope. Lots of meat and muscle to chew on.

Jason moaned, slipping back down a few feet through pine needles and bushes in his eagerness to reach food.

Alerted by the sounds, the man stopped his work.

"Hello?"

Jason moaned again, this time in frustration as he slithered another foot down the slope away from his intended prey.

"Who's there?"

The words meant nothing—all Jason registered was the sound of food. He tried to stand, but his feet slipped on the damp needles and gravel. He fell forward on his face with a thud, and gave another piteous moan.

"Shit."

The man came to the edge of the slope and looked down, catching sight of Jason's struggling form.

"Shit. Kid, are you okay?" He dropped the pliers, but kept hold of the wire-cutters and rapidly descended the slope, maintaining his footing with easy grace.

"Kid?"

Jason moaned again, the only sound in his new vocabulary.

"Jesus…" The man slid to a halt next to him and knelt by his side. "Hang in there, kid," he said, putting a gentle hand on Jason's shoulder and turning him over. "You're gonna be fi—"

He stopped, mouth agape in shock as he saw Jason's face for the first time.

"Oh, you have got to be fucking kidding me."

Before the man could react any further, Jason whipped his head to one side and sunk eager teeth into the man's forearm, worrying the flesh like a rabid dog, then ripping a piece out.

The man yelled in outraged pain, but instead of trying to get away, he flipped Jason back on his stomach and put a knee on his back, using both hands to open the bolt cutters.

Jason's face smushed into the dirt, but he kept chewing on the morsel of flesh even as something cold and sharp was placed against his neck and snapped shut.

His head, partially separated from his body, listed to one side, but he kept chewing until repeated blows to his skull put the lights out once and for all.

CHAPTER THIRTEEN

I slept for almost twenty-four hours after I got back to my room. There could have been a full-scale zombie invasion and it wouldn't have been able to wake me.

Gabriel had stayed while Dr. Albert gave me a quick exam, leaving only after I'd crawled under the blankets.

When I finally woke up, I felt amazingly well rested. I stretched like a cat. The aches and pains were gone. I checked out the wound on my arm, now just a faint scar.

Sweet.

I was also hungry, the kind of ravenous I used to get after several weeks of banana-and-water dieting. I wanted food, and I wanted it now.

As if on cue, the door opened and I smelled something savory and mouth-watering. Simone came in, immaculately dressed in a black trumpet skirt and hunter green blouse and bearing a tray loaded down with food. I briefly wondered if she used lacquer to keep her hair in that perfect upsweep, or if it just didn't dare fall out of place.

I sat up expectantly as she set the tray on my lap, sat in the chair next to the bed, and poured herself a cup of coffee from the carafe on the tray.

"How did you sleep?"

"Better than I have in ages," I said, trying not to drool at the veritable buffet of food and beverages set before me. "How did you know…?" I nodded at the tray.

Simone smiled.

"If my own experience is anything to go by, you'll be ravenous about now. Eat up."

And I did. It was one of the best meals I'd ever had. Something struck me, and I paused briefly from devouring strips of bacon.

"Why does this all taste so good?"

"You'll find that all of your senses have been elevated. Food will taste and smell better."

I thought about that.

"So does it work the opposite way, too? Like, if someone farts, does that mean I'll be the first to smell it?"

Simone gave a bark of laughter.

"I'd never thought of it that way," she said, "but unfortunately, yes. Heightened senses work both ways. On the bright side, you'll also be alerted to the presence of the living dead, because you'll smell them long before they're close enough to attack. There are meditation techniques to help filter things when sounds and smells become too overwhelming, but eventually it becomes second nature."

"Okay, then." I attacked a chocolate croissant. Buttery goodness melded with rich, dark chocolate in an almost orgasmic experience. If food tasted this good, the downside would be totally worth it. I'd just avoid chili cook-offs.

When I finished decimating the meal, I settled back, holding a cup of coffee laced with cream and honey.

"So what's next?"

"Ah," Simone said. "Training. You and the rest of your team have a lot of work to accomplish in very little time if we're going to contain this outbreak."

"Couldn't we just do a montage, like you get in the movies?" I wondered if I could blame my knee-jerk tendency to be a smartass on the wild card effect. *Probably not.*

"Unfortunately it's not that easy." Simone sipped her coffee. "You'll have to make do without 'Eye of the Tiger' playing in the background." She took another sip. "When you're done eating, you can have a quick shower and I'll take you over to meet the others."

"Is the… is the outbreak still contained to this area?" I asked. "I mean, it hasn't gotten to Lake County yet, right?"

"Your parents are still safe," Simone assured me without actually answering the question.

"And Matt? Is he…?"

Simone nodded.

"Gabriel told me to tell you that he took care of it himself."

I absorbed that for a few seconds, trying to sort how I felt about Gabriel putting Matt down like a rabid dog. Gratitude warred with a grief I couldn't even put into perspective, so I gave up trying to work it out and moved on.

"What about General Heald?"

Simone shook her head.

"All signs indicated typical onset of the walking death virus even before he was taken out of the red zone a few hours ago via medivac."

"In other words, he's not our problem, one way or the other." I couldn't bring myself to have too much sympathy for a sociopath like Heald.

Simone smiled.

"You have a way of cutting to the quick of things, Ashley. I have a feeling it will serve you well in the days to come."

A half hour later I was clean, clad in yoga pants, red baby-doll T-shirt, and expensive running shoes. And oh, it felt good to be wearing something other than hospital chic. I followed Simone into a large gymnasium-style room under the main floor of Patterson Hall, where five other people—including Gabriel—were seated on folding chairs gathered in a semi-circle.

There were three men and two women, one of the latter barely old enough to be in college. They all stared at me when I walked in and I immediately wondered if I had, like, a hole in my shirt or food stuck between my teeth.

I hate being late to a party.

"This is Ashley," Simone announced. "Ashley, you already know Gabriel." I nodded.

"And this is Tony—" She indicated a tall, dark-haired punk-looking kid in his late teens, piercings in uncomfortable places and legs far too long for the chair he sat in. He shot me a bored nod. Simone continued.

"Kai—" A Will-Smith-type-of-cute black guy I recognized from my creative writing course, who waved with a smile that said, *Yeah, I know I'm good-looking, and I know you know it.*

"Mack—" He was a man in his fifties with a face like a sweet-yet-mournful basset hound. At her words, he smiled sadly.

"Lily—" Her face was mostly covered by a long swath of thick, shiny light-brown hair, and she looked barely out of her teens. Bright green eyes peeked at me from behind the curtain of hair.

"—and Kaitlyn." A skinny blond woman in her thirties whose appearance screamed "Hollywood trophy wife," right down to her sun bed tan. She looked at me suspiciously, as if she expected me to sleep with her husband or something.

"That's Kaitlyn with a 'K,'" she said brusquely.

Stifling a retort and stiffening my spine, I pasted on a smile and grabbed a folding chair, wincing at the sound of rusty metal as I opened it. Gabriel shifted his own to make room for me between him and Kaitlyn-with-a-K, who shot me a look as if I was something she'd just stepped in.

Jeez, whatever, lady.

I didn't have the energy to deal with whatever had crawled up her butt.

"Is this all of us?" I tried not to sound disappointed, but five of us against the zombified world seemed like crappy odds.

"For the moment, yes," Simone answered. "We're still waiting to see if two other candidates pull through. We should know within the next twenty-four hours." She took a seat across from us. "And five wild cards, found in such a relatively small radius, is actually rather promising."

"What's the usual percentage of wild cards versus the normal population?" Kai asked.

"Point-zero-zero-one percent. Basically, one out of every ten thousand. But that may be because those who actually survive the initial attack are rare. Most victims are either devoured outright or are so badly injured that they die before we can tell if they would have become a zombie or a wild card."

We all looked at one another nervously.

"So," Simone continued, "since you will be working together for the foreseeable future, I'm going to ask you to enlighten us with what brought you to this point."

From the looks on their faces, I could tell everyone in the group was as eager as I was to relive the nightmare.

First he checked the police scanners, until static rendered them useless.

Then, when he went to check the usual online forums, he couldn't get onto the 'net. His reliable backdoor entrances into military communications frequencies were locked tight. Always a bad sign. And damned if he hadn't spotted several military helicopters buzzing overhead on their way toward the college.

Time for reconnaissance.

He took a quick peek under the bandage on his arm as he drove. Still no sign of infection, but it hurt like a motherfucker.

Fucking zombie rugrat.

He took the winding mountain road with the absent-minded ease of familiarity, his mind chewing on the implications of what he'd heard over the scanners. A lot of truly fubar shit was going down in Redwood Grove, enough to convince him there was an outbreak. What he didn't know was how widespread it was.

Reaching the end of what was essentially a very long private driveway, he turned the truck east onto a paved road heading towards the 101 Freeway. Empty cars were scattered on both sides of the road.

Definitely bad.

The road dipped down, rising back up in a steep grade. He hit the accelerator and roared up the hill at forty miles per hour, getting respectable airtime when he crested the top.

It took him approximately five seconds to realize he was barreling toward a roadblock of military vehicles.

"Shit!"

He hit the brakes and jerked the truck hard to the left, tires squealing as he avoided a collision with an olive-drab Humvee. He pulled over to the side of the road, adrenaline pumping with the near miss.

There were a half-dozen or so abandoned civilian cars on the side of the road. One of them, a Saturn, had two flat tires and several holes puncturing the side. The smell of burnt rubber hit his nostrils as he stepped out of the truck, almost at the same time as he heard a disembodied voice.

"Sir, I'm going to have to ask you to turn your vehicle around and go back the way you came."

A soldier in combat gear and a bio-chem mask stood in front of the Hummer, firearm pointed in a way that meant business.

"You want to tell me what's going on, son?" He kept his hands open at his sides, seeking to convey harmlessness.

Nothing to hide here, right?

"Please get back in your vehicle and turn around, sir."

Several more armed soldiers in bio-chem masks stepped out from behind the other vehicles, all pointing the business end of their M-4s in his direction.

"You can't even tell me why?"

"Sir, we are authorized to use force if you try to leave the quarantine zone."

"Quarantine?" He knew better, but took a step forward anyway. "What fucking quarantine?"

There was the soft but unmistakable sound of weapons being cocked.

His gaze flickered past the soldiers to the woods behind them. Bloodied limbs—several adults and at least one child.

He hoped to god they'd been infected.

"Sir, we are authorized to terminate anyone attempting to leave the quarantine zone. Please return to your vehicle and go back the way you came."

He did what they said with no further argument.

Things were well and truly fucked up here.

CHAPTER FOURTEEN

Tony, the punk teen, raised a hand. Not the kind of courtesy I'd expect from someone with that many pieces of metal stuck in him.

"Like what?" he said. "What do you want us to say?"

"Whatever you'd like," Simone replied. "Where you're from, what you do, how you came here."

Wow, I thought. *This is like the world's weirdest encounter group.* But I didn't say it aloud.

"Oh, *please*." Kaitlyn scowled at all of us. "Why waste our time? Who gives a crap what any of us did before we found out that we're freaks. What does it matter?"

No one said a word. Simone peered at Kaitlyn, and I couldn't tell for the life of me what she was thinking.

Kaitlyn squirmed uncomfortably in her chair. It squeaked in protest. We all winced at the sound.

Finally Simone spoke, her tone carefully neutral.

"The way things are now, the people in this room are more important to you than your closest loved ones," she said. "You'll be trusting them quite literally with your life. It would be to your advantage to know about the people who will be watching your back on a daily basis."

Kaitlyn flushed, her expression more angry than embarrassed. I got the feeling Ms. Rodeo Drive wasn't used to having someone stand up to her. Hopefully the 'tude would come in handy when she was slaying zombies.

I took a quick peek at Gabriel. His expression was as unreadable as Simone's. I wondered when he'd learnt to hide his feelings, 'cause he sure hadn't bothered when I met him. He glanced in my direction, and my gaze flickered away almost as quickly as his.

I felt heat rising in my cheeks.

"Ashley, why don't you go first?" Simone suggested.

Well, crap. Maybe she didn't *mean* to put me on the spot, but I still hated it. But I wasn't about to let her down, so I took a deep breath and dove right in.

"Um… well, I'm Ashley and—" Suddenly I couldn't resist it. "I'm Ashley, and I'm a wild card."

Blank stares. All except Kai, who let out a little snorting laugh.

"They say the first step is admitting it," he said with a grin. Damn, he was cute, even if he'd be the first person to say so.

Gabriel frowned.

Okay, not serious enough.

I continued.

"I, uh, go to school here at Big Red, including Professor Fraser's course on pandemics." I looked at Simone. "Guess this is a field trip, huh." That got a laugh from everyone but Kaitlyn and Lily, although it was hard to tell what was going on behind all that hair.

"Anyway, I'm here because my boyfriend and I were attacked in the woods behind campus. We ran for it. I was bit, and survived." I swallowed hard and stared straight ahead. "Matt didn't."

Kai reached across and patted me sympathetically on my knee.

"That's rough."

Tears stung my eyes for a brief second. I forced them back and managed a quick smile.

"How about I go next?" he suggested. "I'm Kai King, double major, English and Drama."

A soft voice emerged from behind the veil of hair that was Lily.

"How'd you get… how did you find out you were a wild card?"

Whoah, she talks!

Kai winced and rubbed his forearm.

"Roommate was down with Walker's and he… well, I came back to our dorm after classes, and he bit me on the arm before I knew what the hell was happening. About that time, this guy—" He gestured towards Gabriel. "—came through our dorm with a bunch of dudes with guns. Brought me here, and I… I guess I was one of the lucky ones."

Kaitlyn made a rude noise.

"You think this is *lucky*?"

Kai bristled.

"Did you see any of the people who were dying from this?" He held up his arm where the marks of human teeth were still visible. "It's a nasty way to go. So, yeah, I'd say I'm damn lucky." His gaze went around the room. "Just like the rest of you."

Kaitlyn shook her head defiantly.

"I watched while my best friend and her daughter were ripped to pieces at a rest stop a few miles down the road," she said. "We were on our way home to Arcata. They had to use the bathroom. I didn't." She wrapped both arms protectively around herself as she talked. "So I stayed beside the car while they went inside. Total tourist trap, with those chainsaw carved redwood statues of bears and pigs. They'd just reached the doors when a bunch of those things burst out of the building and around the sides of the porch.

"We… we froze. One of them bit me, but I got in the car. Sharon and Megan—they didn't stand a chance."

She shot Kai a hostile look.

"So yes, if I had a choice, I'd rather be dead than remember the sound of their screams." She glared at all of us, as if daring us to offer her any sympathy.

Stupid me, I tried anyway.

"I'm sorry," I said quietly.

"Oh, *are* you?" I'd never heard three words infused with quite so much venomous sarcasm. I'd have been impressed if I hadn't been the target. "That's funny, because you don't seem capable of anything beyond making shallow jokes. I wonder how your boyfriend would feel if he knew how seriously you're taking his death."

Oh, no, you DI'n't.

I stared at her, not quite believing I'd heard her correctly.

The rest of the group looked equally stunned.

It took a few seconds for my brain to process the fact that, yes, she really *did* just go there.

Taking a few deep breaths, I sat up very straight in my chair.

Both Gabriel and Simone tensed.

"I don't think you're in any position to judge me, or decide how my boyfriend would feel." I kept my voice level, even though I was right at the edge of losing it.

Simone stepped in.

"Everyone deals with trauma differently," she said, and she looked directly at Kaitlyn.

"That doesn't mean it's all right!" Kaitlyn's voice trembled with rage.

Simone started to reply, but I'd had enough.

"You're right," I said. Everyone looked at me. "It's *not* always appropriate. For instance, Kaitlyn, you're dealing with your own grief by focusing on me. I'm not sure why, but I really don't give a shit. Because I'm not your whipping girl, and it's *not* okay for you to be a total bitch."

Another deep breath.

"Because you're not the only one here who's lost someone."

Kaitlyn's mouth opened and closed like the proverbial beached fish, but she couldn't come up with a response. She finally sat back in her seat, red-faced, furious, and thankfully silent. Good thing 'cause I had an itchy right hook.

"Well, then," Simone said briskly. "Tony, what about you?"

Tony still looked bored. After a moment he spoke up.

"Playin' video games at the arcade in Redwood Grove. Manny and I were duking it out on *Resident Evil: Darkside Chronicles*. These totally reeking deadheads came in. Fuckers tore up the place and messed up my high score." A weird smile flashed across his face. "That fucker Manny'd be laughing his ass off, if they hadn't eaten him."

We sat in stunned silence, not knowing what to say. He just shrugged.

"Hurt like hell to get bit, but here I am."

He slouched back in his chair, twiddling his thumbs as if there were joysticks attached. So Simone turned.

"Mack?"

Mack gave her a little nod and gazed at us all with those big, sad eyes, hands resting on his jeans-clad knees.

"I'm a mailman," he said, almost as if it was an apology. "I was on my route, with all those little houses that're off the beaten path." He had a soothing voice, kind of like Garrison Keillor, made for folksy homespun tales. "I know the people real well. They're the kind of folks who make homemade fudge for my Christmas bonus, real nice people."

He swallowed.

"I kind of figured something was wrong when I stopped at the Miller's place. Young couple with two kids, real cute twins, five years old. Those little girls always come out to say hi when they hear me at the door.

"Well, this time…" he swallowed again. It looked like it hurt. "They didn't come out. Even though the front door was open, just the screen door shut, but not all the way. Shantal—that's Mrs. Miller—well, I knew she was home 'cause her car was in the driveway. But she didn't come out to say hello, either." Mack wiped his forehead on a blue and black plaid flannel sleeve.

"At first I tried not to worry. You know, maybe they were out back or something. But then I noticed… well, the flies. They were buzzing on the inside of the screen and… and on the floor… it looked like blood. Mrs. Miller had one of those scented candles lit, cinnamon or something. But underneath it, I could smell something rotten."

He looked guilty.

"We're not supposed to go into anyone's house on our routes. We're not supposed to do that. But I then thought, what if the twins were hurt? So I went inside."

Even Kaitlyn seemed to be holding her breath.

"There was stuff—a cast-iron pan, half-cooked hamburgers, blood and other stuff on the floor. Maybe a finger. I'm not sure. It was covered with flies.

"One of the stove burners was still on, so I turned it off before it started a house fire. Then I heard a sound from the living room, a moan, like someone in pain.

"The girls, the twins—" He looked up again, directly at me this time, eyes deep wells of pain. "They were eating their mom." Kaitlyn made a choked sound, hand flying to her mouth. Mack gave her an apologetic look, but kept going.

"I didn't know what to do. I guess I yelled or made some sort of noise, 'cause the girls—those little girls all covered in their mother's blood—they looked up and saw me standing there and, well, they left their mom and attacked me." He pulled the cuff of his pants up on his right leg to show several healing wounds. "I didn't want to hurt them, but they kept coming. I made it to the kitchen, grabbed the fry pan and—"

He stopped for a moment.

"I didn't want to do it. But I had to. I had to hit them. Those sweet little girls." He stopped, tears running down his cheeks.

Surprisingly, it was Lily who spoke first.

"You had to do it, you know." She reached out and put a hand on his shoulder, somehow still managing to keep her face covered by hair. "They weren't little girls any more."

Mack nodded, dashing the tears from his eyes with closed fists.

"I know," he said quietly. "But when I hit them, I still saw their faces like they were when they were alive." His voice choked up as sobs wracked his body. Simone handed him a package of tissues she seemed to conjure from thin air.

After a moment she spoke again.

"Lily, what about you?"

Lily had started to shrink back into her chair, like a blow-up doll that was deflating, but Simone's voice stopped her in mid-shrink.

"Me?" she said. "I... I just... I live in an apartment in town. Above my mom's bead shop." She kept her head down as she talked. I ached to push the hair away from her face. It was kind of like talking to Cousin It. "I work there on weekends and afternoons after class. Mom's in San Francisco on a buying trip, although she was supposed to get home tonight."

She stopped, as if uncertain where to go from there.

"Do you go to Big Red?" I smiled encouragingly, hoping she could see it through the hair.

Lily nodded.

"I'm studying art and photography," she said "My boyfriend and I were at the student union. He was texting—he does—*did* that all the time, and I got mad at him because I was sick of it. So I went outside to get some fresh air and I saw these people—these things— heading toward the union. They didn't look right. And I could smell them."

She jerked her head toward Mack, hair briefly lifting to reveal pretty features.

"Like you said you could smell something rotten in the house, right?"

Mack nodded. Then she vanished back beneath the hair.

"I could smell them on the breeze." She paused, fiddled with a strand. "They started attacking people. At first I thought it was a joke, like one of those flash mobs, but then I saw the blood. I ran back in the union, tried to get Casey to listen to me."

"But he just thought I was still mad at him, and kept on texting. Ignored me." She gave a little shrug that could have meant anything. "He did that a lot. Ignored me, I mean."

Jeez, this really *was* like an encounter group. I kept the thought to myself, though. Last thing I wanted to do was spook the girl now that she was talking.

"So they came through the front door. Lots more blood, bright shiny blood, red like an apple. Casey didn't take it seriously, just kept on texting." She shrugged again. "Before you know it… I tried to help him, but there were too many of them. One of them bit me on the shoulder, and I saw them tear him to pieces before I ran out the back door.

"They bit his arm off, and it was still holding his iPhone."

With that, Lily heaved a great sigh and sat back in her chair, a wind-up toy whose key had run down.

CHAPTER FIFTEEN

Kai raised a tentative hand.

"How bad is it out there?" he asked, looking at Simone and Gabriel.

Simone hesitated briefly.

"It's not good," she replied, "But so far it's contained within a hundred-mile radius around Big Red. The relative isolation of Redwood Grove and the sparseness of residences and businesses in the surrounding area have worked in our favor. But if even *one* carrier makes it through to a more populated area, we could easily lose control.

"Which is why it's important that we move forward quickly. We're going to do our best to prepare you, but I'm afraid the majority of your training will come in the field." She smiled. "Welcome to the *Dolofónoi tou Zontanoús Nekroús*."

"Delta Zeta Nu," Kai grinned. "I guess we've made it through rush week."

Simone nodded at Gabriel.

"It's your show now," With that, she walked to the doors, but turned back to face us.

"I'll see you all in a few hours for dinner. I've no doubt that you'll have worked up quite an appetite." Then she left.

Tony spoke up, wearing the same bored expression he'd worn since I'd met him.

"So when do we start training?"

"You've already started," Gabriel said. He stood up and paced as he spoke. "If you're smart, you'll remember everything you've just heard, what it's taught you about the zombies and your fellow wild cards. You need to know what to expect from each other when the pressure's on."

Tony smirked.

"I don't see how any of these sob stories could make a difference, one way or the other."

Gabriel gave him a total hairy eyeball.

"Then let's hope you're better at fighting than you are at listening."

Tony's smirk deepened.

"Seriously, dude. Tell me what I'm supposed to get from knowing that Redwood Barbie here—" He jerked his head toward me. "—outlived her boyfriend."

I hooked a foot under one of his chair legs and pulled hard. There was a metallic crash, and Tony was flat on his back. I just stared down at him.

"For starters, jerk," I said, "You've learned that I won't put up with any shit from you."

"And she might outlive you, too." Extending a hand, Gabriel pulled Tony to his feet. "Unless you learn how to pay attention." He surveyed the rest of the motley crew. "Ready to get started, everyone?"

Tony eyed me with new respect.

"Shit, yeah," he said. "Can I have her watching *my* back?"

"You call me 'Barbie' again and I'll be kicking your butt," I growled.

Gabriel slapped Tony on one shoulder.

"We'll switch round so you all get a chance to work with one another," he said firmly.

Thank you, I mouthed at him when Tony wasn't looking.

One corner of Gabriel's mouth lifted in reply.

Well, what do you know, I mused. *There may be hope yet.*

"Let's go then," he said. "Since it's going to be your first session, I'll take it easy on you."

―――――――――――――

"Got you, you pus bag."

Pvt. Cletus Hudson watched in satisfaction from the roof of the Sciences building. The zombie he'd targeted—a skinny gangbanger wearing baggy jeans and a hoodie—went down on the quad, a red hole in its forehead. He waited a minute to see if it needed the old double tap, but the ugly fucker didn't move.

"Heh, did y'see that, Tucker?"

Tucker didn't answer. Come to think of it, Hudson hadn't heard a peep from him in a while, not even a cough. Which was weird, seeing how Tucker'd been hawking up his lungs for the better part of the afternoon.

"Tuck...?"

Still no answer.

Hudson turned to find Tucker slouched on the opposite end of the roof, face planted against the roof edge, his M-4 lying next to him.

A chill went up Hudson's spine. There was black gunk trickling out of Tucker's left ear.

"Oh, shit."

Hudson reached for his walkie-talkie, hands suddenly clumsy as he tried to unhook it from the carbiner on his belt. As he fumbled with it, Tuck's body suddenly twitched as if it had been hit with a taser.

Once.

Then again.

Hudson froze those crucial few seconds as what used to be Tucker rose unsteadily to its feet, eyeballs filmed over, a milky white bleeding into bloodshot yellow. It looked like he'd vomited up oil, black shit drizzling down his mouth, out of his eyes, nose, and ears.

"Fuck!"

Hudson forgot about the walkie and wrestled with his M-4 as his buddy lurched across the roof toward him, closing the distance between them even as Hudson fired.

He missed.

CHAPTER SIXTEEN

Simone hadn't been kidding about the whole "working up an appetite" thing.

We started with basic hand-to-hand, what Gabriel called "methods of disabling without grappling." In other words, how to not let the ravenous ghouls get a hold on you. And if they did, how to disengage without being bitten or otherwise mauled.

He also stressed the importance of maintaining an awareness of our surroundings, the better to keep any eye out for escape routes, objects that could be used offensively or defensively, and more damned zombies. Sure, wild cards didn't have to worry about infection, but we could still have our necks ripped out or our limbs torn off.

Our corpses wouldn't reanimate, but we'd still be dead.

We spent two full hours just learning how to fall, roll, and deflect an opponent's energy. Lots of blocks, throws, joint locks, and shit like that.

I'd never done anything like it, yet it was weird—the skills came easily. Kind of like being turned into a vampire in the Buffy-verse, where you're suddenly given martial arts skills even if you were a total nerd before the bite.

Our newfound strength helped us perform the things Gabriel demanded of us, and the enhanced senses were amazing. We all discovered that our coordination and muscle memory were seriously amped. But it didn't always jive with what we'd known before. It took a lot of repetition to overcome ingrained fear based on years of physical and emotional limitations. But once we got it?

It was sweet.

"Excuse me," I said.

I was in the process of jerking on Kai's arm while knocking his legs out from under him with my foot, sending him to the mat. It was a move I'd latched onto pretty quickly. I still didn't like being on the receiving end of it, though. I hated falling.

Gabriel paused, one arm wrapped around Mack's throat, the other pinning an arm behind his back.

"Won't some of this stuff just, like, rip off a limb or two?" I asked. "I mean, we're talking rotting corpses."

Gabriel shrugged.

"It could happen," he admitted.

"Schweet," Tony said in a passable Eric Cartman.

"So if we can't really hurt them or hold them, won't they just keep trying to snack on us?" I persisted.

"If you rip off an arm," Gabriel replied, "that's one less limb your opponent has to grab you with. A leg? It can't run after you. And where most people would run the risk of infection from the splatter, you don't have that problem.

"So all of this gives you more time to take the brain out of action. No brain, no zombie."

I nodded, wondering if I could beat a zombie's brains out with its own leg.

Probably not, I decided. *Too squishy.*

"Nice take down, by the way." Gabriel nodded.

"I'll say," Kai groaned, lurching slowly to his feet.

"Um…" Mack raised his unpinned hand, neck still gripped in Gabriel's chokehold. "Is this going somewhere? 'Cause this isn't a comfortable position."

* * *

When we finally stopped for dinner, I was dripping with sweat, exhausted, and so ravenous I didn't care that there wasn't time to shower. We were pretty much all sweaty and smelly. *Really* smelly. I could detect the acrid odor wafting off myself and my fellow wild cards with a clarity that made me regret the enhanced senses. We ate in a small cafeteria adjacent to the gym, where Simone joined us. I wondered how much of this underground space lay directly beneath Patterson Hall, and if any of it spread out further.

Medical staff, soldiers, and clerical types drifted in. They'd load their trays with food and scarf it down before heading back out. A few nodded at Gabriel, but for the most part our little bunch was treated as if we didn't exist.

Wow. Zero popularity points for being zombie retardant superheroes.

"Is it just me," I whispered to Lily, who was sitting to my right, "or are they acting like we just farted on their pillows?"

She giggled, and tucked her hair behind one ear so half of her face was visible.

Progress!

"Don't worry," Simone said, overhearing us from the other side of the table. "It's natural for people to be intimidated by things they don't understand. They'll get over it."

"Since we'll be putting our asses on the line for them, I sure hope so." I stabbed a piece of steak with my fork.

"Here, here." Mack raised his glass of milk. I picked up my water glass and clinked against it. Lily followed suit, along with Kai, Simone, and Gabriel.

"Jeez, that's gay," Tony said. But he lifted his soda and waved it in our direction.

Kaitlyn ignored us, huddled in her own little world at the end of the table. She'd done the work during training, but always reluctantly, as though it pained her to have to touch any of us. And she hardly made a sound. I wanted to feel sorry for her but she pretty much made it impossible.

Bitch with a capital B.

"Hey, everyone."

Speaking of bitches, Jamie—Miss Hot Topic herself—stepped up to our table dressed in black and fuchsia striped tights, a short black tattered skirt, a sparkly fuchsia T-shirt, and some truly amazing black platform boots that would have been appropriate on a '70s pimp. She looked like Tinker Bell's evil twin.

Wonderful. Another person who didn't like me.

She set a tray of food on the table and inserted herself between Simone and Mack. She didn't quite do a hip check on him, but close enough. Mack raised his eyebrows and shrugged, then moved aside with good grace.

"Are you a wild card, too?" Kai asked, looking Jamie up and down. I could have told him he was wasting his time, but he'd figure it out for himself. Or not.

Jamie flicked him a brief glance.

"No, I'm Professor Fraser's assistant." Her gaze went back to Simone as if drawn by a gravitational pull. I wondered if Simone had any idea just how gargantuan a crush Jamie had on her, or if it was even a blip on her gaydar.

At least Jamie didn't have the hots for Gabriel.

"Hello, Jamie," Simone said, smiling. "You remember Ashley, from Pandemics in History?"

"Yes," Jamie responded, giving me a laser stare of death.

Oh, well. What's one more?

After dinner we had a welcome break from kicking each other's butts, and focused on a more esoteric form of training: watching zombie movies. We're talking the good, the bad, and the really shitty.

The campus was closed down by the quarantine, so Patterson Hall was empty. We sat in one of the lecture halls—room 217, in fact. Jamie ran the DVD player while Simone and Gabriel did a running commentary, pointing out the facts and fallacies.

"OMG," I whispered to Lily, "we're in the film class from hell."

Lily giggled, then immediately shushed when Jamie shot a dirty look our way. I stuck my tongue out at her and grinned as she turned away.

Childish, I know, but satisfying.

"Killer…"

"Yeah, dude!"

Tony and Kai gave each other a high five as a zombie got its head taken off with a scythe, and special effects blood spurted everywhere. Personally, if I saw one more rotting ghoul doing the taffy pull with someone's intestines…

"Fast-moving zombies such as the ones portrayed here," Simone commented as the heroes slammed a mall door in the face of a really creepy one-armed ghoul, "are products of the MTV generation of filmmakers. Short attention span."

I raised my hand and she nodded.

"So you're saying there's no such thing as a zombie who can run?"

Simone opened her mouth to answer, then paused and exchanged an indecipherable look with Gabriel.

"Let's pause the film here, shall we?" she said, and then she stepped up to the podium. For just a moment, things almost seemed normal. "Some of these movies are fictionalized versions of incidents that couldn't entirely be suppressed, while others have been planted in order to relegate zombies to popular culture, thus obscuring the existence of the walking dead behind a celluloid smokescreen.

"Based on the records compiled through the centuries,

fast-moving zombies do not exist. They may be ambulatory, but their bodies are rotting. Zombies shamble, stumble, lurch, and crawl. They do not run."

"Yes!" Tony punched the air in a victory sign. We all looked at him. "I had a bet with Manny. If he wasn't dead, he'd totally owe me twenty bucks."

Kai raised his hand.

"What about the smart zombies?"

"We're looking for a zombie no one's ever seen before," Tony explained.

"I think you've both already had your brains sucked out," I growled. "Now would you shut up so Simone can finish?"

Simone smiled and shook her head.

"Actually, it's a valid question," she said. "But aside from the rudimentary motor functions, nothing remains from when they were alive. So no, no smart zombies."

Mack interrupted the proceedings with a huge, jaw-cracking yawn.

"I'm sorry," he said sheepishly.

"Let's call it a day, shall we?" Simone gestured to the back of the room. "On the table are a variety of fiction and fictionalized reference books on zombie apocalypses. Some are survival techniques, others—much like these movies—are works of fiction with kernels of useful information tucked into unexpected places. Consider them homework."

"You mean the shit in all these books is real?" Tony looked skeptical.

"Not all of it," Simone replied. "Like the movies, some were written by people who know—or knew—that the threat is real. Some are meant to warn and teach, others to veil the truth. The rest are simply entertainment.

"They're rated from one to ten as far as accuracy and efficacy go. I'd particularly recommend *Zombie Survival Guide* and *Zombie Combat Manual*. The combat techniques in both have been field tested and the historical accounts in the survival guide will give you an idea of how previous outbreaks were contained."

If my mind hadn't already been blown, I think that would have done it.

Yes, Virginia, there really is a zombie apocalypse.

Two armed soldiers escorted Lily and me to a room on the same floor as the cafeteria and gym, thankfully above the med ward and the lab. It was very much like a college dorm room, with two twin beds and—joy of joys—our own bathroom.

"I am *so* glad we don't have to share a toilet with everyone else," I said as I collapsed onto one of the beds.

"Me, too." Lily smiled at me shyly. "I wonder who has to share a room with Kaitlyn."

I grinned, relieved that I wouldn't have to hide my inner bitch with my new roomie. And a happy thought occurred to me.

"Bet she and Jamie have to share. Maybe they'll cancel each other out." I stretched, feeling aches and knots in muscles and joints I hadn't known I possessed. "Is it okay with you if I take a shower? I promise I'll be quick."

She nodded, and I sprinted for the bathroom. I forced myself out of the hot water in record time and pulled on a pair of sweats and a tank top I'd found in the little dresser between the beds. The bathroom medicine cabinet held basics like soap, deodorant, toothpaste, and toothbrushes, as well as a few luxury items—face cleanser, moisturizing cream, and lip balm. The balm had a slight rose tint to it.

Even the hint of color made me feel more human. I looked like death without lipstick.

That thought reminded me of Zara, and once again I wondered what had happened to her. Had she recovered from Walker's, only to be torn apart? Or had she caught whatever was turning people into the walking dead? All I could do was hope for the best.

Crawling between the sheets, I skimmed over the *Zombie Survival Guide* while Lily showered. By the time she came out of the bathroom, clad in green scrubs, I'd learned that plate armor is a bad choice for zombie combat and chain mail—while slightly preferable—would hamper you just as much unless you'd trained in it for years. Go SCA!

Lily jumped onto her bed, burrowing under the covers like a little kid hiding from the bogeyman.

"Do you want to read some more?" she asked.

"Nah." I put the *ZSG* on the dresser next to a little banker's lamp. "Lights out?"

"Yes," she said. "Please."

I reached out and pulled the switch. The room was immediately cast into pitch black, no ambient light at all. Suddenly I realized how much my eyes took in when there was light. The absence of all of that detail was shocking.

This must be what it's like to be blind. It only took a minute or so, however, before I could make out shapes and outlines.

Cool. My very own low-budget night-vision goggles.

We lay there in our respective beds for a few minutes, one of those thick, aware silences meant to be broken. Lily sniffled.

"You okay?" I asked.

For a moment she didn't answer. She moved slightly, and I heard every crinkle of the sheets.

"Yeah," she said finally. "I'm just worried about Binkey and Doodle."

"Er… are they your roommates?" *And if so, who the hell named them Binkey and Doodle?*

"No," she answered. "They're my cats."

"Are they outside cats?"

"No, they're locked in my apartment."

"Do they have food?"

Another pause, accompanied by a sniffle.

"I have a feeder, but it won't last too long. They like to eat a lot. I bought a bag of dry food a couple days ago, but I didn't refill the feeder."

"Is the bag out where they can get it? Because if they're anything like my parents' cats, they'll have ripped that puppy wide open by now."

"You think so?" Lily sounded distinctly hopeful.

"I know so," I said, trying to sound certain.

Another pause.

"They had a bowl of water, but they go through it fast."

I thought about that one for a moment.

"Can they get into the bathroom?" I asked. "Do you leave the seat up?"

"Um… I don't, but my roommate boyfriend does. Or did. Casey was crashing there while Mom was out of town, until he found his own place." Then guiltily, "My mom doesn't know."

"Hey, be thankful she was out of town when the shit hit the fan," I said. "Hopefully he did the guy thing and left the seat up, so they'll have plenty of food and water for now."

"You think?"

I could tell Lily wanted to believe what I said.

"I think," I said. "I also think we should get some sleep, 'cause you know Gabriel's gonna kick our asses tomorrow."

"Yeah…"

I heard her yawn, followed by another long pause.

"Thanks, Ashley," she said. "You make me feel like things are going to be okay."

She must have fallen asleep right after her last sentence from the way her breathing evened out and lengthened into the gentlest of snores. They still sounded like thunder in my ears, though. Earplugs were in order, at least until I learned how to dial down my enhanced senses.

I lay awake for a few more minutes, feeling an unaccustomed warm glow. I'd calmed Lily down, and that felt as if I'd made a small difference in what had suddenly become a very bleak world.

CHAPTER SEVENTEEN

The researchers and support staff weren't expected to see combat, but they were required to take part in training with weapons and combat techniques, just in case. Even the medical staff had to participate.

This meant—joy of joys—that Jamie joined us while we learned the basics of handling firearms, edged weapons, and pretty much anything you could use effectively against the walking dead. I did my best to ignore her, and she returned the favor.

I loved the edged weapons training. Both Kai and I pretty much kicked butt at it. I'd studied theatrical combat and fencing beginning in high school, and he and I discovered that we'd had the same instructor, a thirty-something wannabe swashbuckler with an age inappropriate soul patch and carefully cultivated mustache. Kind of pretentious, but a good teacher.

If I ever saw him again, I'd thank him.

Honestly, you would not believe the things you can do with wooden kabob skewers if you know where to shove them. And if all you've got is a book? Shove it in the attacker's mouth and reduce the risk of being chomped.

Basically anything can help you survive if you use your brains and don't panic. That's what a lot of the training was about—keeping your cool when facing off against a horde of carnivorous corpses. To panic is to die, whether you bolt or you freeze.

To give in to sentimental attachment will kill you, too. If your loved one has been turned, they will not recognize you. They will try to have you for dinner.

We learned these things and more through a combination of training techniques. After the edged weapons, my favorite sessions were with the firearms.

Gabriel took us to the range, which turned out to be a closed off hallway with a bunch of sandbags stacked against the far wall. That's where I discovered that I love shooting things. And somebody actually makes zombie targets for shooting ranges—I'm pretty sure they weren't government issue, either. Before you knew it, I blew the shit out of Zombie Steve.

The first half hour was pure fun because Gabriel operated on the assumption that nobody had ever handled a gun before, so we got to start 'plinking' with little 22 caliber pistols and rifles.

"Even a small bullet, placed in the right part of a zombie's head, will do the necessary brain surgery to put them down," Gabriel explained.

The 22s had no kick at all, kind of like a pellet gun or even one of those old rat-rubber pistols my friends and I used to play with. Lots of hours spent shooting each other in parks and playgrounds, and even *more* hours picking up the little yellow 'bullets.'

Then we moved up to military grade stuff, which is when Gabriel went all anal and practically fingerprinted each of us before letting us play with the weapons.

The Colt M-4 was okay. I mean, everyone's seen them on TV, anytime there's police action or a swat team. Jack Bauer used one on 24. Still not much of a kick, and pretty easy to shoot.

Next we played with military pistols, Beretta 9 mms and some other stuff. A Glock, blocky and ugly looking, but fun.

There was a .45 pistol Gabriel called a 1911. A bad boy that looked as if it came straight out of a gangster film. As far as I was concerned, it could stay there; it was a pain in the ass to shoot.

Finally the shotguns were wheeled out, and they made the 1911 feel like a .22 in comparison. Winchesters and Remingtons, all 12 gauge that kicked like a pissed-off mule. Then I spotted a little cut-off double-barrel number that totally looked like something from *The Road Warrior*. Immediately I wanted to try it, but Tony beat me to the punch and snatched it out from under me.

"Creep," I muttered.

"You snooze, you lose," he said with a smirk.

He aimed and gave the target both barrels. The shotgun bucked back and smacked his chin hard enough to knock him on his ass.

"Way to go, Mad Max," I said, helping him to his feet. "Bet you wish you'd snoozed a little more."

"No way," Tony replied. He rubbed his jaw while staring at the double-barrel monster with a look of love. "This thing rocks!"

Gabriel also gave us a few shots with an autofire shotgun, and weirdly, it had damn near no kick at all, which was really cool.

So cool, in fact, that they were only given to the trained military personnel—which *didn't* include the wild cards.

"You all," Gabriel informed us, "will be using the M-4s."

Tony clutched his double-barreled baby to his chest. I wouldn't be surprised if he tried to smuggle it out under his shirt.

Jane huddled behind the desk in her manager's office, doing her best not to make any noise that could draw their attention.

They'd descended on the store without warning, at least a dozen of them. They were people she recognized, but… wrong. Bloody wounds, chunks of flesh missing, black fluid running out of noses, eyes and mouths. She'd watched The Walking Dead. *She knew what they were, didn't waste time telling herself that it was impossible.*

So while the rest of her co-workers and the few customers were busy screaming in disbelief as they were pulled down and torn to pieces, Jane had run into the office, locked the door, and shoved a filing cabinet in front of it. She added another cabinet behind the first. If they did manage to break open the door, she hoped they wouldn't be able to push it open far enough to squeeze inside.

Then she hid, just in case one of them should peer in through the small office window and try to break the glass. If they didn't see her, maybe they'd go away.

After they finished eating.

Everything was happening quickly, on a super-accelerated schedule, as we had to process concepts and emotions we could never have imagined. To paraphrase *Predator*—one of my favorite testosterone-drenched flicks—we didn't have time to bleed.

Gabriel believed in repetition, the old 'practice makes perfect' routine for each and every thing he taught us. Luckily part of the wild card legacy is great stamina.

Mack kept up with the rest of us, despite his age. I spotted a pleased grin on his face one day, after he executed a drop-and-roll maneuver as smoothly as a twenty-year-old. From that point on, I started ignoring his muttering about aching joints and creaky knees.

Gabriel, on the other hand...

It struck me in the middle of a training session. He still looked gorgeous, but he also just looked, well, off. His skin was sallow and his eyes had developed deep hollows under them. I thought about asking him if he was okay, but couldn't quite summon up the courage.

Plus I was busy fending off Kai and Lily, both of whom were coming at me with bokkens. Kai had wanted to use steel instead of wooden training swords, but Gabriel nixed that.

"Shouldn't we just be practicing head cuts here?" I asked. "I mean, what's the point of sparring?"

Gabriel shot me an irritated *don't be stupid* look.

"The best way to learn is by facing the *real* possibility of being hurt."

"Then why aren't we using *real* swords?"

That's when he'd sicced Kai and Lily on me.

Bastard.

Simone came in around four or so, accompanied by Dr. Albert and a soldier lugging a bunch of bottled waters. While the rest of us collapsed in mid-grapple, I stifled a laugh as Jamie stood up straight and sucked in her non-existent stomach.

Simone handed Gabriel a bottle of water.

"How's it going?" she asked, and she looked at him intently.

Gabriel grunted in response, twisting the cap off the bottle and downing most of its contents in one gulp. Beads of sweat gathered on his forehead.

"Gabriel," Simone said, "Dr. Albert needs to have a word with you."

He nodded.

"Take five, everyone," he said, and I wondered if anyone else noticed the odd gravelly undertone to his normally smooth voice. He followed Dr. Albert out of the room while Jamie jumped up to help Simone distribute the rest of the bottles.

Lying on the floor on my back, I rolled the ice-cold plastic over my forehead, neck, and chest. It was both shocking and refreshing. Shutting my eyes, I focused on deep breaths as my heartbeat returned to normal. The respite was so good as to be almost orgasmic, like a hot shower after a few days of camping and hiking.

Come to think of it, a hot shower sounds pretty good about now too, I mused.

I wondered what was up with Gabriel. Simone had said he was 'different.' Not wild card different—I was sure of it. Something else. But what? I was curious, but also concerned. He drove me crazy at times, but I found myself appreciating him a lot more than I had back when our entire interaction had been based on pissing each other off.

Not that it wasn't still fun, in its own way.

"Is this our new team, Professor Fraser?"

I jumped as a rich, hearty baritone voice spoke above me, sounding like the words of a Shakespearean hero—totally James Earl Jones. My eyes flew open and I sat up, dropping my water bottle in surprise. Jamie smirked. But I ignored her and checked out the newcomer.

Dressed in army fatigues, he was skinny and short, and his features looked like the sad side of a comedy-and-tragedy mask. His eyelids drooped and his mouth actually turned down at the corners.

"Did I startle you, young lady?" he said. "My apologies."

Ohmigod, it was like watching a dubbed Chinese movie, the type where the voiceovers didn't match the actors at all. I mean, the words and his mouth were in sync, but the voice *so* didn't go with that face.

I tried not to giggle.

"Ah, er, no… No problem," I said.

"Team, this is Colonel Paxton," Simone said. "He's replaced General Heald as commander of this operation." Her tone, while not effusive, was warmer than it had been when addressing Paxton's predecessor. I hoped this meant he was less of an asshole.

The Colonel nodded.

"It's good to meet you all," he said, nodding to each of us in turn. "Welcome aboard."

I swear, he had the sort of voice you'd follow into battle, but coming out of the face of a court jester. There was nothing funny about what he said next, however.

"Professor Fraser, we have an emergency."

CHAPTER EIGHTEEN

"Well, shit."

Standing in the lobby of Patterson Hall and looking out onto the quad with the rest of the wild cards, I had to agree with Tony's assessment.

What I could see of the campus looked to be crawling with the walking, rotting dead, including at least a dozen in military uniforms. The protective neck and headgear they were wearing would make it fun to try and deliver a killing blow, I mused.

The setting sun lent an eerie crimson glow to the scene.

Colonel Paxton nodded.

"Shit, indeed, young man," he said. "Until this morning, we had control of the campus and were moving into the town to sweep it clean and rescue survivors. But with the increased infection rate among our own teams, the zombies have been coming from the outlying areas and overwhelming our forces, which in turn are joining the ranks of the enemy. We need to clear the immediate perimeter while our engineers erect a protective barrier around the campus."

"Wouldn't it be safer to get the barrier in place now, and then clear the interior?" Kai asked.

Paxton frowned.

"If we had the luxury of time, yes. But the barrier needs to go up so we can establish a safe base of operations, and a place to house additional survivors. Patterson Hall is dangerously overloaded, and we don't dare wait any longer.

"This operation will be dangerous," he said, turning to face us.

Wow, total understatement.

"I hadn't wanted to put you into the field so soon," he admitted. "Unfortunately most of our soldiers will be protecting the engineers who are building the barrier, so we can only spare a small number of personnel to support you as you sweep the area. Those will mostly be snipers."

"Guess it sucks to be us," Kai muttered.

I jabbed him with my elbow.

"Hey, at least we won't die if we get bit again."

"Will we get sick again?" Lily hugged herself protectively. She had pulled her hair away from her face in a tightly woven braid pinned up and under a snug-fitting helmet with a chin-guard.

All of the wild cards had any excess hair braided, pinned, or otherwise tucked out of harm's way. We were wearing lightweight but effective sectioned Kevlar armor covering our upper and lower arms, chests, and thighs.

The Kevlar covered sturdy but flexible, fire retardant pants and long-sleeved shirts. Black knee-high, lace-up boots discouraged any pesky shin or ankle biters. Very *riot gear chic*.

We were armed with our M-4s and had each chosen some sort of hand-to-hand weapon, based on personal preference. Kai, for example, hefted a crowbar. I had a lethally sharp blade somewhere between a katana and a wakizashi. The slanted tip was sharpened enough to slide in and out of flesh with ease. It had what is cheerfully called a 'blood gutter' running down its length, which insured that it wouldn't get trapped by the suction of the muscle tissue and fat.

Icky, but practical.

As soon as Gabriel had noticed my interest in the sword, he'd made me wear its scabbard so I'd be used to its weight. I also carried a shorter blade called a tanto in a crossover sheathe, blade up over the left side of my chest. If I lost my gun and primary blade, I'd have easy access to the tanto.

Thank you, Zombie Combat Manual.

My fellow wild cards carried an assortment of goodies—machetes, axes, and crowbars. Lily had a little pickaxe, the wide edge and point honed to razor sharpness. It hung from the right side of her belt. Between that and her firearm, she looked like a lethal Care Bear.

No fooling ourselves on this one, though. Lily would be fighting. *I* would be fighting. Fighting for my life, as well as those of my fellow wild cards, the military personnel, and the poor hapless engineers trying to build a wall.

Suddenly I wanted to throw up.

A hand rested on my shoulder.

"You okay?"

I looked up to find Gabriel at my side, looking much healthier than he had earlier. His color was better and the haggard circles under his eyes were gone. Whatever he'd done, it was reassuring to have him back to normal.

"Yeah…" I said. "No. No, I'm not okay. I mean, it's real. This is really happening. We're all going out there to fight an enemy that's trying to eat us and… and we might die." I gulped.

"I might die."

I felt like an idiot, but couldn't stop myself from continuing.

"I might screw up. Someone could die because I screw up." I started to hyperventilate. Gabriel took hold of my shoulders and looked me in the eye.

"You're not going to screw up, Ashley."

I wasn't buying it.

"How do you know? We've only been training for, what? Not enough time to rehearse for a monologue, let alone to prepare for this." I gestured toward the zombie-infested quad.

"I've seen you in action." He spoke quietly and intensely. "You're quick, smart, and you think on your feet." He put a hand under my chin, lifting it so he could look me in the eyes. "And I'll be out there watching your back. *All* of your backs. Okay?"

I searched his gaze for any sign of bullshit, but didn't find a trace.

"Why are you being so nice to me?" I couldn't resist asking. "I eat meat and sugar, remember?"

Gabriel stiffened a bit.

"Guess I've learned we're not always what we eat."

He let go of my chin, his hand brushing the side of my face so quickly it might have been an accident. His touch made my skin tingle.

Or maybe it was just nerves.

That's what I told myself as he turned back to the rest of the group, all of whom were eyeballing us curiously.

"Okay, everyone," he said, all business. "It's time to do this. We're going out in two teams, Team A and Team B."

"How come we have to be Teams A and B?" Tony grumbled. "It's boring—no *style*. Can't we be, like, Team Romero and Team Fulci?"

Kai rolled his eyes.

"Dude, that is so fucking cliché, I can't believe you even suggested it. It's like being a *Star Wars* geek and naming your kid Lucas or Jar-Jar."

"*No one* would name their kid Jar-Jar," Tony countered.

"Whatever, dude," Kai said. "I rest my case."

Gabriel cleared his throat, shooting them both a withering glare.

"*As I was saying*, we'll divide into two teams and do a sweep of the campus. Team A will move out to the perimeter where the barrier construction will be taking place, moving inward in a clockwise direction while Team B moves counterclockwise slightly inside of the perimeter."

We stared at him blankly.

Gabriel sighed, and pulled out a campus map.

"Each team moves in ever tightening circles until they arrive back here at Patterson Hall, which is dead center."

Fitting, I thought, but I kept quiet.

"The idea is to clean out the zombies from the outside in—not exactly normal procedure when securing a perimeter, but we're stuck with it. Team A will hopefully catch anything Team B misses. As soon as we've removed the majority of the threat, the military personnel will bring out the engineers.

"Later we'll need to do a sweep of each and every building on campus, to check for targets and survivors."

He folded the map and turned to face us.

"Team A will be led by myself and consist of Ashley, Kai, and Lily," he said. "Team B will be led by Sergeant Gentry here—"

A baby-faced man in fatigues stepped forward, favoring his left leg slightly. The name rang a bell.

"He's seen plenty of this sort of action overseas."

Overseas?

"*Dolofónoi?*" I asked.

Gentry nodded.

"Good old Delta Zeta Nu." He slapped his right leg. "And a wild card, as of a few days ago."

Gabriel continued.

"His team will consist of Mack, Tony, and Kaitlyn."

Tony looked less than thrilled by his teammates, and Kaitlyn shared his enthusiasm. Mack, bless him, smiled at both of them.

"First step is making our way through the zoms currently surrounding DBP Hall."

Zoms? Cute.

"We have snipers on the roof, and others will move into position on the top of other buildings to help cull the herd. Don't engage in combat at this point unless absolutely necessary. The point is to make it to your starting positions and begin the sweep inwards. Then you'll see plenty of action. Understood?"

We all nodded.

Simone stepped in at this point.

"If necessary, use your weapons to enable you to get into your starting positions. If one of your team falls, do your best to rescue them even if they're bitten. Remember, you're immune to infection, but not to being ripped to pieces.

"We can't afford to lose any of you," she added.

"Aren't you going with us?" Lily's voice shook as she stared with huge green eyes.

"No," Simone said shortly. "The powers-that-be consider my expertise more important than my combat ability."

"And quite rightly so." Colonel Paxton stepped forward. "Not only is Professor Fraser tracking the source of this outbreak, she's working on a cure. Her knowledge is even more invaluable than her wild card status."

Simone didn't look happy, but Jamie did. I'm pretty sure Miss Hot Topic would have tackled Simone had she tried to leave the building. And I actually agreed with her.

"What about survivors?" Mack asked. Trust him to think of other people when his own life was on the line.

"If they're in a safe location, or you can get them to one quickly, leave them and we'll go back for them as soon as the campus is secure. If not, try to get them back here."

From the look on Mack's face, I could guarantee that he wouldn't be leaving anybody behind.

"What if they're bitten?" We all looked at Kaitlyn, surprised that she'd actually volunteered something.

Gabriel hesitated.

"Every infected person is a potential wild card," he said. "If you can get them back here, do it. But put your own safety first. I repeat, we cannot afford to lose any of you."

I gave a little shudder, knowing what would happen to any infected victims if they weren't wild cards.

"If things go fubar," he continued, "fall back to Patterson as quickly as possible. I don't expect they will, but there's always that possibility. Team B, if something happens to Sergeant Gentry, Mack is in charge."

Mack's surprised expression mirrored Kaitlyn's and Tony's.

"Oh, I... I don't think that's such a good idea," he stammered. "I'm not—"

"No arguments." Gabriel stared sternly. "We don't have time to dick around." Mack subsided, looking both nervous and a little pleased.

"Team A, if anything happens to me, Ashley will take the lead."

Huh?

My mouth fell open in surprise. Kai reached over, put a finger under my chin and pushed upward.

"You heard the man, little girl," he said. "You lead, we follow." Lily nodded her agreement.

"But nothing's going to happen to you, right?" I said.

"I'll do my best." Gabriel slapped my shoulder, and I resisted the temptation to yell *hooyah!* mainly 'cause I thought that was a Marine thing, and didn't want to offend anyone.

"Any questions?" he asked.

"Yeah," Tony said. "How do I get out of this chickenshit outfit?"

Gentry looked at him, completely deadpan.

"Look into my eye," he said, scratching his cheek with one finger.

After a moment of stunned silence, Tony answered.

"Dude," he said solemnly, "I'm totally ready to follow you into battle."

CHAPTER NINETEEN

Kaitlyn shook her head in disgust, trying to mask what I suspected was a massive—and justifiable—case of nerves.

Gabriel nodded at her.

"Kaitlyn, you ready?"

"Do I have a choice?" she replied. Wow. There was enough bitterness in her tone to sour a bowl of Hawaiian punch.

"You already made your choice." Gabriel's voice was no-nonsense. "But you're either up for this, or you're not."

"Spare me the *rah-rah* bullshit." Kaitlyn stared at all of us. "I'll go because there's nothing else to do."

"Good enough for me," Gabriel said. "Let's go." He nodded, and a soldier standing at the door moved to unlock it. Then Gabriel turned back. "Everyone got their nose plugs and walkie-talkies?"

We all nodded and pulled out soft plastic nose plugs that attached to elastic bands hung around our necks. While our super-sensitive schnozzes would help us when we needed to detect the walking dead, there was no point wallowing in the stench.

Simone opened the interior glass double doors, and then unlocked the reinforced steel mesh outer doors. Immediately moans rose through the air as our movement attracted attention. Heads swiveled on rotting necks, and ghastly eyes turned in our direction.

Fresh meat.

"Marines, we are leaving!" Sergeant Gentry grinned at Tony, and dashed onto the zombie-infested quad.

"I think I love him," Tony said, and he ran out after Gentry, followed by Mack and Kaitlyn.

"Let's go!" Gabriel said grimly. No clever movie quotes for us, but Kai, Lily and I were right behind him anyway. It was either that or freeze like a rabbit gone tharn.

Lurching corpses honed in on us as we ran down the stairs and onto the quad itself. My heartbeat accelerated and I broke out in a bona fide cold sweat.

Trees and benches became obstacles as greenish-gray hands clutched at me, gaping mouths opened, snapping for my flesh. Zombie heads exploded in splatters of gore as the snipers did their job. I tried to ignore the indescribably foul goo that spattered across my face and body.

It can't hurt me, I thought. But it was still totally gross.

As I ran, my gaze focused on Gabriel in front of me. He didn't falter, just kept moving no matter what lay in his path. There were hideously dismembered and gutted corpses, some of which still twitched with unnatural life even though there wasn't enough left of them to be ambulatory. I wondered how many students and faculty had died on Big Red's campus while I had been recovering from my wounds.

One of the ghouls stepped into Gabriel's path, then another. He used the butt of his gun to knock them to the side so they wouldn't fall in the way of the rest of the team. I flashed back on Matt charging through the field as if he'd been going for a touchdown, toppling zombies that landed right in my path.

Nausea rose in my throat. I felt those germ-infested teeth digging into my shoulder and arm, brambles trapping my hair as more fetid corpses closed in for the kill. Things spun in a hellish merry-go-round of memories as I tried to focus on the here and now.

A clawed hand clutched my left arm. I jerked away from it as a particularly ripe male zombie in the remnants of a band uniform reached for me. Its arms may have said *you need a hug*, but its gaping, hungry mouth sent a different message.

"Motherfucker!"

I screamed the word like a war cry as I bashed zombie nerd in the forehead with the butt of my M-4. Except with the nose plugs I sounded like a profane munchkin. I started giggling, and once started, couldn't stop.

Lily caught up with me.

"Are you okay? she asked in a pinched, nasal tone.

The sound set me off even more. She looked at me like I was insane. I guess I was, just a little bit.

"We sound like we're on helium," I choked as we ran side by side in the path Gabriel had cleared through the quad.

Lily smacked a putrefying cheerleader in the face as it lurched out of the shadows of what used to be my favorite coffee kiosk.

"Take that, you stuck up zombie bitch!" Then she burst into laughter. "Omigod, we do!"

I'm not saying we suddenly lost all fear. Not even close. I still felt like throwing up, but the spinning flashback had stopped. The horror was still there, but it was real, and it was something I could deal with.

I could run, I could fight, and I could kill.

Fuck you, zombie hordes.

CHAPTER TWENTY

Gabriel reached the far side of the quad, pausing on a ghoul-free patch of grass to make sure we were behind him, then set off in-between the student union and Fine Arts building. Trees and bushes lined the sidewalk between the two buildings, ideal cover for opportunistic zombies if they had the brains to stage an ambush.

But they didn't.

The few that tried to grab at us just shambled, grabbed, and tried to bite. It wasn't too hard to dodge them; they were slow and uncoordinated, especially when faced with our wild card reflexes.

I wondered if zombies felt frustration when their would-be meals evaded their clutching fingers. I thought about how I'd feel if my dinner jumped off the plate whenever I reached for it.

That would suck.

A really disgusting male zom lurched directly in front of me. We're talking a face not even a mother zombie could love, and one I recognized from my creative writing class. He'd asked me out and I'd turned him down, not so much because of his looks, but because he'd been an impossibly pompous asshole.

He'd also suffered from mega acne, and zombification had done nothing to clear it up. His skin was covered with little volcanic eruptions. The word 'juicy' sprang to mind.

I wished it hadn't.

I skidded to a halt. Lily slammed into me and Kai completed our Three Stooges moment by barreling into her. The impact sent me stumbling forward, right into Acne Boy's eager arms. In what had to be luck, its fingers clutched my arms at the elbows, slipping in-between the padding. Bloodstained teeth gnashed in anticipation of its first bite, graying tongue lolling out between its blubbery lips.

"No way, pal," I growled. "I wouldn't date you, and I sure as hell won't let you eat me." Jamming the M-4 between us, barrel pointing down, I drove the stock up and into its chin. Its mouth snapped shut and a piece of tongue plopped onto the sidewalk.

Okay, eeuww.

"Oh, that is just so wrong," Kai choked.

Fighting the urge to throw up, I used the length of the gun to shove against the zombie's chest, trying to pry its fingers off my arms. Amazing how much strength there was in those rotting hands.

As a young and stupid five year old, I'd had my finger pinched by a pissed-off crab. I'd screamed and hopped around until my dad pried it off. The zombie's grip felt a lot like that.

Lily and Kai, recovering from the collision, each grabbed one of Acne Boy's hands and yanked the fingers backward. I could hear the snap of its bones breaking as they forced it to let go. I gave one more shove with the gun, then hip-checked it off the sidewalk into a bush.

Kai swatted me on the butt.

"Nice hip action, girl!"

I considered clipping him with my gun, but then Gabriel spoke up. He was already at the next intersection, the Science and Administration buildings behind him.

"Stop playing around and move your asses!" He glared at us. I rolled my eyes, but moved my ass. Rising moans from behind told us that the zombies we'd bypassed were headed our way.

Up ahead, their numbers thinned out when we reached the dorms, but I saw lurching silhouettes through some of the windows. Was anyone alive in there, maybe cowering behind their doors, hoping against hope to go undetected? Maybe Zara was one of them. Or maybe she stalked the campus, looking for flesh instead of face scrub.

No time to think about that now. The search and rescue mission would have to wait until after we'd cleared the open areas.

Don't I sound all military and shit.

The number of zombies thinned further as we passed the dorms. We jogged easily through their decreasing numbers until we reached the gymnasium, athletic fields, and parking lots, the last part of campus before the surrounding fields and old growth redwoods.

Suddenly there was *lots* of activity. Large, sturdy military looking vehicles, klieg lights set up on temporary wooden platforms casting their glow over the parking lot as dozens of men and women in protective suits hustled around like large, sterile ants.

Some were unrolling coils of razor wire that looked like the world's nastiest Slinkies, while others fiddled with the nozzles of hoses attached to small tanker trucks. Gabriel stopped by one of the trucks and we all gathered around him.

"What are they gonna do?" I said. "Zombie wet T-shirt contest?"

Gabriel snorted.

"Those tanks contain an experimental foam designed to harden on contact with air, in order to create effective barricades as quickly as possible. In this case, it'll be the secondary barrier. The razor wire will be the first."

"Wow, that's totally James Bond," I said, impressed. "Does it work?"

He nodded toward one of the trucks.

"Watch."

One of the suited engineers aimed a nozzle at the ground behind a Slinky and flicked a lever. Immediately a flood of white foam poured out. The man moved the nozzle slowly back and forth, bisecting the parking lot with a wall of what looked like shaving cream. As we watched the stuff went from snowy white to a dingy gray as it hardened.

"How much of that stuff do they have?"

"We have twenty of those trucks," Gabriel said. "They each hold enough foam to put up a hundred yards. So if we use the outermost buildings—like the gym and dorms—as part of the overall barrier, we should have enough to protect the entire campus."

"Why bother with the razor wire?" I asked. "It's not like they're gonna go 'ouch, sharp' or anything."

Gabriel gave a half smile.

"They may not feel pain, but they can still get snagged in it. And even a few moments' delay can be the time we need."

I watched in fascination while the engineers continued to position razor wire and back it up with foam. Hard to believe it could stop a crowd of hungry zombies.

"It won't hold them forever," Gabriel added, as if he'd read my mind. "But it should do the trick long enough for us to clear the campus and erect something more permanent."

"You think we're going to need something permanent?" The thought horrified me.

"Just a figure of speech. If we handle this right, the outbreak soon will be just another file for the archives."

Somehow, I wasn't reassured.

"And if we don't?"

Gabriel put a hand on my shoulder. I felt its warmth, even through the body armor.

"Then it's end of the world as we know it."

"I so didn't need to hear that," I said.

"Don't worry." He looked at me intently. "We can do this."

"I know we can," I said just as seriously. "But now I'm gonna have that damn song running through my head all night."

Gabriel laughed, as if I'd startled it out of him.

I grinned up at him, noticing how the corners of his eyes crinkled up when he smiled. I suddenly remembered all the lustful thoughts I'd had about him when I'd first met him—before he'd opened his mouth, that is.

I don't think he could read my mind, but even in the weird illumination thrown off by the klieg lights I saw his eyes darken from denim to indigo. I caught my breath as his hand tightened on my shoulder and something sparked between us.

"Incoming!"

Thank you, ravenous zombies. Talk about lousy timing.

The shout came from one of the lookouts. Beyond the half-finished barrier, shambling, staggering corpses were making their way out of the redwoods and into the fields. A few had already reached the parking lot and headed toward the engineers with a frightening single-mindedness.

The dull pop of gunfire intertwined with the ululating moans of the undead as the sharpshooters went to work. None of the zombies made it closer than twenty feet to the men and women who were erecting the barrier.

Gabriel's hand dropped off my shoulder and his expression morphed back into dead serious mode.

"Wild cards, listen up!" he said. "You know the plan. Follow the perimeter and start closing the circle. Kill every zombie you see, rescue survivors if you can without compromising the mission, and meet back at Patterson Hall. Watch each other's backs. You've got walkie-talkies if you get separated from the rest of the team.

"Let's go."

With one last unreadable look in my direction, he

took off, following the line of the trucks, razor wire, and super-duper shaving cream. Adrenaline kicked in. I unsheathed my tanto and katana and nodded to Lily and Kai.

"Ready to kick some zombie butt?"

Lily grinned and nodded back.

Kai slapped us both on our behinds.

"Let's do it!"

Lily and I exchanged looks.

He's gonna pay for that.

CHAPTER TWENTY-ONE

Search and destroy.

I'd heard the words before, but just among many clichés uttered by macho characters in any one of dozens of movies, good and bad. Pretty straightforward.

But until you've actually spent time actively seeking out an enemy for the express purpose of killing them, you cant really understand what they mean. After an hour of splattering brains and the vile black sludge over an ever-shrinking spiral around Big Red campus, the true meaning of *search and destroy* was embedded in my soul.

And as I was putting a bullet through the brain of a guy who used to sit next to me in History 109A—"Race Gender, and Power in the Antebellum South"—it hit me.

I'm not afraid!

Terror had vanished in a mind-numbing routine of violence. I kept telling myself our targets were no longer human, that their souls or whatever gave them humanity were long gone. Every time more than one of the things converged on a member of the team, the rest were there to take it down. I'm not saying it was a walk in the park—in fact, it was totally gross. But the fear of dying evaporated as the hunt continued, and the zom body count rose.

"To your right!"

Kai's shout alerted me to a female zombie lurching out

from the shadows of the Fine Arts building. Remnants of a bubblegum pink "Juicy" tracksuit hung from its rotting body.

The zombie was juicy, all right, but not in a good way. Its pink-tipped nails raked harmlessly across my armor-protected bicep and I promptly kicked its legs out from underneath it, sending it to the ground. Before I could deliver the killing thrust, something swooshed by me in a rush of air and crunched into the zombie's skull with lethal impact.

Lily grinned at me, a wild light in her eyes, turning a wholesome prettiness into kind of a scary beauty. Like, imagine Melanie Wilkes from *Gone With the Wind*, but possessed by Kali.

"I've always hated those stupid Juicy clothes," she said, an edge to her voice. "I mean, who wants to have 'Juicy' stamped across their butt? That's just kind of gross. I mean, right?"

"Totally," I agreed, conveniently forgetting the fact I had a favorite pair of teal Juicy sweats in my closet.

A yell brought our attention back as Kai was attacked by three ex-jock zombies that must have come staggering around the corner of the gymnasium, football uniforms still intact.

Shit. The helmets were going to make it hard to take out their brains.

All three of them piled on him as if he were about to score a touchdown for the opposing team. Kai went down with another yell and a bone-jarring thud, his crowbar falling uselessly to the sidewalk.

Gabriel was already out of sight. Lily and I glanced at each other, shrugged, and dove in, each of us grabbing one of the jock zombies and peeling him off. My zombie snapped at me, but I'll be damned if it didn't still have a mouth guard in there. Between that and the facemask, no way this dude was taking a bite out of anyone.

Its grip, however, still showed some of the strength it

had possessed in life—enough to rip off one of my arms if I didn't take it down quickly.

Fine.

At such close quarters, I had to use my shortened katana to whack my opponent. As I did so, I discovered that it takes a lot of *oomph* to decapitate a human, even for a wild card.

Lily, in the meantime, used the sharp edge of her pickaxe to crack her jock-zom's helmet open like a hard-boiled egg. As it fell away, she flipped the weapon over in her hand and brought the pick down to penetrate the brain. The blow took the zombie to the ground, and Lily braced a foot against its shoulder, pulling the point out. She used it again on the still-wriggling corpse to make sure she'd finished the job.

This left a beefy zombie still pinning Kai to the ground, its face buried in his neck. Kai was hollering at the top of his lungs. Lily and I each grabbed the zom by a shoulder and hauled it backward. Shoulder pads make for great leverage.

Between the two of us, we threw it on its back where it thrashed like an upended turtle. I reached down and gave Kai an arm up while Lily dispatched what I think was once Big Red's star fullback.

"Thanks, Ash." Kai looked a little shaken. He ran a hand over his neck and grimaced. "Zombie drool. Ah, that's just nasty."

"Big wuss," Lily said as she pulled her weapon out of the latest kill.

So much for my shy roomy, I thought.

Kai looked offended.

"*You* say that after one of these pus bags macks down all over *your* neck, Miss Thing."

Lily wrinkled her nose at him, wiping the business end of her weapon on the zombie's team jersey.

"Couldn't be any grosser than my first boyfriend," she replied.

Kai shook his head and patted her on the back.

"Girl, that is just sad."

The walkie-talkie at my belt gave a sudden squawk.

"*Ashley?*"

Gabriel. I grabbed the walkie-talkie and hit the relay button.

"Here, Red Leader!" Was I supposed to say *over*, or something official like that?

"Where the hell are you and the rest of the squad?"

"Peeling what's left of Big Red's forward offense off of Kai."

"He okay?"

I nodded, then realized he wouldn't see it.

"Yeah," I replied. "We're all fine."

"Good. Then get your asses over to the Biology building, *stat*."

I couldn't resist it.

"Just our asses?"

I heard a snort, or maybe just a burst of static. Turning, I smirked at the rest of Team A.

"Our fearless leader wants us to join him. *Stat*, he says."

Kai shrugged.

"Gabriel wants stat, we give him stat."

The three of us took off at a run, rounding the corner to spot Gabriel waiting under a light at the entrance to the Biology building, M-4 in hand. As we drew closer, he nodded toward the doors.

"I heard screams inside."

"Survivors?" I looked up at the building, its featureless institutional windows dark and foreboding.

"We can hope so," he replied. "It would be much safer to tackle this in the daytime, but if we wait that long—"

"It might be too late," Lily broke in.

Gabriel nodded again.

"You guys up for this?"

A muffled cry came from inside, frantic and hopeless at the same time.

CHAPTER TWENTY-TWO

"Let's go," I said, and I ran through the doors almost before Gabriel pushed them open. He grabbed my shoulder as I moved past, jerking me to a halt.

"Don't be an idiot," he growled. "Use your flashlight until your eyes adjust to the dark."

I stopped and pulled a small olive-drab LED flashlight out of my belt pouch. I hit the 'on' switch and a surprisingly bright blue light emanated from the head. What it revealed wasn't good.

Blood, lots of it, smeared the floor and the walls of the main hallway. Bits and pieces of stuff I didn't even want to think about.

"Oh, god, please help me!" A female voice with the same notes of frantic despair as the previous cry carried down a flight of stairs off the main hallway.

"We're coming!" I screamed the words at the top of my lungs, hoping the zombies would be drawn by the sound of fresh meat. Moans answered me.

Hot diggity, I thought. *It worked.*

I took off toward the stairs seconds before Gabriel's "GO!" echoed through the hall. I'd probably catch hell for it later, but, oh well.

Skidding on a patch of blood or something even worse, I nearly slid past the stairs. Catching myself on the polished brass banister, I took the steps two at a time.

The reassuring thuds of footsteps clattered close behind.

The moans increased in volume. I saw why as soon as I hit the second floor hall. If not quite seething with zombies it was, at the very least, crawling with them. In some cases quite literally—there were a few partials with entrails and shattered limbs trailing behind them as they dragged themselves along the tiled floor. Looking at what oozed out, I was profoundly grateful for my nose plugs.

They were gathered at the far end of the hallway. At least half of the things focused on me, already following the sound of my voice. The other half gathered around a closed door, scratching, pounding, clawing in a frenzied yet single-minded effort to get to their prey.

Even at that distance, I could hear sobbing coming from behind the door—uncontrollable wrenching sobs from someone fully expecting the worst.

Time to improve her expectations. Waving my flashlight I shouted.

"Hey! Dead things!" Okay, so my witty repartee was kind of lame. "Over here! Free dinner this way!"

"What the hell are you doing?" Kai reached the top of the stairs just in time to hear my attempts at zombie whispering.

"Drawing them away from that room so we can kill them and rescue whoever's inside."

"How about we kill them while their attention's on the door?"

Oh. Yeah.

Lily and Gabriel joined us.

"He has a point," Gabriel said neutrally.

Lily snorted, almost dislodging her nose plugs.

"What fun is that?" she countered. I couldn't decide if I should be proud of her, or worry about her. I chalked it up to the adrenaline rush.

Gabriel rolled his eyes.

"I can see that I'll have to keep you two separated."

Lil and I grinned at each other.

"Fine," he continued. "Let's clear the hall."

We started to charge forward, but Gabriel stepped in front of us.

"Let me begin." Raising his M-4, he opened fire with a precision I could only admire. There were no wasted shots; each bullet hit its target. When he finally ceased fire, the hall was littered with twice-dead corpses.

We stared silently at the carnage.

"Wow," Kai said.

Lily pouted.

"You didn't save any for us."

Okay, maybe a little too much adrenaline.

Gabriel shot her a look.

"There'll be plenty more." He turned to me. "Ashley, you and I will see who's behind the door. Lily, Kai, check the unlocked rooms. We might as well clear the entire floor while we're here."

Lily ran down the far end of the hall with a little war whoop while Kai made his way in the opposite direction with a bit more stealth. Gabriel and I approached the door that had been under siege, shoving corpses out of the way to clear a path.

I tried not to look at any of the faces of the fallen zombies. Seeing former classmates or teachers would make it that much harder. Maybe I was just tired, but I could feel myself losing my much-needed detachment.

"Thanks," I said to Gabriel as we muscled aside a particularly hefty male zombie wearing a *Simpsons* T-shirt.

"For what?"

"Taking care of this batch. I think I'm on overload here."

Gabriel nodded.

"I understand," he said. "But we're not finished yet. I mean tonight."

"I get that." I broke eye contact. The intensity in his

gaze flustered me, and that was the last thing I needed in this situation. Getting back to the business at hand, I rapped on the door.

"Hello?"

Silence, then a muffled whimper.

"It's okay," I said. "It's safe now. You can open the door."

Another pause.

"They'll get me." The voice was feminine, barely above a whisper.

I shook my head, then stopped. Not like the person could see me.

"No, they won't," I said, trying to sound reassuring. "We killed them."

"But—" There was infinite horror in her next words. "But they're *already* dead."

I shivered despite the warmth of my armor and the adrenaline coursing through my system. She was right. These things went against all known laws of nature.

I shook my head again—this time mentally.

Enough of that shit, I told myself. *Job to do, right?*

"I know," I said. "But now they're *really* dead. We shot them in the head." I hoped that was reassuring, but as soon as I said it, I wasn't so sure. "And we'll protect you," I added.

"Promise?"

"You bet."

I heard the rasp of metal on metal, and then the door slowly opened outward. I moved one of the bodies to allow it to do so, then angled my flashlight so the beam wouldn't shine directly on the face of the person timidly emerging from what looked like a large storage closet.

Our rescue-ee appeared to be middle-aged, probably a teacher, dressed in the remnants of what was once a sensible dark jacket with matching skirt and a light-colored blouse, now ripped in places and spattered with blood.

She took a tentative step outside of the closet, legs so

wobbly she nearly fell. I shouldered my M-4 and held out an arm to give her support.

"Thank you." Her voice was raspy, probably ripped raw from screaming, but the depth of her gratitude came through loud and clear. I don't think she was just thanking me for the arm to lean on.

"Are you all right?" *Okay, stupid question.* "I mean, did any of them bite or scratch you?"

She shook her head.

"No… at least, I don't think so."

"Ashley, check her for open wounds." Gabriel stepped toward the woman, and spoke directly to her. "You don't want to get any blood near your mouth, nose, or eyes, either. It's infected with a virus."

I did a quick scan of all exposed flesh. Given the circumstances, I wasn't going to ask her to strip.

"She looks clean." I said, then I looked her in the eye. "How long have you been up here?" I asked gently.

"Two… no, three days."

"In this closet?" That triggered my borderline claustrophobia, and the thought horrified me.

She shook her head.

"I was hiding in one of the classrooms with a fellow teacher, Professor Gough," she said. "We found a couple of energy bars and a bottle of water in the podium, but it wasn't enough. They—" She made a vague gesture toward the bodies. "They'd stopped moaning and clawing at the classroom door. Something else had caught their attention."

Her voice became almost eerily calm.

"We thought it would be safe to try and reach one of the bathrooms, get some water. We were so thirsty…" She swallowed. It looked like it hurt. "We made it to the men's room, but there were more of those things inside. They grabbed Professor Gough before he could even scream.

"Oh, he screamed plenty after that, though. I could hear him even through the walls."

She shook her head as if trying to dislodge the memory.

"When I backed out, those things were just… just flooding the halls again. Ian's screams… they heard him. This—" She gestured toward the closet. "—was the closest door."

I shone my flashlight beam in the direction she had indicated. Sure enough, there was a deadbolt on the inside.

"Why would anyone put a deadbolt on the inside of a storage closet?" I asked no one in particular.

The woman gave a faint laugh, surprising me.

"We had a janitor who liked to drink during his shifts, so he installed them on the inside of a few closets around campus so he wouldn't be disturbed." She reached out and fingered the bolt almost lovingly. "He was fired, but the administration never got around to removing the deadbolts.

"Lucky thing, that," she added.

"That's an understatement," I said. How many more people might still be alive because of an alcoholic janitor? It was, excuse the pun, a sobering thought. "What's your name?"

She took a deep shuddering breath before responding. "Jan Blandsford."

"Jan, I'm Ashley. And we're going to need to get you out of here and to safety. Can you run?"

Another deep breath, this one determined.

"Yes. Yes, I believe I can." She took a step and skidded on a piece of… well, some body part or another.

"Here, let me help you." Gabriel stepped forward and put an arm around her to help her navigate through the mess.

"Thank you," she said again, this time with what I could swear was a slight flirtatious note to her voice. Gabriel might not be a wild card, but he had a way of helping a woman deal with a life or death situation.

Just look into these blue eyes and you'll forget all *about it.* At least he was using his powers for good, instead of evil.

Lily dashed back along the hallway, pickaxe dripping

with gore. She skidded to a halt next to us, as happy as a kid on a really gross Slip 'n' Slide.

"Found some in the men's room," she said, only a little out of breath. "A couple more in one of the classrooms." She hefted her axe with a satisfied grin. "I took care of them."

Gabriel nodded.

"Good job," he said. "Let's find Kai and get out of here."

As if on cue, Kai appeared around the corner at the opposite end of the hallway, the pronged end of his crowbar just as gore-encrusted. He grinned at us.

"Did I hear my name?"

Jan lifted a hand and smoothed a stray strand of hair out of her face. Obviously Kai had the same ability as Gabriel. But I'm pretty sure he never gave much thought to the whole "with great power comes great responsibility" thing.

"Everything clear down there?" Gabriel asked.

"Yup." Kai smacked the crowbar against his open palm.

Suddenly Jan screamed. A lone female zombie staggered out from a doorway behind Kai, clawed hands clutching at his back and shoulders, black fluid running out of its mouth as its jaws gaped open.

Kai gave a high-pitched yelp and whirled around, smashing the thing over the head once, twice, and then a third time with his crowbar. There was an audible 'crack' on the third hit as the thing's skull shattered under the impact and it went down to the floor.

Kai lifted the crowbar above his head like a spear and thrust the pointy end into the zombie's head. Once he was confident that the job had been done, he walked over to us.

"Now we can go," he said.

Lil and I looked at each other as he stepped past. Two minds with the same thought. We both smacked him on his ass, as hard as we could.

He turned, raised an eyebrow, and grinned.

"Why, thank you, ladies," he said. "Normally I have to pay for that."

"Hey, Kai?" I said.

"Yeah, Ashley?"

I smiled at him.

"You scream like a girl."

Betty glanced at the clock on the Mini Cooper's dashboard. Nearly four o'clock, which meant maybe an hour of daylight left. But at least an hour and a half drive still left before reaching Redwood Grove.

Sighing, she took another sip of lukewarm Starbucks coffee and wished yet again that the Mini's radio worked. She tended to zone out, and music helped keep her focused. Hell, she'd even listen to talk radio or the news, though she usually avoided both like the plague.

Anything to distract her from worrying why Lil hadn't been answering her cell for three days.

Brake lights blinked in front of her. Betty slowed and caught sight of a flashing sign to the right. Freeway closed, detour ahead.

Resisting the impulse to curse, she went into her yoga ugia breath, forcing herself to stay calm as traffic slowed to a crawl—four lanes of freeway funneling down into one.

Breathe in, breathe out.

Forty minutes later she reached the exit. At the bottom of the ramp she saw what looked like an alcohol checkpoint, except it was manned by military personnel instead of cops.

This can't be good.

Breathe in, breathe out.

She finally pulled up to the checkpoint, unrolling her window as the car drew abreast of a young male soldier. Betty pasted on a smile.

"What's going on?" she asked.

"Ma'am, where are you headed?" The soldier looked younger than Lily.

"Redwood Grove," she replied. "I live there."

"I'm sorry, ma'am, but that area is under quarantine at this time."

Quarantine? *Betty shook her head in disbelief.*

"You must be mistaken," she said.

"No mistake, ma'am."

"But my daughter's there. She hasn't called me—" Then she stopped as she understood the reason for Lily's silence. "Oh god." She looked up at the soldier, no more than a boy. "I have to get to my daughter."

He shook his head firmly.

"I'm sorry, ma'am, but no one is allowed in or out of the quarantine zone until further notice."

"There has to be someone I can talk to!" she responded, trying not to let panic overcome her.

"Here, ma'am." He drew a card out of his breast uniform pocket. "This is a number you can call to get status updates on anyone inside the quarantine zone."

Betty took the card; it was a 1-866 number.

"You'll have to move along now, ma'am," he said, and he stepped away from the car, motioning in the direction she was supposed to go.

Betty nodded and hit the accelerator, following the detour signs until she was out of sight of the checkpoint. Then she turned off the main road and doubled back parallel to the freeway, crossing over to the west side a few miles south of the checkpoint.

It would take her a few hours, but there were old logging trails and back roads that weren't on any maps. She'd try them all if she had to.

One way or another, she was going home to her daughter.

CHAPTER TWENTY-THREE

"Well done," Simone said as we staggered through the front doors. I ached in muscles I didn't even know I had.

Gabriel looked crappy again, his skin pale and running with sweat. We hadn't run into Team B, but he'd already had confirmation via walkie-talkie that they'd completed their sweep, and had returned a short time before us.

Kai was supporting our civilian survivor, and Simone immediately stepped forward.

"Professor Blandsford!"

Jan's eyes widened with recognition.

"Professor Fraser?" she rasped. "You're alive, too?" She started quietly weeping as Simone enfolded her in a reassuring hug.

"You're safe now," Simone said. "Jamie will take you to get a checkup—you remember Dr. Albert, don't you? And then you can have a shower and a hot meal."

Never far away, Jamie stepped forward quickly and led Jan off toward the stairs.

"Oh, lord, a shower." Jan started crying even harder. "I never thought I'd take another shower again."

I sidled up to Simone.

"They're not taking her to the med ward, are they?"

"Oh, good god, no." Simone sounded appalled. "Dr. Albert will check her over to make sure there's no possibility of infection. If she's clear, she'll be given a room. If not, well, we'll sedate her before taking the appropriate measures."

Appropriate measures. I shuddered. Waking up in that hellhole was something I wouldn't wish on my worst enemy.

Colonel Paxton appeared and beamed at us. At least I *think* he was happy. With his expression, it was hard to tell.

"How many zeds do you think are still within the confines of the campus itself?" he asked.

"Hard to say, sir," Gabriel replied. "We'll need to go out tomorrow and clear the rest of the buildings. We can take them two at a time, one per team. Open the main points of entry and lure out as many as we can before doing a room-by-room check."

Paxton nodded.

"Excellent," he said. "Team B brought back several survivors. Unfortunately some had been bitten, but at least two were uninjured."

We went to shed our unimaginably filthy clothing, which was placed into hazardous waste containers. Then we were hosed down with some sort of disinfectant that smelled like Lysol and bleach on steroids, wielded by our hazmat-suited pals. Finally we went back to our rooms, wrapped in towels.

Lil and I thumb-wrestled for first dibs on the shower, and I won.

"It's not fair," she grumbled. "My thumbs are longer than yours, I should have won."

"T'ain't the length," I replied, "It's the dexterity."

Lil stuck her tongue out at me as I shut the bathroom door, anxious to smell like something other than zombie guts or kitchen cleaner.

Hot water never felt so good, but I took pity on my poor filthy teammate and made it quick. Swiping my underarms with deodorant, I quickly put on a little moisturizer and lip balm, slathered my body with lotion, wrapped a towel around myself, and vacated the bathroom.

My wardrobe choices were limited to yoga pants, T-shirts, tank tops, sweats, and long-sleeved olive-drab thermals. I had another set of combat wear, but I'd had enough of that for the night, even if it did look kind of ginchy.

I chose yoga pants and a thermal.

As exhausted as I was, I was also wide-awake and totally ravenous. I sat on the bed for a few minutes, listening to the sound of Lily humming slightly off-key show tunes as she enjoyed a long soak.

Next time I'd throw the damn wrestling match.

After five minutes or so of humming and an amazingly loud series of growls from my empty stomach, I knocked on the bathroom door, opened it a crack, and yelled over the sound of running water.

"Lily, I'm going to the cafeteria. See you there?"

She stopped humming.

"Okay!" As soon as I closed the door, the show tunes started up again, more off-key than before.

I definitely needed to look into earplugs.

The cafeteria was empty except for Team B—Gentry, Mack, Tony, and Kaitlyn—who were all seated and chowing down on what looked like steak dinners complete with salad and corn on the cob slathered in butter. I could see steam rising from the bread basket on the table. There were bottles of beer and wine lined up on a counter.

Oh, yummy…

No one else from my team was there yet. Probably enjoying nice *long* showers.

Tony saw me first and waved his fork in the air, sending a piece of steak flying off to the side, narrowly missing Gentry.

"Hey, Ashley!" he called out.

The rest of the group looked up. Mack toasted me

with a glass of red wine and Gentry wiggled an ear of corn by way of saying hello.

Kaitlyn just went back to her meal. You'd have thought all of the zombie killing would have given her an attitude adjustment, but no such luck.

I waved back to those who gave a shit, loaded up a tray with food, and took a seat near the end of the table. Close enough to be sociable, but leaving room for anyone else who might want to sit next to me. Like Lil or Kai… or maybe Gabriel.

"How'd it go?" Tony grinned at me, a Band-Aid over one eyebrow.

"Good, I guess," I said. "Still alive."

"Cool." He grabbed a bottle of Dos Equis and took a swig. I guess if Tony was old enough to kill zombies for his country, he was old enough to enjoy a cold beer.

"What happened to you?" I gestured to the Band-Aid.

Tony turned red, took another swig of beer, and muttered something unintelligible.

"Dumbfuckzombippedabarbul."

I raised an eyebrow.

"You don't say."

Mack chuckled.

"What he's trying to say is that a zombie got up close and personal with one of his piercings. Guess it liked bright and shiny things."

I gave a shout of laughter.

"Yeah, well…" Tony drowned his mortification with more beer, and shot Mack a pissy glare.

I grabbed a bottle of water and downed it in three long gulps, then poured myself a glass of Napa Reserve cabernet. Matt would have approved. I took a dainty bite of steak—actually, I ripped into it like a starving tiger—and followed it with a sip of wine.

Pure bliss. Hooray for the enhanced taste buds. Guess it didn't always suck to be a wild card.

For the next few minutes I ignored everything to

focus entirely on eating. The hot rolls were probably just Brown'n Serve with I Can't Believe It's Not Butter or something like that, but home-baked and freshly churned never tasted so good.

I was nearly through my first steak and contemplating a second one when someone sat down next to me, on the left. I didn't have to look to know it was Gabriel; that side of my body suddenly went on hyper alert, all warm and tingly. A moment later I saw Lily and Kai heading toward the table from the other end of the cafeteria.

I turned and smiled briefly, noticing that he looked much better, then focused on my food again during the hullabaloo of greetings.

Kai plopped himself down in-between Tony and Sergeant Gentry, and Lily sat on my right, setting a copy of the *Zombie Combat Manual* next to her plate.

"More homework?" I asked.

She nodded. Without saying a word, she opened the book with one hand and picked up an ear of corn with the other, munching as she flipped through pages, thoroughly ignoring the rest of us. Our death-dealing extrovert had evidently retired for the night.

"Hey," Gabriel said to me under cover of the babbling going on around us. It was amazing how much awkwardness could be conveyed in one syllable.

"Hey, yourself," I replied, going for three times as much awkwardness.

"Enjoying the food?"

I nodded.

"Maybe it's just 'cause I was starving—" I took another sip of wine. "—but I don't think I've ever tasted anything so delicious. I mean, if you like this sort of thing."

Gabriel gave a half smile.

"Don't worry. No lecture today—not after everything you've been through."

"Glad those zombies are good for *something*." I kept my tone neutral—maybe flirting just a little. I checked out his plate, piled high with baked potatoes, salad, rolls, and corn.

"No offense," I said, "but where are you getting your protein from? Seems like you'd need some, after… well, after everything."

Gabriel rolled his eyes. "Haven't you heard of tofu?"

I wrinkled my nose.

"Gross," I said. "It's all white and wriggly and kinda weird."

"This from a woman who just waded through zombie entrails." Gabriel poured himself a glass of wine.

"Yeah, but you didn't see me eating them, did you?"

Gabriel chose to ignore that.

"Ever had a tofu hot dog?" he asked.

I shook my head.

"I've always equated it with non-alcoholic beer," I said. "I'd rather have the real thing."

"Don't knock it until you've tried it."

I noticed something red sticking out from under a pile of salad on his plate, something that looked suspiciously like a small piece of exceptionally rare steak. Gabriel looked down, and frowned.

"Doctor's orders," he said. I could tell he was pissed off at being caught.

Not long ago I'd have read him the riot act. Now I grabbed another roll from the basket.

"God, I love bread and butter." I cocked my head and looked at him. "Does being a wild card mean I can eat as much butter as I want without getting fat?"

I felt him relax.

"Only if you continue to work out the way you have been."

"So once the zombocalypse is over, then it's fat city, huh?"

Before Gabriel could respond, Gentry started laughing from across the table. Suddenly I realized that everyone else had gone quiet, and had been watching us.

Shit.

"Zombocalypse," Gentry said. "You just come up with that?"

I shrugged.

"Makes it sound kind of manageable, don'tcha think?"

"I like it," Tony said. I could tell he'd had his share of the beer, and maybe more.

"'Course you do, bro." Kai patted him on the shoulder. "Doesn't hurt that Ashley thought it up, does it?"

Uh-oh.

Kaitlyn sniffed audibly.

"Trust Ashley not to take things seriously," she said into her plate.

And trust you to take any opportunity to be a bitch. I took a few deep breaths, not wanting things to escalate. I felt Gabriel tense up beside me, but to my surprise, Lily snapped first.

"Back off, Kaitlyn," she said. "Just because you don't have a sense of humor doesn't give you the right to be a bitch to someone who does."

Whoah! Unleash the attack kitten!

Kaitlyn looked as if a Smurf had just bitten her. It was enough to shut her up, though, and let the rest of us enjoy our meal. I noticed that she was the only one who wasn't indulging in beer or wine.

"So if we can't have cool team names, what about our own code names?" Tony suddenly declared. "You know, like Snake Eyes or Matador."

Kai was all over that.

"You can be Ash," he said to me.

"Wow, that's original," I replied.

"No, really," he said. "Like for Ash in the *Evil Dead* movies. He totally kicks ass."

"My point remains the same," I said. But I actually kind of liked it.

Tony waved a hand.

"Whaddya want?" he asked. "Killer Barbie?"

I shot him the look he deserved.

"I'll take Ash, thanks."

Kai grinned.

"And Tony's gotta be Joystick." But "Joystick" looked less than thrilled.

"Aww, jeez," he said, "It makes me sound like a vibrating dildo."

Kai shrugged.

"If the shoe fits…" he said.

Gentry leaned back in his chair, causing it to creak. We looked at him, and he grinned.

"I ain't saying a word."

"How about X-Box?" Lil offered shyly.

"Better than Joystick," Tony admitted.

"Wii would work, too." Kai smirked, ducking before Tony could put him in a headlock.

"Mack can be Postman," I suggested. "The movie sucked, but Costner makes a good action hero."

Mack nodded his approval.

"At least I'll remember it," he said.

"I'll be Ladies' Man," Kai announced.

"In your dreams," Tony shot back.

"Even better," I said, "Lando."

Kai looked pleased.

"Gorgeous and geeky," he said. "Gotta love it." Then he and Tony turned their attention on Kaitlyn. She scowled back.

"Don't even *think* about it." Wisely, they dropped it.

"What about me?" Lily said, a hint of eagerness in her voice. I was glad to see her coming out of her shell—especially for something other than zombie killing.

"Cutie Bunny?" Kai suggested. She punched him on the arm, and it didn't look as if she held back much. "Damn!" He rubbed his arm. "Okay, not so cute."

"Gremlin?" Tony made sure to move out of Lily's range. She chucked her copy of the *Zombie Combat*

Manual at his head, and he barely ducked in time. Scooping it up, he protested, "It's just so wrong to use this book against a fellow wild card."

Lily looked to me for help, but I was drawing a big old blank. Feeling a bit light-headed, too. Problem was that she *was* cute, so all of the wrong names were suggesting themselves.

Finally Mack held up his hand.

"I got it!" he said proudly. "Diamond Lil. Just Lil for short."

"I like it," she said, "But where does it come from?"

"Diamond Lil was Lillian Russell, an actress and singer from way back. Beautiful and tough."

Lily nodded, favoring Mack with one of her rare smiles.

"Even cooler," Tony said, "she's a super hero!"

"Oh, well then…" Mack looked amused.

"In the comics," Tony continued, getting into it. "Sometimes she's a super villain. "She's also, like, a mutant, hits twice as hard as a normal person. Totally kick ass at street fighting."

That should do it. Sure enough, Lily beamed.

"What about Gabriel?" Sergeant Gentry said, grinning with the pleasure of someone who enjoys stirring the pot. "He needs a code name, too."

Gabriel's look was deadly.

"That's not necessary," he said flatly.

"Easy one," I said, wiping a sheen of sweat off of my forehead. "Tofu."

"Tofu" shot me a glare. I just smiled back sweetly.

But Tony wasn't done. He turned his attention to Gentry.

"You're next, dude."

"Yes, *Willard*," Gabriel said. "I think it's your turn."

"Ooh, cold, Tofu," Gentry said, sounding wounded. "Very cold." But he didn't seem particularly upset, really.

"Willard?" Kai grinned hugely. "Like the rat?"

"That was Ben," Tony corrected. "The rat was Ben. Willard was the dude who controlled the rats."

"That works," Kai said, "since he's in charge of *your* team."

Mack cleared his throat and put on a look of mock pain. Kaitlyn shot a glare, and she wasn't pretending.

Kai flushed.

"Sorry."

Mack just grinned.

"Actually, you wanted a nickname for the team," he said. "How about Rat Patrol?"

As everyone laughed, a sudden wave of heat swept across my face, neck, and chest, and I felt nauseous. I wondered if I'd gotten a bad piece of steak—like I really needed another case of food poisoning. My stomach roiled and I decided it was time for an emergency trip to the bathroom. I stood up, and was unsteady on my feet.

What is this? I'd only had two glasses of wine. Or maybe three.

"You okay, Ashley?" Lily smiled up at me with a slightly unfocused gaze.

"I'm fine," I lied. "I'll be back in a few."

I carefully made my way across the cafeteria and into the hallway, heading to the nearest ladies' room. Once I got there, I spent a few minutes deciding whether or not I was going to throw up.

CHAPTER TWENTY-FOUR

But I didn't.

I splashed cold water on my face and on the back of my neck, cooling off what had to have been an alcohol-induced hot flash.

Maybe it's a side-effect of the hyper-senses, I thought through the receding nausea. *Wouldn't that be a rip-off?* I hoped my fabulous new wild card powers included dodging a hangover, though, and decided to down some ibuprofen with a big glass of water, just in case they didn't.

Drying my face off with a paper towel, I turned and pushed the bathroom door open, smacking right into someone on the other side.

"Crap!" I yelped, giving out the kind of sound small dogs make when they're stepped on. Then I stumbled back from the impact—whatever I'd hit must have been a brick wall on two legs.

Pushing the door open again, slowly this time, I found Gabriel standing there, looking pissed.

"Jeez friggin' Louise," I growled. "What were you trying to do, scare the crap out of me?"

"Just checking to make sure you're okay." Now he looked both pissed off and embarrassed.

What the hell was going on?

"Well, next time see if you can do it without giving me a heart attack." I'd have said more, but I was hit by another hot flash, spiking my temperature a couple of degrees and leaving me flushed and dizzy.

I shut my eyes and swayed on my feet.

"Watch it," Gabriel said, reaching out and steadying me with both hands.

"Yeah. Just…" I just started babbling, without knowing what I was saying. "Y'know, I think I should have stopped after one glass of wine." I opened my eyes to find him peering intently at me. "Seriously, I'm okay. Other than whatever years were taken off my lifespan from the shock." But there was no anger now. The hot flash seemed to have burned all of it away.

"Were you…" I started, but I wasn't sure how to ask. "Were you looking for me?"

"You didn't look too good when you left the table," he said, and he was still holding my arms. "I wanted to check on you. The scaring you to death bit wasn't part of the plan."

"Just a little bonus, huh?"

"Something like that."

An awkward silence fell between us, the tension palpable.

"Is this about the whole tofu thing?" I asked, trying to lighten the mood.

"I could have lived without it." There was an edge to his voice that surprised me.

"Well, you know what they s—"

I gasped in shock. Without warning, his hands tightened painfully on my upper arms and he pushed me up against the wall, his body pressed against mine. His eyes darkened so much I thought I must be imagining it.

My breathing quickened as his hand shifted from my arms up to my face, fingers twining through my hair. Anger and desire warred in his gaze. Heat coiled in my stomach even as fear shuddered up my spine.

I tried to shake my head, but his fingers held it in

place as he muffled any protests by covering my mouth with his.

Fingers massaging my scalp, he slowly increased the intensity of the kiss, his tongue entering into play as he tilted my head back and slid it in.

I felt like I was following along in a dance, being led by someone who knew the steps much better than I did. I discovered that I was content to follow, matching the pressure of his lips with mine, letting my tongue play with his as he pressed his body into me, emphasizing the move with with a low, throaty sound.

He was definitely packing heat, and it wasn't his sidearm.

I gasped and arched against him, arms going around his body to pull him closer. He made another sound— one that was half low laugh, half growl—and took a quick step back out of the circle of my arms, only to seize my wrists with one hand and pin them against the wall above my head. I pulled against his hand, testing his strength, but he restrained me without even trying.

It was kind of scary… and incredibly sexy.

He insinuated a knee between my thighs, then kissed me again, all gentleness out the window, tongue exploring my mouth as his knee rubbed back and forth against my most sensitive areas. His free hand crept up beneath my shirt and he rubbed his palm over the peak of one nipple, pinching it.

I gasped in a combination of pain and ecstasy. My breath came short and fast as I rocked my hips against his knee, my tongue doing some exploring of its own, teeth biting his lower lip. He moved his mouth from mine, down my jaw to my arched neck. He bit it, teeth on either side of the pulse that throbbed there, hard enough to hurt in the most pleasurable way possible.

Maybe it was the adrenaline-filled experiences of the day, but I wanted Gabriel like I'd never wanted anything before. I wanted him even more than I'd wanted that steak dinner. And that was saying something.

We were both close to the point of tugging off each other's clothes and doing the nasty right there against the wall when a door slammed somewhere down the hallway. The effect on Gabriel was instantaneous.

His hand slid away from my breast and the other let go of my wrists as he stepped away from me so suddenly I would have fallen over if I hadn't been leaning against the wall. My breathing ragged, I stared at him.

His breathing was a little choppy, too, as he spoke.

"I'm sorry," he said. "That shouldn't have happened."

"What the fuck?" Or not, as it seemed. Frustration made me blunt. "What the hell *should* have happened?"

"I lost control," he said. "It's not... I can't allow it."

What, and I can? I thought angrily.

"So it's not okay for Mister 'I'm better than everyone else,' but it's something you'd expect from the slut," I countered. Hurt wrestled with anger. "Thanks, but no thanks, Gabriel." No way I was crying in front of him.

He looked as though I'd slapped him. Then his expression went unreadable.

"That's not what I meant."

"Then what did you mean by 'this is wrong?' What, are they gonna court-martial you for making out with a recruit?"

"No, but—"

"Then maybe you're allowed to screw anyone below your rank."

"That's not it at—"

"Then near as I can figure, this was all just some kind of sick joke. *Wasn't* it?"

He stopped trying to speak, and just stared at me.

"What, did you make a bet with the rest of the guys? Tony owe you a twenty?"

"That's enough!" Gabriel was getting angry, too. I knew I was pushing him, but I didn't care.

"Gee, let's see how fast can I get Ashley all hot and bothered, and then dump her ass and—"

Gabriel grabbed my shoulders and shook me once, then twice before slamming me up against the wall.

"Stop it," he gritted.

I shut up. Something in his tone scared me enough to cut through the rage.

Another door slammed shut, someone coming or going. He let go of me, and I steadied myself again.

"That's enough," he repeated, and he took a deep breath. "This isn't about you."

I shut my eyes, fighting the urge to punch him. When I thought I had myself under control, I opened my eyes again.

"Then as usual, it's all about you," I said.

"Yes." For some reason, I didn't think he was taking it the way I'd meant it. "It has nothing to do with you at all."

Another deep breath.

Then I punched him hard, right in the solar plexus, catching him by surprise. He doubled over with a grunt and I shoved past him, moving to a safe distance down the hall. Then I stopped, and turned back to him.

"You know what's funny, Gabriel?" He slowly straightened up, hands on his knees as he regained his wind. "For a moment there, I could have sworn it was about both of us. I thought I'd been wrong about you." I paused before adding, "I won't make that mistake again."

With that, I turned and walked away quickly, heading for my room.

CHAPTER TWENTY-FIVE

I wasn't hung-over the next day, unless you count an emotional hangover, in which case I had a doozy. No time to nurse it, though, either physically or emotionally. There was work to do.

We spent two days clearing the buildings on the Redwood Grove campus, one by one. After the zombies were eliminated in each building, hazmat-suited teams would come in and take away the corpses for disposal. Any survivors were taken to Patterson Hall.

The entire time I was luring zombies out of buildings, killing them, sweeping the buildings for the ghouls too clueless to answer the dinner bell, and locating survivors too terrified to answer our calls, I was going through my own personal hell.

I was doing it all under orders from the guy who had humiliated me.

Worse, there wasn't anyone I could talk to about it.

I'm here to tell you, it sucked.

But I did it all. I can't say I had a smile on my face, but I gritted my teeth, determined to do my job and kick ass. Though I wished it was Gabriel's.

"Yo, Tofu!" Kai hollered from the front door of the Poly Sci building, mid-afternoon on the second day. "You've got zoms on their way out the front door."

"Roger that, Lando."

"Ashley," he added, "You'll be on the front door after we dispatch the zoms." He used nicknames for Kai and Lily, but for me it was all formal.

Whatever.

I hated the fact that he made me feel like a high school kid with a crush. Somehow he managed to tap into every insecurity still lurking in my psyche.

Faint moans grew louder as Kai—"Lando," that is—dashed through the doors, clearing the stairs in one jump. He whirled around and opened fire as the hungry zombies staggered outside, looking for food.

At least thirty of them poured out and down the stairs, most of them looking to be former students with maybe a couple of teachers thrown in for good measure. I didn't recognize any of them, for which I was thankful. Anonymity made it easier to put bullets in their heads. Something in those flat, freaky pale irises and bloody corneas made it easy to forget these things had once been human.

Kai, Lil, and I did pretty damned well, without wasting time or ammo on body shots unless totally necessary. I couldn't help but be proud, though, that out of the three of us, I was the best shot.

Once we had taken care of the crowd that had followed Kai outside, he, Gabriel, and Lil went inside to finish the job while I kept an eye out for stragglers. As I waited I thought about Lily… Lil, that is. She insisted on being called that now. I suspected it was more than an affectation to her, more than Tony's geeky need for movie-type labels.

For Lil, the new name was a way to differentiate between the girl she'd been and who she'd become. She'd seen more horror in a very short time than most people see in a lifetime, and had gone from an almost neurotically introverted student to a member of a killing team. All of the wild cards could say much the same thing, but from what little that Lil had told us, it was obvious she'd led a particularly sheltered life before the attack.

She still worried about her cats. And her mom, too, who may or may not have returned from her trip to San Francisco. But it was easier to focus on the killing than think about what might have happened to them, so she'd thrown herself with gusto into zombie killing. Only time would tell what this was doing to her on a deeper level.

Hands clutching at my shoulders pulled me from my thoughts and I turned to find a male zombie in chef's whites, arms outstretched by way of the standard zombie greeting.

I stumbled backward, nearly falling on my ass as I narrowly avoided the bloodied teeth snapping at my neck. Regaining my balance, I unsheathed my long blade. I suddenly felt the need for a more visceral activity than just putting a bullet in its brain.

As the zombie Chef Ramsay lurched toward me, I slipped to its left and sliced through the back of its knees. The razor-sharp blade cut the rotting flesh and tendons as if going through butter. Zombie chef fell forward.

I pulled the blade to my right and used the momentum of the body and hips to put all my strength into a parallel cut that took its head right off the neck. A final—and unnecessarily vicious—thrust through one eye finished the job.

I paid more attention after that, keeping my thoughts to the task at hand. A couple more ghouls stumbled around the far corner of the Political Science building. I dispatched them each with a bullet to the brain, thus satisfying the need for target practice.

The rest of the team emerged from the building about twenty minutes later, a trio of trembling co-eds and an equally shaken male teacher's assistant in tow. All four hung on Gabriel's heels like a paddle of ducklings following their mommy.

"Any trouble, Ashley?" Gabriel's gaze flickered somewhere between my left ear and the middle of my forehead.

Asshole.

"Nope," I said, all business. "Six stragglers, six shots." I remembered the one I'd sliced and diced. "Oops, seven stragglers."

"Not too bad." Gabriel nodded. "We're definitely making headway. That's half again what we had at the drama building."

"And nothing compared to what we found at the dorms." Kai shuddered at the memory even as he spoke.

The dorms had been slaughterhouses, walls and floors slick with blood, both congealed and fresh. There were very few bodies, however, since most of the corpses had gotten up and joined in the feeding frenzy. Plenty of *pieces* of bodies though, some recognizable and others reduced to unidentifiable lumps of raw, bloody meat.

What few students had survived the massacre were nearly catatonic, given over to Dr. Albert and the medical team.

Gabriel radioed our status to the Powers That Be and we waited for the hazmat team to arrive so they could clear the corpses for incineration and take the survivors back to safety… or the med ward. Kai sat with them in a huddle, softly sweet-talking the girls to set them at ease.

"When are we going to start on the town?" Lil asked, taking a sip of water from her canteen as we waited.

"Hopefully in the next couple of days." Gabriel took off his helmet and wiped sweat from his forehead. Lil offered him her canteen. He took it with a nod of thanks and drank some water.

"We have that much more to do here?" she said.

"It's going to be far more dangerous out there than it's been in here, you know," he said. "We're talking plenty of businesses and hundreds of personal residences, including several apartment complexes. And we're not going to be able to contain the town the way we have the campus.

"Even though the military established a perimeter around the infected area," he continued, "we're talking a hundred square miles of mountainous woods, rocky terrain, and a lot of houses and homesteads tucked away off the beaten path. That's a lot of places for the zoms to hide, and we are desperately short of manpower."

"Oh." Lil's voice was very small. I glanced sharply at her. Something was going on that she wasn't saying.

Gabriel handed her back her canteen. She offered it to me. I shook my head 'no.' Call me immature, but I didn't want to take a drink after he had touched it with his lips.

The hazmat team showed up and began piling bodies in the back of their big old garbage truck. A jeep with a similarly protected driver pulled up right behind them. We loaded the three co-eds and the teacher's aid onto it for their trip to Patterson. All four looked to Gabriel as the jeep drove off.

Was no one immune to his manliness?

Feh. Screw him.

We met up with Team B on our way back to HQ. Gentry and Tony were supporting a heavily limping and deeply chagrined Mack. Kaitlyn lagged a few feet behind, sullen as ever.

"Mack, you okay?" I hurried over to them.

"You weren't bitten or anything?" Lil joined me, green eyes wide with concern. Lil liked me, but she loved the Postman.

"Nah, no bites," Mack said, looking embarrassed. "I just took a bad step and torqued my ankle a little."

"Tripped on a dead zombie," Tony explained helpfully.

"It's true," Mack said. He shook his head and looked disgusted. I patted him on the shoulder.

"At least you didn't step in it," I said. "That would have been gross."

Mack laughed.

"Thanks for the silver lining, Ash."

"Bad news is that he sprained it pretty thoroughly," Gentry said. "Good news is it'll heal up pretty quick if he elevates it and ices it for a day. Wild card perk number twelve."

"What are the first eleven?" Kai asked.

Gentry grinned and shrugged.

"Heck if I know. Maybe we should start a list."

After dinner we had another session of training by watching zombie movies. The night's selection included Lucio Fulci's *Zombie* and the rest of the remake of *Dawn of the Dead*—the movie that started the trend of sprinting zombies.

Zombie was notable both for its 'zombie vs. shark' action and the propensity of the women to throw their heads back and scream when attacked.

"This is totally unrealistic," I grumbled. "It's like they *want* to get eaten."

"The point," Gabriel said in his "lecturing" tone, "Is that everyone reacts differently under stress. *You* might not panic like that, but most people do. And you'll need to deal with the results. That's your take-away."

"That, and don't make out in a graveyard," I said with open disgust. "I mean, seriously. When you're on the run from zombies, who thinks it's a good idea to rest *and* make out? In a cemetery!"

"Don't take it all too seriously." Simone sat in the front row next to Gabriel. Jamie was in her usual place next to the DVD player. "We may be able to glean some discussion points from these movies—" Somehow, I had the feeling she didn't really think so. "—but you should also take the opportunity to kick back and relax."

"In that case," Tony offered, "we need to watch *Zombie Strippers*. It's a classic!"

That earned him dirty looks from all of the women in the room—especially Kaitlyn.

"Wouldn't it be nice if once in a while it was a *man* who froze?" Kaitlyn snapped. I agreed, but wasn't about to say so. Not and give her a shot at me with those claws.

"Now *that* would be unrealistic," Kai replied with a distinct lack of self-preservation. Kaitlyn looked as if she was about to respond, but she just crossed her arms and glared. If I was Kai, I'd sleep with one eye open for a couple of days.

We finished *Zombie* and moved on to *Dawn of the Dead*, picking it up from the scene where they first arrive at the mall. Gabriel hit pause after the young ingénue put everyone in danger by trying to rescue her dog.

"We call this Ripley's Syndrome," he said. "After the scene in *Alien.*"

You've got to be kidding me...

"The key," he continued—proving that he wasn't a mind reader— "is that if you want to increase your odds of surviving, don't go back for the cat."

"Well, no shit." Tony looked scornful. "Who the hell would be *that* stupid?"

Lots of people, I thought.

"You know that," Gabriel replied, "but you're going to be dealing with survivors who won't have your rational instincts. In order to keep them alive, you may have to use force."

"Like this chick," Tony continued, pointing at the screen. "I mean, they just said in the last scene that the deadheads aren't interested in eating anything but people, right?"

"True," Gabriel said, "but she's exhibiting an emotional reaction, not a rational one." I didn't like his tone. "That sort of emotion-based response can get you and your teammates killed."

"Heaven forefend that anyone have an emotional reaction," I muttered loudly enough for him to hear. I had the satisfaction of seeing the muscles in his jaw clench.

Score one for me.

Lil raised a hand, looking tentative. Gabriel nodded toward her.

"Is it really true the zombies aren't interested in eating animals," she asked. "Just people?"

"At this juncture, the evidence points to a definite preference for humans," he replied, either missing or ignoring the edge in her voice. "But lacking an immediately available food source, they may eat any warm-blooded creature. We just don't know for certain."

With that, he resumed the film.

As we watched the rest of the movie, he cut in a couple more times to bestow upon us some nugget of wisdom we were supposed to appreciate. As far as I could tell, it was all bullshit. Finally, the last of the survivors were eaten, and the credits rolled.

I snuck a sideways glance at Lil as she tried her best to wipe tears from her eyes before they trickled down her face. I didn't have to be a psychic to know what was wrong.

CHAPTER TWENTY-SIX

Lil managed to hold it together for another hour of cinematic games, but the minute we got back to our room she lost it.

Tears came out with loud, gut-wrenching sobs. She cried for so long and so hard, I thought she was going to make herself sick. I sat with her—handing her tissues as needed and pressing a cold washcloth to the back of her neck—until she had cried herself out.

This wasn't the first time, but it was the worst I had seen her.

"I can't do this, Ashley." Lil looked at me, eyes puffy, reddened wells of pain. "All I can think about is my babies. They're probably out of food and think I've abandoned them and—"

Tears started welling up again. I took the washcloth and gently blotted her face.

"Look," I said, trying to sound matter-of-fact. "You told me before that you'd just bought a bag of food, right? Well, it would take them a while to go through that. And if your roommate left the toilet seat up, they've got water."

"But what if some of those *things* got into the apartment?"

I thought about that.

"They're cats. Cats are better than any other animal at

running and hiding. Zombies are only so smart, right? So even if they *did* get in, the odds are your boys are fine."

She wasn't buying it.

"But sooner or later, they're gonna run out of food." She blew her nose again. I handed her a glass of water; she had to be dehydrated about now. "Ashley, all I can think about is them all alone and wondering where I went. I just can't stand it."

That's it, I thought. And it all came together. *What the hell.*

"So let's go get 'em." I said. The words were out of my mouth before I knew it.

"But you heard Gabriel." Lil said miserably. "If you want to live, don't go back for the cat."

Yeah, like that bastard's gonna tell me what I should do. Not fucking likely. I hunkered down in front of her chair and took her hands in mine.

"You know what?" I said. "Fuck him. People risk their lives all the time to go after animals in burning houses, floods—all kinds of disasters. Because if they didn't try, they'd never forgive themselves.

"If they don't try, then it's the kind of thing that'll eat a person alive from the inside out." I'm not sure who I was convincing—her or me. Not that it mattered.

Lil bit her lip.

"Do you really believe that?"

"I do." And I really did, too. "I'm not gonna let that happen to you. So if you want to go after… Binkey and Noodle?"

"Doodle."

God help me.

"If you want to go after Binkey and Doodle, I'm with you," I said.

More than once now I'd seen her take glee in killing ghouls, reveling in the blood and gore. But for only the second time since I met her, Lil's face brightened with something like genuine hope.

"Really?" she said.

I nodded.

"Yup. The rule should be, if you want to live with yourself, go back for the cat."

Lil looked excited and horrified at the same time.

"Gabriel's gonna be so pissed if he finds out," she said, and a part of her sounded thrilled at the prospect. I had to laugh.

"That's just an added bonus," I said. "And there are *so* many things worse than having Gabriel pissed off at us."

Like getting eaten alive, I thought, but I didn't say it out loud.

"If we're careful, he won't find out," I lied. "And if he does find out, what's he gonna do, spank us?"

An unexpectedly mischievous look flashed over Lil's face.

"I dunno, that might be kind of fun."

Damn, girl. I really hoped Lil was joking, and at that moment I was glad I hadn't confided in her. So I *tsk-tsk'd* and shook my head.

"Lil, I am shocked and appalled," I said, and I shot her a look. "Not that I necessarily disagree with you."

She grinned, but the glee disappeared almost immediately.

"Are you *sure* you want to do this?"

"Have you seen *Alien*?"

"No."

"Again I am shocked and appalled," I said. "But all you need to remember is that both Ripley and the cat survive."

You'd think it would be difficult to sneak out of a secured facility in the middle of the night, especially armed with M-4s, a pickaxe, and a couple of wicked sharp blades. But Lil and I walked right out the front door of Patterson Hall without a peep.

Simone hadn't been exaggerating how short-handed we were. And our teams must have done a brilliant job of clearing the campus, because we only saw two soldiers walking the perimeter, and no zombies at all. Once we left the safety of Big Red, however, we'd be dealing with god knows how many hungry ghouls, and soldiers whose orders were "shoot to kill."

We stuck to the shadows, hugging the sides of buildings and using trees and bushes as cover until we reached the foam barricade—what I called Mount Gillette— where it butted up against the parking lot in back of the gymnasium. There again, the snipers were few and far between, forced to patrol the barrier in broad sections.

So it was just a matter of waiting until a lone soldier moved to the next section down. Once he was out of sight we clambered up to the top of a big-ass SUV.

"We can jump from here," I whispered.

"What about the razor wire?"

I shrugged.

"How far can you jump?" I asked. "Think you can make it?"

Lil thought for a moment, then nodded.

"What about when we come back?" she asked.

I pulled a pair of wire cutters out of my belt pouch.

"Last resort, though," I said. "I'm hoping we can snag some heavyweight gloves at a hardware store, to pull it out of the way, but if not, we've got these." I shoved the cutters back in the pouch.

"Gabriel's *really* gonna kill us if we screw with the barricade."

I couldn't argue with that. But there was no way I was going to back out at this point.

"Last resort, I promise."

We waited for a few minutes, listening intently. When we were convinced that there was no one around, I smacked Lil on the arm.

"This is it," I hissed. "Let's go."

The foam barricade was about six feet tall and five feet wide at the base, tapering to three feet at the top.

Easy enough.

Glancing around once last time, I jumped from the SUV onto the hardened foam, my boots finding easy traction on its rubbery surface. Lil joined me a few seconds later, bouncing up and down on the balls of her feet like a kid on a trampoline.

"This stuff is *awesome*." She gave another experimental bounce.

I shook my head impatiently.

"We can play on it later," I said. "Let's just do this."

There looked to be about two feet between the foam and the razor-wire slinky, which itself was about four feet tall and maybe three feet wide.

Beyond that I saw movement, and once my eyes adjusted I spotted at least a few dozen zombies staggering through a field toward the parking lot. A few more were closer, but a bunch of unmoving bodies attested to the skill of our sharpshooters.

"I've always hated the standing broad jump," I muttered, trying not to think what would happen if either of us got hung up on the razor wire.

Lil nodded solemnly.

"If we miss, it's gonna hurt," she agreed. "A lot."

I took a deep breath.

"Then we won't miss." I flexed my knees once, twice. Swung my arms back and forth a few times, then positioned myself at the very edge of the wall, Lil standing next to me. "Remember, think forward, not upward.

"Ready?" I hissed.

She nodded.

"One. Two." We bent our knees and swung our arms on each count.

"Three…"

"*Go!*"

We flew through the air together, arms pinwheeling to give us more forward momentum, like a half-assed version of Butch and Sundance. I landed on the ground with a bone-jarring *thud*, hitting feet first with bent knees. My teeth snapped together and I felt the shock through my entire body.

But I cleared the Slinky of Doom.

So did Lil, who landed right next to me.

Straightening up, I held out a hand and pulled her to her feet.

"Let's go get those cats of yours." We took off into town, running as fast as we could. I knew we could avoid the zombies, but it would really suck to be shot by our own people.

Almost immediately I realized I'd forgotten my nose plugs.

A fleshy female, wearing the tattered remnants of criminally tight jeans and a tank top several sizes too small, staggered towards us. She stunk.

I mean, we're talking ripe, señor.

Oh, crap.

I glanced over at Lil, whose expression said that she shared my pain.

"I won't puke if you won't," I said.

She nodded.

"Can I kill it?" she asked eagerly.

"Be my guest."

Lil raised her pickaxe and slammed the pointy end down into the zombie's head before it could take another step. Then, placing one booted foot against the zom's shoulder, she gave a heave and extracted her axe with an unpleasant suction sound. The smell seemed even worse after that.

"That *really* stinks," I said.

She nodded.

"Yeah."

"Let's get the hell outta here."

We reached the cover of the trees, and headed in the direction of the road. The only light was an ambient gleam from the kliegs and a little bit of moonlight filtering through the trees, but we had no trouble seeing in the gloom. We ran as quickly as the terrain allowed, pine needles and leaves crunching under our feet.

Otherwise it was eerily quiet, no crickets, birds, animals or any other noises at all. I didn't share my observation with Lil. But more than ever, I hoped her cats were okay.

We reached the road, a cracked and weathered stretch of asphalt connecting Big Red to Redwood Grove, long overdue for maintenance. Cars sat off to the side, doors flung open and ominous dark stains splattered on the seats and the road. Several had broken windows, bits of cloth and what looked like shredded flesh caught on the jagged edges.

Whatever happened here had not ended well for whoever had been in those vehicles.

We stuck close to the tree line along the side of the road, jogging at a steady pace now. For the most part we ignored any zombies we spotted lurching along toward campus. If any posed an immediate threat, either Lil or I took them down with sword or pickaxe—or in one case, both.

Synchronized slaying, the sport of champions.

"Do you think there are any survivors out here?" Lil asked as we neared our destination. It didn't take a genius to figure that she was thinking about her mom.

"Sure," I replied. "We had survivors in the dorms, so there's no reason to think people couldn't hole up in a safe spot off campus. A lot of the older houses have attics and crawl spaces."

"Yeah, I guess you're right." Lil fell quiet as the first cluster of buildings became visible a few hundred yards down and across the road.

Redwood Grove had one main street running in and out of town, with the rest of the streets laid out in your basic grid. You'd have to really work hard to get lost there.

Normally the lights from town would have lit the sky above it, but a lot of them were out. Not all of them, however—some streetlights, probably on automatic timers, still gave a comforting glow, and it looked like a few buildings had lights burning in windows.

Closest to the college were the fraternity and sorority houses, big old Victorians with the Greek letters either hanging from banners or on signs in front of the buildings. Normally they'd be well-lit, music blasting from the windows.

Now the windows were dark and the silence downright eerie. Alpha Chi Kappa's front door stood wide open, the entryway a black throat leading inside. My enhanced night vision showed splotches of dark liquid on the porch.

I didn't look too closely at what lay scattered about on the lawn next to an aluminum keg. Time enough for that when we came back in the daylight to search for survivors.

The sound of shuffling feet caught my attention. I grabbed Lil by the shoulder and held a finger up to my mouth. We hunkered down behind a Prius as a lone zombie made its way unsteadily out of the nearest house. It might have been a frat boy, drunk-off-his-ass, but the blood on its L.L. Bean flannel shirt said otherwise.

Lil and I stayed hidden behind the car until the zombie lurched out of sight, then resumed our careful journey toward the town's business district.

I still wasn't sure exactly how we were gonna get two freaked-out felines back to Big Red. We could always try to find a car with keys in it, although driving up to the barricade wouldn't exactly contribute to the stealth part of the mission. If there was any way of getting back in without letting Gabriel discover that we'd been gone, I was determined to take it.

We cut through several front and back yards to save time. The quiet continued to spook me. No dogs barking, no babies crying. No sounds of insects or cars or televisions... nothing.

"Where are they?" Lil whispered as we crept through past a swing set in the backyard of a Craftsman bungalow. "The zombies, I mean."

I shrugged, stepping over an overturned tricycle.

"Maybe headed up to Big Red because of all the noise up there," I offered as I edged through a narrow side-yard leading to the front of the bungalow. "Maybe they've eaten everything there is to eat. Or maybe—"

I stopped short, words drying up in my mouth.

We'd reached the front of the house, a chain-link gate separating us from the yard, which faced out onto the main drag.

I swallowed once, then twice.

"Or maybe they're all hanging out on Maple Street."

CHAPTER TWENTY-SEVEN

Lil and I crouched down behind the gate, peering out between the gaps at what had to be the majority of the zombie population of Redwood Grove.

"Where's your mom's store?" I whispered.

Lil pointed to the right, where a seemingly nonstop parade of shamblers was headed.

"Pretty much dead center of town," she said.

I snorted and she shot me an apologetic look.

"I know, but seriously, the store's in the Courtyard."

That explained it. The Courtyard was a little shopping center made up of individual cottages ringing an enclosed patio with a rose garden in the center. The overall affect was "quaint" with a capital "Q."

I shook my head, getting my brain back on track.

"This is gonna be tricky," I muttered. "Odds are those things are all over the patio."

"There's a back entrance off an alley." Lil patted one of her many pockets. "I've got the keys that'll get us in either way."

I nodded slowly.

"So the real trick is to get down there without every zom in town seeing us."

We decided to backtrack a few blocks and cross over to the other side of Maple Street where it dead-ended into Oak, which ran perpendicular to Maple. Oak had the public library, the high school and a couple of small shops on it, and it didn't seem to be zombie central like Maple Street. Guess no one wanted to read or go to class in the afterlife.

Slackers.

Better for Lil and me. We dashed down Oak and across the end of Maple Street, heading for the alley that ran the length of the business district. Dumpsters and trashcans lined the way, giving us plenty of cover.

"How many blocks?" I hissed as we made our way as quietly and quickly as possible.

"Maybe four or five?" Lil guessed. "It's in-between Aspen and Beech. I don't usually take the alley."

"Get your keys out now," I suggested. "Just in case, y'know?"

"Good idea. Hang on a sec." We paused next to a wickedly stinky dumpster so Lil could fish the keys out of a pocket. One thing I'll say for military fashion, you never run out of pockets.

We continued down the alley, our feet crunching on broken glass and other debris. The moon had come out from behind the clouds, making it easier to see.

One of the restaurants we passed, Baxter's Brewery, had a light on inside, the glow filtering out through a filthy window overlooking the street. We paused, and heard shuffling and moans coming from within. The light was probably attracting more zombies to the restaurant, a sort of "dinner is served" sign.

Lil smacked my arm.

"We're almost there." She kept her voice to a whisper. "It's the next block up. We just have to cross Aspen Street." Although not as busy as Maple Street, Aspen was home to several restaurants, a trendy boutique, and an Albertson's grocery.

At least a dozen zombies shambled, staggered or lurched up and down in either direction. One of them, a female dressed in ragged layers that may or may not have been filthy before its reanimation, pushed an empty shopping cart. *Bag Lady Zombie.*

Lil and I ducked back and hugged the wall of the alley next to a white panel van, the kind serial killers used. I poked my head out and looked both ways. A pretty much sparse but steady trickle of zombies wandered in either direction.

I ducked back.

"We're going to have to run for it," I said. "I think we can make it to the shop, but unless we get lucky they'll know we're in there. That'll make getting out again a real bitch. So we'll have to be fast."

Lil nodded.

"I've got a cat carrier inside," she said. "We'll grab Binkey and Doodle and run for it."

"Can you handle the carrier and your pickaxe?"

Lil hesitated, then nodded again.

"Whatever it takes."

I sucked in a deep breath.

"Okay. Let's do this." I slapped her shoulder just as a rotting hand shot out of the driver's side window of the van and sunk into Lil's shoulder. She gave a startled shriek as a zombie, a gaping hole where its nose used to be, began pulling itself out of the window, using Lil as leverage.

My sword was already out. I used it to slice through the zombie's wrist and free Lil. She smacked the hand still clutching her shoulder, knocking it to the ground.

"Go!" I gritted. We took off across Aspen Street, dodging several zombies that immediately started moaning and clutching at us. We knocked them aside and dashed into the alley on the other side of the street. Bag Lady Zombie turned her shopping cart around and slowly wheeled it after us as we sprinted for the back of Betty's Bead Emporium.

"Here!" Lil slammed to a halt in front of a non-descript metal door situated between two dumpsters. I barely stopped myself from running headlong into her.

"That's my mom's car!" Lil stared at a green Mini Cooper parked haphazardly next to the front dumpster.

"That's great," I said as I unholstered my M-4. "Maybe she's inside. Let's get in there and find out, okay?"

"Sure, yeah… of course." Lil set her pickaxe down and fumbled with the keys. The moon went behind a patch of clouds, and the light in the alley was almost non-existent.

"You got it?" There was a rattling behind us, and I took off Bag Lady Zombie's head with one solid stroke of my blade, then sent the point through the brainpan. The body slid slowly to the ground, releasing its hold on the shopping cart. The weight sent the cart rolling away as Lil finally managed to slide a key into the lock.

The tumblers clicked as she twisted.

"Got it!"

Acting on impulse, I grabbed the cart and hauled it up to the door as Lil pulled it open. She raised an eyebrow as I muscled the cart over the doorjamb and into a dark hallway.

"Considering we have two cats and probably some supplies to haul back to campus," I explained, "it seems like a set of wheels might come in handy."

She nodded and shut the door. I pulled out a flashlight and shone it around. The hall led past a stairway that headed upstairs.

"Apartment's up here." Lil bounded up the stairs. I left the cart and hurried after her.

"Lil, wait a sec, okay?" If her mom's car was there, then mom might indeed be upstairs, but not necessarily alive. I didn't know if Lil was ready or able to cope with that.

I caught up with her just as she reached the door to the apartment, grabbing her wrist before she turned the key in the lock.

"Go slow, okay?"

She glared at me, like a sweet cuddly kitten suddenly gone feral.

"Why?" she hissed.

"Because you don't know who… or what might be in there."

She started to answer, then stopped as it dawned on her what I meant. Her eyes went wide, the whites startling in the flashlight's glare.

"It's… you mean, my mom?"

"Probably not," I said quickly. "But we have to be careful."

Lil took a deep breath.

"Yeah." And then another. "Yeah…"

She turned the key, then deliberately tucked it back into her pocket before cracking the door about an inch.

"Hello?"

Nothing.

"Mom…? Mom, are you there?"

"*Prroww*?"

Lil's face lit up.

"Doodle!" She ran into the apartment, caution thrown out the window at the sound of a cat's meow. I followed, sword and flashlight at the ready, and did a quick sweep of the place.

The apartment was small, but cute, decorated with Maxfield Parrish prints on the walls, eclectic secondhand furnishings, and enough toys to entertain an entire colony of cats. It definitely *smelled* of cats, but not as bad as I'd have expected.

Two doors stood open down a little hall. One was a bedroom, the other a bathroom. I looked. The toilet seat had indeed been left up.

Thank goodness men are pigs.

A partially shredded jumbo-sized bag of dry food sat in a corner of the little kitchenette, kibble spilling out onto the floor. There didn't seem to be anyone else there and, thankfully, no bloodshed and no body parts.

There were, however, two extremely fat felines, one a brindle-colored fluff ball with long fur, the other a shorthaired and absolutely huge black cat. Both sat with Lil smack in the middle of the overstuffed couch, purring loudly and staring at us expectantly.

The black one meowed again and Lil started crying.

"Oh, Doodle… you're okay!" She scooped both cats up against her. They looked confused, but tolerated the embrace. They did not, however, look as if they'd missed any meals.

"Damn, they're fat." I shook my head, thinking of the poundage we were going to be hauling back to Big Red. "Will they both fit in one carrier?"

Lil nodded.

"It's kinda big, and they like being together."

"Good." Because at least one of us would have to have both hands free as we headed back through Zombie Town. "Let's get everything together and get out of here."

Lil hesitated.

"But my mom…"

Isn't here, I almost said. But I didn't. Instead I put a hand on Lil's shoulder.

"I've done a sweep of the apartment," I said as reassuringly as I could. "There's no sign of violence."

"The shop," Lil said firmly. "She could be hiding in the shop."

The logical place for her mom to hole up would be the apartment, with access to food and water. But I didn't say so. If it were my mom, I'd be grasping at straws, too.

"Let's get the supplies ready and the cats into the carrier and then we'll check the store," I said. "That way if anything… well, if anything goes wrong, we'll be ready to run for it."

Lil took another deep breath.

"Yeah, okay."

She retrieved a decent size carrier from the back of a closet and unceremoniously stuffed both cats inside, one after the other. The offended howls began immediately.

"I know, babies," she murmured, latching the carrier gate securely. "But you'll thank me for it later."

"Or they'll pee on your bed," I commented. "What else do we need?"

"Food and litter."

We grabbed everything we could find with military efficiency. When we were done, I turned to her.

"You ready to go?"

Lil started to nod, then stopped.

"Two more things." She dashed off down the hallway into the bathroom, reappeared and then vanished into the front bedroom, re-emerging seconds later with a stuffed lamb that was distinctly worse for the wear. What had once been plush fur was now threadbare and nappy.

"You've got to be kidding me."

"It's Lambiepie," she said defensively. "He was my very first toy."

"Just don't let Tony see it," I warned her. "You'll get a new nickname."

Lil stuffed the lamb in the waistband of her pants and pulled her shirt down over it, looking like she'd suddenly grown an oddly shaped tumor.

"Now I'm ready," she announced.

Sheathing my sword, I grabbed the bag of food and the litter while Lil got the litter box and hefted the carrier. She listed to one side with the weight of the carrier.

"You two have got to go on a diet."

Mournful howls answered her.

"They're worse than hungry zombies," I said. And then looked at her. "The howling… it's going to attract some attention, you know."

"Maybe they won't pay attention because it's not people?" But she didn't sound like she believed it, any more than I did.

"Will they stop after a while?"

"Last time I took them to the vet's, they cried all the way there and all the way home."

I nodded. So *much for stealth.*

"Okay then," I said. "Let's just worry about getting back in one piece."

CHAPTER TWENTY-EIGHT

Back downstairs, we put the carrier and its unhappy cargo—still howling—into the shopping cart, then packed litter and food around it. No way it was going to be a smooth ride back up to Big Red.

Then it was time to check the shop. I wasn't religious, but I pretty much prayed that we didn't find Lil's mom. Better for Lil to have some hope.

"You got the key?" I asked, but Lil already had it out. She inserted it into the deadbolt, which unlocked with a definitive *clunk*.

She slowly cracked the door open an inch.

"Mom…?"

We both listened carefully. The cats even paused their non-stop howling.

"Mom?" A little louder this time. And still no answer. Lil glanced back at me, hefting her pickaxe with one hand, flashlight with the other. I nodded and unsheathed my blade as she opened the door all the way, then stepped inside. I followed close behind.

The shop looked as if it had remained undisturbed during the outbreak. Zombies milled about in the courtyard, visible through two picture windows on either side of the wooden front door.

Lil shone her flashlight around the store. Rows and rows of bins held beads separated by shape, size and color, a magpie's paradise, all bright and shiny under the LCD beam.

Pretty.

"This is cool," I whispered.

"Yeah, it's a great place to work," Lil whispered back. "Mom used her divorce settlement to start the shop when we moved here." She shone her light around. "Doesn't look like anyone's been around at all since I closed it the night before, well, before Casey got eaten. I guess Annie didn't make it in to open the store."

She looked around the room again, eyes bright with unshed tears, and an expression that was way too bleak.

"Ashley, do you think my mom is dead?"

"I…" I stopped, unsure of what to say. The odds were pretty good that she was, but there was still a chance. I didn't want to raise her hopes, but I also didn't want to dash them. I finally went middle of the road.

"She probably went looking when she didn't find you here," I said, trying to sound sincere. "She might have holed up with another survivor. Your best bet is to hope for the best." I paused for a moment, then continued.

"We should get back to Big Red. The sooner they send us here to clear out the town, the sooner we might—*holy crap!*"

A loud thump from the front of the store made us both jump. A female zombie pressed up against the picture window to the right side of the front door. Long, black hair worn in a single braid, flowing, gauzy ethnic skirt and top in purples and browns. Dead white pupils stared in at us with unnatural hunger.

Lil gasped.

Oh, shit.

"Oh, no." Horror and sorrow mixed equally in her voice. "Annie."

I don't know if it could hear us or it was just coincidence, but it looked up when she said its name, smacking the window with its hands as it moaned its hunger. Its hands left dark smears on the glass. Within a few seconds it was joined by another zombie, and then another.

"We've got to get out of here now," I said urgently. Lil's expression went blank, as if she'd shut off her emotions. She shut of her flashlight, as well, and moved toward the back door.

"Give it a minute," I suggested. "If their attention is here at the front, we'll have an easier time sneaking out the back without being spotted."

"Should we make some noise?" Lil asked.

"Couldn't hurt. The old okie-doke?"

She gave a ghost of a smile. "The old okie-doke."

I rapped on the window and shouted.

"Hey, you!"

"In here!" Lil joined me and banged on the front door. We watched as zombies peeled off from the steady stream wandering past and staggered to join the ever-increasing crowd in front of the store. I glanced at Lil, and could tell from her set expression that she was scanning the crowd for a familiar face.

One I hoped she didn't see.

"Maybe we should—" I stopped short as the zombie that used to be Annie suddenly let go of the gate and veered off to its left, pushing through the crowd with what almost seemed like a sense of purpose.

"Okay, now that's just weird."

"Do you think she remembers the back door?"

A chill ran up my spine.

"We'd better get out of here now." Lil looked worried, and I added, "Yeah. It looks like some of the others are following her."

We hightailed it to the back of the building where Binkey and Doodle started howling again in their carrier, paws emerging through the mesh. All they needed were tin cups and a sign reading "dirty screws!"

"Shush, babies," Lil crooned. "We need you to be quiet now."

I snorted. *Like logic ever worked on a cat.* Then I put my left hand on the doorknob, the right holding my sword.

"You handle the cart and I'll handle the zoms, okay? If we both need to fight, we'll make sure the cart is between us so they can't get to the cats.

"Ready?"

Lil nodded, gripping the cart with both hands.

I shoved the door open hard and felt it connect with something on the other side. Whatever it was hit the ground. The smell and accompanying moan told me that at least one zom had figured out there were snacks behind Door Number One.

The moon had come out from behind the cloud cover again, giving me enough light to see several figures already approaching where we stood, with more rounding the mouth of the alley. The smell of putrefying flesh was just nasty.

The zombie I'd knocked down reached around and grabbed at my ankle. I jerked away from its clawed fingers, stepped past the door and plunged the end of the katana into the back of its skull.

Sploosh. Dead zombie.

The moans to our left grew louder and the smell grew worse as at least a dozen zombies staggered toward us. One of them was Annie. More filled the mouth of the alley.

I glanced to the right. That end was still zombie free, and I didn't see any movement on the street beyond it.

"Go right," I said, "then left out of the alley. Double back a few blocks down."

The first few zombies reached us, clutching at Lil as she pushed the cart through the doorway. I kicked the closest one, a good ol' boy who'd drunk a few too many beers when he was alive. My foot sank into its substantial gut. The impact caused a farting sound as gas escaped through God knows where. The accompanying smell was horrific, but the kick knocked it back into two other zombies, bowling them over like nine-pins.

That bought us some space.

"Get the cats out of here," I yelled, caution scattered to the wind. "I'll cover you." Lil sprinted toward the other end of the alley, the rattle of the wheels painfully loud. No way we were sneaking onto campus with that thing.

Some of the fresher zombies moved faster than the others—not running, but their shamble still covered more ground than I liked. Trading my blade for the M-4, I took aim for the closest one and fired. My shot grazed the zombie's ear, but didn't take it out.

Damn. I wasn't nearly as good as Gabriel, and right about now we needed his precision.

Well, it wasn't gonna happen.

Fuck it.

I switched over to semi-auto and sent a spray of bullets at their legs, aiming for the knees. They fell in a writhing mass.

More zombies appeared at the mouth, blocking my view of Aspen Street beyond. Luckily for us they all still seemed to be coming from that direction. I sent another spray into the oncoming crowd to create a temporary roadblock for those behind them, then took off after Lil, who had reached Beech Street.

As she pushed the cart out of the alley, hands reached for her from the right. She yelled in surprise as a skinny male zom wrapped his arms around her shoulders, yanking her off balance. The cart wobbled as she lost her grip on it, but stayed upright. I hauled ass the remaining distance, shoving my forearm under the thing's chin and slamming its jaw shut before it could take a bite out of Lil's neck.

She wriggled out of its grasp, grabbed her pickaxe from the cart, and sent the business end into the zom's skull, splattering me with all sorts of nasty brain goo.

"Oooh, sorry," Lil said, yanking the pickaxe out again.

"I ain't got time to barf," I muttered, trying not to puke. If I'd had time, I would have spewed all over the damn place, but the moans were coming from all directions as the undead residents of Redwood Grove honed in on us.

They shambled from both directions on Beech Street, dozens filtering down from Maple Street and enough coming from the opposite direction to make our escape route far more dangerous than I'd anticipated.

The alley to the back of us was impassable, seething with bodies. The alley entrance across Beech was blocked by one of those huge trucks with big-ass wheels, what I call "penis compensation trucks." Lil and I might be able to climb over or around it, sure, but we'd have to leave the cart behind.

Shit.

"There are so many of them." Lil looked as scared as I felt, so I tried to hide my own fear from her. This whole thing had been my idea, and I was going to get her *and* her cats back to Big Red. Or die trying. Although I preferred to do it without the dying part.

"We can still move faster then they can," I said. "We just need to clear a few out of our way. You take the ones coming from Maple Street and the alley. I'll clear us a path down Beech. Don't worry about head shots, just slow 'em down!"

Lil hesitated, eyes wide with panic as the reeking corpses closed in on us, the stench nearly unbearable.

I smacked her on the arm, hard.

"Ouch!"

"Remember!" I shouted. "Ripley doesn't die!"

This snapped her out of her deer-in-the-headlights look. While she dropped the pickaxe into the cart and unholstered her M-4, I sprayed my last few shots at the zombies coming at us from the south side of Beech Street. I ejected the magazine and slammed another one home as quickly as possible. I had one more full magazine in my belt pouch, and plenty of ammo, but no time to reload the empties. So I had to make the shots count.

We shot their legs out from under them, but more took their place. It was like trying to dig a hole in the sand before the tide filled it in. And those we'd mowed down were crawling toward us, trailing bits and pieces of themselves as they did so.

"This is *so* not good." Lil changed out magazines, keeping herself between the oncoming zombies and the shopping cart. The cats were thankfully quiet, probably catatonic, so to speak, from the moans and the gunfire.

"We need to make a break for it." I shot her a glance. "It's not going to get any better, and if we don't go now, we're gonna get ripped to pieces. And then Gabriel's gonna really be pissed at us."

Lil gave a shout of surprised laughter that turned into a yell as one of the kneecapped zombies grabbed her foot, pulling her off balance. She fell on top of it, her M-4 skittering a few feet away as the thing rolled so that it was on top, gore-drenched teeth inches from her face.

Several others reached the cart, hands grabbing for the carrier as if they thought something tasty was inside.

"Shit!" I slammed the stock of my M-4 into the head of Lil's attacker, giving her a chance to throw it off. Then I dealt with the ones trying to get at the cats, again using the M-4 stock as a bludgeon to back them off before flipping the weapon forward and firing point blank into their faces.

Lil scrambled to her feet and did a mean stomp on her attacker's skull before retrieving her firearm.

More came at us, the moans nearly deafening and the smell overwhelming. The gap I'd made had closed again, zombies crawling and staggering from all directions.

We were so screwed.

CHAPTER TWENTY-NINE

We both backed up against the cart.

"I'm sorry, babies," Lil whispered. She grabbed her pickaxe and swung at the nearest zombie as it reached for her.

Before she made contact, however, a shot rang out, making a loud bang as the top of the zombie's head vanished in a spray of blood and brain matter.

What the fuck?

Another shot, and the head sheared off of what was once maybe a five year old. The little ankle biter had been about to grab me and I hadn't even noticed.

"Over here!" It was a man's voice.

More shots, each one resulting in a dead zombie. Lil and I looked around for the source.

"*Here!*"

It came from the monster truck. A man dressed in what Matt would have called "weekend warrior" style—army fatigues tucked into combat boots, black T-shirt under a matching jacket—stood on the cab of the truck, aiming a really big rifle with cool precision, another firearm slung over his shoulder. He had a bandana pulled up over his nose, covering the lower half of his face.

He looked tall and imposing standing up there—in fact, downright heroic—but honestly, I think I would have viewed a midget the same way had he appeared out of nowhere to pull our asses out of the fire.

"Get in the truck!"

We didn't hesitate. Lil swung her pickaxe like a melee weapon, whirling like an armed Tasmanian devil while I grabbed the cart by the handle and sprinted across the street, using it as a battering ram to knock a thankfully skinny male zombie out of the way.

The man on the truck kept taking out the zombies that posed the greatest threats. Between his precision shooting and Lil's pickaxe of death, I made it to the truck with the cats in one piece, zombies trailing closely behind.

"Get in!"

"We're getting!" I wrenched open the passenger door, flipped the seat forward, tossed my M-4 inside, and wrestled with the cat carrier.

"Leave it," the man shouted, capping two more zombies.

"Are you crazy? This is what we came for!" I yanked hard and the carrier jerked upward. Binkey—or was it Doodle?—chose that moment to resume howling.

The man's eyebrows shot up.

"I'm not the one who's crazy here." But he didn't argue any further.

I muscled the carrier into the back of the cab and climbed in as Lil tossed the litter and food in after me. She then shoved the cart into a knot of ghouls, knocking them off balance long enough to allow her to jump into the front seat and slam the door shut, locking it.

Zombies immediately swarmed the windows, bloody hands slapping and clawing against them, green faces pressing to stare in at us hungrily.

The roof of the cab creaked as our rescuer jumped onto the ground on the driver's side. The door opened and he climbed in, slamming the door shut as several enterprising zoms pulled themselves into the truck bed behind us and began hammering on the back window.

Our rescuer's bulk seemed to fill the cab as he turned the keys that were hanging from the ignition.

"Hold on or fasten your seatbelts!"

I did both, holding onto the "oh shit" handle with one hand and stabilizing the carrier with the other. He floored the accelerator and the truck surged forward with an almost animalistic growl. The momentum jolted us all backward, including the zombies.

They flew out of the truck bed to land on the asphalt. Those clutching the sides of the truck either lost their grip or their hands as the vehicle sped north on Beech Street and across Maple.

Our rescuer didn't slow down, and zombies thumped off the bumper like bugs hitting the windshield. They continued to trail after us even as the truck picked up speed. Once they were out of sight, I let out the breath I hadn't realized I'd been holding while Binkey and Doodle kept up their own harmony of the damned. After a few minutes they shut up. Maybe they felt more secure.

More likely they were exhausted.

My stomach rolled with motion sickness, but I didn't complain. The driver slowed down and looked at me in the rear-view mirror.

"You risked your lives for a couple of cats?" The bandana wafted out as he spoke. His eyes looked black in the almost non-existent light, his brown hair was cropped close to his skull, military style.

"Um… yeah," I said. "Pretty much."

"They're my cats," Lil explained.

"But it was my idea," I added, not wanting her to take the heat.

The man nodded slowly. There were a few beats of silence before he spoke again.

"I like cats." His gaze went back to the road ahead.

Lil glanced at me over the back seat.

"Is he crazy?" she mouthed.

I shrugged, hoping he hadn't seen her. At least he liked cats.

"I'm Ashley," I said. "And this is Lil. Thanks for saving our butts."

"No problem."

"You gonna tell us your name?"

"Nope."

I sat back and shut up. We drove along for a few minutes in oddly comfortable silence, reaching the outskirts of town before he spoke again.

"You two with the military, up at the college?"

"Not exactly," I answered. "I mean, we're with them, but we're not military."

His eyebrows shot up again.

"You want to be more specific?"

I shrugged again.

"We're both college students who were in the wrong place at the wrong time."

"We're wild cards," Lil chimed in.

"Well, you're *something* wild if you're willing to risk your lives for a couple of cats," he observed dryly. He may or may not have been smiling under the bandana.

"It means we're immune to the zombie virus," I explained. "We were bitten and survived."

"Is that so?" Oddly enough, he didn't sound particularly surprised, and I had to wonder why. Before I could pursue it, he continued. "How many of you wild cards are there?"

I did a quick mental count.

"Seven that I know of." Then I remembered Simone. "No, eight."

"So you're not military, but you're *working* with the military." His tone was neutral, but something told me he wasn't a big supporter of the armed forces.

"You don't like them?" I asked.

"Not much of a fan of any branch of the government, military or civilian. Especially when they've got me under quarantine and threaten to 'terminate with extreme prejudice' when I go too near the border they've set up."

"Wow." Not much to say to that.

Lil stared at him, shocked.

"They told us the army had the infected zone quarantined," she said, "but there's no way they'd kill someone trying to get out, right? I mean, not if the person were alive."

He gave a short, humorless laugh.

"Guess you haven't spent a lot of time around the feds." He went silent for a moment, then continued. "So tell me why you two are all tricked out like baby mercs in a Syfy original movie."

Okay, I had to like the guy for that crack.

"Like Lil said, we're wild cards," I answered. "That's the name they give to people who are immune. And not that you could tell from what happened back in town, but they've been training us so we can clear the college and then the rest of the quarantine area, because a lot of the soldiers on the *inside* are getting the virus and they're not sure why."

"Were you drafted into this?" he asked tersely.

I shook my head.

"No," I said. "At least I wasn't. It was my choice." I didn't see any point in bringing up General Heald's attempts to bully me. "Anyway, since we can't get the virus, we take risks other people can't."

"Like rescuing cats in the middle of a dead town."

"Actually we'll be in deep shit if they find out we did this," I confessed.

"So you need to get back into campus quietly."

"That would be nice," I said hopefully. "Any ideas?"

He thought about it for a minute.

"Old logging trail on the other side of Big Red," he said. "Leads up pretty close to the Administration building. Should give you some cover to sneak back in. They put the barrier smack up against either side of the building, so you could break in through a window or door, although you'll have to deal with the razor wire."

"How do you know all this?"

He shrugged.

"I make it my business to find things out."

"What's with the bandana?" Lil asked.

"Filters the smell out a little," he replied. "Not a lot, but enough to stop me from puking up my dinner when I have to deal with the deadheads. You girls might try it next time."

"We normally use nose plugs," Lil muttered.

"So why are you still wearing it?" I challenged, staring at him. "I know we're not exactly fresh out of the shower, but we don't smell *that* bad."

He raised one eyebrow this time.

"Either you smell worse than you think, or those cats are farting to beat the band."

He was right. My nose was still recovering from the zoms, so I hadn't noticed.

"They do that when they're stressed." Lil looked embarrassed.

"Besides that," he added, "you don't need to see my face." With that he shut up.

"Don't you want to stay at Big Red?" I asked. "It's safe there. Well, safer than it is out here."

"I prefer staying where I am," he said. Then, before I could reply, he added, "I have my reasons."

"Good reasons?"

"Good enough," he replied. "As good as yours for sneaking out on your own."

Can't argue with that.

He turned onto a narrow road overgrown with hanging branches. Even the truck's suspension and shocks couldn't ease the jolting as the wheels hit numerous ruts. We hit a particularly deep pothole, and I winced as I felt the jolt up through my tailbone.

"Jeez Louise," I said. "Guess our tax dollars haven't made it this far."

"This road hasn't been used since they built the university," our rescuer said. "No need to keep it up."

"Glad you knew about it."

"It pays to know how to get in and out of places."

"Paranoid much?" Okay, it just slipped out.

Surprisingly he laughed.

"Yeah, you might say that." He dodged another crater. "Now let's see if my paranoia can get you back into the college without getting caught."

CHAPTER THIRTY

Mystery man turned off his headlights, and almost immediately my eyes adjusted to what little light was filtering through the trees. Waiting for him to slam into something, I gripped the door handle until my hand hurt, but we made it without incident.

He stopped the truck at the edge of the tree line, far enough away from the campus for the sound of the engine to be muffled by the forest. Lil and I hauled cats, litter, and food out of the truck. They hadn't gotten any lighter during the trip, but they had, thankfully, fallen silent—probably shell-shocked from the rough ride up the logging road.

Our savior got out of the truck and stood nearby.

"It's about a hundred yards to the back of the Admin building," he said, his voice low. "I'm not seeing any dead heads between here and there, so you should be okay."

Yeah, if we don't collapse under the weight of Binkey, Doodle, and all of their shit.

I hefted the bag of litter, wondering why the hell we thought it was a good idea to bring it. Lil lifted the cat carrier, but even in the gloom I could tell she was near her limits.

Mystery dude looked at us for a beat, then reached into the bed of the truck and pulled out a folding dolly, complete with straps.

"This should help."

"You were a Boy Scout, weren't you?" I said.

"Close enough." He pulled the dolly open. "Litter first, carrier next, then the bag of food." We followed his directions, watching gratefully as he strapped everything securely into place.

"Wait a sec." He reached into the back of the cab and pulled out a pair of sturdy leather-and-canvas gardening gloves. "Ought to help you hold the razor wire out of the way, at least long enough to get inside the perimeter."

I took the gloves.

"Thanks." The word felt inadequate. I stuck out a hand, and he shook it solemnly.

Lil started to put out her hand, then when he reached for it she threw her arms around him. I saw his eyes widen with the same surprise I felt as he stiffened, then softened enough to gave her a quick squeeze. He gently set her away from him, hands on her shoulders.

"You take care of those cats of yours."

Lil nodded solemnly.

"I will."

He looked at me.

"And you take care of this one." He thrust his thumb in Lil's direction.

I nodded.

"I will," I replied. "Better than I did tonight. Thanks again."

"I'll wait until you're inside before I leave."

"Gee, kind of like a date." So much for solemnity.

He snorted and got back in the truck.

"Who was that masked man?" I said, mostly to myself. "Come on, Lil." She nodded wearily. I wondered if she had enough juice left to get back to Patterson Hall. "Just a little further and we'll be in our beds," I said. "I'll take the dolly. You just keep an eye out for zombies and soldiers."

"How about zombie soldiers?" Just a little ghost of a smile with her words.

"Those, too."

We made it between the trees and the Admin building. I slipped on the gloves, several sizes too big but thick enough to allow me to pull a section of wire up far enough for Lil to crawl under, dragging the dolly on its back behind her.

The cats stayed miraculously quiet.

It was a little trickier to hold the wire up and crawl under without having it snap back down on me, but I managed by going through feet first.

I stood in the narrow space between the wire and the building, and gave a thumbs-up in the direction of the woods. The man had to have better night vision than a wild card, 'cause the lights blinked on and then off again and I heard the engine turn over. The sound of the truck receded back down the old logging road.

"We've cleared this building, right?" Lil stood by a closed window.

"I think Team B cleared it," I answered. "We're pretty much done with the campus after tomorrow. Only a few buildings left."

"Then we can start on the town." She had an anxious edge to her voice. I just nodded.

We pried open a window. Lil boosted me up and I wriggled through, landing with an ungraceful thump. I froze, listening for any sound. When there wasn't any, I reached out and Lil hoisted the dolly through. Then she crawled in after it.

We shut the window again, locking it for good measure.

The building was quiet and sterile, with an antiseptic smell—bleach and faux citrus—that told us that the clean-up team had taken care of the blood stains, viscera, and body parts.

There were two soldiers on guard duty at the front of Patterson. We quietly pulled the dolly up the handicapped ramp, staying just out of sight, and I tried the most cliché trick in the book. I hefted a medium sized rock and pitched it into the darkness, as far as possible on the other side of the front doors. It landed in the bushes with a satisfying *crack*.

By golly, it worked.

Both soldiers immediately trained their firearms in that direction, then went over to investigate. Lil and I hurried the rest of the way up the ramp and inside, stifling laughter the whole way. Not that it would have been funny if they'd heard us and opened fire.

The lobby was empty—not too surprising considering it had to be around two in the morning. I hit the "down" button on the elevator, and the doors slid open immediately. Lil pushed the dolly in, and I hit the button for the basement level.

We both leaned against the back of the elevator, quivering from exhaustion and the sudden weakness brought on by the aftermath of what had been basically a three-hour adrenaline rush. We stared at our reflections on the inside of the shiny metal doors.

"You have brains on your face," Lil observed.

I snorted.

"You've got blood on yours," I replied. "And bits of skin."

"We both look pretty gross."

That we did. Our clothes were disgusting, too—covered in tacky blood and that black fluid that ran out of zombie orifices.

Then it hit me.

Infected blood and bodily fluids.

"Shit." I pushed myself away from the wall.

"What?"

"We need to be decontaminated."

Lil looked confused.

"We can just put our clothes in the hazmat bags, right?" she suggested. "Take hot showers?"

I shook my head.

"We can't afford for any infected crap to get into the

common areas—like this elevator. Maybe *we* can't get sick, but a lot of other people might."

A pained look swept across Lil's face.

"Can't we just use lots of soap?" she pleaded. "I mean, we went through so much to keep anyone from finding out that we've been gone."

"I know," I replied, shaking my head. "But we can't risk it. What if someone turned, just because of us?"

I couldn't read the expression on her face, but I was pretty sure she wouldn't put her need for sleep ahead of human beings.

At least I hoped so.

The doors opened, letting us out right next to our room.

"Let's put the stuff away, then go get hosed off," I suggested. "We can say we were out on campus and ran into a couple of stray zombies. We'll probably still get in some trouble, but not nearly as much as we will if they find out we went into town.

"Then we'll bring some bleach back and clean off the elevator," I added.

Lil nodded.

"Just make sure to wipe up any blood you get on anything, okay?"

"Yeah, I will." Her tone was definitely snappish, like a kid up way past her bedtime. Then she looked sheepish. "I'm sorry. I'm just so tired."

I patted her arm.

"I know, honey. I am too."

We put the cat carrier in the bathroom, leaving the cats inside so we wouldn't get any goo on them.

"We'll be back in just a little bit, babies," Lil cooed. "Then you can come out and we'll feed you."

I snorted again.

"Yeah, like they really need the food," I said. She shot me a look.

We slipped back out. The halls were quiet, most people sensibly asleep, at least on this level. We had to go down one floor for the decontamination area. It was quiet down there, too.

Maybe, just maybe, we'll get away with this.

Decon was a revamped bathroom with several portable shower stalls hooked up to tanks full of Super Lysol or whatever the hell they used to spray us off. We could do it ourselves, so ten minutes and we were both hosed down and wrapped in white towels. We wiped our weapons down with bleach and slung them over our shoulders.

We padded in bare feet back to the elevator, breathing a mutual sigh of relief when the doors slid shut and the car began its one-floor journey upward.

"Shit," I said for the umpteenth time that night. "We forgot to bring bleach with us to clean this stuff off." I heaved another huge sigh, this one in frustration, as the doors slid open. "You take your shower, and I'll go back down to get the bleach."

"Are you sure?" Lil asked. Clearly she hoped I was.

"Yeah," I said, trying to sound sincere. "Can you take these?" I handed her my M-4 and swords. "I'll be right back."

I jogged back to Decon, grabbed a bottle of bleach and some paper towels, and hightailed it back to the elevator. Feeling a bit like a human yo-yo, I rode it up yet again and stepped out into the hallway...

Right into Gabriel.

CHAPTER THIRTY-ONE

I yelped in surprise and dropped the bottle of bleach. It bounced painfully off of my bare foot and rolled against the far wall, lid still in place.

Gabriel stared at me as I clutched my suddenly way-too-small towel to my bosom like a Victorian maiden. He wore nothing but a pair of sweat pants, six pack abs and well-defined chest bare to the world.

My face flushed with heat.

"Ashley, what are you doing?"

How to answer that? I thought quickly, if not wisely.

"I wanted to clean our bathroom."

As soon as I said it, it sounded lame. Nothing to do but brazen it out, though.

"So I... I got some bleach. From downstairs where the bleach is." Going on the old adage that the best defense is a good offense I added, "What are *you* doing here?"

"I heard someone in the hallway," he replied. "Guess it was you." He looked me up and down. "Why aren't you dressed?"

"I didn't want to get bleach on my uniform." *Lamer and lamer.* "So if you'll excuse me—" I tried to step around him to retrieve the bleach, but he blocked my end run with his arm. There wasn't a lot of space between our bodies.

He sniffed the air.

"You smell like disinfectant."

"One of the hazards of being a wild card, right?" I made another attempt to scoot to the other side, but he boxed me in with his other arm, not quite touching me. I could feel the heat rise between us and wished I had my body armor back on.

"Ashley, what the hell have you been up to?"

"Nothing!" I snapped, fed up with his interrogation. "At least nothing that's any of your business. So you can stop the strong arm tactics and let me go back to my room."

"To clean your bathroom." You could cut the sarcasm in his voice with a tanto.

"Yeah, and clean my bathroom." My towel slipped down an inch and his gaze dropped. His eyes darkened and the heat ramped up a notch.

"It's cold," I said. "Get out of my way, and I'll get some clothes.

"Besides," I added with deliberate nastiness, "we've been here before and it didn't end well, remember?"

Ooh, score one for me. Gabriel looked like I'd slapped him. He dropped his arms and stepped backwards, letting me move past him to pick up the bottle of bleach.

I might have brazened my way out of it had Lil not chosen that moment to open the door to our room.

"Ashley?" she said, rubbing a towel over her head. "I let the cats out of the carrier, so watch the—" She saw Gabriel, gave a gasp of horror and slammed the door shut.

"Cats?" he repeated.

"Er…" Nope. I had nothing.

Comprehension dawned on his face, along with slow-burning anger.

"You two went into town, didn't you?"

"I…"

"You two *idiots* risked your lives, and the security of this campus, by going after a couple of *cats*?" He grabbed my arm and shook me. So much for slow-burning anger. His voice rose as he went straight to full-on rage.

A door opened down the hall and Tony stuck his head out.

"Sleeping down here. Or *trying* to." He vanished back inside his room, then poked his head back out. "Will you two get a room?" He disappeared again, and slammed the door shut.

Gabriel hauled me by my arm to a nearby stairwell door, causing me to drop the bleach again. He pushed me into the stairwell and shut the door behind us. He dropped his voice, but the level of fury was still there in his eyes.

"Do you have any idea of how stupid you are?" he gritted.

"We didn't compromise the security," I protested, wincing as his fingers pressed deep into the flesh of my bicep. "We jumped over the barrier and the razor wire to get out, then crawled under the wire and got in through an unlocked window in the Admin building." I paused and added, "We locked the window."

He grabbed my other arm and dragged me close, face glaring down into mine.

"This is a military operation," he said, his voice flat. "You're a civilian member of a military team."

I glared back.

"A civilian *volunteer*, remember?"

"Volunteer or not, you do *not* do *anything* without a direct order from your team leader." Every word was clipped as if bitten off between clenched teeth.

"Look," I said, determined not to let him intimidate me, "Lily has been miserable. Her boyfriend was ripped to pieces in front of her, and her mom might be dead. As far as she knows, all she has left are those two cats.

"She's been crying herself to sleep, worrying that they might have starved to death—or worse," I continued. "Sooner or later her concentration would've gone wonky at the wrong moment. Then she would have gotten herself or someone else killed."

Gabriel's grip didn't change.

"That was *not* your decision to make! "Why the hell can't you follow orders?"

Something snapped in me.

"If I'd wanted to be a mindless drone," I growled, "I'd have stayed with my control-freak husband. But I didn't, because I do *not* need that kind of shit in my life any more!"

I tried to knock his hands off my arms, but he shook me again, eyes blazing hot blue fury, as he spoke.

"You. Could. Have. Been. Killed!" He emphasized each word with another shake. On "killed" he threw me away from him, the back of my head smacking into the wall hard enough to rattle my teeth.

I barely managed to catch my towel before it slipped all the way off my body. Gabriel couldn't stop his gaze from tracking it, which pissed me off even more.

I'd had enough.

I wrapped the towel around my upper chest, tucking it securely in place as I stared defiantly at him, silently daring him to touch me again. I was angry enough to hit him if he tried.

"Maybe it's not enough for all of us just to survive," I hissed. "Who the hell are you to place a value judgment on the worth of Lil's cats? She has to be able to live with herself, and if she'd left them to die, she might not have been able to do that.

"You've seen how close she is to the edge. She needs something to love and something she thinks is worth fighting for. And if you don't get that, you can just go to hell!"

"Ashley—" He took a step toward me. I held a hand up in warning.

"Don't. Just… *don't.*"

He stopped and sucked in a deep breath.

"Why didn't you come to me?" he asked.

I rolled my eyes.

"Because you would have said no."

He ran his fingers through his hair, making it stand on end.

"Jesus, Ashley…" He started to reach for me, then dropped his hand by his side, shook his head and repeated, "You could have been killed."

"But we weren't." I swayed on my feet as this latest adrenaline rush subsided and left me even more drained than the first. Gabriel reached out to steady me. I stepped back.

Uh-uh. You so *don't get to touch me right now.*

"Is your head okay?" The anger had left his voice.

"No problem," I lied. I actually had the beginnings of a headache. "I still have to scour the elevator, and I really just want to shower and get the smell of disinfectant out of my skin. So let's just call it a night, okay?"

He took another deep breath.

"Okay."

I turned away from him toward the door.

"I'll go with you," he said.

"Just… just don't yell at Lil," I warned him. "She's been through enough tonight. And—" Might as well get this out of the way. "—the whole escapade was my idea."

Gabriel gave a sharp laugh.

"Why does this not surprise me?"

We left the stairwell and headed back to my room. Gabriel picked up the bottle of bleach from where I'd dropped it the second time.

"I'll go first," I whispered. "She's probably hiding in the bathroom about now."

I opened the door.

"Lil?" No answer. *She wouldn't have bolted, would she?* Worried, I stepped inside, stopping short.

Gabriel came in behind me.

"What is it?" he asked. "Is she okay?"

I pointed to the bed where Lily had collapsed, giving in to exhaustion. Binkey was draped around the top of her head like a furry halo, Doodle curled in the crook of one arm. Lambiepie's threadbare head stuck out from the crook of the other. Both cats purred loudly and the contented smile on Lil's face—even in her sleep—brought tears to my eyes.

"Yeah," I said quietly. "She's okay."

CHAPTER THIRTY-TWO

The next day we finished clearing the rest of the buildings on campus. Gabriel and I seemed to have come to an understanding. It made for a much more positive search-and-destroy experience.

There weren't a lot of military personnel left—maybe a quarter of the original Alpha and Beta teams. We still had sharpshooters to cover us, but the soldiers on the ground had been dropping like sexually active teens in a slasher film. Each time it was the same. They developed flu-like symptoms, and then things went downhill from there.

We'd rescued thirty or so survivors so far—not a lot when you consider that Big Red's average daily population is two thousand students, plus teachers and staff. Still, we'd rescued people, and had high hopes for finding pockets of survivors in Redwood Grove itself. There were several tourist stops in the quarantine zone, and a bunch of isolated homes, gas stations, and random businesses just off of the highway.

Every now and then I wondered about our mystery man. I hadn't mentioned him—didn't see any reason to do so.

A lot of borderline survivalist types lived in the area. If they hadn't succumbed to the virus, odds seemed reasonable that they could hang in there. And our dude seemed like the kind of guy who'd've sussed out the whole 'shoot 'em in the head' thing, too.

The military did regular aerial supply drops, so we were good for food and other basic supplies. Too bad they couldn't drop in additional personnel, but each new soldier would become a potential zombie time bomb. So they couldn't risk it.

To my surprise, nothing was said about the previous night's clandestine mission. It didn't seem like Gabriel to play with the rules, though, so I found myself waiting for the other shoe to drop.

"Good job today, everyone," Colonel Paxton said as we returned to Patterson. "After you clean up and get some dinner, we'll go over tomorrow's tactics."

Dinner! Hoo-ha! I was starving.

"Ashley?" the Colonel said. "Would you and Lily please come see me and Professor Fraser in room 217, as soon as you've showered?"

Shit. Should've known it would hit the fan sooner or later. I shot a dirty glance in Gabriel's direction.

All I got back was an unapologetic shrug.

Clean but hungry, Lil and I reported to the lecture hall in record time. No sense putting off unpleasant business, and the sooner we finished, the sooner we got dinner.

"This sucks," Lil said, and she frowned nervously as we neared the door to room 217. "Couldn't they have let us eat first?"

"Nah. They want us weak and hungry so we'll crack and spill the beans."

"Spill *what* beans?" Lil turned her frown on me. "I mean, at this point, what beans would we *not* spill? It's not like we have anything to hide."

"Good point," I admitted. "But it sounded good."

Lil gave a little snort and we went inside. Simone and Colonel Paxton waited for us at the front of the hall, seated at a table. Lil and I approached with the air of two prisoners waiting to be sentenced.

Colonel Paxton came to his feet with a chivalrous—and theatrical—little bow. He was a strange one.

"Have a seat, ladies."

We sat across the table from our interrogators.

"It's come to my attention that you went on a little spur-of-the-moment excursion last night," he said, and I couldn't read his tone. "Is that correct?"

We both nodded. No use denying it.

"Where to begin?" he said. He looked down, then up. "Tell me, how did you get off campus?" There was no way to tell where this was going. All I could read in his expression was friendly interest. Maybe he was just biding his time before opening up a Colonel-sized can of whup-ass.

Lil hid behind her hair, letting me do most of the talking. I described our route out of Big Red, including our leap over the Slinky of Doom and subsequent trek into town through the woods.

"We did our best to stay out of sight," I explained. "Figured we didn't want to draw any attention to ourselves going in or out."

Both Paxton and Simone nodded.

"Go on," Simone said. I couldn't read her, either.

I described our adventure, keeping it as short and succinct as possible. I felt like I was narrating a History Channel show. "*Zombies were a way of life in the twenty-first century…*" But when I described how many zombies had converged on downtown, Colonel Paxton frowned.

"That matches what we've gleaned from aerial recon, and it's not good." He paused, then continued. "I would have thought they'd have gone through their available food source by now, and wandered out of the area."

I felt Lil wince.

"Maybe there are still a good number of survivors

holed up somewhere in town," I suggested. "Most of the zombies were headed down Maple Street before we attracted their attention."

"Good point," Simone said. "Is there a school or church, or some other establishment where people might hold out for an extended period of time?"

Lil emerged from her veil of hair.

"There's the Albertson's shopping center," she offered. "That would provide food. There're a few other shops, too, like a coffee house and a hardware store."

"There's an old Lutheran church down that way," I added. "One of the old-fashioned stone kind. And the fire station."

"All viable possibilities," Simone said.

Lil shot me a sideways glance.

"We have to get those people out of there, right away," she said.

Simone looked at her with compassion.

"It's not as simple as that, Lily—"

"*Lil*," my partner-in-crime snapped back. "Call me Lil."

Simone nodded, unfazed.

"Very well," she continued. "Lil, we have limited personnel, without the option of bringing in any more. And judging from what you've told us, we would be bound to incur casualties if we tried to mount a rescue operation. "

"But wouldn't it be worth it to save those people?" Lil's voice crackled with anger. "We're being asked to put our asses on the line every day! Why can't the military spare a few more soldiers to help us?"

Whoah.

Simone heaved a weary sigh.

"I know it seems unfair, but it won't do us any good to rescue a group of survivors, only to have the zombies find their way back to campus and swarm *en masse* before we've had a chance to reduce their numbers.

"It could mean death for everyone here," she added,

"as well as any survivors we bring back. That won't do anyone any good."

"Professor Fraser is correct." Colonel Paxton tapped his fingers on the table. "We need to clear the zombies out entirely, before they discover there's more food to be had here, and swarm us."

Swarm? It was the second time they'd used that word. *I don't like the sound of that.* But Paxton moved on.

"How did you get past the zombies when you were returning to camp?" he asked. "Why didn't they follow you?"

Once more Lil and I looked at each other. Somehow it felt wrong to rat out our rescuer, especially given his attitude about the military, but it seemed just as wrong to withhold information. It's not like the guy had done anything wrong, after all. If anything, he'd saved two of the Zombie Squad's precious wild cards.

Lil retreated back behind her hair, abdicating responsibility. I gave a mental shrug and spoke up.

"Well… erm, we had help." I then proceeded to spill the beans about our rescuer, playing up his heroics. I also talked about how he had been threatened on the borders of the quarantine zone.

"He took an old logging trail so we could get back in without being seen. Dropped us off outside the Admin building."

The Colonel wrinkled his brow. But for some reason, he didn't pursue it.

"Are you certain none of the zombies followed you?"

I shook my head.

"No. Coming out of the middle of town, he drove like some sort of insane Nascar driver. And the trail itself was pretty small and winding, so I don't see how any of them could've kept up with us—or figured out where we went."

Colonel Paxton nodded.

"Did he tell you his name? Where he came from?"

"We asked, but he wasn't talking."

"He wasn't interested in coming back here with us, either," Lil said.

"He was the survivalist type," I added. "Kind of like Burt Gummer in *Tremors*, but better looking."

"Ah, yes. Very helpful, I'm sure." If Colonel Paxton had seen *Tremors*, I'd eat my helmet. Actually, about now I was hungry enough to consider eating *anything* if it had been sautéed in enough butter.

Colonel Paxton stood up, signaling the end of our conversation. We'd gotten off light, and for the life of me, I couldn't figure out why.

"Go get some dinner," he said. "We'll see you back here after you eat." We got to our feet. "You've brought us some valuable intel, ladies. But if you leave campus again, without direct orders, I will have you placed under arrest so fast your heads will spin. Is that clear?" His voice remained amiable throughout.

"Can you do that?" I asked. "Arrest civilians?"

"Young lady, I'm the commanding officer, and this is a military operation. I can do anything I like." He smiled, yet somehow he sent a chill down my spine, and I realized I'd been underestimating him.

Never again.

Simone's face was carefully neutral.

Lil and I scurried up the aisle and out of the room.

"Do you think he was serious?" Lil's eyes were huge.

"I'd lay money on it," I said. "So unless you've got more cats stashed away in town, I think it'd be a good idea to take him *very* seriously."

After eating a rushed dinner, we hurried back to the lecture hall. The rest of the wild cards sat in the front row—all except for Kaitlyn, who was sitting by herself several rows back.

She really ought to wear black, I thought, *and just become a full-time Goth*. She sure as hell took herself seriously enough to qualify. Sure, this was a shitty situation, but what was the point of alienating everyone around you?

I truly did not understand the bitchy enigma that was Kaitlyn.

I plopped down next to Mack, who gave me his sweet smile as I sat down. Lil cozied up between Kai and Tony. I noticed Tony checking her out as she did so. He'd gotten rid of any visible piercing—no more barbells or hoops. But he still had the steel post in his tongue. I only knew because every once in a while he'd click it against his front teeth in a nervous tick.

Simone, Colonel Paxton, Gabriel and Sergeant Gentry sat at the table up front. Gabriel and Gentry looked fresh out of the shower and comfy in jeans and T-shirts. It took some effort to focus my attention on Colonel Paxton as he began the briefing.

"Our original plan was to send you into Redwood Grove tomorrow, to start clearing out the town," he said. "But recent intel has made us revise this strategy. There are substantially more flesh-eaters there than we anticipated. The numbers need to be culled, yes, but we're going to start further afield and try to lure some of the zombies out of the town proper. Then we can dispatch them accordingly.

"By circling around and approaching from the far side of town, we hope to eliminate a substantial number of them, and avoid the possibility of leading a swarm back to Big Red."

"A swarm?" Mack raised his hand. "What constitutes a swarm?" He frowned. "How many are we expecting to find?"

Paxton looked at Simone and raised his eyebrows. She fielded the question.

"It depends entirely on the situation," she said. "Depending on the number of humans versus the number of zombies, it can mean hundreds, if not thousands."

Simone shook her head. "If they move in unison, toward a single food source, it's a frightening sight."

Kai shrugged.

"We kicked the asses of hundreds of the suckers here on campus," he said. "What's the big deal?"

"The zombies on campus were spread out," she replied, "their attention focused in different areas. A swarm takes on a sort of hive mentality. We don't know why it happens, but imagine the difference between a thousand bees all buzzing around different flowers in a field. Then imagine that same thousand honing in on the same flower. Or person."

Kai squirmed.

"Okay, I get the picture."

Colonel Paxton nodded.

"If the zombies trailed you back to campus, a big enough swarm might break through the barrier. And we don't have the manpower to destroy that many—not all at once. If the situation got out of hand, we'd have to call in an air strike."

"Nuke it from orbit," Tony muttered. "It's the only way to be sure."

"If need be, young man." Paxton wasn't joking. "If need be."

"What happened to the whole 'wild cards aren't expendable' thingy?" Kai looked as if he'd been betrayed.

"You didn't really buy that shit, did you?" Kaitlyn wore her usual expression of disgust. If she hadn't been so determined to be a bitch, I'd have had sympathy for her point of view. I mean, things really sucked in a world where the dead came back to life and ate your friends and family.

Kai leaned back in his chair and shot her a nasty look.

"Yeah. I bought that shit," he replied.

Kaitlyn snorted derisively.

"Then you're an idiot," she said. "Of *course* they want us to feel special. Why else would we risk our lives, day after day, just to take care of *their* problem? We die, they can always find someone else."

Okay, I'd officially had enough.

"Jeez frickin' Louise," I snapped. "This isn't just 'their' problem. It's everyone's problem, and if we're the only ones who can get down and dirty with the zombies, of *course* we're special. God, Kaitlyn, I know you're a bitch, but I didn't think you were stupid."

She sprang to her feet, fists clenched.

Oh yeah, go ahead and throw the first punch, I thought. *Just give me an excuse.*

Simone cleared her throat. Loudly.

Kaitlyn sat back down without another word, and I kept my mouth shut. Simone looked at both of us.

"Thank you." How she found it in her to be polite, I'll never understand. "We do not have time for this sort of divisiveness. Of *course* you're important to us." She paused, then continued. "But if the only way to contain this infection is to eradicate the hot zone, then we may *all* be deemed acceptable collateral damage."

Colonel Paxton shook his head.

"We'd do everything in our power to get you all out of here first, believe me."

And I did. It made sense, especially when you considered Simone's extensive body of knowledge. How could they have a Zombie Squad—excuse me, DZN—without her? It would be like the A-Team without Hannibal.

There went my brain, off-roading again.

Gabriel and Gentry took over the discussion.

"Here's the plan," Gentry said. "We're going out as one team to a truck stop called Bigfoot's Revenge, on the far side of Redwood Grove. We'll start there, then fan out to the residences on the outer perimeter of town.

"While we search for survivors, the zombies we engage will raise a ruckus. This should draw more of them out of town and thin out their numbers enough that we can get to any survivors. And then—hopefully—we can get back to Big Red without being swarmed." He looked at all of us.

"Any questions?" No one said a word. "Good. Let's get this show on the road."

With that, the briefing ended.

Word must have leaked.

Shortly after we went to our room, Lil and I had a parade of visitors wanting to meet Binkey and Doodle, both of whom had obtained unofficial celebrity status.

Our fellow wild cards showed up first, with the not surprising exception of Kaitlyn. Mack seemed especially happy to have something on which he could lavish affection, and both cats responded with non-stop purring. So much for the myth that cats are "mysterious and aloof."

The evening turned into an impromptu party, with med techs, soldiers, special ops, and other personnel, all bearing wine, beer, or munchies of some sort. Even Dr. Albert stopped by, still wearing his white doctor's coat. He had a can of StarKist tuna in hand.

"For the cats," he explained.

Colonel Paxton was absent, as was Gabriel, but Simone showed up briefly, looking as weary as I'd ever seen her, yet somehow managing to appear impeccably groomed.

Maybe that's her wild card power.

No surprise, Jamie accompanied her. What *did* surprise me was the shy smile she gave me when she came in.

"I love cats," she murmured, heading straight for Binkey and Doodle.

"These felines are, in a word, rotund," Simone observed, sitting on the edge of Lil's bed and scratching Binkey under the chin.

"Lil was worried that they would starve to death," I said. I grinned at my roommate, who was sitting on Tony's lap and drinking a local microbrew—her third already. I myself resisted the urge to drink more than one beer. Nothing says "stupid" like zombie hunting with a hangover.

"Nonsense." Simone raised an eyebrow at Doodle as he stretched out a lazy paw. "You, my feline friend, could live off your fat longer than a camel could live off its hump."

Doodle yawned, unimpressed.

Simone scritched his tummy absent-mindedly as she turned toward me and dropped her voice so that only I could hear.

"You realize what a foolhardy thing you did, don't you?"

I shrugged and nodded.

"Yeah. But I'd do it again."

It was Simone's turn to nod.

"I know."

"*Hey.*"

We both looked up to see Gabriel standing there. Lil waved at him from Tony's lap, splashing beer on Kai.

"Gabriel!" she cried. "Meet Binkey and Doodle!"

Jamie moved aside and Binkey allowed Gabriel to rub his belly, followed by Doodle. Their purrs rumbled above the conversations in the room. "Affection sluts" didn't even begin to do them justice.

"It's getting late," Simone announced. "Probably best if everyone gets some sleep. Tomorrow is not going to be an easy day."

Jamie immediately got to her feet. Gabriel clapped his hands together to get everyone's attention.

"Lights out!"

"But I want another beer," Lil said, upending her now empty bottle with a pout.

"Here, here!" Tony raised his own bottle and chugged it.

"That's enough!" Gabriel said. "What you'll face tomorrow will make a sweep of the campus look like a walk in the park. We need you in top mental and physical condition."

Kai got to his feet in an effortless move that belayed the beers he'd already consumed.

"Well, when you put it that way..." With Lily still on his lap, Tony tossed his empty bottle in the trashcan, grabbed another full one from the little table, and popped the top.

Gabriel grabbed it before he could take more than a sip.

"You're pushing it," he said, and there wasn't a trace of amusement in his voice.

Tony scowled at him.

"C'mon, man," he protested, "It's a free country. We've earned a couple of brews."

Gabriel stared him down. Tony tried staring back, but lowered his eyes after only a few seconds.

"You suck, Tofu."

"Yeah, Joystick, I guess I do."

"That's X-Box," Tony grumbled.

Lil looked a little pie-eyed as she slid off Tony's lap, wobbling slightly. I got the feeling she hadn't done a hell of a lot of drinking before becoming a wild card. Grabbing a bottled water, I twisted off the top and handed it to my loopy roomie.

"Here, kiddo," I said." I'll get you some ibuprofen."

Lil took the water, but frowned.

"I wannanother beer."

"And I want world peace, so we're both shit out of luck tonight."

I ducked into the bathroom and grabbed the ibuprofen out of the medicine cabinet, shaking four into my hand. Two for me, and two for Lil. As I put the bottle back, I noticed a brown prescription bottle next to the toothpaste—some drug called Clozapine with the name Lily Kiputh on the label.

Huh. Wonder what these are for?

Shutting the cabinet door, I dry swallowed my pills and rejoined the dwindling party, making sure Lily took her dose with what was left of her water.

"Let's go, troops," Gabriel commanded. I stood by the door with folded arms as he herded the rest of our visitors out.

"You really know how to kill a party, don't you?" But I smiled as I said it.

Mack stopped for a quick hit-and-run scritch for both of the cats, and then a hug for me.

"You done good, kid," he whispered.

Then it was only Gabriel in the room.

"Get some sleep, okay?" And then he was gone.

CHAPTER THIRTY-THREE

The next day dawned way too early for my taste.

And it dawned without a hint of sunlight. The trees and buildings were masked with the kind of fog filmmakers conjure up by using machines. All that was missing was the blue backlighting. It was also one of those thick, drippy fogs that soaked hair and clothes after just a few minutes. Shitty for the work at hand, but great for the skin.

All the wild cards were stuffed into a Chevy Suburban, the back row of seats folded down to make room for our gear. Gabriel drove and Gentry rode shotgun.

We took the main road leading down toward Redwood Grove, then cut to another one that bypassed the town and headed twenty miles west to Bigfoot's Revenge. There we would start our search and destroy, and if we attracted any undead attention, it would be easy enough to lead them away from campus. At least, this was the working theory.

The whole strategy thing gave me a headache.

After about half an hour, Gabriel pulled the SUV into a cedar-chip-and-dirt parking lot. The tourist trap had been around since the 1950s, one of the more popular stops on the way up through Northern California. It boasted a souvenir shop with carved bears, eagles, totem poles, and bootleg Disney characters carved from redwoods. There was a motel comprised of twelve quaint log cabins, and a coffee shop claiming "the best mochas in the Pacific Northwest." There was even a drive thru redwood on the property, but it had been blocked off ever since a Hummer got wedged in the middle and had to be extracted with a winch.

There were about a dozen other vehicles in the lot, some parked neatly at the edge, others skewed haphazardly as if the drivers had skidded to a halt in a hurry. The front passenger door of an old blue Chevy Impala hung wide open, and I could see blood pooled among the wood chips underneath.

No sign of unlife as we piled out of the truck, but the fog was thick enough to mask a lot of activity.

Piles of redwood burls were stacked up on the porch along with the wooden sculptures. A seven-foot redwood Bigfoot, arms outstretched menacingly, loomed at the base of the stairs. Donald Duck peeked out of the fog from his perch on the landing and a large eagle sat on the railing, wings in perpetual flight.

The eerie silence combined with the mist actually made old Bigfoot look kind of scary.

I adjusted my gear, making sure my weapons were in place, my M-4 at the ready, and my hair still tucked beneath my helmet. The rest of the wild cards were all doing the same—including Kaitlyn, who seemed unusually tense, even for her.

Her expression was pinched, almost haunted, as she looked around. If she'd been anyone else, I'd have asked what was wrong and tried to help. But I preferred not to have my head bitten off, thank you very much. Especially by a fellow human.

We'd opted to go without nose plugs this trip, to give us the advantage of an extra warning system. The heavy fog was deceptive, dispersing scents and muffling sounds, making it hard to pinpoint directions. Given that the zombies could approach from any direction through the surrounding woods, it seemed better to have all our enhanced senses up and running.

In fact...

I caught a whiff of something rotten. A branch cracked beneath a foot, off to my left at the edge of the parking lot.

"Incoming," I said as a friggin' ginormous male lurched out of the fog like something out of—you guessed it—a horror movie.

This porker was fatter by far than the pudgy businessman who'd first taken a bite out of me. Its blue-and-red checked flannel shirt could have doubled as a tablecloth, and I didn't know they made jeans that size. Rolls and ripples of pasty sallow-green flesh flashed where the hem of the shirt couldn't quite meet the waistband, which was doing its best to hide under all the stomach fat.

I didn't see any obvious causes of death—no bites, scratches or other injuries. In fact, other than a little gore around the mouth and the definite undead tint to its flesh and eyes, this guy looked fairly normal. I'd have put money on a heart attack.

Can you turn after you're already dead? I wondered.

It stretched out its arms as best it could, gave a pathetic, hungry moan, and continued to lurch toward us.

"Whoa, dude!" Tony laughed. "Last thing you need is more food." He turned to us. "He's as big as the fuckin' Death Star."

"Jenny Craig time for you, fellah," I muttered, unsheathing my sword.

"Oh, come on," Tony whined. "Lemme have this one, Ash."

"No fair," I protested. "I smelled him first."

"Pu-leeeeze?"

I rolled my eyes and gave a little gesture.

"Go for it."

"You're too nice," Kai said. "That one's gotta be worth a lot of points."

"Nah," Gentry replied. "Too slow. Easy target. Biggest problem is if it falls on top of you. But Tony would have to be pretty damned clumsy to let that happen."

"Wanna place bets?" Kai grinned.

"Hey, I heard that, Lando," Tony growled.

"You just be careful there, Joystick."

Tony growled again, but chose not to reply.

We all watched as he plucked a sledgehammer from the porch, then casually strolled up to the Death Star zombie, easily hefting the weapon with both hands. It cracked me up, 'cause I expected him to see how hard he could ring the bell at the fair.

Unable to resist the cheap shot, Tony swung the hammer like a baseball bat and hit the zombie in its gut, no doubt expecting to knock it on its ass.

Whomp!

The hammer bounced back as if made of rubber, and the unexpected rebound knocked Tony on his ass.

Even Gabriel smiled.

Death Star moaned again, its attention now fully on its fallen prey.

"Get a move on, kid." Gentry said, tapping an imaginary watch. "Plenty more to kill without you messing around."

Tony scowled and scrambled to his feet. He circled behind Death Star and without further ado smashed the sledgehammer against the back of its skull, once, then twice. The zombie staggered forward, and then toppled over onto its belly with the slow majesty of a downed redwood. The ground shook as it hit, bits of dust and redwood chips flying up and out from the point of impact.

It was unfortunate the thing landed face down, because we were all treated to the unlovely sight of very fat, rotting plumber's crack.

Tony raised his hammer for one last blow to its skull. *Keee-runch.* Dead zombie.

Wiping the head of the sledgehammer on Death Star's flannel shirt, he grinned in satisfaction.

"Let's see how many ghouls heard the big fat moaning dinner bell," he said.

Sure enough, more moans drifted through the fog, coming from all around, signaling the approach of more zoms. A door creaking on its hinges turned our attention to the souvenir shop. A tiny female tugged open the heavy wooden door, squeezing through the opening. It couldn't have been more than five years old when it had died, filthy blond hair in braided pigtails tied off in jaunty pink ribbons that matched the color of its T-shirt and frilly little skirt. Large chunks of flesh were missing from its neck, arms and shoulders.

It saw us and eagerly staggered towards the stairs, sad hungry mewls emanating from its mouth.

Someone gasped.

I turned to find Kaitlyn staring at the little girl zombie with an expression of such sorrow and agony it almost hurt me just to see it. I remembered the story she'd told about watching her friend and the friend's daughter being ripped to pieces in front of her.

Oh jeez… it can't be.

"Megan…"

Kaitlyn's agonized whisper told me it could, and it was. A wave of pity swept over me and it didn't matter that I knew it wouldn't be welcome. The raw pain on her face demanded it.

Mack stepped forward and unholstered his M-4. His eyes were leaking slow, steady tears as he took careful aim and pulled the trigger. The zombie collapsed at the top of the stairs and Kaitlyn gave a great keening wail, knees crumbling underneath her as if they couldn't support the weight of her grief.

Mack went to hug her, but she pushed him away and

then held herself, arms crossed protectively across her chest as she rocked back and forth in time to her sobs.

But we didn't have time to comfort her. Other zombies staggered out of the trees on all sides, and from the interior of the gift shop. I heard thumping sounds coming from some of the cabins as the zombies inside tried to get out to see who'd come to dinner.

We all formed a rough circle around the still stricken Kaitlyn, covering all angles of approach, M-4s in hand. Tony tossed his sledgehammer onto the ground next to the SUV.

"Pick your targets, and don't waste ammo," Gabriel barked. "Clear space, and if you miss the head, finish the job."

Almost instantly we had upwards of thirty zombies closing in from all directions, gory phantasms clutched by the mist. Gunfire filled the parking lot, the sound oddly muffled by the heavy fog, the smell of cordite mingling with the scents of pine, cedar, and zombies.

Especially zombies.

Even in the heat of the moment, I was impressed at how well my fellow wild cards kept their heads under pressure. The sight and smell of these things were truly horrible, and having them close in like that—arms out, mouths stretched wide to reveal teeth dripping with blood and black fluid—was a sight to freeze the heart of most people. Which is probably why a lot of folks died without running. I'd been through it in town, and still it gave me the creeps.

But the wild cards never faltered, and within minutes all the zombies we could see were sprawled dead around us.

We stood in silence for a moment. The only sounds remaining were those of Kaitlyn's grief, which had trickled down to a few choked sobs, and the steady thumping on the inside of some of the cabins.

Gabriel knelt alongside her and put his hands on her shoulders.

"You need to pull it together," he said quietly. "You're going to get yourself or one of your team members killed if you can't."

Kaitlyn's eyes flashed with a look of wild hatred that quickly diffused into an almost bewildered expression, as if she suddenly realized where she was, and why... and didn't like it much.

Gabriel's gaze held steady.

"Can you pull yourself together?" he asked. "Can you do this?" Then he added, "We need you."

Kaitlyn gave a wrenching, watery sigh, and then nodded.

"Yes. I can do this." She took a deep gulp of air, and it was as if something she'd been carrying suddenly dropped off her shoulders. She got to her feet, actually letting Gabriel help her. Then, even more surprisingly, she squared herself, and looked at Mack.

"Thank you," she said. "I couldn't have done it. But it needed doing."

Mack reached out and squeezed her shoulder.

"I know," he said. "I'm sorry."

She nodded, then looked around at the rest of us, pausing when she reached me.

"I am, too," she said. She held my gaze for a few seconds, then walked off to the edge of the parking lot. Not exactly touchy-feely, but more than I ever expected.

Gabriel gave her a few moments before speaking.

"Time to check the shop and the cabins." He pointed in my direction. "Ashley, Kaitlyn, Mack, and Kai, take the cabins. The rest of us will check the souvenir shop and the back area. Everyone, keep an eye out for more flesh-eaters trailing in from the woods. Any trouble, give a holler." He patted his walkie-talkie. "Any questions?"

I cleared my throat.

"Any reason we're not working in our normal teams?"

"We may not always have the time to divide into specific teams," he replied. "You need to know you can count on any member of the wild cards to back you up."

I nodded. *Okay then.*

"Kaitlyn?" he said.

Kaitlyn turned her head in response to Gabriel's call, then rejoined us, shoulders straight, the set of her jaw determined.

CHAPTER THIRTY-FOUR

Four cabins were lined up in a row next to the souvenir shop. There were three more in a rough semi-circle off to the right, front doors a few feet back from the right side of the parking lot, backs nested among the trees.

We hit the row of cabins first.

"Think there are any survivors?" Mack said anxiously.

I shook my head. "There'd be zombies trying to get into the cabins if there was anyone left alive."

It was easy to tell which cabins were currently occupied. The steady thumping of fists on wood was an undead giveaway.

So, ladies and gents, we definitely have flesh-eating prizes behind doors number one, three, and four.

Kai jerked his head toward the second cabin.

"Ashley, how 'bout you and Mack check out that one. Kaitlyn, you wanna cover me here?"

Kaitlyn took her place without argument.

I raised an eyebrow at Kai.

"Who died and made you Mister In-Charge?" I said with mock indignation.

He shrugged.

"I'm just going with the flow, baby girl."

"Did he just call me 'baby girl'?" I asked Mack.

"Yes, he did," Mack replied.

"I'll have to kick his butt for that later."

Ignoring us, Kai moved purposefully toward the door of the first cabin, kicking it in with one booted foot and then quickly leaping to one side, back flat against the cabin wall, so Kaitlyn had a clear shot.

"Very macho," I commented. "Mel Gibson would be proud."

Kai grinned.

"Thank you for noticing."

"It wasn't a compliment."

There was method to his macho madness, however, because his kick had knocked a zombie ass over teakettle. As it struggled to its feet, Kaitlyn stepped up and shot it in the head. Kai nodded his approval and the two went inside.

Mack and I turned to the second cabin.

"You wanna kick it open, or shall I?" I asked.

Mack grinned.

"How about we try the doorknob instead? I'd rather leave the showy stuff to other people."

"Works for me," I said.

Putting my hand on the doorknob, I paused, listening for any movement inside. Nothing. Water dripped into my eye from my forehead, where moisture had condensed under the rim of my helmet. I wiped it away, turned the doorknob and pushed the door open, copying Kai's evasive move just in case Mack needed a clean shot.

"Looks clear." Weapon ready, he entered the cabin and I followed close on his heels.

There wasn't much space inside—a bedroom, bathroom, and an indentation in the wall with a clothes pole running the length of it. The bed was queen-sized, with its headboard against the wall to one side. No sign of occupation and, thankfully, no body parts, either.

A quick peek in the bathroom, and we moved on to the next cabin while Kai and Kaitlyn took care of number four. He kicked the door in on that one, too.

Several headshots later, the four of us met outside and headed across the parking lot to the three remaining units. A painfully skinny and totally androgynous zombie wandered out from the trees and I shot it almost as an afterthought.

"Is it just me, or are we getting used to this?" I asked Mack quietly.

He shook his head.

"I don't know that we'll ever get used to it. But what's the point of jumping every time one of them staggers up? We know what they are, and we know how to stop them."

We reached the last three cabins. A couple of weathered glider rockers sat in a small clearing to the left, a little table in-between. A wine bottle lay on its side, its contents having long since trickled away.

Somewhere on the periphery of my hearing there was the sound of sobbing. The placement of the cabins, along with the tricks played by the fog, kept me from pinpointing it.

Kai and Kaitlyn headed to the cabin on the far left, so Mack and I took the middle one, both grinning when Kai kicked his cabin door open. Then I put my hand on the doorknob and listened. With an inward hiss of surprise I realized that the sounds of sobbing were coming from within, intertwined with a human voice muttering something over and over. It was too faint for me to make out the actual words.

"Mack," I said, "I think we have a survivor!"

Mack's face brightened with excitement. Nothing made him happier than finding someone alive in the midst of all the chaos and death.

I turned the doorknob, but the door wouldn't budge. I rapped on the wood with my knuckles.

"Hello?" I said. "Hello, can you hear me? We're here to help!" I put my ear to the door. The sobs continued, along with the muttering. Stepping back, I used the barrel of my gun to knock, in case they hadn't heard me the first time.

"Hello?" I said, louder this time.

Still no answer.

I looked at Mack and frowned.

"What's up with that?" I said. "You'd think whoever it is would be jumping with joy about now."

"They might be too scared to answer," Mack offered. "Or injured."

Kai and Kaitlyn emerged from the first cabin. I motioned to Kai.

"You feel like kicking down another door? Sounds like we have a survivor inside, but he or she isn't answering, and the door's locked."

Kai nodded enthusiastically.

"Oh, yeah! I'm likin' the door kickin'."

I put a hand on his arm.

"Let me take point after you get it open. If whoever's in there is scared, I'm probably a little less intimidating than you."

"You find me intimidating?" Kai looked pleased at the thought.

I snorted.

"As if," I said. "But someone else might."

"You know how to knife a man's self-esteem right in the gut, girl."

I knocked on the door again, and raised my voice.

"Whoever's in there, we're going to break open the door. We're here to help you, okay?"

Still no answer.

Without further ado Kai stepped back and kicked with enough force that the door swung inward, hit the wall, and bounced back to a nearly closed position. I winced, hoping he hadn't just given the person inside a coronary.

"Thanks a lot, Lando."

He gave me a little salute and dashed off to the third cabin. Kaitlyn followed, shooting me a little smile over one shoulder. I nearly fainted with shock, but managed to smile back.

"I've got you covered, Ashley." Mack kept his gun trained on the door as I pushed it back open with my free hand. When nothing appeared, I slowly stepped inside.

The smell hit first—the coppery, thick stench of blood and other bodily excretions. I choked and almost grabbed for my nose plugs, but quickly forgot about them when I took a good look inside.

Blood splattered the walls and floors in thick, viscous smears. A trail of bloody handprints, followed by more smears of blood, led from the far side of the room to the closed bathroom door, as if someone had tried desperately to crawl away from an attacker.

It looked like they never made it.

The sobs continued, rising from the other side of the queen-sized bed. The words continued as well, only now I could hear what they were.

"I'm sorry, I didn't mean it."

The same six words repeated over and over, interspersed with the choking sobs and… some other sound I couldn't quite place. Blood and other things were thick on the white crocheted bedspread. My heart froze in my chest and the hair rose on the back of my neck.

Something was seriously wrong here.

"I'm sorry, I didn't mean it."

"Hello?" I slowly walked over to the bed, conscious of the blood making sticky sounds beneath my feet, and peered cautiously around the corner.

"I'm sorry, I didn't mean it."

Two partially devoured bodies lay there on the floor, of a woman and young boy, still a toddler, clothing in shreds. A man in blood-soaked jeans and a blue flannel shirt now dark with gore crouched over them, sobbing and muttering. He showed no yellowing of the skin, or decay—no symptoms at all of having turned.

"I'm sorry, I didn't mean it."

Then, as I watched in disbelieving horror, he lowered his face to the woman's abdomen and took a bite of flesh, wrenching the meat away from her body with a feral snap of his jaws.

CHAPTER THIRTY-FIVE

His sobs didn't stop as he chewed and swallowed.

"I'm sorry, I didn't mean it," he repeated as soon as he could.

I made a choked sound in my throat and stumbled backward, yelling as I backed straight into Mack, who'd come up behind me. He braced me with his hands on my shoulders. Looking past me, he made a gurgling sound in his throat.

The sound of my yell was enough to distract the man. He looked up at us, eyes red and swollen with tears, mouth and teeth dripping with blood and pieces of flesh.

"I didn't mean to do it," he whimpered. "I didn't *want* to do it. But I couldn't help it. I couldn't help myself. I was so hungry, and I could feel myself rotting... the inside, everything decaying."

"Oh, god, I'm sorry. I didn't mean it. I'm so sorry..."

He curled back up over the bodies of what must have been his wife and son, rocking and crying and muttering and eating.

"He's bat-shit crazy," I whispered, willing myself not to throw up.

"You're not kidding," Mack agreed, sounding as sick as I felt. "Question is, what do we do with him?"

I swallowed hard.

"We'll have to get him back to Big Red, I guess." My gaze was drawn almost against my will back to the weeping man. "Where are Kai and Kaitlyn?"

The sound of gunshots answered my question before Mack did.

"Cleaning up incoming."

"Let's get this guy outside and find Gabriel."

"You sure that's a good idea?" Mack asked doubtfully. "He's dangerous, no doubt about it."

"I'm a good husband," the man said suddenly, as if in response to Mack's words. "A good father. I love my family. I tried to save them when those… those things attacked us. But they… they smelled so good and it burned inside." He started rocking again, but the tears seemed to have stopped for the moment.

I took a deep breath, and immediately regretted it.

"What's your name?" I asked.

"Jake," he said slowly. "Jake Konig."

"Mr. Konig… Jake, how long have you been trapped in this cabin?"

He thought about the question for a moment.

"I'm not sure—maybe a week?"

Oh, god. The combination of hunger and the sheer horror of seeing the dead walk must have taken his mind right over the edge.

"You really need to come with us now," I said, struggling to maintain a calm, neutral tone.

"Oh, no, I couldn't do that." He shook his head. Drops of blood flew off his lips. I did my best to suppress a shudder.

"Jake, you're ill," I pressed. "You need medical attention." I spoke as soothingly as possible, as if trying to calm a spooked animal. Mack stood stock still behind me, but I could feel the tension thrumming through him as he waited, poised for trouble.

"I can't leave Shanna and Tyce." He shook his head again. "They need me." He tenderly stroked his son's forehead, then leaned over to kiss his wife's lips… before taking a bite out of them.

I nearly lost the battle with my rising gorge, but somehow managed to keep everything down.

"They'll—" my voice cracked. I pulled myself together. "We'll bring them with us, too. You can all go together and get some help, okay?"

"All of us?" Jake looked up at me, pale blue eyes sincere in the bloody mask of what had once been a pleasantly handsome face under a shock of curly brown hair, now matted and tangled.

I nodded, wanting nothing more than to get out of this claustrophobic cabin with its smell of death.

"All of you, I promise."

Mack and I backed up a few feet as, ever so slowly, Jake got to his feet. I hoped he didn't need a helping hand because I didn't know if I could touch him without throwing up. Besides, I didn't trust him not to attack me, too.

He managed it on his own, though, swaying slightly as he stood up all the way. He put a steadying hand on the bedpost, his shirtsleeve pulling up to reveal his forearm. A circle of teeth marks stood out against the pale skin, crusted with dried blood.

I inhaled sharply.

"When did you get that bite, Jake?"

"This?" he rubbed his arm, a vague look on his face. "Those things… first day here. I got Shanna and Tyce back into the cabin, but one of those things bit me. I got really sick. Shanna, she took care of me, nursed me until I felt better. But then I started rotting inside."

Great. What we have here is a totally loony wild card. Super strong, super senses, and super psycho.

I gestured toward the door, trying not to be too obvious that I had my gun aimed in his direction. Just in case.

"Come on," I said. "We'll send someone in to get your family. Okay?"

He nodded hesitantly.

"Yeah... yeah, that'd be really good. I think Tyce needs a doctor."

Mack and I backed away slowly to give him space to exit the cabin before us. I didn't trust him at our backs.

He neared the door, then paused, glancing toward the bed and what lay on the other side.

"You'll bring Shanna and Tyce?" he asked.

I nodded.

"Yeah, we will." I held my breath when he took a step back toward his dead wife and child. "Jake? You just need to come outside now." My eyes flickered back to the bite on his forearm.

He heaved a huge sigh, and all the tension seemed to run out of his body.

"Yeah, okay. That's probably a good idea. It smells funny in here." He again moved toward the cabin door, his gait stiff and unsteady as if he hadn't moved a lot in the last few days.

Kai chose that moment to poke his head in the cabin.

"Hey, everything okay in here?

Jake's head snapped up and reared back on his neck, looking freakily like a human cobra as he bared his bloody teeth and hissed at Kai.

Kai took one look at Jake's gory face, hands, and clothes and immediately raised his M-4, pressing the trigger.

"*No!*"

I lunged forward and knocked the barrel to one side. The shot missed Jake by inches. He yelped and cowered down against the bed, hands and arms over his head.

"Damn it, girl," Kai snarled, "Are you fucking crazy?"

"No," I snapped. "But he is." I jerked my head toward Jake. "He's human, Kai. He's not a zombie."

"But his mouth..."

I shook my head.

"Look, we have to get him back to campus. He was

bitten and he's still alive. He's a wild card."

"Mother fu—" Kai stopped and got himself under control. "Okay, got it." He shook his head. "I gotta rethink my membership in this particular club."

"Go get Gabriel, okay?" I said. "Just ask Kaitlyn to help us cover him. But tell her to stay outside!" Kai ran out of the cabin and I hunkered down next to Jake, still not willing to touch him. "Jake, we're sorry about that. Kai thought you were a zombie. But he knows better now."

"One of those things?" Jake's eyes narrowed, his expression switching from terrified to dangerous in the space of a few seconds. "I'm not one of those things. Don't you call me that!" A drop of blood trickled down his face to his upper lip. He flicked it off with his tongue, eyes closing briefly as he savored the taste. Then his eyes went wide with horror and he wiped the back of his sleeve across his mouth.

"I'm *not* one of them," he whimpered.

"No, you're just sick. We have to get you to a doctor. Let's go outside." I felt like a broken record as I repeated this several more times, but Jake responded to my words or my tone, and finally left the damned cabin.

Mack and I were right behind him. Kaitlyn waited for us outside.

"Just sit here," I said, pointing to one of the gliders. He sat, limbs folding up underneath him as if someone had cut his strings. He rocked slowly back and forth in the chair, pushing off with his feet. It creaked in protest, hinges in dire need of oiling.

"I'm hungry." *Creak. Creak. Creak.*

I ignored him, scanning the fog-shrouded parking lot, then the buildings, looking for Gabriel and the rest of the team.

"I'm *hungry!*" Feeling the urgency in his voice, I looked back at Jake.

"We'll get you food when we get you to a doctor." It took an effort to keep my voice calm. I'd seen his last meal.

"I've got a protein bar," Kaitlyn offered, reaching into one of her pockets and pulling out a Think Thin bar.

She held it out in front of her.

Jake's eyes flickered toward the bar. He reached for it.

"Kaitlyn, no!"

I lunged forward as Jake grabbed Kaitlyn's arm, jerking her off balance into his arms as he sank his teeth into her neck. She shrieked with surprise and pain, dropping her M-4 as she clawed frantically at his head and hands, trying to throw him off.

I heard footsteps running toward us from across the parking lot as Jake clamped onto her like a leech, biting deep, chewing and worrying at her flesh, ignoring whatever pain he must have felt as her hands clenched in his hair, pulling with all her strength.

I managed to wedge my arm in-between his neck and her body, getting him in a chokehold and cutting off his oxygen supply. Kaitlyn jabbed a finger into one of his eyes. He screamed involuntarily, teeth losing their hold.

She immediately jerked away from his mouth, neck pouring out blood through the ragged wound he'd inflicted.

He still had hold of her arm, however, and yanked her back toward him, growling in his throat even as I pressed my forearm harder into his neck.

The stock of Mack's gun smashed down against Jake's wrist, shattering bone and forcing him to let go of Kaitlyn. She staggered back, hands clasped against her bleeding neck as blood spurted out between her fingers.

Deprived of his prey, Jake twisted like an eel in my grip and went for my neck. I managed to shove my arm against his Adam's apple before his teeth sunk into my flesh. He snapped at me like a rabid animal, his breath wafting over me like a week's worth of spoiled meat.

I heard yelling, and out of the corner of my eye saw Mack raise his weapon and smash the butt end down on Jake's head with a sickening crack. Jake went limp and crumpled to the ground, blood oozing from an indentation in his scalp.

I scrambled out from under the dead weight as Kai and Gabriel sprinted up, Lil, Tony and Gentry hard on their heels. I scanned for Kaitlyn, who swayed on her feet, hand still clasped over the wound on her neck, blood seeping between her fingers.

Her face was chalky white from shock and blood loss. Mack and I grabbed her before she collapsed on the dirt next to her attacker, leading her to the glider as her hand slipped off the wound and fresh blood spurted out.

"Shit!" Slapping my hand over the wound, I looked frantically up at Gabriel. "She's bleeding to death!"

CHAPTER THIRTY-SIX

Things happened really quickly after that.

Mack dashed into one of the cabins, emerging almost immediately with a red flannel pillowcase. As he knelt by Kaitlyn's side and pressed the cloth against the wound in her neck, Gabriel's gaze flicked from Jake's body to Kaitlyn, then to me and my blood-splattered hands and clothing.

"Ashley, are you okay?"

I registered the concern in his voice, but didn't have time to think about it.

"I'm fine, but Kaitlyn... her neck. He bit her."

Gabriel started to reply, then tensed.

"What—" I began.

He shushed me with a slashing hand gesture, his posture one of intense concentration. Then we all heard it—rising moans coming from all directions, the sound muffled, yet echoing all around us as if rebounding off the thick fog. Nothing was visible yet, but they had to be close.

Gabriel didn't waste any time.

"Get to the truck."

"You're not leaving me here." Jake pushed himself up on his hands, blood streaming from the wound on his head. I thought I could see brains through the blood.

How is he even alive?

He raised his head slowly and saw me.

"You can't leave me," he said. "Please, help me!" I hesitated as zombies appeared in the woods behind the cabins. We had to take him with us.

Didn't we?

"Please…" He tried to stand, but fell back.

I took a step toward him, one of those stupid *yeah, I know better* moves we all do on occasion. Kai grabbed my arm and yanked me away, hard.

"Leave him."

"But—"

Kai shook his head.

"I don't care if he's a wild card. He nearly killed Kaitlyn. He can stay here and get ripped to pieces. You got me?" He stared me down until I nodded. He was right, but I didn't have to like it.

Kai let go of me, then helped Mack get Kaitlyn. They half carried, half dragged her between them to the truck. The rest of us fell into a loose formation around them as rotting figures began shambling toward us out of the fog.

"Please!" Jake wailed from behind us. "Don't leave me! You have to help Shanna and Tyce." I risked a look back and saw zombies converging on him.

And then they lurched right past as if he didn't exist. Jake continued to screech, even though he remained untouched.

And suddenly it hit me. There hadn't been any zombies trying to get into Jake's cabin. They would have known there was prey in there, and would have been pounding on the door and walls to get at it. Jake wasn't just crazy, and I didn't think he was a wild card.

Zombies continued to pour out of the forest. Gabriel took out three of them in rapid succession with precise headshots. Time to get the hell out of Bigfoot's Revenge.

"Don't try to take them all out!" he shouted. "Just get to the truck!"

"Someone open the door!" Mack yelled, stumbling under Kaitlyn's dead weight as she started to lose consciousness. Kai helped prop her up, but that put three of them out of the fight.

Slinging his M-4 over one shoulder, Tony retrieved his sledgehammer from the ground and swung it in a vicious arc as zombies closed in from either side. He knocked two of them backward, roaring like a wrathful god with each swing—a teenage punk version of Thor.

Lil ran up next to him, ducking the sledgehammer with almost choreographed grace. She reached the passenger side of the truck and pulled open the doors. Tony beat the zombies away as Mack and Kai got Kaitlyn into the backseat.

Gabriel and Lil covered the rest of us, Lil using her M-4 with good effect, if not with Gabriel's lethal accuracy. Gentry and I clambered into the rear of the Suburban.

Tony's sledgehammer was spinning in rapid figures of eight, so fast it looked like some sort of massive eggbeater. Gabriel tossed his rifle into the truck and slid across to the driver's seat, starting the engine. Lil jumped in next to him as Tony continued to bludgeon the approaching zombies, his face a mask of bloody rage.

"Tony!" Gabriel roared, "Get your ass in here now!"

Swinging his sledgehammer one more time and cracking the heads of several zoms, Tony dove into the back seat, slamming the door behind him as Gabriel hit the accelerator and peeled out of the parking lot.

This was one of those times I wished I didn't have enhanced senses. Mingling with the unnatural moans and growl of the engine, I could still hear Jake's wails, even as we drove into a roadblock of more zombies.

Undead hands grasped at the vehicle. The sound of fingers squelching on the windows mixed with the thud of metal hitting flesh as we lurched forward. The Suburban shuddered with each impact, but held the road.

The perfect family vehicle. Seats a family of eight and holds the road while skidding through a bloody horde.

I had to get a grip.

Peering out the back window, all I could see were ghouls staggering through the fog, lurching after us down the road. And out the side windows I saw more flesh-eaters among the mist-shrouded trees.

Where the hell were they all coming from?

Gabriel drove like the proverbial bat out of hell, toward the highway that would take us back to Big Red, without even slowing for turns or potholes. Gentry and I didn't have seatbelts and were forced to brace ourselves against any handhold we could find. After about five minutes the zombies receded into the foggy distance and Gabriel slowed down minimally.

He looked into the rear-view mirror.

"How's Kaitlyn?"

Mack glanced up at him, still holding the pillowcase firmly against Kaitlyn's neck.

"The bleeding's slowing down, but her breathing is rough. And the wound is probably infected."

"She's a wild card," Gabriel countered. "She can't get infected."

I shook my head, then realized he couldn't see me.

"The guy that bit her... he wasn't a zombie," I said. "He was still alive when we found him."

"What?" The word was explosive, like a bullet.

"He'd been bitten," I said softly. "He said he could feel himself rotting. But he was alive, and he was eating his wife and son."

Gabriel blanched, his skin actually turning pale as I watched in the rear-view mirror.

"Dude had to be fucking crazy," Tony said.

"No. He wasn't crazy." Gabriel spoke in a carefully controlled voice. But some emotion lurked very close to the surface. "Or perhaps it would be more accurate to say he wasn't *just* crazy."

He paused, and through the rear-view mirror I saw a play of emotions rippling across his face so quickly I couldn't identify any of them. An instant later he'd schooled his expression back into Stoic 101. He started to speak again, but whatever he had to say got lost as the Suburban rounded a curve and headed straight for a knot of figures standing motionless in the middle of the road.

Gabriel twisted the wheel to one side in a knee-jerk reaction. As the SUV left the asphalt and veered off into the trees, I got a glimpse of the would-be road-kill Gabriel had swerved to avoid. Zombies. At least six of them, just standing there as if they'd been waiting for us.

Our truck bounced over uneven terrain and off of redwoods before hitting something, maybe a stump. It teetered for a microsecond, then rolled over and over, all of us inside thrown around like rocks in a tumbler, only without the shiny polished finish at the end of the ride.

Gentry and I had the worst of it, without any seatbelts or "Oh Jesus" handles to hang onto, our weapons flailing around as we rolled. Gentry did his best to shield me by wrapping his arms around my upper body, one hand pressing my head against his chest.

Something hard hit the back of my head, but my helmet protected me from more than an uncomfortable *thonk* and a little bit of brain rattling.

When we finally came to a halt, passenger side on the ground and the undercarriage pressed up against a huge redwood, Gentry and I were smushed up against the window, limbs entangled with scabbards, M-4s, and each other.

I pushed his forearm off my mouth.

"You okay?" I asked.

He nodded, wincing as he did so.

"Yeah, I think so."

The SUV's engine gave a final death rattle and cut out.

Assorted groans and little cries of pain filled the vehicle as the shock of the accident wore off enough for us to start moving around. We were all bruised and bloodied.

Shaken, but not stirred.

Shut up, brain.

"Everyone okay?" Gabriel hung awkwardly from his seatbelt, suspended sideways next to Lil, who was pressed up against the passenger door.

"Kaitlyn's in bad shape," Mack said, voice thick with concern. "The bleeding started up again."

"Let's get her out of the vehicle." Gabriel unlatched the driver's side door and gave a mighty shove. It swung open and then slammed shut again, gravity being what it is.

"Shit," he said. "Lil, I'm probably going to step on you a little bit here."

"That's okay," Lil responded.

He unlocked his seatbelt and fell on top of her. I heard a small "Oof!" sound, but otherwise she didn't complain. Somehow Gabriel ended up feet first on the passenger window so he could use his height and long arms to open the driver's door with enough leverage to insure that it didn't slam shut again.

He pulled himself out of the SUV, then reached back in and helped Lil, as well. I heard the sound of his feet crunching on the ground as he moved around to the back of the SUV, where he popped the latch and opened the rear door, holding it up as Gentry and I slithered awkwardly out into the fog, grabbing our guns as we did so.

I hit the ground, wincing as my body protested any movement after being put through an automatic spin cycle.

"You okay?" Gabriel put a steadying hand on my shoulder.

"I think so." I gave him a brief smile.

"Good." He reached out and touched my face, so quickly it might not have happened. Then he was all business as he leaned in the back. "Can you get Kaitlyn out through the back?"

"I think so," Mack replied. "Tony, you go first, then we'll hand Kaitlyn to you."

Tony gave a grunt before squirming through the gap between the back seats and the roof, hunkering down as best he could against the side rear window while Mack and Kai slowly and carefully passed an unconscious Kaitlyn through to him.

He emerged back first from the rear of the SUV, hands hooked under Kaitlyn's armpits as he dragged her outside. He did everything he could to hold the pillowcase, now tacky with blood, still pressed against her neck. He stretched her out on the ground as assorted thuds and grunts preceded Mack and Kai's exit from the vehicle.

We did a quick inventory. Blood dripped from Gentry's nose where something—probably my head—had clipped it during the roll. Tony had a gash across one cheek. We all could have used a bucket of ibuprofen, but all in all, we'd gotten lucky and escaped without any broken bones.

Kai thumped his helmet.

"Guess there's a reason for these things after all."

I did a quick check of all my weapons, and was gratified to find that the various sheaths and straps had held. Then I listened for any signs of movement around us. Whether it was because of the fog, or because we were alone, I didn't hear anything.

That can't last, I mused. *Those zoms in the road aren't that far away.*

Kaitlyn groaned, eyes fluttering open.

"Wha—what?" she rasped. Mack immediately dropped to her side.

"You're okay, sweetheart," he said gently. "We're getting you back to Big Red."

She looked up at him, eyes glazed with pain and shock. And then she gave a small smile.

"You're a liar, Postman." Her voice was weak, but the words were clear.

Mack smiled back.

"I don't lie," he protested. "It's part of the whole 'neither rain nor sleet' thing, didn't you know that?"

Her eyes shut again, the little smile still on her lips.

Mack looked up at Gabriel.

"How far is it back to the campus?"

"We're at least twenty miles out." Gabriel shook his head. "We'll have to call for extraction."

"I'm on it," Gentry said, and he reached down to his belt, then frowned, fingering a bent clasp. "Radio must have come off in the crash. Hang on, I'll get it." He turned back to the SUV, but Gabriel shook his head.

"Listen."

We did. The moans of the walking dead penetrated the fog.

CHAPTER THIRTY-SEVEN

The sound of unsteady yet relentless footfalls headed our way through the trees.

Gabriel tensed.

"We don't have time," he said. "We'll have to run for it, find some kind of protection where we can make a stand. We'll have to carry Kaitlyn."

"I can walk," Kaitlyn said faintly.

"Sure you can," Mack said as he and Gentry helped her to her feet, supporting her weight between them. "You just can't stand."

The moans grew closer, the dripping fog and echoes off of the trees making it hard to tell exactly how far away they were, and from how many directions they were coming.

"This way!" Gabriel bounded away from where we'd gone off the road, the rest of us following as closely as we could, given the thick undergrowth of bushes, saplings, and vines.

Trees, trees and more friggin' trees. It's so easy to forget how big the redwood forests are when you just drive through them now and again. Being on foot made me aware of how very small I was, in comparison to the giants all around me, and how easy it would be to get lost.

Gabriel kept up a good pace, but made sure not to outstrip the rest of us. It would have been all too easy for stragglers to get disoriented in the fog, especially Mack and Gentry as they did their best to support Kaitlyn. She tried to walk, but was practically a dead weight between them.

A low hanging branch smacked me in the face.

I was tired, hungry, and had to pee.

My breath came in shorter gasps as the ground suddenly rose up in a steep gradient, moist pine needles and mud slowly giving way to eroding granite and rocks, all of it slippery beneath our feet. Lil sprinted just ahead of me while Mack and Kai struggled to maintain their footing. Tony and Gentry brought up the rear, helping Mack and Kai when they stumbled.

Even with our added advantages, we couldn't go at this pace for much longer, and the moans of the undead weren't fading off into the distance. I could see movement through the trees and fog, brief nightmarish glimpses of our pursuers. They were tracking us, whether by smell or sound or both, and they had the advantage of never getting tired or needing a bathroom break.

We needed to find shelter, and quickly.

We reached a particularly steep and treacherous slope, clumps of earth and rock crumbling beneath our feet as we clambered up, using scrub brush and trees as handholds. Lil slid back into me once, nearly sending us both tumbling back down the incline, but I managed to grab a nearby tree and dig my feet in until she regained her footing.

"Over here!" Gabriel's voice came further up the slope. The rest of us scrambled until we finally hit level ground, and a high chain-link fence. About three feet of packed dirt and pine needles separated the fence from the slope in what looked like a well-worn path.

"This way," Gabriel said. "There's a house over here."

We followed the path along the fence toward the right and the sound of Gabriel's voice. The flat terrain was the first break we'd had since the accident. Mack's face was red with the effort of hauling Kaitlyn up the slope and Kai didn't look too fresh, either. Kaitlyn's skin looked moist and the pale—almost bluish tinge—screamed shock. We had to get her inside quickly.

I moved ahead and nearly ran into Gabriel where he stood in front of a locked gate. A narrow dirt road led up to it from the woods below. Thankfully, there wasn't yet any movement on the road. Beyond the gate I could see what looked like an adobe structure, set back against a steep tree-studded hillside, really almost a cliff.

The color of the building blended in with the rocks behind it, looking almost like part of the natural environment. The walls were gently rounded, reminding me of the hobbit houses in *The Lord of the Rings*, and followed the curve of a rocky overhang, which provided added shelter.

The two ends of the chain-link fence butted up against either side of the hill. Both fence and gate were at least six feet tall and had barbed wire strung across the top. To the right of the house was one of those portable garage thingies—a metal frame structure covered by canvas. Just beyond that was another, smaller, portable shelter, this one surrounded by pieces of redwood, burls and cross-sections stacked like wooden cucumber slices.

The gate itself consisted of your basic tubular bars made of galvanized steel, set too close to allow a person to climb in-between them. A thick U-shaped latch flipped down around an equally sturdy metal post on the side. A heavy-duty padlock latched the two together.

"Can you open it?" I asked as Gabriel examined the mechanism.

He shook his head.

"It's a Medeco lock," he said. "The military uses them because they're nearly impossible to cut. We'll have to climb over."

The rest of the team caught up.

"No way we can get Kaitlyn over this," Gentry said.

He wiped sweat from his forehead as it drizzled down beneath his helmet.

"You got any better ideas?" Gabriel snapped.

A fresh wave of ululating moans rose from the trees below us. I could hear the distant sounds of zombies struggling with the same treacherous conditions we had just left behind.

"Yeah," I said. "I have an idea." Grabbing the gate, I started shaking it as hard as I could and yelled, "HELP! IF ANYONE'S IN THERE, PLEASE LET US IN!"

The look on Gabriel's face was almost comically surprised. I shrugged and continued hollering. It only took a few seconds before Gabriel, Gentry, Tony, and Lil joined me in rattling the gate and adding their voices to mine.

The ruckus excited the zombies, and the volume of their hungry cries ratcheted up a level as they blundered upward through the trees. It couldn't be long before the first ones reached us.

And then what? How long could we hold them off, even with gravity on our side? We could charge back down through the woods on the far side of the path, but it sounded as if they were coming up from all directions.

Even if we could make it past them, there was no way Kaitlyn could manage it.

I shook the gate with renewed determination, hollering at the top of my lungs. There had to be someone inside this mini-compound, damn it, and he or she had to hear the racket.

They have to help us, I thought grimly, *or I swear I'll come back and haunt them, even after I've been ripped to pieces and divvied up between a dozen zombies.*

The moans and thrashing sounds grew closer. I took a quick peek over my shoulder and thought I saw movement through the fog, beyond some trees about a hundred yards down the hill.

Shit.

Turning back to the gate, I opened my mouth to yell again.

And froze, mouth wide as I found myself staring into the business end of a very big gun held by a very tall and very pissed-off man.

Square-jawed, dark-eyed, with graying dark-brown hair cut close to his skull, he looked about as welcoming as my dad did when he got cold-called by salespeople or Jehovah's Witnesses. He wore baggy cargo pants, a dark green thermal shirt, and one of those photographer's vests with tons of pockets.

The rest of the wild cards shut up, as well. The zombies, however, kept moaning.

The man glared at us.

"What the hell are you people doing here?" he demanded. "This is private property."

That voice. Lil and I looked at each other. Pulling her up next to me, I ignored the gun barrel, and smiled brightly.

"Hi again," I said. "Can we use your bathroom?"

Everyone looked at me as if I'd gone insane—except for Lil, who put her hands on the gate and stared up at him with the winsome gaze of a kitten trying to persuade a human to part with food.

The man looked from me to Lil, then back again. One eyebrow shot up. His eyes narrowed, then widened imperceptibly as recognition kicked in.

"Suuuure," he said. "Come on in." And he shouldered his gun.

"You know this man?" Gabriel didn't sound happy.

"He's the guy who helped me and Lil out in Redwood Grove," I explained.

Lil nodded.

"He saved Binkey and Doodle," she said.

Without further ado our rescuer pulled a key ring from one of the seemingly endless pockets, flipped rapidly through the keys, then inserted one into the padlock. It popped open and he quickly slid it out, and then unlatched the gate.

Before he opened it, he looked the group over, gaze lingering on Kaitlyn, who was hanging limply between Mack and Kai.

"So these are your fabled wild cards, eh?" He didn't sound impressed.

"What were you expecting?" I snapped. "The A-Team?"

"Hell, girl, a cheerleading squad would be more impressive than this bunch."

"I've known some pretty nasty cheerleaders," Tony said.

The man snorted.

"Truth that." His gaze raked over Lil and me again. "Hell, at least you left the cats at home this time. Binkey and Doodle…" He shook his head, but opened the gate wide enough to let us in and barked, "Come on, haul your asses. They're almost here."

"That falls into the category of totally unnecessary advice," I told him as we stumbled inside the relative safety of the fence. He shot me a look before shutting and relocking the gate.

"Watch it, or I'll charge you a quarter to use the toilet."

"I'll owe you," I shot back.

"You already do."

I couldn't argue with that, so I didn't bother to try.

As our reluctant host led us to his house the first zombies reached the fence. Several of them smacked into the chain link, rattling it loudly and sending us scurrying.

"Will it hold?" Gabriel asked.

The man shrugged.

"It should. Not a lot of room for them to mass up against it, but enough zombies with enough time on their hands might bring it down, eventually. How many you figure followed you here?"

It was Gabriel's turn to shrug.

"Hard to tell. But we were swarmed pretty heavily at Bigfoot's Revenge. They seemed to come out of nowhere, too."

The man rolled his eyes.

"Great. If I'd wanted to hold a dinner party, I'd have sent out invitations." He glared at the zombies, then turned. "Well, we'd better get inside and hope the ones in front have short attention spans."

CHAPTER THIRTY-EIGHT

The interior of the house was surprisingly spacious, with high arched ceilings and an airy, open feel to it.

The front door opened into a large living room on the right, a kitchen-and-dining area to the left, and a hall straight ahead with doorways on both sides and at the very end. Definitely bigger on the inside than it was on the outside, and a good thing, 'cause our host was a lot taller than your average hobbit.

"Um, excuse me," I said, pulling off my helmet. "I wasn't kidding—where's your bathroom?" Mystery man looked amused.

"Down the hall," he said. "Last door on your left, past the gunroom." He turned to Mack and Kai, who were still holding Kaitlyn. "Let's get her on the couch."

They moved into the living room.

"That's a nasty neck wound," he said. "Keep her head elevated."

"Gunroom?" Gabriel raised an eyebrow. "Most people just have rec rooms."

"Depends on your definition of recreation, I guess."

Gabriel just nodded. I noticed hollows under his eyes and a slight sallow tone to his skin.

"You don't look so good," I said, and I reached up and touched his face. It felt hot and clammy. Sweat trickled down from his hairline.

"Just tired." He grabbed my hand, moving it away. I hoped he was okay.

The bathroom was impeccably clean—not what I'd come to expect from a single man. There wasn't anything that hinted at the presence of a resident—or even visiting—female.

Thick black towels, hung from wooden pegs on the walls, matched the toilet. A razor lay on the sink, carefully lined up next to a bar of soap in a black stone soap dish. A stack of *Military History* magazines sat in a large basket next to the toilet, along with a how-to book on building cob houses, a copy of *The Anarchist's Cookbook*, and the unabridged edition of Stephen King's *The Stand*.

Interesting selection of reading material.

I noted the address label on the back of one of the magazines. It read "Nathan Smith."

That's got to be an alias.

Finishing up, I washed my hands, then took advantage of the hot water, soap, and one of the black washcloths to try and get the dried blood off of my face and neck. I also wanted to wipe away any trace of Jake's saliva. Whatever he was, I didn't want that shit on my skin.

I glanced in the mirror on the medicine cabinet above the sink.

Yup, I look about as crappy as I feel. My lips were chapped and pale, their natural rose color leached out by stress and exhaustion. The circles under my eyes showed me what I'd look like when I was old... if I lived that long.

There was a knock on the door. I grabbed my weapons belt from where I'd dumped it on the floor in my haste to get my pants down. Then I turned the knob and found Lil practically dancing in the hallway. She dashed past, shutting the door behind her.

I went back up the hall at a more leisurely pace, glancing curiously at the closed door to what had to be the gunroom as I went by.

Every home should have one, right? I thought. *You don't get a spotlight in* Architectural Digest *without one.*

Across the hall was an open door leading to what had to be his office. A brief glance inside told me that our host was a Mac man all the way. Whatever he did for a living, he could afford all the latest models, too.

Reaching the living room, I looked around more carefully. It had been furnished by *Redwoods'R'Us*, with burl tables of various shapes and sizes scattered about. The large couch was redwood and leather, with a matching chair and ottoman tucked in an alcove boasting a curved window that must have cost a fortune.

There were books everywhere—on shelves, on the tables, under the tables, in stacks next to the tables. All subjects, from lavish photo books to more how-to manuals, paperback fiction, biographies—a little bit of everything.

Not a bad place to be holed up in during the apocalypse.

They'd settled Kaitlyn on the large brown leather couch, head resting on two thick pillows. She shivered despite the two plaid blankets they had draped over her body. She didn't look good, but at least she was conscious.

Our host knelt by her side, checking out her wound. He glanced up when I walked into the room.

"Ashley, right?"

I nodded.

"Yup, that's me." I couldn't resist it. "Nathan, right?"

Up went his eyebrow. Then back down again.

"You've been reading my mail."

Lil came back from the bathroom, and Gabriel immediately vanished down the hall. I hoped our host had plenty of toilet paper stashed away.

Nathan nodded toward me.

"Ashley, I need you to go into the kitchen and get a glass of water. You'll find the glasses above the sink. There's salt and baking soda in the cupboard to the right of the stove. Put two pinches of salt and one of soda in the water." By way of explanation he added, "It'll help with the shock, so hurry."

Normally someone giving me orders sets my back up, but this guy had already pulled our asses—not to mention Binkey and Doodle's furry butts—out of the fire. Besides, while he talked like someone who expected people to obey him without question, it didn't seem like a power trip. More like he knew what needed to be done.

Everything was where he said it would be—Nathan was frighteningly organized. I made the mixture as quickly as possible and trotted back into the living room.

Nathan took the glass with a nod and held the rim up to Kaitlyn's mouth, supporting her head with his other hand so she wouldn't choke. She took a sip and made a face, almost spitting it out, but Nathan kept the glass in place.

"It may taste like shit," he said, "but it'll help. Sip it slowly." Using a combination of coaxing and bullying, he got her to drink most of the mixture.

Kai elbowed me out of the way, carrying the granddaddy of all first-aid kits. Working as quickly and efficiently as any nurse, Nathan proceeded to disinfect, salve, and then bandage up Kaitlyn's wound.

She stayed quiet throughout, drifting in and out of consciousness, still shivering every now and then. Nathan finished his first-aid and moved away from the couch. Mack followed him and spoke in a hushed tone.

"Is she going to be okay?"

Nathan hesitated. He looked at Kaitlyn and then motioned Mack over by the front door before responding.

"I don't know," he admitted. "It's a good thing you stopped the bleeding when you did, or she would have died. But she's lost a lot of blood and isn't responding as well as I'd like. She needs better medical attention than I can give her. And even then, I'd say it's iffy."

"But she's a wild card." Tony flopped down on the ground. "We heal faster than other people."

"Then that's probably the only reason she's not dead,"

Nathan responded bluntly.

"So we have to get back to Big Red." Mack looked at the rest of us. "Right?"

Nathan shook his head.

"You were lucky to get here. Getting out isn't going to be as easy, at least until the zombies that followed you here decide to look for another diner."

Gabriel reappeared, looking almost back to normal. Amazing what a trip to the bathroom can do. He took off his helmet and wiped sweat and blood from his brow.

"That's not going to happen," he said. "As long as those things know there's food in here, they'll try their best to get in until they rot where they stand or break down the fence."

Nathan stared at him for a few seconds, expression unreadable. He strode over to the living room window, pulled the curtains aside and looked out. Still expressionless he dropped the curtains back into place and turned back toward the rest of us.

Another pause before he slammed a fist against the wall and growled.

"I can't fucking believe you people led them here," he said. "FedEx and UPS can't find me, even with Google Maps, but you guys? You zero in on the place like you've got a goddamn homing beacon."

"Sorry to have inconvenienced you." Gabriel didn't sound sorry at all.

Nathan snorted.

"But how about you?" Lil asked. She looked at Nathan with a mixture of hero worship and curiosity. "How do you get back here without them following you?"

Nathan's expression softened fractionally.

"I know all the back roads, like the logging track I showed you two. I also have a little bit of experience when it comes to finding and losing people."

"I'm guessing ex-military," Gentry said. "Special Forces."

"Something like that," Nathan admitted. "And glad to be out of it." He shook his head again. "Christ. Fucking zombies."

"You don't seem too surprised." Gabriel folded his arms across his chest.

Nathan shrugged.

"I'm not. I saw a lot of weird shit over the years, and had my suspicions about a few things my superiors tried to cover up. And that was before I had a close encounter with one of those things."

"You were bit?" Lil's eyes got big.

Nathan nodded.

"Yeah. More than once."

No wonder he hadn't blinked when we told him about wild cards.

"This isn't the first time this has happened," he said, and he glared at Gabriel and Gentry. "Why the hell weren't you people better prepared for it?" His gaze swept the room to take us all in.

As grateful as I was for the use of his bathroom, this still pissed me off.

"*You people*?" I said. "What the hell is *that* supposed to mean?"

"You people who have been covering this up all these years," he said, as if that was supposed to explain everything. "You can't tell me you're not part of it."

"Dude, until we nearly died and became mutant zombie fighters, we were just minding our own businesses," Kai said, glaring at him. "Just like y—well, just like normal people. This is all new to us, man, so don't mix us in with your 'the truth is out there' bullshit."

"It's not bullshit," Gabriel said.

Everybody looked at him.

"He's right."

CHAPTER THIRTY-NINE

"Big of you to admit it," Nathan said.

"But we don't have time to talk about it right now," Gabriel continued. "We have to get out of here, get back to the campus. Judging from what Ash and Lil experienced in town, and what we've seen here, the situation is worse than we'd thought. It's only a matter of time before the zombies make it past the perimeter of the quarantine zone.

"That, or the government nukes us." He turned back to Nathan. "Do you have a vehicle we can borrow?"

"You want me to turn over my only means of transportation, after you out me to a horde of hungry flesh-eaters."

Gabriel nodded.

"Actually, I'd prefer it if you'd drive. By your own admission, you know the roads."

"Jesus jumped-up Christ in a sidecar." Nathan laughed, but there was no real amusement in the sound. "I suppose you'd like to raid my weapons supply, while you're at it."

We all looked at one another.

"You got extra ammo for M-4s?" Gentry asked hopefully.

"What do you think?"

Nathan was the master of the non-answer. But after

a moment, he nodded, looking like he'd just stepped in zombie shit.

"Come on," he said. "You're gonna need help lugging stuff."

"So we get to see the gunroom?" Tony nodded. "Sweet."

Nathan rolled his eyes.

"Where are those bad-ass cheerleaders when you need 'em?"

He strode down the hall, and I admit that I was hot on his heels, curious as hell to see what the gunroom looked like. I had a picture in my head of Burt Gummer's basement, racks and cases of guns and ammo lining the walls.

The image wasn't far off.

Turned out the door opened onto a staircase. That descended into a room with a concrete floor and walls, and what looked like an ammo tumbler on a workbench in one corner.

When the hell did I start recognizing things like ammo tumblers, I asked myself. I wondered if Nathan had an elephant gun. He had a lot of stuff California law enforcement would frown upon, although it was probably legal in Texas.

Gabriel looked around, eyebrows raised. He could have been reading my mind.

"I hope you realize you're in possession of some highly illegal materiel," he said.

"Depends on who you talk to," Nathan replied coolly. "Let's just say I've earned the right to bear arms."

"And flamethrowers?" Gentry slapped one of two green tanks attached to a metal and canvas frame, with what looked like a high-tech gasoline hose and nozzle. "Military issue, no less."

Nathan shrugged.

"It's impolite to question a man who's about to loan you munitions," he said.

Way to evade, I thought. But I agreed with him. He didn't have to help us. We'd led a shitload of zombies to his front door. And while I'm not usually an anarchist, as far as I was concerned, he had the right to all the privacy he wanted.

Gentry, Kai, and Tony wandered the room, *oohing* and *ahhing* over weaponry the way my mom waxed enthusiastic over luxury yarns in her local knitting store. Even Lil was looking around with an expression of curiosity mixed with awe.

"Okay, people," Nathan said. "Stop gawking and get your asses over here." He pointed to one of the modular storage containers, neatly labeled "M-4."

"There's your ammo." He pointed to another drawer. "Magazines." Then he opened a locked metal cabinet that held half a dozen M-4s. "Extra rifles."

Nathan pulled a couple of firearms out of another cabinet. I have no idea what type they were, but from the looks on Gabriel and Gentry's faces, they had to be a weapons lover's wet dream.

"How the hell did you get K-11s?" Gentry was practically drooling.

Nathan just gave a lopsided grin.

I noticed a second door at the far end of the room.

"Does that go outside?" I asked.

Nathan nodded.

"Up to the carport. Always have a backup exit."

"He's one of those survivalists," Tony observed.

"Pretty smart there, Captain Obvious," I said.

He flipped me the bird.

Nathan handed out M-4s and let us replenish our ammo pouches with rounds from the drawer. I felt like a pirate running my fingers through treasure as I scooped out enough rounds to stuff my pouch. I shoved a couple of magazines into my pockets.

I was, as they say, loaded for zombies. Okay, maybe they don't say that, but I do.

"We should leave this way," Nathan gestured toward the back exit, addressing Gabriel. "If we can get to my truck without the zombies seeing us, we stand a better chance of making it out of here."

Gabriel frowned.

"Whoever opens the gate will be ripped to pieces."

"Like I said," Nathan replied, "Always have two exits." He grabbed the flamethrower. "And a little extra firepower."

Gabriel just gazed at him while Tony and Gentry grinned at one another, high on testosterone. Nathan held up a couple of backpacks.

"These are already full. Who wants 'em?"

Kai took both.

"I'll give one to Mack," he said, "and help him bring Kaitlyn down." He stuffed a few more rounds in his pouch and headed back up the stairs.

Nathan shut the gun lockers, then turned to me.

"Ashley, can you grab the first-aid kit?"

"You mean that big honkin' mini-fridge?"

He grinned.

"Yeah, that's the one. But don't worry, it's lighter than it looks." He held up the flamethrower. "Any of you know how to use this?"

Tony reluctantly shook his head. I could see he was itching to try it out, though.

Gentry stepped forward.

"I'll take it." Nathan held the tanks while Gentry slipped it on over his shoulders and fastened the canvas buckle around his waist.

"You look like a Ghostbuster," Tony said enviously.

I grinned involuntarily as I ran back upstairs. I'd been thinking the same thing myself.

I almost ran into Mack and Kai helping Kaitlyn down the hall. She was supporting a little of her own weight now, but there was something about her skin tone and the tight, fragile look around her eyes that still didn't bode well.

"They're all over the fence," Kai said, jerking his head toward the front window. "It's only a matter of time before they get past the razor wire—probably because it'll be clogged with zombie flesh. We'd better get out of here fast, or we're not going anywhere."

"I'll be right down," I said. As soon as they cleared the hall and started down the stairs, I dashed to the living room and grabbed the first-aid kit. It really did weigh a lot less than you'd think.

Either that, or I can lift a lot more than I think.

Before I went back downstairs, I couldn't resist a peek out the living room window. When I saw what was out there, I wished I'd had better restraint. Zombies lined the fence, two and three deep, more pushing against those in front as they reached the top of the slope. They were packed against it so thickly, I couldn't see anything beyond.

Even though the house seemed to be soundproofed, I could hear their keening, as if it was distant. How the hell Nathan expected to get the truck past them was anyone's guess. I assumed he had a plan.

Letting the curtain drop, I hurried back downstairs, carrying the first-aid kit. Everyone but Gabriel and Nathan had already headed out the back door. Gabriel came forward to meet me, and he put a hand on my shoulder.

"You okay with that thing?"

"I'm fine," I said. I don't know if it was possible seeing how I was wearing body armor, but I swear I felt heat from his hand pouring into my body.

Nathan cleared his throat.

"We need to get out of here," he said. "Take this." He tossed a full duffle bag to Gabriel, who took his hand from my shoulder just in time to catch it.

I shot Nathan a dirty look as we passed him. But he just shut the door and followed us down a short cement hall to another staircase, this one leading upward to a metal door which opened into the back of the canvas carport.

Out here the moaning of the zombies was loud, coming from everywhere. I recognized the big-ass truck Nathan had driven the night he'd saved me and Lil, and somehow I didn't think he was driving it to compensate for a small penis.

Kaitlyn was already settled into the bed of the truck near the cab. It was lined with furniture pads. Mack settled in next to her, wearing one of Nathan's backpacks. Gentry climbed in, too, and hefted the flamethrower. Lil started to join them, but I put a hand on her arm.

"How about you go in the cab, and I'll help Mack with Kaitlyn."

"You sure?" Lil's face was strained. I could tell the thought of curling up in the back of the cab appealed to her.

"Definitely." I caught Nathan looking at us with what looked like a small smile of approval.

Gabriel frowned.

"Ashley, you ride in the cab, too."

"Hell, no," I said. "I got carsick the last time I rode in that thing. You ride up there."

"I'm the best shot here," Gabriel insisted. "So I'm in the truck bed. No arguments."

"Fine," I said. "So Tony and Kai can ride in the cab. I'm a better shot than both of them put together."

"She has a point," Kai said.

With that, Gabriel gave up. Weapons and first-aid kit stowed, we finally got everyone in the truck. Mack and I hunkered down on either side of Kaitlyn, like two protective bookends. Gentry and Gabriel perched at the foot of the bed, looking like action figures. Our helmets were back on, straps secured.

"You people ready?" Nathan started the engine without waiting for an answer. At the sound of its growl, the moans of the living dead rose in volume. They knew it meant food.

Mack looked out at the zombies and shook his head.

"They'll just swarm the truck."

I shared his concern, but hid it.

"This guy is good," I said. "He has something up his sleeve—I'd bet my life on it."

"Whatever it is," Mack answered, "I hope it explodes."

CHAPTER FORTY

The monster truck roared out of the carport and around to the far left side of the fence where there was, indeed, another gate—also thick with zombies. Stopping a few feet from it, Nathan leaned out the driver's side window and shouted.

"Fire in the hole!"

With that he tossed something over the barrier.

We all ducked down, Mack sheltering Kaitlyn with his body as the something exploded, sending dirt, rocks, and zombie debris flying through the air. We stayed down until it stopped raining pieces.

When I stuck my head back up, there were a lot fewer zombies, but the gate was still intact.

He sure knows how to build 'em.

A low hum sounded as it slowly rumbled open on its tracks. Nathan pulled the truck up to block as much of the opening as possible. As soon as enough space had been cleared, he edged the truck through the opening.

Zombies immediately closed in on us. Gabriel began taking out the ones on the left, while I took aim at the ones on the right. For each one I hit, he took out three.

As soon as we were clear, the gate reversed on its tracks. Most of the zombies lurched after the truck, which had yet to pick up speed, but a few headed into the compound. Gabriel took care of those with casual ease while Gentry sent a blast from the flamethrower into the ones right behind us.

The truck headed down an incredibly narrow, bumpy stretch of dirt that didn't even qualify as a road. Mack did his best to shield Kaitlyn from the worst of the bone-jarring jolts, but every so often she gave out a gasp of pain.

Even over the rumble of the engine we could hear the moans of the living dead. The woods seemed to be full of them, resulting in a foggy Dante-esque landscape.

We hit the bottom of the trail, which thankfully opened up onto a respectable paved one-lane road. As Nathan picked up speed, I glimpsed a couple of scattered houses on either side, barely visible in the mist.

"Anyone know where we are?" Gabriel asked over the increasing roar of the wind.

"I think this hooks up with Redwood Highway," Mack said. "We should be in the clear once we reach that."

The zombies thinned out, but their ululations followed us down the road, and more appeared on either side. It was as if they were tracking us via a sort of hive mind or something equally Stephen Kingy.

"How are they all finding us?" I asked Gabriel, who was perched against the truck gate as he reloaded clips for his gun. "It's like they're all on the same frequency or something."

Gabriel slapped a new clip into the M-4.

"Remember what Professor Fraser said about swarms?" he said. I nodded. I hadn't liked the sound of it then, either.

"Well, this is a classic example. It doesn't happen very often, but every now and then they'll fixate on one target—or targets—and the moans act like a series of signal beacons."

Suddenly I understood.

"That means they'll follow us to campus, doesn't it?"

Gabriel nodded.

"Unless Nathan can shake them," he said.

"And if he can't?"

"Then we have to make a stand at Big Red," he said. "And if we can't hold out..."

He didn't have to finish his sentence.

Nuke 'em from orbit. It's the only way to be sure.

"Here's Redwood Highway," Mack said, his voice optimistic.

Gentry turned to look at him.

"This goes right past Redwood Grove, doesn't it?" Mack nodded.

"Right on the outskirts, yeah. Then it heads straight up to the college." Gentry frowned at that.

"If the zombies in town hook up with the ones on our tail now, that's asking for trouble," he said.

That didn't make sense. Nathan was smarter than that. Then it hit me.

"I bet he's going to take the logging trail." I peered into the woods, trees and dim figures passing by in a blur.

We neared the town and Nathan took a sudden hard left. Trees butted up against the road on one side, and what residents jokingly referred to as the 'burbs lined the other. Our path was refreshingly clear of the walking dead, but their wails could still be heard behind us. The eerie sound seemed to fill the entire redwood forest.

Nathan slowed the truck down a bit—just enough to take the Mr. Toad's Wild Ride out of the experience, at least for the moment. I can't say I exactly relaxed, but a little bit of the tension left my body.

Then the road curved around to the right, every bit of tension returned, and it brought some friends along. The route heading east crawled with zombies, the thickest I'd seen them since we'd left Nathan's compound. They were already turning toward us, their moans joining those of their brethren.

Nathan sped up again, fast enough to plow through those in front and avoid the clutching hands of the ones closing in from the sides. Gabriel, Gentry, and I held on as best we could while trying to keep our weapons at the ready.

I so did not envy Gentry that flamethrower. He looked pretty steady, though, and kept his balance like a sailor dealing with rough seas.

"This is bad," Gabriel muttered. "I think we've got two separate swarms, and now they're both going to follow us back to the campus. If we can even get through."

Nathan abruptly hit the brakes, the truck slamming to a stop so suddenly that it nearly dislodged Gabriel and Gentry from the back of the bed. My helmet banged against the window of the cab before I went sprawling forward, almost landing on top of Gabriel. We quickly recovered our positions, and saw why Nathan had stopped.

We'd reached Maple Street, and if we thought it had been occupied by a steady stream of zombies before, the stream had turned into a river, with waves of them rolling toward the little stone church nestled among the trees on the left.

"Shit," Gentry muttered. "I sure as hell hope he has another grenade."

Gabriel took careful aim and took out a pajama-clad zombie approaching the truck.

"They might not follow us after all," he said. "They really want whoever's in that church." Even as he said it, though, a current of the undead turned toward the truck.

"Shit," he said. "I think we've got their attention."

A groan next to my ear caused me to jump. Kaitlyn rolled over and winced.

"I think I'm going to be sick," she whispered. She tried to say something else, but Nathan hollered and drowned her out.

"Fire in the hole, fore and aft!"

We hit the deck as he lobbed two grenades this time, one into the crowd on Maple Street, the other behind the truck as far as he could pitch it. Luckily the man had an arm worthy of an All-Star pitcher.

I heard Mack cry out as the concussion from both blasts rattled the truck and our brains. Once again it rained zombie bits. I raised my head and some indefinable goo dripped off the front of my helmet. Grimacing, I wiped it off, and then noticed that Kaitlyn was no longer in the truck bed.

Mack lay a couple of feet away, stunned by the blast, his expression dazed.

"Kaitlyn?" I shouted, my ears still ringing.

"Over here!" came the muffled response. I sat up, looking over the edge of the truck toward the sound of her voice.

She was staggering across the road, her way cleared by the grenade. Looking as clumsy as any zombie, she paused at the edge of the tree line. Swaying unsteadily on her feet, she waved both arms above her head.

The wound in her neck started to bleed again.

And then I froze as I realized she hadn't been talking to me.

"Over here!" she yelled again. "This way!"

"Kaitlyn, what the *hell* are you doing?" I bellowed.

She flashed me a weak smile and continued yelling.

The engine gunned, and I pounded on the back of the cab.

"Nathan, don't go yet!"

"Are you bat-shit?" he yelled back. "Why the hell not?"

"It's Kaitlyn!" I pointed in the direction of the trees where she continued to holler and wave. Zombies started to notice her, turning toward the sound like compass needles discovering true north.

Gabriel scrambled unsteadily to his feet.

"Kaitlyn, get back here!" he shouted.

She just ignored him. Cursing, he shouldered his M-4 and began picking off zombies as they neared her. Some still honed in on the truck, but Gentry switched to his rifle and took care of those.

"Get that woman back in the truck!" Nathan yelled. "We've got a very small window to get across the River Styx here before they close the gap."

"Kaitlyn, get your ass back here!" Gabriel tried again. She just shook her head.

"I'll lead them away." With that, she slowly backed into the trees, waving and yelling, "Come and get me! This way!" More zombies followed, moaning louder as they did.

Gabriel swore again, slamming his hand against the side of the truck.

"I'm going to get her."

Mack, in the meantime, had struggled to a crouching position.

"Jesus," he said, "she'll be torn to pieces." He watched in horror as she vanished into the trees. "She'll never be able to outrun them."

Before any of us could stop him, he grabbed his gun and leapt out of the truck bed. He hit the ground, stumbling forward before recovering his balance, then dashing across the road and disappearing into the trees after Kaitlyn.

"Mack!" I screamed. Lil yelled his name, too, her nose plastered against the side window.

More zoms headed toward the truck even as a steady number continued to trickle into the woods. I could still hear the sound of Kaitlyn's voice as she taunted them, and Mack's as he called for her.

God damn *this wild card shit.* For once, I didn't want any senses, enhanced or not.

Nathan stuck his head out the window.

"We have to go, people!"

Gabriel hesitated briefly.

"Go."

His voice was flat.

Nathan gunned the engine and drove quickly across Maple Street. From there he headed out of the town.

Soon enough we turned onto the logging trail. Nathan took the road as fast as possible, but I didn't even notice the jolts this time. My mind still couldn't process what had just happened. Why had Kaitlyn suddenly gone all kamikaze on us? And why had Mack...

Well, I knew why Mack had done what he'd done. To do anything else would have killed his soul.

We'd only seen a few zoms since we left Redwood Grove, but those were enough to start the zombie version of telephone. Which meant that eventually the swarm would find their way to Big Red.

Nathan pulled up alongside the razor wire and we quickly and silently unloaded the gear. There was no time to find a security checkpoint. Gabriel and Tony slipped under the wire, then he stood on top of the cab and we did an assembly line, passing stuff up for Nathan to hand it down to them on the other side.

When we'd gotten everything over the fence, Gabriel and Tony held the wire apart for the rest of us to crawl through. We made our way across campus to Patterson Hall.

No need for secrecy this time.

Whenever one of the soldiers appeared, though, Nathan's expression clearly said that he'd rather be somewhere else.

Colonel Paxton, Simone, and Dr. Albert were waiting for us in the foyer.

"We lost Mack and Kaitlyn," Gabriel said bluntly. For once the Colonel's sad clown features suited the occasion.

And then Nathan and Simone saw each other. They stared for a full beat.

"Hello, Nathan," she said in a voice cool enough to chill wine.

What the hell?

"Oh, Christ on a crutch." Nathan shut his eyes and rubbed a hand on his forehead, as if trying to massage away reality. "Simone Fraser. I should have known you'd be part of this whole clusterfuck."

CHAPTER FORTY-ONE

Exhausted and heartsick, the remaining wild cards gathered in the cafeteria.

Gabriel and Gentry didn't join us.

We huddled dispiritedly together as we picked at our food. I was certain all of us were thinking the same thing. We weren't invulnerable, and we lost two people as a result. Until today none of us had really confronted the fact that our lives were still fragile things and could be lost at any second.

Lil was devastated, silent tears slipping down her face as she stared at her hamburger and fries without touching them. Tony's face was unreadable, but his usual barrage of banter with Kai was totally MIA.

I forced myself to eat, convincing myself that I'd need the fuel for what we'd face when the swarm caught up with us. We might have a few days or we might only have a few hours, so we had to be ready. Yet all I wanted was to forget that the last few hours had ever happened. I wanted Mack to be there with his basset hound eyes and warm smile. I'd have even paid to hear one of Kaitlyn's bitchy remarks. Anything but face the reality of their loss.

So I forced my mind down another path.

"I should have known you'd be part of this whole clusterfuck."

I mean, how weird was that? Nathan had somehow vanished almost immediately, and we'd been hustled off for decontamination before I could corner Simone.

Lil gave a small, choked sob, bringing my attention back to the present.

"There were so many zombies out there," she said. "Why did Kaitlyn do it? If she hadn't, Mack would still be here. We were almost home."

The venom in her voice startled me.

Kaitlyn, I thought. She couldn't have been in her right mind, but she must have thought she was doing the right thing. After what she saw at the rest stop, did she want to die? Or did she just think it was inevitable?

"She was probably delirious," I said carefully. "And I think… she must have heard Gabriel talking about needing a diversion. She probably thought she was helping us."

"But they're still coming," Lil countered. "So it was pointless!" Her voice rose. "Mack sacrificed himself for nothing!" The angry tears were streaming down her face now.

I tried again.

"We don't know that he's dead."

"He *is* dead," she shouted. "He is! I hate her!" With that Lil burst into loud, braying sobs.

"Oh, Lil…" I reached out to hug her, but she shoved me away with enough violence to send me flying out of my chair. I hit the floor with a bone-jarring thud, staring up at Lil in shock.

The room went quiet, the only sound coming from Lil's frantic sobs.

I got to my feet, took a deep breath and put my arms around her, refusing to let go as she thrashed like a child throwing a tantrum, striking out with fists and feet. I held on tightly until she finally subsided, crying heart-brokenly into my shoulder as I stroked her hair, holding back my own tears.

Tony looked uncomfortable with Lil's display of emotion, while Kai seemed sympathetic. But it was Tony who got a couple of damp napkins and handed them to me so I could press them on the back of Lil's neck and forehead as her sobs slowly tapered off.

When she finally had herself under control, he handed her a wad of dry ones so she could blow her nose.

"Thanks." Her voice was small and shaky, but the edge of hysteria had left it. I pushed a hank of hair away from her face.

"You okay?"

Lil nodded.

"I'm sorry," she whispered.

"S'okay." I held her close again.

Someone cleared his throat. We looked up to see Nathan, clean and dressed in fatigues and a black T-shirt, a plate piled high with food in one hand, a glass of milk in the other. We hadn't even heard him come in.

I righted my chair and sat in it again, then took a much-needed sip of wine.

Nathan sat down across from Lil, Tony and Kai scooting their chairs over to make room.

"You okay, kid?" he asked solemnly.

Lil took a deep, quavering breath and nodded.

"Yeah."

"Good. 'Cause while your teammate did a stupid thing there, it was also a brave thing. She figured she was saving the team."

"But Mack…"

"Also did a stupid thing, but it took guts."

Lil looked down at her plate.

"She wasn't worth his life."

Nathan shrugged.

"That's not your call to make. People are who they are, and they're going to do what they think is right. Like you risking your life—and hers—to save those cats." He gestured toward me. "You think if you two had died, the rest of your teammates would've said, 'Gee, they died, but at least they tried to save the cats'?"

"If you want to live with yourself, go after the cat," Lil said softly. Then she gave another coughing sob, and nodded. "Mack wouldn't have been able to live with himself if he hadn't gone after Kaitlyn."

"Probably not." Nathan took a bite of burger, chewing and swallowing before adding, "Now eat some food. We're in for a fight, and I don't want you fainting on us."

To my astonishment, Lil picked up her burger and started eating it without saying another word.

I looked across at Nathan and mouthed *thank you*. He gave an imperceptible nod and took another bite of his burger. I almost asked him about Simone then, but thought twice about it.

It'd wait.

Simone, Colonel Paxton, Gabriel, and Gentry waited for us in room 217, the four of them sitting at the table in front.

Gabriel's expression was grim, but when he glanced up he shot me a smile. It didn't reach his eyes, however.

Nathan sauntered down the aisle and plopped down comfortably in the front row. Simone made a point of not looking at him.

"Just like being back in college," he said.

Once we were all seated, Colonel Paxton stood up.

"Before Dr. Fraser addresses the issue at hand," he said, "I want to tell you how deeply sorry we are for the loss of your fellow wild cards, and how proud we are of you for your bravery." He sat back down.

Short, succinct, and, I thought, sincere. Yet somehow it didn't do anything to ease the pain.

Simone took the floor. She took a deep breath, then finally spoke.

"Early on in this outbreak, we ran across an anomaly, and—"

Tony raised his hand.

"What do you mean, an anomaly?"

"It's a deviation from a common rule," Nathan said, leaning back in his chair, an unreadable expression on his face as he stared at Simone. Just then, I would have killed for the wild card power of telepathy.

"Thank you, Nathan." Simone said pointedly, as she ran a hand through her perfectly coiffed hair. Several strands pulled free, and I feared for them. "As I was saying, we ran across what we thought was a unique case early on in the outbreak. This person contracted the virus and started exhibiting certain characteristics of the undead, but without actually dying.

"We tested a vaccine on him... this person. A vaccine we'd hoped might cure the zombie virus itself. It didn't, but the vaccine *did* halt the progressive deterioration of his immune system."

A picture flashed in my head, of Jake huddled over his wife and child. I knew where this was heading.

"We thought that incident was unique, some sort of a mutation, not unlike the one responsible for the wild cards." she said. "Now we know that it wasn't unique." Simone looked at us gravely, then continued.

"As long as these individuals eat human flesh, they retain their personalities, and slow the progress of the disease. If they don't, however, their bodies will slowly decay, along with memories and cognitive abilities.

"Eventually they will die, and then resurrect as one of the walking dead."

"So it's Hannibal Lecter time, or else," Tony said.

Simone nodded.

"As I said, we thought this was a unique condition. But there have since been two other persons exhibiting these symptoms. One of them was here in the lab, kept under controlled conditions. She did not respond to the vaccine and became violent. And the other—"

"Jake," I said. "It was Jake."

I didn't need Simone's expression to tell me I was right.

And then I looked at Gabriel, whose face was as white as it'd been in the Suburban before we'd crashed. He'd known, too.

I stared at them both in disbelief.

"Why wouldn't you tell us something like this? And Gabriel…" I stopped, heartsick. "I thought we could trust you," I added, looking back and forth between them.

Her expression stricken, Simone spoke.

"If we'd had any idea you'd run into this in the field, I assure you, we would have told you, Ashley."

"But how could you *not* tell us?" I demanded. "Kaitlyn might still be alive if we'd known about this.

"We trusted you. Both of you!" I stood and strode up the aisle. I'd made it halfway to the door when Gabriel's voice reached me.

"We didn't say anything because I was the first person to exhibit the symptoms."

I stopped in my tracks, then slowly turned.

"Until a few days ago, we thought I was the only one," he continued. "We've been wrestling with it ever since. How comfortable would you—all of you—" He gestured around the room. "—have been following me into combat situations, if you'd known the truth?"

I couldn't respond. All I could see was Jake's gore-smeared face. Only this time, the features were Gabriel's.

"We've been trying to find a cure for a very long time—decades, even more," Simone said. "And this vaccine—" She held up a vial. "—proves that we can keep the symptoms at bay, at least in some cases."

I stared at the vial, then at Gabriel, flashing on the difference in his appearance before and after he'd vanished into Nathan's bathroom.

Guess he was carrying.

"Gabriel felt he'd be a more effective team leader if we kept his condition confidential," Simone said. "I agreed to honor his request."

Nathan raised his hand.

"May I say something?" He didn't wait for an answer. "Simone, you need to stop trying to justify an honest mistake on your part. And Ashley, you need to sit your ass down and stop acting like a high school kid who didn't get invited to a party, just because your boyfriend has a few secrets."

My face flamed in embarrassment.

"Fuck you, Nathan!"

He waved a dismissive hand.

"Whatever. You're a civilian combatant in a military unit. Secrets are a part of the game, especially in a black ops unit like this one." He looked me straight in the eyes. "Get over it and get used to it, or get out. We don't have time for this juvenile shit.

"You're better than this," he concluded.

I swallowed a couple of times, and tried to choke out an apology. Then in my mind's eye, I saw Jake biting his dead wife's lip off, and imagined Gabriel doing the same to me.

My stomach lurched and my gorge rose. I gagged and pressed a hand against my mouth, then ran out the door. The last thing I heard before it shut behind me was Gabriel's voice.

"Damn it, she has the right—"

CHAPTER FORTY-TWO

I barely made it to the bathroom before losing my dinner in one hot gush, and then another. I hung over the toilet bowl, shaking with reaction.

Finally, when I was sure nothing else was going to make its return appearance, I moved to the sink, splashing cold water over my face and rinsing my mouth to try and get rid of the nasty-ass aftertaste of vomit.

I hate throwing up.

The door opened.

"Ashley?" I looked in the mirror and saw Gabriel staring at me, as uncertain as I'd ever seen him. "Are you—"

I held up a hand.

"Please don't ask if I'm okay. I am so *not* okay I can't even begin to figure out where to begin." I began to pace back and forth as I continued. "I saw a man, a living, breathing human, eating his wife and son. And now I find out that the man could have been you.

"And I get why you and Simone didn't want to tell the team, I really do. But—"

I stopped pacing, and faced him.

"Is that the only reason?"

Gabriel took a deep breath, eyes dark blue with turmoil.

"I mean, is this why you didn't, you know, you wouldn't, with me…" God, could I sound any stupider?

"Ash, you have to understand," he said. "I don't know what's going to happen with this condition."

"Oh, for fuck's sake." I slammed one hand against the sink. "So you have some zombie STD. I'm a wild card, remember?"

His eyes narrowed and he took a step toward me.

"That doesn't guarantee a goddamn thing."

"Fine, but I want to know if it's the reason you wouldn't go to bed with me or—" I closed the gap between us and glared up at him. "—if it's just some lame-ass excuse."

"Damn it, Ashley, you don't understand!"

"Then explain it to me." We had approximately a half-inch of space between our bodies, every bit filled with heat.

"It's worse than being a zombie, because zombies can't think or feel. But being alive—or half dead—and knowing you're eating human flesh, that you *have* to if you want to stay alive…" He shuddered. "It's disgusting."

"So you decided to reject me before I had the chance to reject you," I countered.

"Of course not! That's abs—"

I stopped him short with just a stare. I could feel the anger welling up in me.

"As far as you were concerned, it was okay for me to think there was something wrong with me," I said. "*Much* better than having me think there might be something wrong with *you*."

"That's not—" I held up my hand, and he stopped again.

"Yes it is," I said. "That's *exactly* what it boiled down to. And you know it."

"Ashley, damn it—"

I grabbed a handful of Gabriel's hair with one hand and locked lips with him. He responded by wrapping an arm around my waist, pressing his other hand against my butt, lifting me up to set me on the edge of one of the sinks. We continued to kiss feverishly, hungrily as if this were our last night on earth. Our hands roamed up and down each other's bodies, finding curves and muscles, hardness and softness.

Parting my legs with his knee, he pressed himself against me, the heat and the hardness of his arousal almost enough to make me come on the spot.

I pulled his T-shirt over his head and tossed it on the floor. My long-sleeve thermal followed. He dipped his head down to my breasts, teasing each peak with teeth and tongue until the sensation was just short of painful, a real 'it hurts so good'-type of feeling. I gasped as his fingers slid past the waistband of my yoga pants, slipping into my warmth with smoothness and ease, showing us both how ready and eager my body was to get down to business.

I arched against him, wanting more than his hands and fingers, as talented as they might be.

"Do you want this?" Gabriel whispered, nipping at my earlobe.

"Shut up," I growled.

He withdrew his hand, hooking those clever fingers in my waistband as he lifted me up with his other hand and pulled my yoga pants and underwear down and off my legs and feet. They joined the growing pile of clothes on the floor.

I reached down greedily to unbutton his jeans and started to shimmy them off his hips when he pulled away.

"Wait a second," he said

Going to the bathroom door, he flipped the lock and went to the condom machine on the wall, giving it a hard *thwack* with one fist. The little metal door creaked open and several foil wrapped condoms dropped to the floor. Gabriel scooped one up.

"We can owe them."

He then slid out of his jeans, kicking them to the floor, and came back over to me. I watched as he approached, admiring his physique. He was built like a classical Greek statue, rather than a gym junkie.

He stared at me just as hungrily.

We didn't waste any time. We couldn't indulge in a long, languorous session of hot-monkey love. We had to get back to the briefing.

We also knew that we might be dead in the next forty-eight hours.

But the moment Gabriel slid inside of me and we began rocking our hips together, the world went away for a while. Everything was centered around the heat of our bodies, the sensations building in me as I wrapped my legs around his hips, the sink cold against my butt.

His mouth trailed from my lips to my ear, where he nibbled on the lobe, moving down to my neck. A brief vision of Jake's bloody mouth flashed into my head.

No!

I forced it away. Instead, I reveled in the feeling of his teeth gently scraping against the skin. My hips began to rock faster of their own accord, the first flickers of an orgasm starting to pulse in all the right places, spreading through my body in waves of liquid heat. My muscles tightened around Gabriel, who groaned with pleasure as the pace of his thrusts increased in speed and power.

The words 'harder, faster' came to mind, followed by 'pussycat, kill, kill' and I started laughing even as I came in a great quivering wave of pleasure.

Gabriel's orgasm followed almost immediately, the shudders that racked his body sending more ripples through my loins along with another, smaller orgasm.

Two for the price of one.

Then his hands cupped my face. For a moment we just looked at each other, each catching our breath as the last aftershocks left our bodies.

He cocked an eyebrow, still breathing just a little heavily. "Why did you laugh?"

I told him, figuring he might as well know how my

brain worked. A bemused smile flickered across.

"I know I'm weird," I said, "but—"

"Yes, you are." The smile became a grin. "But you're sure as hell not boring." He kissed me again, then looked at me.

"Ashley…" He stared at me so seriously it almost made me laugh again. Luckily I didn't. "You know what I could become. You've seen it. Are you sure about…" He paused.

"About what? About the fact I want you so badly that I just had sex with you in the women's bathroom?" I nodded. "Yes. I'm sure. Just promise me you'll trust me next time."

"Next time…?"

I shrugged.

"Next time you have some horrible secret that you think you shouldn't tell me. I mean, I'm a mutant too, y'know?"

"Fair enough."

He kissed me one more time, then reluctantly slid out of me. I let him go just as reluctantly, but we had serious business to attend to, and I'm sure everyone was already wondering why we'd been gone so long.

Doing a quick clean-up, we both hurriedly dressed. I splashed water on my face again and checked for any obvious signs of our activity.

"You gave me a hickey," I said, looking at the bite marks between my neck and shoulder.

He pulled my thermal up a little higher and hid it.

"No one will notice."

I gave a little laugh.

"Besides, Nathan already thinks you're my boyfriend." I unlocked the bathroom door and reached for the handle, but Gabriel grabbed my wrist and turned me around to face him.

"So. If we survive, would you like to go out some time?"

"As long as it's not for tofu burgers, you got a date."

We walked down the hall hand in hand, unclasping our fingers only when we reached room 217. I took a deep breath and went inside, Gabriel close behind.

Was I embarrassed? Sure. No one likes to lose it in front of friends and colleagues. But as Nathan pointed out, now wasn't the time for high school shit, so I'd suck it up and act like an adult.

CHAPTER FORTY-THREE

Nathan had joined Simone, Paxton, and Gentry at the table in the front of the room. Taking his place in the pack as one of the alpha dogs.

Simone looked concerned when we walked in.

"We have a swarm headed our way," she said, and my blood ran cold. "With arrival estimated in approximately twelve hours. Nathan—" Her tone became oddly formal. "—if you'd be so kind."

Nathan nodded.

"We have around eighty trained soldiers, fifty noncoms, two hundred civilians, and an additional thirty or so survivors who may or may not be of any use. Doesn't sound like a lot when you think about what's going to be coming at us."

Sure doesn't, I thought, sitting back in the front row next to Lil. She sat stiffly, and didn't say anything.

"You ever see a movie called *Zulu*?" Nathan didn't wait for a reply, even though Tony's hand shot up immediately. "Less than a hundred and fifty British soldiers held off between two and three thousand Zulu warriors at a place called Rorke's Drift by erecting barricades of wagons and sacks of grain, then employing a classic military tactic.

"Stand fast, fire in ranks. Three lines." Nathan got to his feet and started pacing. "First rank fires, drops down.

Second rank steps up while first rank reloads. Third rank fires while second rank reloads. Oh, yeah, and these Zulus—who happened to be some of the fiercest warriors in the world—were charging the Brits at a dead run, with shields, spears, and even some rifles of their own. But at the end of the day it was the English who walked away from that fight."

Wow, I thought. I'd been expecting something along the lines of, *They can take our brains, but they'll never take our freedom!*

He looked at us intently.

"We've got less than a hundred soldiers against a few thousand zombies. But the zombies don't have weapons and will be coming at us a lot slower than the Zulus, with none of the strategy. Plus we'll have a few other tricks up our sleeves."

"What if it doesn't come down like that?" Tony said. "You ever see *Zulu Dawn*? In that one the soldiers are, like, totally obliterated by the Zulus."

Nathan just looked at him, then scanned the room.

"Anyone else got any movie trivia to share?" He came back to Tony, who pushed himself deeper into his seat.

"No? Good. So let's discuss the rest of our assets."

"Damn, I so want one of those."

Tony stared enviously as Gentry walked up, carrying his flamethrower. Gentry grinned and brandished the nozzle, the tanks already strapped to his back.

"Maybe when you're a little older, X-Box."

"Can I have a flamethrower?" Lil poked her head up from behind a bench where she sat loading ammo into a clip. As usual, it took the promise of mayhem to get her to join the conversation. But given how devastated Mack's death had left her, I was cautiously relieved.

Gentry patted her on her helmet. "If you're very good,

Santa might put one in your stocking." She answered with a dirty look.

The wild cards crouched on the inner side of Mount Gillette where it ran the length of the main parking lot. Gabriel was out with Nathan and the rest of the soldiers, setting up lines on the far side of the barricade. They'd built a couple of makeshift wooden ramps on either side, so our people could go back and forth with relative ease.

Most of the remaining soldiers, Alpha, Beta and assorted personnel, were already in position at various points along the barrier, watching for the swarm. Aerial recon confirmed that the majority of the zombies were approaching along the road that ran directly from town, right up into the parking lot—flat and empty, easy to cross.

Abandoned cars had been moved, parked nose to tail across the outer edge of the lot to create an additional barrier. We had sharpshooters up in strategic places to take out as many zombies as possible, and several lookouts spread around the perimeter of the campus to catch stragglers coming from other directions.

The fog lay heavy in the air again, thick and moist and cold. Once again the cosmic FX designer had given us the perfect day to battle hordes of the undead.

What's wrong with a little sunshine? I wondered.

The air itself smelled of eucalyptus, sea salt from the ocean, and something else—a faintly rotten taint wafting in on the currents. What breeze there was carried the moans of the damned—or was that my imagination?

It didn't matter. The swarm was on its way, and soon enough the smell of putrefied flesh would fill our senses.

I still wanted to know what the story was with Nathan and Simone. And why was it that Colonel Paxton seemed content to have Nathan take the lead in what was his operation? But explanations would have to wait.

We'd stayed up late into the night figuring out how we were going to face what could be several thousand zombies with a ragtag group, some of whom would be more liability than asset on the battlefield. And then there were the survivors who still hadn't come to grips with the fact the dead had returned to life. They could barely function on a day-to-day basis, let alone fight against something they refused to accept was real. They'd stay in the secure lower floors of Patterson Hall while the rest of us fought.

If we lost, well, they'd be blissfully unaware of it right up to the moment the military dropped a tactical nuke.

For the moment, though, we had to unload the stuff we'd lugged from Nathan's armory and divvy it up among the soldiers and those civilians who were willing and able to fight. We had little canvas backpacks piled up, each one waiting to be stuffed.

Tony and Kai dragged out a pair of battered metal cases from the cache we'd brought with us. Tony opened one that held racks and racks of tiny little metal darts, each about the size of a six-penny nail with bright red and yellow fins.

"What are these?" He held up one of the glittering little arrows. Fingers immediately plucked it from his hand.

"I call them 'déjà vus.'" Nathan didn't quite materialize from the fog, but his appearance was unexpected enough to make us all jump. I suspect he did it on purpose. "You can fire them from a rigged handgun like this—" He reached into the larger case and picked up what looked like a modified paintball gun.

"We've also got them packed into claymore dispersal platforms which we'll plant in strategic locations. Those will launch a shitload of them all at once, sending them in a specifically aimed arc.

"Nice for crowded parties."

He loaded the dart into the gun he was holding, took aim at the closest trashcan, and fired. There was a deep metallic *thunk*.

I raised a hand.

"Um, I hate to say it," I commented, "but that was kind of underwhelming."

Nathan shot me a look.

"Not done yet. Two things: One, each flechette—"

"Flechette?"

"Dart. Each dart has a little RIFD chip in it, just like the tags they use in department stores to prevent shoplifting." He took out a small rectangular object from his vest pocket. "This is the transmitter. It sends a radio signal to activate the dart, wherever it might be, like so.

"Fire in the hole," he added.

We dove for cover as Nathan knelt and thumbed the big red button. The trashcan vanished, blossoming into a fireball with an earsplitting explosion.

"Item two," he said. "The dart's fins are made of plastic explosive."

"Okay, that's impressive," I said, ears ringing.

"Totally awesome," Tony breathed.

Nathan held up a hand.

"But here's the downside, party people. The signal strength is severely limited. You've got an effective range of about thirty feet, tops. So the transmitters have to be carried onto the battlefield. And that's a suicide mission for anyone not immune to the zombie virus, what with all that hot blood and goo splattering around.

"So the wild cards will be the ones carrying the transmitters out into the swarm."

"How is that *not* a suicide mission?" Kai muttered.

Nathan tossed him a knapsack.

"Load these puppies in with the ammo. I'll get the rest of them out of the truck." He strode back off toward Mount Gillette as a golf cart pulled up, driven by Jamie with Simone as passenger. Both wore combat gear, and both made it look good. Jamie smiled at me as they stepped out of the cart and I gave a little wave.

That still feels weird, I thought. But I didn't say anything.

Tony checked her out with an appreciative eye.

"You look sharp in Rambo gear," he said, oozing charisma. She eyed him back with a noticeable lack of appreciation and turned away without saying a word. Yet he didn't seem to mind. He was too busy checking out her butt.

Simone took in what we were all doing, picking up a knapsack stuffed full of ammo clips and déjà vu darts.

"Almost done then?" she asked, and I nodded. "Good. Jamie and I will help hand them out. We'll each need one, too."

"You're going with us?" I didn't bother hiding my surprise.

"You need as many capable fighters as possible." Simone picked up an M-4 and several clips. She looked *very* capable. "Although I did promise the Colonel that I'd fall back if necessary."

"What about Nathan?" Okay, I couldn't resist it. "Did you promise him, too?"

Simone shot me a sideways look.

"Nathan," she said, "has no control over my actions."

I was still wrestling with tact when Tony decided it was completely unnecessary.

"Like, did you guys used to date, or what?" he asked.

Simone raised a patrician eyebrow.

"Now is hardly the time to discuss this."

"But you knew each other, like, before, right?" Lily popped up like a little Whack-A-Mole. Nice to see her interested in something other than bloodshed.

Simone looked as if she'd just stepped in something foul, but we all stared at her expectantly.

"Come on, Simone," I wheedled. "We may all die in the next few hours. Don't make us die with our curiosity unsatisfied."

She stared at me.

"Some would call that emotional blackmail, you know." She sounded entirely serious.

I shrugged, grinning at her.

"Inquiring minds wanna know."

Simone took one more glance around. Even Jamie looked hopeful. So she threw her hands in the air.

"Oh, good god," she said. "Nathan was an Army Ranger in Pakistan. We met in Kyrgyzstan. Our missions… overlapped."

"Did he know about the zombies?" I asked. I figured there had to have been zombies if Simone was involved.

"Nope. But I figured it out." Nathan reappeared, carrying more cases of déjà vu darts.

Simone bristled, as out of sorts as I'd ever seen her.

"Probably wouldn't have gotten definite proof if I hadn't got bit," he added, then he nodded to Simone. "Your crew was really good at the cover-up. But I saw and heard enough to confirm that some of the things in our nightmares are real. It also confirmed that I had a damned good reason to be paranoid about the military.

"And women," he added.

Simone looked like an irate feline who'd just had its fur stroked the wrong way.

"You, of all people, knew the importance of maintaining secrecy in covert operations," she replied. "Yet you expected me to disobey my orders, just for the sake of a pair of brown eyes and strong shoulders." She stopped, as if grasping for words. "Well, that was long ago. I suggest you simply get over it."

She turned and stalked off, as angry as I'd ever seen her. Jamie shot Nathan a glare, and hurried after her.

Nathan shrugged.

"Oh, well, at least the sex was great." Then he walked off in the opposite direction.

"Ohmigod," I muttered. "Definitely TMI."

"Totally," Tony agreed.

CHAPTER FORTY-FOUR

A shout went out over the barricade.

The tension in the air went from palpable to physical, so thick I could cut it with my katana. The slight tinge of rot in the mist thickened to a visceral stench of putrefying flesh and rotten blood—to the point that I fumbled for my nose plugs.

The dead were walking, and headed straight for us.

A hand came down on my shoulder. I recognized Gabriel's touch even through the armor and padding.

"The first ones have reached the edge of the woods," he said quietly.

I nodded, suddenly shy.

Of all the stupid times to go tongue-tied.

Gabriel peered around.

"A lot of these people will never be ready for what's coming," he said. "They're just doing the best they can in a situation they could never have imagined would be real." Then he looked at me. "But you take what comes at you, and roll with it. Not bad for a Liberal Arts major."

I smacked him on the arm.

"Thanks. I think." We stood in silence for a few seconds.

"Can we win this?" I didn't really expect an answer.

"I don't know." Gabriel looked out toward the edge of the campus. "Nathan knows what he's doing, and

Colonel Paxton is smart enough to check his ego at the door. But the numbers and the odds…"

"Let's hope we do a *Zulu* instead of a *Zulu Dawn*."

"Pretty much."

We stared at each. I leaned closer, and—

"It's okay, Rico… *cough cough*." Tony grinned at us. "I don't mind dying, because I got to have you." Another dramatic cough.

Kai snickered.

"I hate you, Tony." I spoke with great sincerity.

Gabriel looked at him.

"One of these days, Tony, you'll be old enough to have a sex life," he said. "And when you are, I hope you've got something more meaningful than movie quotes up your ass.

"That is, if you live past today."

A shout went up from the barricades. Gabriel's expression went totally grim.

"You guys ready?" he said, and we all nodded. "Good. You have five minutes to finish up here and get your asses into rank." He gave me a last look before vanishing up over the ramp to the other side.

I got nose to nose with Tony.

"If you say 'shit just got real,' I swear I will kill you here and now."

Tony held up both hands in a "who, me?" gesture, and popped in his ear buds. I smacked his arm, hard.

"Hey!"

"What?"

I pulled the bud out of his left ear.

"This! You can't wear your friggin' iPod into battle. What if we need you?"

Rolling his eyes, Tony grabbed the dangling bud and pulled it back.

"It's only for the first few minutes, okay?" he replied.

"Why?"

"Just listen." He stuck the bud in my ear. I listened to

a few bars of a dramatic film score before taking it out.

"So why?" I repeated.

"It's 'March of the Dead' from *Army of Darkness*. I want to be listening to it when the zombies start crossing the field." He looked entirely serious. "I mean, if I might die today, I want good music to go out by."

What could I say? It was like wishing for an orchestral last meal.

"Just leave the iPod behind when we're out on the field, okay?"

Tony gave what might have been a nod or could have been a subtle "fuck you." Then he clambered up onto Mount Gillette to watch for the approaching army of the dead.

Lil stood up, M-4 in hand, pickaxe strapped to her back. I put a hand on her shoulder.

"You gonna be okay?"

She gave me a weary smile.

"Yeah. I just miss Mack."

"We all do." I hugged her and she threw both arms around me and clutched me tightly. Our various weapons and accoutrements clashed and clanked and stuck in painful places, but it didn't matter. I realized again that I'd die to keep Lil safe.

"Wild cards!" It was Gentry. "Time to dance!" He stood on top of the barricade next to Tony and grinned down at us. "You ready to do this?"

Lil, Kai, and I looked at each other and then up at Gentry. We yelled in unison.

"Hell, no!"

"Good! Get your asses into line!" he said. "This one's for Mack and Kaitlyn."

CHAPTER FORTY-FIVE

I glanced at Tony. The ear buds were in, and his eyes were shining with anticipation as zombies slowly poured out of the tree line into the field.

"My lord, the army of the dead approaches," he said softly. Then, as promised, he yanked out the buds, tucked them carefully in his vest pocket and grinned at me.

I gave him a thumbs-up.

An explosion rocked the field as a zombie stumbled onto one of the claymores. One of the soldiers in the front row fired off a few rounds.

"Don't waste ammo!" Colonel Paxton shouted. "They're not in range! Wait for my signal. Then first rank, fire at will."

Blurred faces in the distance started taking on distinct, rotting features as the first of the swarm closed the gap. The zombies' genders became apparent, along with the hideous wounds that had killed them. I could see remnants of designer jeans and tops, dresses, a few business suits, lots of flannel shirts, and—in one heartbreaking instance—Hello Kitty pajamas on what used to be a little girl. Having the time to see the zombies without the distraction of killing them really sucked.

I silently begged Colonel Paxton to give the order to fire.

"First rank, ready… fire!"

Thank you!

The first rank opened fire in controlled three-round bursts, thirty or forty rounds per gun. *Bap bap bap, bap bap bap*, the three-beat staccato, over and over again until their rounds were spent. A light haze of smoke drifted through the ranks, mixing in with the fog.

"First rank, fall back!"

The first rank stepped back as the second rank stepped into position, sighting and firing as soon as we were in place.

Bap bap bap. The little girl went down.

Hello, Kitty, bye-bye.

My rounds went quickly, even with careful sighting. Second rank finished and we dropped back to let the third rank move into place. I ejected the spent clip and someone immediately handed me a fresh one. It was Jamie, still looking terrified but determined. She handed a clip to Lil, too, who had that "Aieee Kali!" light of battle in her eyes again.

Third rank dropped back, the first rank ready to step up. And the dance started over again.

My ears rang with the sound of gunfire, the shouts of men and the moaning howls of the dead providing a muted backdrop for the constant chatter of rifles. Hot brass littered the ground, and now and again an explosion marked the detonation of another claymore.

Our initial goal was to stop them from getting past the cars at the edge of the lot. If too many of them made it that far, we'd have to take the field.

Some of the better marksmen used each shot to lethal effect, every bullet taking out a zombie. I could only aspire to that kind of marksmanship. This went on for what could have been minutes or hours—hard to tell when your ears are ringing and your shoulder's numb from the kick of your gun. All of the shooters were tired, and there was no time for breaks. All each person could do was grab a quick swallow of water when it was their turn to reload.

Very quickly it became obvious the swarm hadn't been thinned by much. Despite the growing number of unmoving corpses now littering the field, more zombies continued to stagger implacably from the road and the street. They were angling in from the sides as well, which meant some of our shooters had to peel off from the straight ranks.

Distant explosions, punctuated by intermittent gunfire, signaled that at least a few zombies were approaching from the other side of campus. The guards stationed there would signal by flare if it got out of hand. Paxton and Nathan were banking that it wouldn't, though, since the zombies weren't capable of strategy.

I hoped to god they were right, because we didn't have the manpower to put up a pitched battle on both sides of the university.

"They're at the cars!" One of the lookouts on Mount Gillette waved frantically as he yelled again, "They're getting through!"

The zombies were crawling under and over the vehicles, slowly but inexorably. Even as we killed the ones in front, more pressed forward, crawling, climbing, and stumbling over the fallen faster than our three ranks could take them down.

If we didn't do something quickly, we'd have to fall back behind the barricade, destroying the ramps. Even that wouldn't stop them forever—they'd just pile up against the Slinky of Death, and then Mount Gillette, until their remains created a rotting walkway up and over.

There were just too many of them.

Lil and I glanced at each other. Time to start taking them down in the field.

"Wild cards!" Colonel Paxton's shout rang out above the gunfire. "Move out!"

Second rank was up and firing, but as soon as we'd spent our rounds, the cards dropped out of rank. The soldier next to me put a hand on my shoulder.

"Good luck out there," he said. "Kick some zombie ass."

I squeezed his hand and grinned.

"You, too. Just hang in there and try not to shoot me." I mean, seriously, not only did we have to worry about getting ripped to pieces and snacked on by zombies, but we ran the very real chance of being hit by friendly fire.

He nodded vigorously, and slapped a fresh clip into his rifle.

"I got it."

I ejected my spent clip and grabbed a loaded one from Jamie.

"Thanks."

"You need some for the road?" She held out several more. I had my M-4, my katana, my tanto, and my dart gun. My various pockets, pouches and knapsacks were pretty full.

But hey, there's always room for Jello.

I checked to make sure the radio transmitter was clipped firmly to my belt. *Time to rock and roll. Or possibly tango.*

"You ready?" Gabriel joined me, dirt and sweat intermingled on his face. He looked irresistible, but I managed to resist.

The next thing I heard was Simone's voice, followed by Nathan's exasperatingly calm response.

"I'm a wild card, damn it!" She glared at him fiercely. Her hair was mussed, her face actually shiny with sweat. She looked like a Valkyrie.

"You're also an expert marksman," he pointed out, nonplussed. "And the foremost living expert on this damned plague. You stay *here*."

Colonel Paxton stepped down from the barrier.

"Nathan's right, Professor Fraser," he said. "We can't risk your life out there. It's dangerous enough here. If you die, it's an irreparable loss."

"Yet if any of them die—" She gestured toward the rest of us, gathered together next to the ramp. "—it's an irreparable loss."

Nathan shook his head.

"Sorry, Simone, but your knowledge is worth all of our lives combined. If we didn't need every competent marksman here, you'd be inside, away from the action. And if the zombies manage to breach the barriers, I'll carry you in there myself."

"That's an order, professor," Paxton added.

I could see Simone seething, but she'd run out of arguments.

"Fine." She turned to our little group. "I expect to see every single one of you safely back here, do you hear me?" Her eyes were bright with determinedly unshed tears. We all nodded silently—even Tony kept his quips zipped. "Good!" Slapping another clip into her M-4 with more force than necessary, she got back into line, a grimly determined look on her face.

Pity the fool zombie who shambles into her sights.

I watched Nathan watch Simone. Judging from his expression, the sex *must* have been great. He caught me looking at him and frowned.

"You heard the professor," he growled. "You kids be careful." I nodded, and turned to Lil.

"I've got your back," I promised.

"No, I've got yours this time," she replied fiercely.

"I'll take care of both of you." Kai used his best Lando Calrissian voice.

"Not to break up the love fest," Gentry said, "but the zombies will take care of all of us if we don't get our asses out there." He tapped his wristwatch. "Time to move, ladies and gentlemen."

We split into two teams again.

"Don't press your transmitters if the zoms are too close," Gabriel reminded us. "Stay at least ten yards away from each other, and keep an eye out for each other when you set off the darts."

Jeez frickin' Louise. This was going to be fun in the fog.

"Move out!"

CHAPTER FORTY-SIX

We took off on either side of the line of fire, running an "obstacle corpse" as soon as we hit the hundred-yard mark. Tony, Kai, and Gentry headed to their left, while Gabriel, Nathan, Lil, and I went stage right.

The crack of rifle fire continued as we ran through the fog, dodging outstretched arms and grasping hands. Every second I expected the impact of a bullet smacking into my back. Honestly, it freaked me out more than the zombies.

We spread out and I took a quick glance to see where the rest of my teammates were. But all three were out of my sight line, lost in a sea of fog and zombies. I heard a gleeful holler—definitely Tony—followed by a rapid succession of little explosions. It sounded like popcorn kernels going off in a kettle.

Half a dozen zombies zeroed in on me, changing their relentless trajectory. I noticed a couple of the little white darts sticking out of the one nearest me, left there by a claymore, and decided to test out the transmitter. It was a little closer than ten feet so I grabbed another zombie, a skinny little thing in a skimpy nightshift, tossed it into the walking pincushion, and flicked the switch.

Pop pop pop! The darts detonated, and several zombies fragmented around me, taking a few undead bystanders with them. The splatter effect was nasty, drenching me in gore, but I'd created a nice little zombie-free zone around me.

For all of about ten seconds.

I whipped the re-jiggered paint ball gun from its makeshift holster, firing a few rounds of darts into random targets while dodging gaping mouths and grasping fingers. Their mottled gray skin seemed to ooze moisture, whether from the fog or the decomposition process I couldn't tell. Either way they looked nasty.

Another explosion went off somewhere to the front and right of me. Someone yelled—definitely male— either in pain or surprise. My heart immediately froze in my chest. What if one of the guys had blundered into the path of a claymore, and was stuck with darts? They'd positioned the mines up against the tree line to prevent this, but who's to say Gabriel didn't lose his way in the heavy fog?

Shit.

I pulled my katana out of its sheathe and took off in the direction of the yell, sliding over the hood of one of the parked cars and into the field. I didn't stop to kill if I could evade, but a few really asked for it. Like one scrawny male zombie with an underbite and no chin. It lurched into my path and clutched at my head, pulling me toward its open, slack-jawed mouth, yellowed teeth champing in anticipation.

Thank you, nose plugs.

I shoved my left hand against its chin, raised my katana and sliced through the skull with one hard cut. A great kill shot, but the blade stuck in bone when I tried to pull it out. The zombie's knees buckled as it sank to the ground. I grabbed the hilt with both hands and yanked hard. The katana came out with a lovely sucking sound.

More zombies converged on me. I cleared some space with wide, arcing horizontal slices.

"Gabriel!" I yelled.

"Over here!"

Recognizing his voice, I ran toward it, hoping my sense of direction wasn't totally screwed up.

Thwack! Off went the head of what used to be a pretty young coed.

Another ten feet or so and I saw him, spraying a bunch of zombies with more darts. He looked like he still had all his limbs.

"You okay?" I asked when I reached him.

"I'm fine." He grabbed me by one shoulder. "But why are you here?"

"I heard you yell when one of the claymores went off. Couldn't risk using my transmitter."

Gabriel snorted.

"One of the mines went off in front of me, but I was on the non-business side of it."

"Heh. Made ya flinch, though."

"Heads up!"

Zombies closed in on all sides.

"Fire in the hole!" he yelled. We ducked down to the ground and he hit the button on his transmitter, setting off a veritable Jiffy Pop series of explosions. A gloopy rain of exploded zombie bits spattered us.

We rose to our feet, goo dripping off our helmets. It'd cleared a substantial area, but already more zombies were filling in the gaps.

He continued to spray them with darts. My sword sliced through countless necks and stomachs as we slowly fought our way out of the thick of the swarm to protect the right flank of our defense. Soon we were slipping and stumbling through the piles of body parts, intestines, and other viscera.

Nathan and Lil must've covered this territory.

The swarm thinned out substantially as we cut back over the cars and across the parking lot, angling back up toward the barricades. But there were still enough zombies headed toward the right flank to potentially put us up Shit Creek if they broke through to the firing lines.

Tony, Kai, and Gentry probably faced the same situation at the left flank.

"Fire in the hole!"

Nathan's voice rang out clearly through the chaos. Gabriel and I dropped again as more déjà vu darts went off.

We joined Nathan and Lil at the far side of the parking lot. They were both equally disgusting.

"Isn't this *gross*?" Lil practically bounced up and down with excitement, eyes shining with unholy glee.

I raised an eyebrow.

"You're enjoying this?"

She shrugged.

"I might as well, 'cause if I die in the next ten minutes, I'd rather be having fun, y'know?"

I couldn't argue with her logic, so I didn't try.

"What are you going to do for excitement when this is all over?"

"String beads," she said firmly. "Whoops!" Staring over my shoulder, she raised her M-4 and fired off a few rounds at some zombies that had gotten too close. One bullet found its mark, but the others hit chest level or missed. "I suck at this," Lil fretted.

"You just need more practice," Nathan said, sighting and firing. Four shots, and four zombies bit the dust. A claymore went off in the near distance.

"I've got this!" Lil dashed off into the fog, and we heard the darts explode a few seconds later, followed by a larger secondary explosion.

Uh oh. That didn't sound good.

Lil reappeared as quickly as she'd vanished, looking worried.

"That took out a few, but it also took out one of the cars. They're pouring through the hole." She shook her head, looking disoriented. "They just keep coming…"

"How many darts do you each have left?" Nathan asked.

I checked my knapsack.

"Maybe ten?"

"I'm out." Lil pulled out her pickaxe.

Gabriel pulled out a handful.

"This is it."

Nathan shook his head.

"Use 'em wisely. And let's hope Gentry is doing damage with his flamethrower."

As if on cue we heard a war whoop from somewhere to our left, followed by a roar. Even through the fog a bloom of hazy light was visible as the zombie barbecue commenced. Invigorated, the four of us grinned at each other and went back to work.

We spread out in a fan, Gabriel and Nathan using their firearms to deadly effect while Lil and I cut down approaching zoms with blade and pickaxe. Body parts flew, the asphalt of the parking lot becoming a treacherous obstacle course of flesh, innards, and that nasty ass black goo.

Lil fell back beside me, panting heavily from exertion.

"They're not stopping, Ashley."

"Sooner or later they have to," I said firmly.

"I don't know how much longer I can do this," she said, voice uncertain.

"Switch to your gun."

"I suck with my gun." She sounded near tears.

"Take your time and aim. I'll cover you so you can give your arm a break, okay?" I didn't tell her that my cutting arm felt like lead. Each stroke of the sword was harder than the last. But to stop was to die.

Or worse, to let Lil die. I'd take a bucketload of ibuprofen later.

She switched out to her M-4 without further argument. I continued slaughtering the incoming, no longer seeing gender or age. They were all just rotting flesh that shouldn't be walking around.

I don't know how long this went on. I sliced, diced,

and decapitated on autopilot, a human Cuisinart running on emergency battery power. Zombie corpses piled up in front of us. But more kept coming.

Finally Nathan fell back next to me.

"I'm out of ammo," he said.

Gabriel joined us.

"I'm close."

Zombies continued to stagger toward us, undeterred by the bodies in front of them. They'd fall, stagger to their feet or get shoved into the body part stew by more zombies pushing in behind them.

"FALL BACK! FALL BACK!"

The shout from the lines chilled my heart.

CHAPTER FORTY-SEVEN

"Back to the lines!" Gabriel snapped.

The four of us ran back along the barricade until we reached the ramp. Gentry, Tony, and Kai ran in from the left, all as disgustingly goo-splattered as we were.

Colonel Paxton and Simone were already urging defenders back over the barricades to the temporary safety of the campus. Some of the soldiers—maybe fifty—still fired in two lines, but you could see the exhaustion in their faces.

Jamie and a few other civilians continued to hand out clips. There was still a good supply, but there were just too many targets and not enough people.

Zombies surged forward into the front rank of shooters closest to where we stood. Dead hands clasped gun barrels, yanking screaming soldiers toward gaping, hungry mouths. I saw the soldier who'd told me to kick ass taken down by a half dozen zombies, hands and teeth ripping at his clothes and flesh.

Without thinking I leapt forward, katana slashing with deadly precision until I'd cleared a path to the fallen man and killed the ones that were attacking him.

Too late. His throat was a mess of mangled, bloody flesh and his eyes stared blankly towards the sky.

Fuck. A quick sword thrust guaranteed he wouldn't come back.

Shots fired around me, into the oncoming mass of walking dead. I felt the wind of a bullet as it whizzed past my cheek and hit the forehead of a zombie a few feet away. Not wanting to be hit, I fell back behind the lines, panting for breath.

Nathan ran up to Simone and grabbed her arm.

"Get back inside the barricades," he said. "Now."

She pulled away with a total "you're not the boss of me" glare.

"As soon as everyone else is safely on the other side," she said, "I'll go."

Without another word Nathan scooped her up in his arms, strode up the ramp and vanished down the other side. He reappeared a few seconds later, stopping to talk to Colonel Paxton.

"Make sure she stays there," he said, and Paxton agreed. Then he jumped back down to rejoin us.

"This is it, kids," he said. He pointed out over the fields and parking lot where zombies continued to pour in, the ranks of shooters barely holding their lines now.

"Most of the lines are going up on the barricade, where they'll continue to take out the advancing enemy. We have enough ammunition left to make a dent in the rest of the swarm, but not necessarily enough to stop them.

"The odds are shitty."

We looked at each other, then back at Nathan.

"We will not go quietly into the night," Tony said. I actually felt a chill run up my spine as his voice rose in intensity, backed by explosions and gunfire. "We will not vanish without a fight!"

"We're going to live on," Kai chimed in.

"We're going to survive," Gentry said.

The three of them linked arms and yelled.

"Today, we celebrate our Independence Day!"

Nathan grinned.

"Good," he said. "Drink some water, load up on darts and ammo, and let's go."

The soldiers continued to fire, fall back, reload, and fire again while we quickly grabbed as many clips and darts as we could stuff into our pouches and pockets. The moans of the living dead were continual, almost white noise by this point.

"Everyone fall back to the barricade!" Paxton's rich voice rang out over the moans, and the remaining soldiers seized the rest of the gear and hustled up the ramp. The Colonel stared down at us, face solemn.

"We'll hold the ramp as long as possible."

"Could you leave a nightlight on?" Tony, of course.

Nathan smacked him on the back of the head.

"Burn the ramp if you need to. We can always get in the back way, if we make it that far."

Suddenly Simone appeared next to Paxton.

"Nathan, I swear I will haunt you if you don't bring every one of them back alive!"

He just grinned. Then he waved his arm at us.

"Let's do this!"

Déjà vu, just like the darts. We dashed back into the fields, spreading out in an arc of controlled mayhem. We sent out more darts into the oncoming zoms, exploded them, cut down stragglers before they could close in on us, and then repeated the process. Gentry used the flamethrower with deadly effect. Heads melted, clothes caught fire, and flaming zombies stumbled like really clumsy stuntmen into other approaching corpses, passing the torch.

We couldn't keep them from reaching the razor wire. There were just too many of them. At this stage of the game, all we could do was take out as many as possible, stem the tide so that the incoming wave wouldn't be enough to sweep over Mount Gillette.

I ran out of darts and switched to my M-4. I had to give my arms a rest. I'd lost sight of the other wild cards, but could hear the occasional roar of the flamethrower, and could feel the heat.

The body count was over the top, and still they kept coming. Rotted faces, gaping wounds, staring white pupils in a bloodshot sea of yellow. How could there still be more when I was so tired?

It wasn't long before the zoms were too close and I had to resort to my katana. Promising my arms and shoulders a massage and icepacks if they stuck with me, I drew from a reserve of strength I didn't know I had, pulled out my weapons, and had at it.

Three figures came at me at once, one of them getting through my guard to grasp at my left arm even as I hacked the head off its friends. I tried to shake it loose, but the thing's grip was like steel and I couldn't dislodge it.

"Motherfucker, let *go* of me!" It was too close for me to use my katana; I would just as likely whack my own arm off. I made a split second decision as it moved in, teeth angled toward my neck.

Stabbing my katana blade first into one of the fallen zombies, I released it, grabbed the tanto from my left hand and shoved the point into the zombie's eye before it could sink its teeth into me. Its grip on my arm loosened as it fell to its knees and collapsed onto the ground. Bracing one foot next to its head, I pulled out the tanto and then retrieved my katana with another quick movement.

I heard a holler to my left and turned in time to see Lil, a few hundred feet away, stumble and go down, her pickaxe flying to one side. A half dozen zoms immediately converged on her before she could get to her feet.

"Lil!" My frantic cry probably carried across campus as I raced across the gore-strewn ground to reach her before the zombies tore her to pieces. I could hear her yelling in anger, but then those yells turned into high-pitched shrieks of pain as the bastards tore into her.

Oh god, please, no...

The space between us was mercifully empty. I leapt

over several fallen corpses, covering the remaining distance, and brought my sword down. A head went flying, then an arm. My ears rang and blood filled my vision. Body parts fell as I hacked and slashed, shrieking like a banshee the entire time, ignoring hands and teeth ripping at me, until all of them lay in pieces on or around Lil's prone body. One of the zombies lay unmoving on top of her, a big, meaty thing that had to weigh twice as much as she did.

Dropping to my knees and, totally uncaring of anything else around me, I muttered an undefined prayer.

Shoving the zombie off to one side, I took in her still face, torn clothes and the bite marks on her arms and legs. They'd managed to get their teeth in-between the armor. She was still breathing, and her limbs were still intact, nothing torn off, but she looked bad.

Nathan appeared next to me and immediately knelt.

"We need to get her back to Big Red."

"Is she going to be okay?" Other zombies were closing in, but I had to know.

Nathan nodded.

"I think so. But she's not going to be able to fight, so we have to get her out of here."

Lil's eyes fluttered open.

"I can *so* fight," she mumbled. "I'm good."

We both ignored her. Nathan put a hand on my shoulder.

"I can carry her back. You gonna be able to keep this up?"

"Just get Lil out of here," I responded. "I'll be fine."

He didn't waste any more words or time, just scooped Lil up and ran back toward Big Red like some sort of super hero. Which in my eyes he kind of was.

I got to my feet, trying to summon up more of the fire of righteous fury that had carried me. Zombies still staggered forward, their unholy moans filling the air, no longer white noise but now an almost unbearable din.

After that I moved through a fog, both figurative and literal. I found my swings getting weaker and sloppier with each kill, and knew it was only a matter of time before I collapsed or made a stupid mistake. I had no idea where any of my fellow wild cards were, or if they were even still alive. The world was reduced to a tunnel vision of zombies.

If I wasn't killing it, it didn't exist.

Then suddenly I reached my breaking point.

Nothing special preceded or prompted it. I decapitated a zombie and then my arms just refused to do any more. They fell to my sides, blades hanging limp in my hands. I stared blankly at the corpses littering the ground around me, and the fresh ones still moving toward me.

I sank down to my knees, exhausted. I knew I should run, at least try and make it back to the barricades, but I just didn't care any more.

CHAPTER FORTY-EIGHT

"Ashley!"

I heard someone yell my name, but I was too tired to respond or even look to see who it was, although I was pretty sure it was Gabriel. But I ignored him. He'd just want me to get up and keep fighting anyway.

I closed my eyes and waited for death.

"Ashley!" Gabriel seized me under my arms and hauled me to my feet.

"Just let me lie down," I protested, eyes still shut. "Okay?"

"Not okay." He shook me hard. "Snap out of it, Ashley!" He shook me again and my body screamed in outrage.

My eyes snapped open and I glared at him. Then he did something I hadn't expected.

He laughed.

"Are you *laughing* at me?" I smacked his shoulder as hard as I could.

"That's better." He kissed me then, hard and quick. "We're falling back. There's too many of them. Can you make it back to campus?"

"Yeah," I replied. "I'm just pissed enough to do it."

"Better than an energy bar," he said. "All-natural, of course."

Gabriel slung an arm around my shoulder and we

turned toward Big Red, only to find our way blocked by zombies who'd decided that we were easier pickings than the meat behind the barricade. There wasn't enough space to dodge between them, and I didn't know if I had another sword cut left in me.

"Do you have any darts left?" Gabriel asked, voice carefully controlled.

"No. Do you?"

He shook his head.

"Nearly out of ammo, too."

"Any chance of the cavalry coming to get us?"

"Everyone else fell back already," he said. "I stayed out to find you."

"So no cavalry." I wanted to be grateful, but couldn't manage the effort.

He shook his head again and shouldered his M-4.

"Let's make every shot count."

Sticking my blades into a corpse, I followed suit. Zombie after zombie fell to his deadly accuracy, and a good number fell to my marksmanship, as well. But for each one that dropped, another took its place, and they were coming from all directions. I slapped the last clip into my M-4, realizing I wasn't ready to die, no matter how bone-weary I might be.

When I'd fired my last round, I dropped the M-4 and retrieved my blades. Time to find out if I had another cut in me or not.

Suddenly a low rumble filled the air, drowning out the moans. The rumble became a roar as something approached through the fog from up the road. The roar was joined by the sound of screeching metal as something shoved a Prius out of its way. A huge, yellow, industrial-strength snowplow careened into view, scattering zombies—whole and in pieces—off either side of the angled blades. The plow slowed to a stop a few feet from us. I thought I'd never seen a more beautiful sight.

Until I saw who sat behind the wheel.

Mack waved at us, grinning from ear to ear.

"Want a ride?"

Gabriel and I scrambled up onto the plow and into the cab, out of reach of grasping hands and gnashing teeth. I gave Mack a bone-crushing hug before settling in. He accelerated the engine and started crushing zombies again.

"How did you make it out alive?" I asked over the roar of the engine.

"I managed to make it through the woods to the back of that church we saw. Got in through a second-story window they hadn't barricaded. Scaled a drainpipe like Spider-Man," he added proudly.

"They?"

"Yup, a bunch of survivors holed up there. They're waiting for me to come back and get them. I figured I'd better get some help first.

"Man, I'm glad to see you guys!"

"What about Kaitlyn?" Gabriel asked.

Mack's smile dimmed as he shook his head.

"She'd lost too much blood."

I reached over and squeezed his shoulder.

"You tried your best, Mack." I paused, then added, "I'm just so glad to see you, and Lil is gonna be over the moon."

The grin reappeared.

"You saved our asses, Mack," Gabriel said. "But where the hell did you find a snowplow?"

"Saw it parked behind the church." Mack veered to the left to avoid a car. Zombies tried to clutch at the sides of the plow to hoist themselves up, but couldn't get any purchase.

"But what made you take it instead of a car?" I asked. "I mean, it's sheer genius!"

"Saw the swarm headed your way and thought it might come in handy," he said with a self-deprecating shrug. "I guess it did."

I leaned my head on his shoulder.

"Yeah, I guess it did."

"And so will this." Gabriel held up a backpack, dipping inside and pulling out handfuls of full M-4 cartridges and, wonder of wonders, déjà vu darts.

He looked at me.

"You up for it?" I nodded.

"I think I just got my third wind."

Gabriel turned to Mack.

"How much gas you got left in this thing?"

Mack grinned.

"You just tell me where you want to go."

We literally plowed through dozens of walking corpses, making broad sweeps up and down the length of the parking lot. Gabriel used his M-4 to lethal effect, his aim unaffected by the movement, while I made the most of the déjà vus, sharing the wealth in as widespread a pattern as possible until the cache was depleted.

Then, while Gabriel kept up his sharpshooting, I used the transmitter to detonate the darts. A few explosions rocked the snowplow, but the cab offered us protection against flying zombie viscera.

We drove along the row of cars at the edge of the lot until we came to the gap where the car had exploded. I peered through the fog at the figures lurching their way across the fields and up the road toward us.

"Is it my imagination or are they thinning out?"

"Déjà vu on your right." Gabriel pointed toward a zombie staggering in our direction, a dart sticking out of its neck. I hit the transmitter, smiling grimly as the explosion took off its head. The thing took one more step before falling to the ground.

"I don't think it's your imagination," Mack said.

A shout rose up behind us, from Mount Gillette.

"Get us back there," Gabriel said urgently.